INTOXICATED
Sleeping Giants Book I

By
Ally Fleming

INTOXICATED

Cover Artwork Courtesy of Melody A Pond~ Cover Artist
(http://melodyypond.weebly.com)

To loyal fans and new readers. Enjoy the ride…

~PROLOGUE~

Wilmington, Vermont~ The Present

"I hear they've got good schools here, Patch. That what drew you to it?" The amusement in Harris Van Deer's chuckle, didn't reach the rather blank look in his unremarkable brown eyes.

"Hell man," Van Deer continued to probe, "what's it like to live in a place with less than two-thousand people?"

By then, Patroclus Kostas had answered enough of Van Deer's seemingly innocuous queries to know that to answer this one would result in the same brutalities his earlier responses had brought on. Renewed dread, along with inward relief flooded Patroclus' wiry build when he heard Harris Van Deer's voice again.

"You will die, Patch," Van Deer's tone then was an unassuming one, "Now I can give you the option of dying quick and painless," he gestured to his colleague Brody Alberts, who wagged a syringe filled with an ominous looking pale green substance.

"Or slow and violently," Van Deer raised his wide hands, curving his fingers in just slightly as though he were gripping a football.

Patroclus heard the firm, distinctive pop of cracking knuckles.

"We know you and your crew were responsible for the jobs on the old men," Van Deer continued. "It's too bad the old guys changed their plans at the last minute. *Still,* you and your men should've waited to make sure everyone who *was* there was dead. That fuck-up made it easy to find and pin down everyone responsible for this little coup. You guys did a good job of layin' low, though. Guess you figured after six years it was safe to come out of your holes. You figured wrong. Now, we know you didn't have the smarts to think this up, Patch," Van Deer's voice adopted a quiet, compassionate tone that would've been believable were it not for the malice lurking in his lifeless eyes.

"We're hoping you'll be smarter than the rest of your guys and give up whoever you've been stupid enough to protect all these years," Van Deer chuckled again. "If your guys had lived to tell you about it, they'd advise you not to play us for fools any longer."

At Patch's surprised look," Van Deer grinned wildly. "Oh yes, whatever you're imagining we've done to them was a hundred times worse. I gotta tell you though, 'ol Corky was especially remorseful when we paid a visit to him and his wife."

Patroclus tried to swallow and failed. With great effort, he fought to get words around the lump in his throat. "They had kids." From across the room, he heard Grant Zubin's chilly rumble of a laugh.

"Yeah, they did." Zubin brushed a thumb over the gleaming, beaked blade of a Bowie knife.

"Cork was mighty helpful," Van Deer went on even as his wild grin defined. "He's how we found you. And his wife," Van Deer released a low whistle, "boy could she beg. We had a good time together. After a while, I wasn't sure if she was pleading for us to go easy on her brats or for me to give her more of what she was getting from my dick."

Patroclus heard the room explode with laughter. The loudest came from Van Deer and Zubin. He swallowed then and relieved himself of the need to vomit by leaning on his anger. "Sons of cunts!" He snarled. "Do whatever the fuck you came to do. I'm the last, so you better make it goddamn good."

"Oh you aren't the last, Patch," Van Deer wasn't grinning then. "You aren't the last by a longshot. Your part- buttfucked as it was- was not the endgame. Which; judging from the fact that our organization has spent the last six years trying to recover from it, tells us that the main objective was royally accomplished."

"Was it Mercuri?" Van Deer's smile returned and was softer. He'd caught the barest flicker in Patroclus' dark eyes. "It was, wasn't it? Damn that son of a bitch- too smart for his own good." Van Deer spoke as if to himself, but soon brought his attention back to his quarry.

"You'll admit it to me, Patch. Before it's all over, you'll admit it to me that it was him." Van Deer leaned in closer. "I've got unfinished business with those cocksuckers, Patch. So does everybody in this room. Did you think we'd just let that go? That we'd have *ever* let it go?"

Patroclus had no interest in the conversation. He was, however, intrigued by Harris Van Deer's momentary lapse in judgement. He took advantage of the proximity of the man's face to his and executed a punishing head-butt. Given the level of abuse he'd already suffered at the hands of the men in the room, he expected the move to have him blacking out at any moment. It was worth it, he thought, worth it to see Harris Van Deer stagger back and bring both hands to his nose gushing blood.

The other four men had surged to their feet. Beefy hands all curled in unison and sent a chorus of crunching knuckles flooding through the soft lit cherrywood paneled study.

Patroclus readied himself for final brutalities. Van Deer's blood red fingers shook and the ferocity of his roar was as savage as the look in the eyes that bulged manically from his bald head.

The imminence of his life ending, did not fill Patroclus with dread or even panic for that matter. Instead, he took solace in the beauty of his surroundings, knowing that he would never give up the four men who had made that possible.

Patroclus knew someone would talk. In a group the size of the one their famed mission had required, there was bound to be someone who would break. Oh yes, he thought, someone would inevitably let some piece of damning info slip and lead this savage crew to the four who had orchestrated their freedom. It wouldn't be him, goddammit! It wouldn't be him.

Cleaving desperately to flailing courage, Patroclus' face contorted into a mask of deep-seated hate. "Come on you motherfuckers. Come on!" Closing his eyes, Patroclus offered a final prayer that he not be the one to break.

6

PART I

Never make a major decision based solely on money

-Chuck Noll

~CHAPTER 1~

Las Vegas, Nevada~ 6 years ago

"Those bangin' heels are gonna wear a groove in this expensive carpet, Tee and I'd say we've got enough expenses we can't cover without you adding more to the list."

Her friend's valid warning, didn't encourage Etienne Shaw to cease her pacing across the large penthouse living room. "We should've never taken that money," she said.

"Well Tee," LuCarolyn Young pushed out of a deep purple velvet sofa. She stalked across the overdone room in silver ice pick heels that added six inches to her own 5'10. "Maybe if it wasn't for the string of hard luck situations we've found ourselves in over the years, without any rich relatives or hell... caring parents to give us a hand, we may've done the right thing and turned it down."

"Shit Lu, Tee's right," Berrill Clayton resisted pacing, but chewed her thumbnail something fierce. "We should've run the other way when Dorinda came to us with this."

"What do you think it means that these guys only wanted black girls?" Etienne asked, distinct dread wedged in alongside her nerves.

"Maybe we should just leave," Prin Holland hadn't set down her purse or wrap since she and her friends had arrived in the high roller's suite. "Those guys who brought us here said to just call them-"

"When we'd done what we came here to do," LuCarolyn finished and then rolled her eyes and whispered an obscenity, "They're not our personal drivers, *Princess*."

"Don't call me that," Prin bristled.

"Yes Lu, don't." Berrill cautioned with a firm wave. "We don't need these clowns knowing our real names. Look guys, just do the job and get it over with. No one here is a virgin. Just moan and bear it- maybe they'll be halfway decent fucks."

"Jesus, Bear," Prin groaned.

"What's wrong with you?" Etienne snapped.

Berrill put her wave in motion again. "It's called psyching myself up. Best I can do since I didn't think to get pissy drunk before we came here."

A panel opened in the rear of the room. A tall, uniformed man emerged pushing a serving cart filled with an array of pitchers, decanters and glasses.

Berrill sent a skeptical look around the room. "God please don't let them be bugging us," she whispered.

"Refreshments, ladies?" The server lifted one of the decanters.

Berrill stalked over to the well-stocked tray. "Hell yes," she took a champagne flute when the waiter offered. "We'll help ourselves if that's okay?"

The waiter bowed formally. "As you wish," he left the room as discretely as he'd arrived.

Berrill sniffed at one of the pitchers. "We've got martinis here, ladies. Drink up."

LuCarolyn went to indulge. Etienne and Prin hesitated.

"You two can't psyche yourselves up for shit," Berrill chided, "Do you really want to go into this thing totally sober?"

The taunt did the trick. Soon, all four women were gathered around the cart where they eagerly and heavily imbibed.

~~~

It wasn't enough, Tee thought as she lay there so much later. She would've needed every ounce of alcohol on that cart to deaden her to the events of such a depraved evening.

Sex for money. It was a line she never thought she'd cross. She'd not only crossed it, she'd kicked, stomped on and all but broke it in half that night. They'd have surely left, money be damned if they'd known what was in store. The ten men who had joined them 20 minutes after their visit from the server, had definitely learned how to share. They'd passed her and her friends around like they were mints, keeping them in separate rooms across the penthouse.

Tee could've sworn she'd heard screams- and not of the pleasured variety. Of course, her... partners didn't offer a break time for an investigation into the source of the cries. They had more in store for her, Tee discovered.

Now, as laborious snores assaulted her ears, she seized her opportunity and went to check on her friends- check on them and get them all the hell out of there. She didn't stop to grab clothes. She didn't know where they were anyway. Besides, she never wanted to see those clothes again.

Tee left her snoring suitors behind. Her dark eyes settled on something gleaming from beneath a pair of trousers discarded near the back corner of an armchair. She veered off from her trek to the door and discovered that the gleam was from a curved knife blade with a grizzly looking wooden handle.

She cast a sideways glance toward the bed and then took the weapon in a surprisingly sure grip. Hefting it slightly, she smiled in grim approval of the weight. She half turned toward the snoring pigs behind her wondering if the weapon might play a part in the next round of sex once the men woke from their slumbers.

Flexing her fingers around the knife handle, she let the blade capture light from a candle burning low on a black lacquer shelf and considered... Later, she promised. She had to find the others. Stealthily, she crept toward the hall. There, her steps took her back to the living room where the night had started.

Tee stood in the middle of the over-furnished room for half a minute, when movement caught her eye on a wide futon laid flat. She swallowed down the need to vomit, hoping she'd not walked in on more sex. Relief seized her when she saw LuCarolyn's silhouette in the gleam of moonlight and Las Vegas beyond the room's immense window wall.

10

LuCarolyn shrieked when Tee touched her arm.

"Shh! Shh! It's okay, it's me- it's Tee."

"Mmm," LuCarolyn pressed her lips together and appeared faint. "I have to throw up."

"Me too, honey, but I'm gonna need you to swallow it." She applied brisk rubs to LuCarolyn's arms and squeezed. "We have to find Bear and Prin first, okay?"

LuCarolyn was nodding. "Right, right. Bear and Prin," she started to stand. "My clothes."

"Come on, honey," Tee urged her friend to stand. "There were robes in a closet in the room where they kept me. Let's go."

"What'd they do to you, Tee?"

Tee winced as her nausea returned. "Things I'll spend the rest of my life trying to forget."

LuCarolyn frowned curiously and glanced back across her shoulder toward the living room. Then, she caught up to Tee who was already retracing her steps through the penthouse.

Together, the women made their way through the dimly lit dwelling. They found Berrill in a second bedroom. She was in the adjoining bathroom heaving into a toilet.

LuCarolyn took in the sight with a look that hinted of longing. "That looks good."

"Later Lu," Tee murmured on her way past to kneel next to Berrill. "Bear? Honey? Let's go. Sweetie, we need to find Prin."

Berrill appeared in no state to leave her perch near the commode. Her blood-shot eyes glistened with fresh tears the moment she looked up at Tee.

"Shh honey, shh…" Tee urged the soother into Berrill's hair. "Later, sweetie. We don't have time for this now." Hastily, Tee finger combed strands of her friend's long hair. She put a hard kiss to Berrill's forehead, consistently squeezing her arm to encourage her to stand.

LuCarolyn came over to help, urging Berrill along with soft words to motivate.

"My clothes…" Berrill murmured as the three of them left the room in the buff.

"We'll take care of it, Bear." Tee soothed, "first we need to get Prin."

Berrill blinked as though the news had suddenly put her on alert. Nodding once, she quickened her pace along the hallway.

11

The heavy carpeting that spanned the penthouse, muffled any sound of shuffling bare feet. The women broke into a sprint toward a set of closed double doors at the end of the hall.

Tee brought a finger to her mouth to order silence. There wasn't much noise from her friends, only the occasional sniffle or shudder of breath. Still, the minor sounds were too much as Tee wanted to listen through the door. She didn't need long to decipher the sounds. She would've preferred the occasional sniffle or shudder of breath over the tell-tale curses and grunts she picked up on instead.

"One of them's up," she said.

"Filth," Berrill muttered, needing no further detail to understand what Tee was hearing through the door.

Tee raised her hand once more for quiet and then began to twist the door's gleaming chrome handle. A lurid curse snaked its way silently inside her head when she stepped inside the room.

One of the ten Tee and her friends had gotten so intimately acquainted with that night, was still vigorously enjoying the evening's activities. The man appeared happily imprisoned in ecstasy's clutches as he claimed Prin from behind.

Tee saw her friend...appropriately positioned. Her cheek lay flat against the pillows, her light honey-toned skin appeared ashen. Her eyes were lifeless orbs of cornflower blue.

LuCarolyn reached out when she saw Tee stalking boldly forward. Her hand only grasped air.

Tee's steps quickly brought her alongside the bed. Coolly, and without a shred of hesitation, she brought the serrated blade to the man's jugular. "I'd ease all the way up if I were you."

"The fuck-?" The foul query rushed out on a choked grunt.

"I think you got your money's worth," Tee breathed, "get off her."

Across the room; illuminated by rose blush lighting from mini chandeliers, LuCarolyn and Berrill traded troubled looks.

Berrill took a scan of the room and noticed the butt of a handgun protruding from a holster slung across the top corner of an embroidered red velvet arm chair. Closing the distance to the chair, she worked awkwardly for a moment to free the weapon. Soon enough, she was gripping it securely.

Tee's order to her stunned quarry, carried on a distorted chord, LuCarolyn thought. She watched her tiny friend standing there nude, her

12

breasts crushed against the back of a man whose throat she held a knife to. She had the look of an enraged, dark hellion eager to lay waste to her prey, LuCarolyn decided.

The comparison of such a destructive force to one as diminutive as Etienne Shaw, should have roused amusement. LuCarolyn didn't as much as smirk. She had never set eyes on a killer, but she knew in that moment, the woman in her sights was poised to becoming precisely that.

Careful then, the man handled Prin as he withdrew. Prin slid down into the tangle of sheets and remained unresponsive.

"Get her," Tee ordered.

LuCarolyn and Berrill knew the words were meant for them. Immediately, they scrambled across the room to gently help their friend up from the bed.

"Check the cabinets in that bathroom. There should be robes in there. Go." She tacked on gruffly when Berrill and LuCarolyn only stared.

"Come on, Hon," LuCarolyn took Prin with her into the bath.

Berrill remained. "Do it," she encouraged.

The man, too petrified to even attempt escape, managed to sob out a word. "Wait-"

"I intend to," Tee's response was meant for Berrill. She moved the jagged blade with one deft shift to the left. Crimson saturated the sheets in a soft, steady downpour.

~~~

"Did you hear somethin'?"

"Damn man, would you stop? For the fifth time, no. The place is soundproofed, remember?"

"They don't belong in there."

"That's the goddamn truth, but it's probably a point we should've acted on several hours ago."

"We should've done somethin', said somethin'," the hard square set to Luke Robb's jaw seemed to define into a more rigid set in response to his partner's words.

"What exactly?" Caleb Stein's voice was a snarl. "Tell our bosses those aren't the girls for them? That they made a mistake and the girls didn't realize what they were getting into? Is that what you're sayin', Luke? Do we tell the folks who pay us that, if they don't mind, we'll just drive the girls back home and no hard feelings?" Caleb tacked on a barely audible curse while tugging a hand through a tousle of dark blonde strands and then setting his head back hard against the wall.

Luke worked the bridge of his nose between thumb and middle finger. "Why the hell did they take that money?"

"Shit Luke, why do most girls take it?" Caleb sighed, "Down on their luck, figure owing the debt is better than being late with their student loan payment or rent. Then they find out that paying the debt involves a lot more than cash with interest. Then they're stuck and what's a little sex if it means you get to keep the cash."

"Cash don't mean squat if you ain't alive to spend it," Luke muttered and set his head against the wall opposite the one his partner had claimed.

The men had lost interest in languishing in the deeply cushioned wing chairs that were vibrantly upholstered in some rich, glossy fabric. Their post, in the private lobby outside the penthouse, had quickly lost its allure. If it had held any to begin with. Both Luke and Caleb had had their fill of such spaces long ago.

Luke's words had held a gruesome truth. He and Caleb had been privy to scenes of a similar nature often enough over the long history of their involvement with The Grodins Alberts Network- The Network or The GAN as it was also known. Luke and Caleb had been among several charged with the responsibility of driving hundreds of girls to their-*deaths?*- nights out with The Ten.

Luke and Caleb had seen the unease filling the eyes of those young women earlier when they'd settled into the back of the car for the ride to the overpriced, overdone hotel. Luke and Caleb had witnessed that unease transition to resolve and could almost sense it when the girls had accepted their fates.

The young women were about to step over a line many women didn't cross without a great deal of soul searching. Sex for money. If only that was all that was in store.

The Ten; as they were known throughout The Network were among the elite in their respective fields. Led by Robert Fritz and Sumter Hamisch, The Ten served as a board of sorts. They determined what jobs required their unique involvement to reach a successful end. Additionally, they advised on how the exorbitant sums earned by those jobs were to be allocated among network personnel and The Network's outside interests.

14

In their… normal lives, the men held posts that claimed position among the highest levels of government and industry. They were, without question, above the law. Given that fact, they believed they were free to explore any and all personal interests no matter how perverse. As long as noone of consequence knew of their indulgences.

"You gotta admit how quiet it is in there, Cale."

Caleb rolled his eyes. "First you're hearing things and now it's *too* quiet. Everyone's not as loud about sex as you are."

"Go fuck yourself, Cale," Luke urged with a slight grin that didn't quite hold as his concern stuck.

"We should check."

"Luke-"

"It's our responsibility to make sure everyone's safe," Luke pushed off the wall.

Caleb took a few seconds to ponder his partner's words before he was nodding his agreement. He fished the room key from the inside pocket of his suit coat and followed Luke toward a short stairway leading up to the penthouse.

The heavy maple door opened soundlessly. There was a brief green flash of the admittance light once the card had been swiped through the reader. The light from the hallway had a garish effect on the room's shallow illumination. The door shut soundlessly behind them as the men assessed their surroundings.

"Christ, this place is tacky," Luke muttered eyeing the display of tapestries, drapes, lighting and furniture that strived for opulence but only achieved mediocrity.

"Different strokes…" Caleb noted. He was unable to dismiss the sensation of hair rising along the back of his neck. He resisted the urge to reach for his gun.

The men worked their way into the room. Nothing overt roused their concern.

Except the quiet, Luke thought. Though it stood to reason that everyone was sleeping, the quiet held an eeriness that didn't solidify the assumption. "Let's get the hell out of here," he breathed, dismissing whatever his sixth sense was trying to tell him.

Caleb grinned. "Are we done being responsible now?" He shook his head. "Come on, the least we can do is give the place the once over since we're already here," he turned to take the corridor to the bedrooms.

"Caleb."

"Damn man, this was your idea, remember?"

"Caleb?" Luke persisted.

Losing patience with his partner, Caleb turned to the man with a clenched fist. He found Luke staring fixedly across the room and followed the line of his stare.

"What the hell?" Slowly, Caleb moved past Luke to take in the living room. With the door closed and blocking the light from the outer corridor, his eyes had adjusted to the dim interior.

Lying spread eagled on the floor and looking like a blood soaked snow angel, was Sumter Hamisch.

"Cale."

Inwardly, Caleb grimaced, reluctant to see what Luke's keen eyes witnessed then. Turning, he found that it wasn't at all what he'd expected. The four beauties he and his partner had left to their fates that night were making their way toward the living room.

"Take us back."

Caleb heard the smallest of the four issue the order when she and her friends were within a few feet of him and Luke.

The four women moved past the two men without stopping or even pausing to offer the slightest acknowledgement of the torn body in the middle of the living room floor.

Luke and Caleb traded bewildered looks and then fixed on the women once more. Their feet were bare and they all wore identical white robes. The scent of fresh blood followed in their wake.

***

Caracas, Venezuela~ 10 months later

"I get that pimp, son of a bitch Roya," a gruff voice crackled through the headset, "a man who can't control his sluts is no man."

"Copy." Mercuri Nikolaides returned confirmation of the transmission from his superior while scanning the outlay of the mountainside villa. Mercuri disengaged his set from the ops commander just as an even gruffer voice filled his ear.

At his side, Mercuri heard a groan that held a lethal cord. Nevertheless, the sound beckoned the sly grin that was Mercuri's trademark.

"A pimp, Christ…" Pope Apostolou's voice carried on such a low octave that every word he uttered seemed wrapped in a soft roar. The effect often had others looking to the man's closest friends in hopes of a translation which was usually unnecessary. Pope added the effect when he wanted to unsettled someone or when he was seriously, murderously pissed.

Mercuri knew it was the latter fueling his friend's tone. Being seriously, murderously pissed was an emotion he shared then as well.

"All this 'cause those old bastards fucked with the wrong women?" Pope's growling tone was then akin to a snarl.

"It happens," Mercuri chuckled.

Pope slanted his friend a wink. "Hell yeah, it does, but most men just suck it up and accept it as a fact of life. Few of us orchestrate a military op on a pimp's vacation home."

Mercuri was on the cusp of flat out laughter by then. "Would you shut the fuck up before you give away our position?" He reached into a flap on his black fatigues and withdrew a two-way radio. "Farm Boy, this is Teacher's Pet, over."

At his side, Mercuri heard another groan though that one wasn't quite as gruff as the one prior to it.

"Do these fuckin' handles have to change over every op or can you guys just choose some you like and stick to 'em?" Pope ridiculed his friends in a tone that was gruff yet tinged with amusement.

"Stowe it," Mercuri ordered just as another voice erupted over the channel.

"Teacher's Pet this is Farm Boy. We ready to do this? Over?"

"Affirmative Farm Boy- order confirmed with Ops Commander. No one takes down the mark, but him. Over."

Rutger Eliades' quiet laughter surged over the frequency. "Someone's gonna be in for a surprise."

"That's a big fuckin' A," Mercuri's response was like stone.

Ops Commander Leonard Fowler had seemed to take the news of his murdered employers harder than their widows.

"Advise your men, Rut. Over."

"Copy. Over and out."

The channel silenced and Mercuri pocketed the two-way.

"Anybody missing Patch yet?" Pope asked, referring to their partner and friend Patroclus Kostas.

"Nah," Mercuri's sly grin emerged once more, causing his extraordinary golden stare to narrow in the process. "But right about now

17

a lot of folks are envying he and his crew for getting the nod to stay behind."

Pope gave a quiet chuckle. "Lemme guess- Brody's at the top of that list?"

"You know him well," Mercuri confirmed. "He pouted for a minute because he and his crew weren't tapped for the security detail on the old men."

That time, Pope snorted a laugh. "Christ, did the idiot really think the commanders would allow that considering how royally they fucked up at the hotel?"

"Well one of those old men is his father, remember?"

"Who gives a fuck?" The growling intensity latched onto Pope's soft voice again. "Not that I could care less, but Fritz and Hamisch might still be with us if that bozo and his crew hadn't been too busy getting their dicks waxed down in the strip club to help Caleb and Luke keep an eye out."

The deaths of Robert Fritz and Sumter Hamisch and the other revered board members of the Grodins Alberts Network, had made world news. Of course, those news broadcasts didn't report how the men had really met their ends. They couldn't. They wouldn't- not when the vast majority of the world's news and law enforcement agencies were either owned or controlled by various members of the board.

The savage multiple murders 10 months earlier in the Vegas hotel had caused more than a stir throughout The Network's fabric. Many, though they dared not admit it, found it poetically justified that the sick indulgences of The Ten had finally bitten them in their high powered asses.

Caleb Stein and Luke Robb had discovered the carnage, but had reported that the women sent to join The Ten that evening were nowhere to be found. But for their clothes and purses carrying only lipsticks and condoms, there were no other clues to their identities.

All anyone had to go on was the name of the man who arranged such evenings of debauchery for The Network and its associates. Enrique Roya however, had managed to keep himself hidden. For a while.

"If it weren't for Brody's screw up, this mission wouldn't have been necessary." Mercuri offered the reminder.

"You think this'll go over like we planned, Merc?" Pope asked.

"It better. I don't think another job like this will fall into our laps again any time soon." Mercuri reached inside the collar of his jacket to

18

massage tightness from his nape. "The guys won't be so easy to convince next time around, either."

"Hmph, easy," Pope's smirk caused his striking aquamarine gaze to sparkle slyly. "Only you would think setting this thing up had been easy."

"Persuasion was never my strong suit," Mercuri gave a self indulgent shrug. All jokes aside, orchestrating the strategy for the mission- the underlying one- had been one of the toughest, if not ballsiest, things he'd ever attempted.

Unbeknownst- he *hoped* it was still unbeknownst- to their superiors, Mercuri had managed to convince the bulk of the Grodins Alberts organization to rebel. Those who joined the rebellion, believed that their well-earned retirement was at hand and long overdue.

The radio in Mercuri's pocket began to crackle with static. "Teacher's Pet, this is Runway Model. Over."

Mercuri shook his head and slid a knowing look to a smiling Pope. "Copy Runway Model. What's your position? Over."

"We're hot and ready. Over." Slayte Miltiades' silky Southern drawl eased through the line.

Mercuri nodded. "Copy that. Standby. Over and out."

"I'll never doubt you, Merc," Pope was saying then, "but if these soap heads suddenly get cold feet and betray us, I say we forget about trying to free them from a life of murder and tyranny, take our payoff and run."

"Copy that," Mercuri had already reached the same decision long before they'd boarded The Network's planes in route to another bloodbath. Their intended target had been very grateful for the advanced warning regarding their upcoming visit. The target had been grateful to the tune of several million dollars- enough for five men, tired of the grind, to not only retire but to retire very well.

Mercuri heard Ops Commander Leonard Fowler's voice in his ear again telling them it was time to do this. He nudged Pope, giving the man a silent nod in indication.

"See you on the other side," Pope clapped a hand to Mercuri's shoulder and then went to team up with his crew.

~~~

"Alright men, let's move. Radio silence from here. Out." Ops Commander Fowler's voice was a violent whisper through various headsets and to the men nearest him.

"Boss."

Fowler was forging on ahead with his guys.

"Boss!"

"Goddammit!" Fowler snatched away his headset with a hiss. "Does radio silence mean anything to you, Rollins?"

Les Rollins already had his hands raised in a defensive stance. "You need to stay behind, Sir."

Those words stopped the commander. "Explain yourself, Captain," Fowler ordered.

"You can't go in there, Sir."

Fowler's full attention was on his subordinate then despite the wave of bodies swarming past them toward the mountainside villa. "And why not?" he demanded.

"Long story, Sir."

Cursing viciously, Fowler looked back toward the swarm already descending on the house. "Well son, it looks like I've just come into some free time."

~~~

Enrique Roya's Caracas villa was a work of art nestled in the Venezuelan mountainside with a view of tropical brilliance from every window. The multi-leveled dwelling with its teakwood decks, glossy hardwoods and Spanish tiles, loomed like an oasis against the late evening skies.

Chief Captain Basil Yost felt the sandy red hairs on the back of his neck stand on end within seconds of clearing the estate's front lawn. "This is wrong," he growled, pressing a hand to his ear to engage his headset.

"What's up, Chief?" Jose Arroyo held back to query his superior.

"Too quiet," Yost said.

Arroyo tugged the visor of his cap and scratched at his brow. "Guess it's past most people's bedtimes even in Venezuela."

"Yeah..." Yost scanned the vast landscape with fresh intensity. "That doesn't play for security, though. We were told it was considerable. Fuck." Yost pressed a hand to his earpiece again. "Chief, Captains, Commanders. Report. Fowler? Dennison?"

The response Yost received wasn't what he expected. A choked gurgle flooded the radio channel.

"Report!" Yost whispered violently.

Two words made their way through the line.

"Set up…"

"Son of a bitch!" Yost was turning for the villa to issue orders to abort when he felt the stinging slice across his jugular. The last thing he saw, before blackness completely descended, was his own blood pooling like the color of crude oil against the palms of his black leather gloves.

Arroyo retrieved a two-way radio from an inside pocket of his jacket. "Big dogs are sleepin'," he transmitted the message and then used Yost's jacket sleeve to clean his knife blade.

~~~

The mission- the true mission- commenced. Once the Commander, Chiefs, Captains, and Ops Specialists had been taken out of play, it was time for the next targets on the rung. Taking heed of Mercuri's tip, the villa's owner fled with his family hours before the assault team's arrival. Now, the immaculate home was primed for battle between those loyal to the Grodins Alberts Network and its philosophies and those who had been turned, persuaded-*wooed*-by the promise of normal lives.

Such were lives many had been promised long ago- promises that had been unfulfilled. The soldiers in the Grodins Alberts organization had finally learned that they would have to fulfill those promises by their own hands.

The dark night was lit by intermittent dispersals of gunfire and shouting. The men Pope Apostolou predicted would be stricken by a case of cold feet, proved him wrong.

The op wasn't an easy one. Not every soldier had been on board with taking down the hand feeding him. Those men fought with a mix of ferocity and confusion. They were either unsure how the tables had turned or unsure how they had so seamlessly turned in favor of the comrades they now fought against instead of alongside.

The mutineers claimed victory after a forty-five minute skirmish. The victorious wasted no time with celebration. Instead, they made quick exits- parting ways for futures that were virtually unknown. They'd all had enough of shedding blood for the advancement of others.

Now, those days were over and they made a point of giving their thanks to those who had made it possible. Mercuri received the king's portion of the handshakes and that was no surprise. While Rutger, Pope and Slayte had played valuable roles, everyone knew it was Mercuri who'd had the vision.

~~~

"How long do you think we'll live the quiet life?" Slayte observed the mountainside villa growing smaller in the side mirror of the Jeep he and his friends took to their next destination.

"I'll take forever," Pope called, eyes closed as he relaxed back on the rear seat.

"I mean, how long do you think *they'll* let us live the quiet life?" Slayte rephrased once a chorus of laughter had softened on the wind. "If it's one thing you can count when it comes to guys like Grodins and Alberts, there's always a group of loyal idiots who'll be set on revenge."

"Everybody out there tonight, knew what they were takin' on," Mercuri said from his place behind the wheel. "They knew what the consequences could be later down the road." He slanted a smirk to Slayte across the gear shift. "You're forgetting what else you can always count on."

"What's that?" Slayte slid down in the passenger seat and prepared to nap.

Mercuri set his head back against the driver's side rest. "Anything worth having is worth walking through hell for and walking back in to defend."

~CHAPTER 2~

Las Vegas, Nevada~ The Present

Dorinda Patterson had finally made it. Entrepreneur, investor, she was even an honorary board member at her 5000 member church. Life was good. She had yet to secure the roles of wife and mother, but life was good.

  Besides, Dorinda knew, those particular aspirations had never been ones she'd obsessed over. It would have been unrealistic to do so anyway. While becoming a mother wasn't such a far stretch, men rarely married women in her line of work. Such truths had stopped bothering her long ago. The income her line of work provided allowed any upset she may've experienced because of certain truths, to be quickly eased.

  That didn't mean the job wasn't without its share of stressful moments. In the field of prostitution, stress was not only a given, it was quite often highly profitable. Men wanted their... sexual recreation to be trouble-free, *stress*-free. After all, trouble and stress were what work and marriage were for. When it came to sexual recreation, men were willing to pay very well to make stress disappear.

Dorinda had considered herself very blessed not to have had stress be a consistent part of her work life. There had been the occasional uprisings of course, but nothing that hovered at the fringes of life and death.

Until, The Ten.

She slid back the lavender suede chair from an immaculate white lacquer desk and surveyed the surroundings she had, on many occasions, demeaned herself to earn. It had all been worth it to pull a nod from Enrique Roya. The stories of how the man had staked his lucrative lifestyle were vast, varied and made her demeaning exploits seem G-rated.

Still, she'd gotten his nod- a nod that had allowed her to put her brothel under Roya's protective umbrella. Protection didn't come without a price, but Dorinda at first believed the price would be worth it. At first. Being one of Roya's associates got she and her girls more than protection.

The Roya name had transferred her brothel from being little more than a penny ante motel, to one of the premiere destinations on the Vegas underground. The transformation had come in the literal and figurative sense.

Gone, was the tacky shag carpeting over which even tackier throw rugs had been placed to hide careless spills of beverages and...other substances. Her floors now shone with gleaming hardwoods. The entire place had been newly painted, treated to resist stains. The walls boasted vibrant colors that she'd allowed her girls to select. Cheap looking curtains had been replaced by privacy blinds in rich, earth toned shades. It was like an entirely new dwelling.

The 'newness' brought on new tricks as well. Gone, were the cheapskates looking for a quick thrill on a budget. Diversion, Dorinda's brothel, then appealed to a better funded set.

As Dorinda wanted to ensure their loyalty, she made certain that her client's needs were consistently met without question. When certain customers complained about the lack of...variety, Dorinda didn't panic. She went out and added new girls to her roster.

When certain customers requested fresh girls regularly, she didn't panic. She supplied. When Roya drew her into the inner circle of his sex trade conglomerate, she thought she'd died and gone to heaven. It wasn't heaven.

She'd heard about The Ten, heard about Roya's involvement with the Grodins Alberts Network. No one who earned a living on the relaxed side of the law, went long without hearing of the organization. The Ten however... The Ten were a group few in her business knew of unless their services were specifically requested.

As Dorinda's reputation for pampering her clients grew, so did her place along the Roya food chain. Not long after that, Grodins Alberts wanted Dorinda's special brand of customer service for its most revered members. Though she was eager to meet the demand, finding new girls wasn't an easy thing to do. High class women for high class clientele, didn't just show up wanting to be paid for sex.

Dorinda had no interest in the women who *wanted* to be paid. She wanted the ones who would've believed they had too much self respect, self worth and good sense to even consider the life.

Those women weren't hard to find at all, actually. Dorinda had ample amounts of the bait required to entice such women, but luring them to that bait... another matter entirely. Dorinda needed only to know what lure to use. And there was always an appropriate lure. Nevermind what a woman thought she'd convinced herself she'd never do. Dorinda could be patient though and let others do the luring for her.

The cafes in and around the university area, were perfect hunting grounds for such researchers- those discreet observers who'd keep an eye out for what she wanted. A gorgeous, good girl with money problems. It had been a good scheme, until The Ten. Until, that night.

Sighing out a breath that ruffled the bangs of her curly bob, Dorinda strode over to a bar fashioned of the same lacquer as her desk. The construction jutted out in a sultry curve along the rear wall of her office. She should've started drinking hours ago, she thought blackly and grabbed a whiskey bottle by the neck with plans to upturn it as opposed to looking for a glass.

Decorum, Dorinda... she reminded herself and reached for a blocky glass on the small chrome drying rack beneath the bar top. Quickly, she sloshed a healthy serving of the drink into the glass and down it in one fiery gulp.

Grimacing fiercely, Dorinda still relished the burn, Silently, she repeated that she should have started drinking hours ago- right after that call. It was no use running, chances were strong that he'd had her place under surveillance weeks before he'd even contacted her. She kicked at a stool skirting the bar. Decorum be damned.

25

It had been over six years. Six goddamn years. Harris Van Deer was still on his mad quest for… she had no idea what exactly. She knew it had to do with what happened inside the penthouse where she'd sent those girls.

Harris Van Deer never asked about those girls, though. He had only been interested in what she knew of Enrique Roya's whereabouts. Like she'd be privy to information like that. She may've charted a stunning climb up the Roya food chain, but she wasn't a member of the inner circle where such knowledge would be shared.

Dorinda hadn't heard from Harris Van Deer in years, not since shortly after that night. What the hell could he want with her now? Had something changed? She slid a quick look to the bottle of whiskey and debated again on chugging down the mind-numbing liquid. Had he come into new information about that long ago night? She wondered. Had all the man's investigating about the events leading up to those brutal deaths finally circled back around to the girls? The girls whose identities Roya said must be protected at all costs?

Dorinda snorted, sloshed another serving of drink into the glass and tossed it back. Protected at all costs? What the hell for? She had never understood why Roya had cared so much about the welfare of four whores who'd yet to earn him a dime?

Perhaps that was why. Dorinda regarded the glass with a furtive look. Those girls hadn't earned Roya a dime before that night, but they *owed* him plenty. They owed him plenty because of her-because of the temptation she'd thrown their way. Now, even years later, Dorinda continued to tell herself that she hadn't forced those girls to do anything to put themselves in Roya's debt. The more she told herself that, the less she believed it. Of course, full disclosure was never the best idea especially in this particular business.

Had she told those four girls what they'd be in for with The Ten that night...she would've lost a very profitable client. Ironically, she lost them anyway and those girls...Dorinda shuddered as she often did when thoughts plagued her of what drove them to the madness they unleashed that night. Perhaps that was why she had and would keep what she knew. She hadn't forced those girls, but she hadn't warned them either. She knew guilt over that would haunt her the rest of her life.

Her hand spasmed around the glass when she heard the knock. She decided against a third hit of the whiskey. It wouldn't do to be too mellowed out around this crowd. With a casual grace, she made her way through the mirrored halls of her establishment.

She had given her staff the night off. This, she wanted to do alone. She'd been instructed to be alone, but would have been regardless. Her girls had no business there tonight.

The liquor worked its magic, already massaging her limbs like a balm. Her stride was a saunter yet; despite all her cool, her heart pounded like a vicious call of thunder. The man she opened her door to, smiled warmly. That warmth belied the distinct chill in his almost opaque stare.

Her ease jostled against sudden disquiet and her large baby blues took a brief scan beyond the man's broad shoulder.

"I thought-"

"He's on his way," Grant Zubin spoke even as he smiled. "He thought we could chat for a little while."

Dorinda stepped back from the door- a soundless invitation for her visitor to enter.

"You don't mind if my guys come in, do you love? It's cold as a bitch out there tonight."

Dorinda only shook her head. It was a totally unnecessary gesture, she knew. Her guests were about to make themselves quite comfortable. She would've rathered not see any of this particular bunch, though. She'd have preferred the one she knew as Harris. There was something dead in his eyes that was more preoccupied than malicious.

The dead element she saw in Grant Zubin's cold metallic blue stare was ominous and alert with dark intent. The unsettling effect of his gaze was only rivaled by the platinum blonde hair he wore in a buzz cut.

Dorinda was moving to close the door once the men were all inside.

"Don't worry about the door, love. I'll handle it," Grant Zubin's voice was as cordial as his warm smile. "You go on and get acquainted with my guys. I'll be right there."

Zubin leaned against the door and watched the madam, flanked by his men, proceed down the hall. His warm smile chilled as he cracked his knuckles.

~~~

Harris Van Deer kept his dark Mercedes SUV parked down the quiet street some distance from the other flashier sports cars and bikes that were littering the curving brick drive of Diversion. Smirking, he considered his partner Grant Zubin's flare for the debased and dramatic.

Harris wondered how the fates had seen fit to bring Zubin such a team of like-minded individuals as the men whose loyalty he commanded. Harris tucked his mobile into a jacket pocket after reading Zubin's text that they were starting the meeting. He could wait, preferring to brave the night's chilly temps instead of witnessing Dorinda Patterson's 'meeting' with his associates.

Harris had never developed Zubin's equal opportunity outlook when it came to interrogation or dispersing pain as punishment. Though he didn't always approve of the methods, he'd do nothing to curb his partner's techniques. This was too important.

Harris pressed a hand over the bridge of his nose. It still bore bruising from the abuse it had suffered.

Patroclus Kostas, the skinny Greek bastard, hadn't betrayed his friends even after the serious working over he'd suffered. That had been disappointing, but a silver lining had presented itself. Harris had taken great and personal pleasure in pummeling the man's face. No one would doubt that he had died very badly.

How he wished he could be there when Mercuri got the news. How he wished he could see the man's face when he saw what they'd done to his friend's. Taking Patroclus Kostas' life had indeed been satisfying, but it had also been rash.

Kostas may not have been willing to give up his friends, but it would've been useful to have him confirm what Corky Lapis had shuddered out during the waning moments of his honorable life. Corky's heroic efforts as a volunteer fireman had earned him a brief spot on his local news station. That spot had been picked up by a regional affiliate that caught the eye of the network's morning news show.

That broadcast had been the catalyst which had added fuel to an old fire. It had given Harris and his associates all the info they'd needed to track him down.

Why would Corky have given them Enrique Roya's name if it wasn't just as Harris had suspected all along? The Roya job had all been a set up, organized by Mercuri Nikolaides. It had all been a carefully orchestrated plan to take out the commanding officers of the Grodins Alberts Network as well as The Network's creators Lorne Grodins and Nathan Alberts.

The incident at the Vegas penthouse had all been part of the plan. Merc, that son of a bitch, had left no stone unturned. While that weasel Kostas and his team were well on task to take out Grodins and Alberts, Mercuri had arranged for Roya's sluts to take out The Network's board.

Yes, the plan had been carefully orchestrated. It had been masterfully implemented, Harris admitted. That type of unwavering focus, attention to detail and frigid ruthlessness had made Mercuri the darling of the GAN. A fucking darling! The snarl of words resounded in Harris' head.

How much had *he* done? What lengths had *he* gone to get those cocksuckers to give him half a shot as something more than a leg breaker? Harris balled a fist, an attempt to douse the memories trying to claw their way to the front of his brain.

He couldn't let them in, he thought, slapping his palms to his shaved head. Harris squeezed his eyes shut and gave his thoughts time to settle. Not too much, though. He needed those thoughts to keep some prevalence in his mind. When he finally got his hands on Mercuri, he wanted to do more than kill him. He wanted to take his time hurting him and not to avenge the deaths of the ten bastards who died at the hands of their bimbos. Mercuri had to pay for what he'd done to the organization Harris would've been on track to take charge of as the head of its soldiers. Now, there was practically nothing to take charge of. If the asshole had just waited, Harris raged. He could've given Mercuri what he'd wanted: freedom. The idiot, Harris thought. All this just to resign.

Harris would have laughed had Mercuri's antics not been so costly. At the helm of the GAN, he could've given Mercuri and all the rest their freedom and more. He *may have*. The GAN had secrets that it wouldn't do well to have former employees blabbing about on the outside.

The only way one became a *former* employee of the GAN was by becoming dead. Harris felt the phone vibrate under his suit coat again. Too soon to be Zubin, he thought. The man had patience for little else aside from his work. He checked the phone anyway, grimacing over the notification that his phone would begin updating in an hour.

He reached for fur-lined leather gloves lying on the SUV's passenger seat. Bringing Zubin in at the onset of an interrogation wasn't his usual method. Zubin's style was usually most advantageous towards the end of things.

Sadly, there wasn't time to play the Q and A dance. Harris needed Dorinda Patterson to talk now. The only way she'd do that was if she was too scared to endure more agony than she'd already been subjected to. With any luck, Zubin would call in to tell him Patterson had already given up Roya and he could avoid a trip inside the brothel to get an actual image of the handiwork.

Perhaps the madam would lead them right to what they wanted and there would be no need to hunt Roya. Oh yes, he thought, tugging on one of his gloves. If only they could bypass the pimp and go right to his working girls.

What would Mercuri do if he knew I had them? Excitement began to churn in Harris' belly until it overcame the dread of witnessing what was happening to the woman inside the large townhome behind the unassuming brick drive.

What were they to him? Knowing Mercuri and his inner circle, they'd most likely sampled the goods and knew they were up for the task. They wouldn't have charged just any four women with the job. Not only would they have to be adept at killing, they'd have to be the kind of lure that would have a man eager to take off his trousers and his weapons without hesitation.

When found, The Ten had been naked as the day they'd been born. The men may've been board member types, but they were too sadistic to be taken out by four hookers. Unless there'd been more to it than that. He'd spent six years looking for a lead to explain that night. It had been six years of his colleagues looking at him like he was even more insane than they'd already suspected he was.

Six years. Aside from Mercuri, Pope, Slayte and Rutger, there hadn't been a peep from anyone else involved with all that madness. Then, just like that Charles 'Corky' Lapis shows up on a morning show as a hero firefighter. Now the players were being recalled to the stage.

Perhaps they'd find Mercuri's four hookers about to kill off another group of unsuspecting saps. There was however an even more interesting theory, Harris mused. How satisfying would it be to find that his old friend had settled down into normalcy. Perhaps Mercuri had finally found what he'd been looking for. Something he'd be willing to give up any part of himself to claim or to keep.

From his coat pocket, Harris retrieved an old magazine article featuring Mercuri at the onset of his new career. The bastard, Harris sneered silently, while scanning the picture of a ship adorned with the Mercuri Fleets logo.

The vessel, already dated when Mercuri had acquired it, was being dry docked at a local shipyard. It had served as Mercuri's first and only ship to launch his business. The first year had been a banner one. The success had allowed Mercuri to dock his dated ship for newer, top of the line models.

Harris wadded the old article he obsessively kept in his possession and hurled it across the dash. How would the darling of the GAN handle losing his revered and powerful lifestyle? How would he handle seeing his dreams reduced to nothing? Harris knew what that felt like. Thanks to Mercuri Nikolaides he knew what it was like not only to lose it, but to see it savaged, ravaged, destroyed…

How delicious would it be if Mercuri finally got to experience the same?

~CHAPTER 3~

Aspen, Colorado~ 3 weeks later

Mercuri Nikolaides could've easily envisioned himself taking part in dozens of scenarios other than the one he currently stood in the midst of. Also worthy of note, was who he stood in the midst of it with. Mercuri's business partner and long time friend Pope Apostolou hadn't found it at all funny when he'd extended a party invite only to have Mercuri laugh in his face or… over the phone as it were.

Nevertheless, there he stood as Pope's 'plus one' at his neighbor's house-warming party. Mercuri didn't know what was more surprising, that the man actually had neighbors or that they liked him well enough to invite him into their home.

Mercuri cut his friend some slack, knowing all too well how easily Pope could turn on the charm when he chose. This, despite the intimidating persona the man could tug on like clothes.

Mercuri returned his focus to the conversation he stood closest to. The hosts were explaining that their gathering was in fact a *re*-housewarming party.

"The place isn't new, just newly remodeled," Steve Brassels explained.

Steve's wife began to laugh while shaking her head. "It's not even that," Denise Brassels put a hand to her husband's arm. "We simply had it modified."

"I don't get it," Pope said flatly. "Is that like something with your mortgage?" He asked.

Steve Brassels chuckled. "Good to know I'm not the only one who was confused."

"Oh…" Denise poked her husband's ribs with a soft elbow and then turned to her guests. "We got into it during a visit to one of our friends in California. We were just as clueless as you are now, Pope. Then we sat down with the modifier who explained the concept." The woman positioned her hands as though she were envisioning a scene.

"Basically, all you see here has been here all along," Denise's shrug sent the sequins sparkling across her black blouse. "With the addition of a few minor details, new life has been breathed into our home." Denise laughed when her guests regarded her with curious and skeptical looks. Next, she was pointing to a suede sectional sofa across the large crowded den. The room, glassed in on three sides, overlooked the Brassels' rear lawn. The acreage was an expanse of winter white lit by shimmers of gold from the yard lamps placed throughout.

"I already had four people ask what we did with our old couch," Denise was saying. "Lots of them remembered it because each section boasted a caddy that could hold everything from drinks and chips, to socks and blankets- very popular on our game days during football season." She slapped her hands to her sides and looked wholly content. "None of them believed me when I told them it was the same sofa we've had since we moved here eleven years ago."

"So why do they think it's new?" Mercuri was somewhat stunned by his interest in the answer.

Denise shrugged as though the concept were elementary. "Our modifier does much of what an interior designer would, but on a smaller scale that's nicer for the wallet."

Looking confused, Pope dragged a hand through a wealth of blue black waves that just brushed his shoulders. "Couldn't you just go out and find your own new pillows for the couch?"

Mercuri bowed his head when his mouth quirked on a smile. He was sure the tidy 60something couple would be unnerved by Pope's harmless, but gruff manner as he towered over them.

The Brassels merrily traded amused looks and then laughed.

Steve Brassels knocked a fist to Pope's bicep. "That's where the science comes in."

"See, it all goes far beyond new pillows and drapes," Denise continued the explanation. "They're little additions the average person might never think of in terms of redecorating. Folks tend to look at the flash and dazzle instead of the tiny elements that bring out the more vibrant subtleties."

Steve chuckled then, his green eyes heavily crinkled at the corners. "If you met our modifier, you'd understand why she's such a big fan of tiny elements."

"Darn it, that's what we're supposed to be doing now," Denise slapped her husband's arm, "the introduction," she whispered.

Steve smacked his forehead with the heel of his hand. "Guys we're sorry, but you're gonna have to excuse us," he told Mercuri and Pope.

"I'll go find her," Denise nudged Steve's arm again, "Honey be sure to give them a card," she said before disappearing into the dense crowd.

"Right," Steve moved to a glass topped end table with granite edging. There, he retrieved a business card from a small silver tin case in the center,.

"Most of her clients are corporations, but she'll do the occasional residence when she finds a place that appeals to her." Steve explained, handing the card to Pope. Then, he was slapping his guest's arms and taking the path his wife had charted through the sea of minglers.

Mercuri cleared his throat following the Brassels whirlwind departures. "Well man, thanks for a very educational evening. I'm sure that's more than I ever needed to know about interior decorating, but I guess you're never too old to learn."

"It's called modifying, not interior decorating," Pope corrected with mock disdain coloring his voice. "And you shouldn't knock it 'til you try it."

"Are *you* going to try it?" Mercuri asked.

Pope shrugged, "A trip to Big Lots is all the modifying I need." He shook his head then. "Rich people…"

Mercuri's eyes were a distinctive golden tint that emphasized the feline intensity of his gaze when he was highly intrigued... or highly pissed. Pope's words had instilled the former emotion- somewhat.

"Seriously?" Mercuri sent his friend an incredulous look that belied his intrigue. "And exactly how many figures comprised your bank balance when you last checked?"

"I'm speaking in terms of old money," the disdain still colored Pope's voice.

Mercuri grunted a laugh. "Last I heard, it all spent exactly the same."

"Aw, can it, man. You know what I mean," the trademark pissed off growl started to underlie Pope's voice. "Maybe our grandkids'll be part of that club, but never us."

Mercuri refused to bite on his friend's favorite argument. They had been 'rich people' for over six years and still the men closest to him refused to accept it. Mercuri couldn't say he was confused by that. The way they'd become 'rich people' wasn't a story they'd ever share over brandy and cigars with the boys at the club. Unlike Pope, Mercuri refused to accept that they hadn't earned their place at the table.

The money earned by way of their ill-gotten lifestyle had been well used or rather, well-invested. Mercuri's decision to stake his claim in the realm of import, export shipping had allowed him to quintuple his friends' net worths as those investments continued to diversify.

Though Mercuri's shipping magnate dream had served them all well, Pope had other interests he'd wanted to let his money play around in. As a result, the man had put funds into an array of commercial and residential properties worldwide.

Slayte Miltiades and Rutger Eliades were sadly not the sort for playing the market or anything that even hinted of work. The two were happy letting their friends put their money to work for them.

In whatever way the four had seen fit to tend their money, it was money well-earned, earned legitimately and tended diligently. Mercuri refused to have any of them ever feeling the need to sink back into what they'd once done to survive.

"Hey, hey everybody let's move it on to the living room!"

Steve Brassels' friendly voice resonated through the house as though amplified. From the den, the living room was a healthy trek along a glass corridor that unveiled more of the staggering snow white property. Steps that were muffled by the corridor's short, dark carpeting, sprung to life with sound when shoe soles began to hit the eye catching hardwoods of the living room entryway. The lofty space also drew the eye to an astonishing skylight made more astonishing by the wrought iron chandelier that washed the room in soft illumination.

Steve Brassels applauded as his guests congregated a few feet below where he stood on the stairway landing. The construction branched off and vanished behind the room's white walls.

"Again Denise and I want to thank you all for coming," Steve had set aside the microphone he'd used to herd in his guests from various parts of the house. His strong tone carried easily over the large living room.

"We also want to thank you for all the compliments we've received on this place," the man continued, "Now, while we appreciate the flattery, we can't take it. Luckily, the young woman who deserves all the praise is here to accept it."

Steve Brassels allowed applause to fill the room for a few seconds before he was raising his hands for silence. "Now many of you have had the chance to speak with her tonight, so you know this already. For the rest, I'll have to warn you that the lady's dance card is filling quickly. If you want her to consider working this same magic for you, then you better grab her while the gettin's good. Ladies and gentlemen, Etienne Shaw!"

Mercuri joined in applauding the designer- er- modifier. When she joined Steve and Denise Brassels on the landing, his applause faltered as he was quite simply intrigued.

Brassels hadn't quite finished his introduction, yet Mercuri moved on closer to the front of the room. He brushed past Pope, who caught the dazed set to his friend's expression.

Smiling, Pope closed the distance to Mercuri who'd stopped several feet away from the landing to watch the dark, waif-like beauty as though he were helpless to do much else. Taking the business card Brassels had passed along, Pope slipped it into Mercuri's coat pocket.
~~~

Tee was certain that she'd already shaken hands with everyone at the party. She promised herself that if no one approached her in the next five minutes, she was going to make a run for it. She adored Steve and Denise for throwing the party in her honor. There was nothing like working for clients who didn't micromanage and left you alone to do what they'd paid you to do for them.

It was even more wonderful when those clients referred you to friends who were hopefully the same non-micromanaging, leave you alone to do your work type. Still, she was beat. The flight from her previous job in New York had given her a little time to unwind, but not nearly as much as she'd needed. That last job had been especially demanding, but worth it once the final results were tallied.

Now, all she wanted was to head up to the guest suite her clients had prepared for her visit. She'd only had a few moments to admire her bed before the party began. She was so looking forward to doing more than admiring it.

Four and a half minutes, Tee regarded the second hand on her watch. With a resolved shrug, she decided that was good enough.

"Leaving your party so soon?"

The clear baritone touched her ears just as she took the second step up. When she turned, Tee sensed her need for sleep only lingering then as though it were an afterthought.

"I..." her voice, naturally cool, usually carried on a steady chord. *Usually*. Just then, her tone was almost whisper soft and fascinated.

Mercuri's voice had been gripped by a fair amount of fascination as well. God, how tall was she? He wondered. Her build, though a beckoning one, was slight. Combined with the boyish cut taming her wavy dark hair, she appeared almost elfin.

Tee was thinking almost the same about the man who had spoken to her. God, how tall was he? Granted, most people seemed excessively tall to her- an easy thing to conceive given that her own height topped out at just under 5'3.

But this guy...he would seem excessively tall to anyone. Well over 6'6 easy. Then there was his build. How many reps, for how many hours over how many weeks and years did it take to carve out a physique such as the one he claimed?

The height and build, though supremely distracting had nothing on the face. Brutally handsome, with enviable bone structure beneath smooth copper-toned skin, the face was a potent attention-getter. His hair, thick and black as obsidian, waved back off a wide forehead to emphasize the harsh beauty of his looks.

Tee knew she was staring, but she just couldn't seem to stop herself. Why couldn't she stop herself? Losing her composure over gorgeous men was something she hadn't done in years. Something she hadn't done since she was a completely different Etienne Shaw.

It had to be his eyes, she thought. Who could resist staring into eyes like that? They were deeply set and intense, but it was the color that gave her pause.

Brilliantly gold; with rich brown flecks that were bolder given the vibrancy of the gold, the combination was a striking one. If she didn't know better, Tee would have sworn she was staring into the eyes of a feline- a colossal, predatory feline.

"They're mine," a quiet sigh colored Mercuri's words as though he'd guessed and wasn't at all surprised by her preoccupation with his eyes.

She smiled. "I didn't doubt it," Tee was pleased to hear that her voice had regained its cool, steady flow.

"They make some people nervous," he said.

Tee was sure the eyes were only partly to blame when pitted against the total package. He was speaking again before she could come up with a response.

"Mercuri Nikolaides."

Again, Tee smiled. "I'm going to have to get you to write that one down."

"Yeah, it's a mouthful."

"I bet," she winced the second the words tripped off her tongue. *Losing your composure over a gorgeous man is something you haven't done in years,* she reminded herself.

Mercuri's mouth, a wide undeniably sensual curve, twitched on the cusp of a smile. He resisted grinning outright over the words he was sure she hadn't intended to utter- not out loud anyway.

"This is uh- some place," he half gestured to the Brassels' living room instead. "Impressive," he added with a curious smile. "So how'd you get into... Jeez, what's it called?" He only pretended to hunt for the name. "Oh yeah- modifying?"

Tee laughed, enjoying the feel of the gesture she rarely indulged in away from her girlfriends. "I'm not really sure where that term came from," she said.

Mercuri sighed again. "Rich people," he grinned when she laughed again.

"What I really do is interior design for corporations."

Mercuri nodded, slipped a hand into a deep side pocket along his dark trousers. "I think our hosts mentioned that," he said.

"Well the thing about design is in the way each designer envisions the space and how well that vision compliments the clients." Absently, she smoothed a hand over the snug sleeves of the creamy powder blue frock that adored her curves.

"Basically, I reimagine spaces," she explained, as her brow quirked. "People like how my mind works. Sadly, most people spend so much time regarding the overall picture, they miss the little things- small touches that make a place sing."

"Like what?" Mercuri stepped in a fraction. Casually, he propped an elbow to the oak railing that sectioned off the staircase landing from the living room. While part of him wanted her answer, a larger part just wanted to listen to her speak- to observe her petite frame and exquisite face as she did so.

"Well there're all sorts of *little* things one can do to add warmth to a space," Tee went on. She was in her element as she spoke of her craft and therefore unaware of how intently she was being studied. "It matters very little what the space is used for."

"A boxing gym?" Mercuri smiled when he saw hers engage.

"Okay…" Tee's luminous ebony gaze twinkled with amusement as she scanned the milling crowd before looking back to Mercuri.

"If it's important for someone to make their gym warm and inviting, they could easily add touches such as comfy lounging chairs and plants… but in a place like that you'd prefer subtlety. Leave the chairs and plants to the lobby- if it's a professional gym. For the actual space, minute additions can make bold impressions on the overall appeal. Something as small as having an outlet concealer for a light fixture decorated with the image of a small pair of boxing gloves or having the weight racks painted to match the gym's overall color scheme."

"And you could paint the little gloves on the sides of the racks," Mercuri supplied, grinning anew when Tee laughed.

"Now you're getting it!" She cheered. "I've never done an actual gym, but if the chance comes my way, I'll be sure to get your permission before I use your idea."

"It's all yours," Mercuri waved a hand. "So how'd you go from conference rooms for corporations to interior design for homeowners?"

"Well, I only got into that part by accident. A friend of mine bought this big, over-the-top place out in Malibu. Just to say she had it, you know?"

"I know the type," Mercuri thought of Pope.

"It was a gorgeous place, but it wasn't a home. I griped so much, she finally told me to do something about it. I did and had a great time in the process."

"So you spend a lot of time in Malibu?"

"Well I live in San Francisco, so…"

"No kidding?" Surprise pooled his vivid eyes. "I'm in Sonoma County- near Kenwood."

Laughter reflected her surprise as well. "Small world," she said.

"Yeah," Mercuri took another patient appraisal of her small, curvy body and then straightened. "I should let you go. It was nice meeting you and I'll call if I'm ever in the market for a modification."

"Sounds good." She gave him a winning smile as she turned to head back up the staircase. "Goodnight Mr. Nikolaides," she called.

"Ms. Shaw," Mercuri watched until she was gone from his sight.

~CHAPTER 4~

Pope smiled, approving of the view that presently had his friends' full attention directed beyond the passenger side window of his Suburban.

"She redesigns homes, reimagines corporate meeting spaces, sketches...Hell..." Pope leaned in to snag a closer look across Mercuri's shoulder. "All that talent wrapped up in a cute, tiny package like that. A guy could forget his ghosts, learn how to live happily ever after, huh?"

Mercuri rested back against the seat, grinning. "Sounds like you're in love. Why don't you go after her?"

Chuckling, Pope used an arm to nudge Mercuri's. "It's a temptation I could go for if I wasn't afraid of having both my legs broken." Pope's aquamarine stare narrowed playfully when Mercuri eased him a chilly look. "I'm guessing the broken legs would just be the start of my torment," he said.

Mercuri directed his golden stare beyond the passenger window again. "Just the start," he confirmed.

"Understood!" Pope laughed, nudging Mercuri's arm again. "So? Why aren't *you* going after her? The Merc I knew would've been waking up next to her this morning instead of pining over her from a car window."

"I haven't been that Merc in a long time," he grimaced suddenly, "and I never woke up next to them. I'm also not pining over her," he muttered the last.

"Right!" Pope's laughter reengaged. "And how many times did you start to come back over here after we left the party last night?"

Frustration began to eat away at Mercuri's trademark calm. "She's too small for me," he suddenly snapped only to feel his agitation mount in response to the gleeful chuckle near his ear.

"Too small? But you don't know for sure, do you? And aren't you just dying to solve that mystery?" Unable to rouse a response from his friend, Pope's laughter continued to mount and he slapped a hand to Mercuri's shoulder.

"Don't worry, man. I'll be happy to wait for you if you're over your shyness by the time I get back," with that, Pope left the SUV and made his way to Steve and Denise Brassels' front door.

Mercuri was fixed on the broad terrace that faced the rear of the Brassels' property. Soon, he'd indeed had his fill of staring.

Tee was bundled up on the terrace where she sat sketching in the middle of the snowy environment. A wide pad in her gloved hands, she merrily scribbled away, oblivious to everything else around her.

Mercuri stood on the terrace then, oblivious to everything else except her. He could feel himself smiling and didn't begrudge the sensation. It felt good to smile over something as missed as admiring a woman. Just...admiring. When was the last time he did that without the admiration following a natural progression to a bedroom?

Not that he didn't want that progression to take place. Only...the chat he'd had with her the night before... Hell, he'd actually enjoyed it-brief as it was. No agendas just... talk. Oh, his interest hadn't been completely platonic. It wasn't everyday a man came across petite and voluptuous in one package. One extraordinary package.

She was covered almost head to toe in white fur and leather. The white was a stark, gorgeous contrast against the molasses dark of her flawless skin. The leather jacket and pants emphasized her body in the most beckoning way as they molded to her ample bust and bottom.

"Do you ever take a break?"

Tee's head whipped round and she let her pad slip to the lounge where she sat as she sketched. "Mr. Nikolaides."

He smiled, appreciating the sound of his name on her voice then as much as he had the night before. "My first name takes less time to say."

She didn't need a second to recall it, but took one anyway. "Mercuri."

He rolled a shoulder beneath the denim jacket he wore. "See?"

Tee clasped her gloved hands into her lap. "Guess that means you'll have to call me Tee. It's what most people call me anyway."

His gaze narrowed, the smile defining. "I'm guessing you don't approve?" He watched her resulting expression confirm the guess. "Why do you hate it? It's... fitting."

"I guess it's better than being called what it stands for," her sigh carried on the still air. "It's short for Itty as in *Itty*enne as in Itty Bitty."

"Ah," Mercuri inclined his head in understanding. "I guess the folks who came up with that aren't the best of friends."

"Hmph, actually they're my best friends," Tee smiled genuinely. "My friends are pretty... Amazonian. We've known each other a long time. Besides... nicknames usually hold a certain significance, don't they?"

Mercuri relayed his agreement with a nod. "It's too bad the significance isn't always complimentary."

"Yeah," she picked at a miniscule thread that had loosened on the back of her glove. "Anyway, it was either Tee or Tiny and that one..." she shivered.

Mercuri's laughter erupted and Tee felt herself shivering then for an entirely different reason. He had an obviously easy manner, one she sensed he could shed easily enough should the need arise. Looking at him, she figured he'd lived a life where those needs rose often.

In addition to making her feel highly overdressed in leather and her fur-trimmed hat, the hoody he sported beneath the lightweight denim molded beautifully to his shoulders. Tee was sure that a build like his made it necessary for him to enter most doorways at an angle.

"If it makes you feel any better, my friends call me Merc. Talk about a non-complimentary nickname," he said once his laughter had curbed.

"Does it have any significance?"

"None I care to talk about."

She could see he meant that and took little time to mull over the meaning. "So did you change your mind about having your house...modified?"

"I'm on my way back to California," he said once they'd exchanged smiles to acknowledge the joke. "My friend just came over to say goodbye to the Brassels."

Tee gave a dutiful shrug. "Well then."

"Well then," he'd returned her sentiment but his feet refused to obey the words next being issued from his brain. Those words were telling him to walk away, reminding him that he was too complicated for anything that went beyond one night. One look at the dark, tiny woman curled up on the chaise, told him he'd want more than one night.

He walked toward her and she pushed to her knees, taking his hand when he offered it to shake. "It was nice meeting you, Etienne."

"Same-oh," Gently, she eased her fingers from his palm to tug off her glove and rest her bare hand against his. "Same here, Mercuri."

Mercuri smiled, nodded and held onto her far longer than necessary. He stroked the back of her hand and the tops of her fingers as though he were trying to replicate an image of the limb in his mind. Then, he was clearing his throat, giving her hand a quick squeeze and turning away.

Tee watched him walk off and then she was studying her hand as if trying to decipher whatever it was that had held him so transfixed. It took less than a minute for her to mutter to herself that she was being a complete idiot. She was certain Mercuri Nikolaides had held many a female hand in his and had regarded it as reverently as he had her own.

Still, such a gesture, offered by such a man and to a woman who had never experienced such a thing... powerful stuff. Rolling her eyes then, Tee tugged back on her glove. It was powerful stuff that she didn't have time for. She didn't have the time, nor did she have a past that would allow such gestures to nudge up against what they could promise.

What the hell had her traipsing off on a tangent like that anyway? The query had her rolling her eyes with a grimace that time. She hadn't thought of such things in years. Maybe that was the problem.

She laughed quietly then. Hell yes that was a problem. One of many.

That night... That night that; even after six years, she hadn't been able to get out of her mind. She hadn't even been able to tuck it away in some rarely visited corner. Most people would probably be on their third therapist by now. She hadn't even considered visiting one.

What would she confess in a session? What *could* she confess? She wasn't seeking closure to the mental tortures associated with sexual assault. Besides, she'd found closure, hadn't she? Sure it'd been closure to guilt, but closure none the less. What did that make her?

She heard an engine gunning in the distance and noticed a massive burgundy SUV pulling off. What would her charming new acquaintance think of her if he knew how she'd gotten closure to her guilt? What would he think of her if he knew what she'd had to feel guilty about? Would he even want to shake her hand much less hold and regard it so tenderly? He'd probably not even be able to look at her. How long had it been before she'd been able to look at herself?

Tee heard her name then and was thankful for the interruption on her runaway thoughts. Her runaway nightmares. Denise Brassels appeared on the terrace wearing a full length sable coat. Tee felt an easy smile on her mouth at the sight of the woman's pink yoga pants appearing when the coat flew against the wintry breeze. White sneakers rounded out the unlikely ensemble.

Denise carried a wide, silver tray laden with a stout, ceramic teapot, wide matching round cups and a plate filled with tiny cakes.

"My word! I'm surprised you're not a popsicle yet," Denise's voice was almost a shriek.

"I'm warm enough," Tee snuggled into the chaise and eyed Denise's fur. "Looks like you are."

Denise appeared sheepish as she set down the tray. "I have to be careful where I wear it, or else the animal rights people will have a fit." She nuzzled her chin into the front of the coat. "I inherited a trunkful of these from my favorite aunt. She collected them back in the days when such things were acceptable." She nodded to the tray. "Hope you're not too cold to have this out here."

"Oh, this is great," Tee waved a gloved hand. "But you didn't have to do all this when you just had company."

Denise looked bewildered for a moment. "Ah," understanding illuminated her attractive round face. "Pope Apostolou. You met him last night, didn't you?"

"I don't think so," Tee frowned a little while trying to place the name. "Is he friends with Mr. Nikolaides? Him I met. Greek, yes?"

"Oh yes," something sly and blatantly feminine crept onto Denise's face then. "And definitely fitting. Those two are a couple of Greek gods if I've ever seen any."

"Denise," Tee called the woman in a hushed chuckle. "What would Steve say if he heard that kind of talk?"

"Please," the woman poked out her tongue. "The man should thank his stars he has a wife who still has a healthy libido. Especially in light of all those little pills he's got to clear out."

Laughter followed as the women poured and prepped their tea.

"So they both live out in California?"

"Mmm," Denise's nod was an eager one. She needed no prodding to dish on her sexy neighbor and his sexy friend.

"Steve actually met Mercuri first. He heads a vast shipping business out there. I remember how impressed we were that someone so young had built something so well run and in such a short span of time." Denise went on to explain how she and her husband had been looking to diversify shipping outlets for the landscaping supply company they had out west. They decided to give Mercuri's company a try and had been happy ever since.

"It's always good to hear about people who begin things from scratch and make them sing in a relatively short period of time," Tee gave an agreeing shrug. "I guess you could say my story isn't much different."

Denise Brassels' expression appeared to sober around the edges then. "I'd be the first to say that I'm sure I don't know a fraction of what there is to know about those sexy Greeks, but I'd be willing to bet all my aunt's furs that your story is completely different from what makes up theirs."

"In what way?" Tee probed. She couldn't fight being intrigued and sensed Denise Brassels wasn't against sharing.

"Well you know," Denise gestured to Tee using her cup. "You run a business after all. I'm sure you make a point of knowing who you're getting into bed with before you pull back the covers, right?"

Tee nodded. Silently though, she acknowledged that wasn't always a two way street. She couldn't claim half the clients she had if they knew about her past bed partners.

"...our check on Mercuri showed that he had an extensive military background," Denise was saying.

"Was that a problem for you?" Tee eyed the woman steadily.

46

"Oh no, not at all," Denise leaned forward slightly as she shook her head. "It's just that there was nothing more to be found. It was as if his life began right there and consisted of only that time," she shrugged and snuggled into the lounge to sip more of her tea. "Long story short, there was nothing that gave us any second thoughts about seeing if Mercuri could solve our shipping problems."

Blissful quiet held for several moments before Denise added more to her explanation. "I suppose it's quite a blessing to be defined by one thing in your life without all the other dark chapters coming out to play." She offered a quiet chuckle. "I guess it's even more of a blessing when that one thing doesn't come from one of those dark chapters, right?"

Following Denise's lead, Tee snuggled into her lounge. "Right," she sighed and blew across the surface of the steamy brew in her mug.

~CHAPTER 5~

San Francisco, California~

Life's dark chapters. Tee hadn't been able to drive the phrase from her mind since she'd heard it the day before. She had said her goodbyes to Steve and Denise Brassels early that morning before she'd headed off to make the flight back home. The words kept popping up in her head all during the flight and had remained during the drive from the airport to her office.

 Now, she sat behind the wheel of her Crossover and studied the attractive but unassuming brick building that bore her name. The phrase hung there in her mind like a dark cloud- ominous and ready to make good on a promised storm. The accomplishment before her eyes would not have been possible were it not for the thing that defined her.

 The thing- that *one* thing- had come from the darkest chapter of her life. Not until Denise Brassels' words touched her ears, had she given them any real credence. Sure, she knew what happened that night had changed her, but that it had… defined her… that was a whole other thing entirely.

Defined… by that horror, by that one thing- that one night she'd become someone, some*thing* utterly different. Perhaps Denise Brassels' words hadn't set off such an epiphany. Perhaps she'd known that truth long ago. Perhaps she'd known it, but hadn't recognized the true scope of what it'd meant for her.

She eyed her building again. eShaw had been her dream and she'd made it real despite the fact that none of her original plans for making it so had been realized. She'd used the change that night had brought in her- it hadn't used *her*- it hadn't… defined her. Had it?

How could it not, Tee? The query, unspoken, blared like a cacophony of sound inside her head. Yes, she answered. How could it not? It *had* defined her. That night she'd become someone unrecognizable, someone capable of killing without hesitation or nerves. She lived everyday with the knowledge that she'd do it again if she had to. She could take another life without hesitation to save her friends.

That knowledge kept her awake many nights. It wasn't that she knew she would spill blood again to keep herself or her friends safe. It was knowing that a part of her could-*would* spill blood for the sheer pleasure of watching it flow. She had heard of bloodlust and had always considered it some fantastical, mythical thing. It was certainly not something that a little black girl from a small town outside Philadelphia would ever experience in her lifetime, but there she was.

That dark chapter. That, as yet unrealized dark chapter. She knew it would be more terrifying than any that had come before it. What would happen when that new chapter began and the opportunity to spill blood (or not to spill it) was in her grasp? Would she go against who-what she had become that night six years ago? After six years, was she now too far gone to be anything other than what she was? A monster.

Her stomach muscles clenched then and Tee recognized the churning in her belly as the onset of nausea. Quickly, she gathered her things and made the escape from her car. The street, beautifully shaded by Red Flowering Gum Trees, was quiet at mid-morning. Crossing wasn't the chore it often was.

Tee was grateful. Such was not the day for a battle with streetcars and other forms of traffic. The nausea had yet to begin a steady, bile-bearing climb along the back of her esophagus. Perhaps no one would notice she was dog sick when she arrived.

She breezed through tinted double doors and into the inviting lobby of her office building. Despite the nausea, her proprietor's sixth sense kicked in and she paused mid-stride. Though hers wasn't a business to have customers steadily filing in and out of its doors, the place rarely appeared quite so abandoned at that time of day.

Her receptionist Moira Kent was usually chatting with other members of the crew. Moira however, usually did her socializing there at her cream colored console desk or on the matching midnight blue sofa and armchairs furnishing a lobby that always tended to carry the wondrous aroma of brewing coffee.

There was still another possibility. Perhaps there was a birthday party or some other event she'd overlooked. Tee took a quick mental recap and couldn't recall any special dates she had missed.

Her stomach rolled more insistently then, but she bypassed the lobby level restroom for a quick check upstairs. Her brow furrowed when she found the main level as deserted as the lower floor. A lunch outing could've explained it-only it was too early for lunch and the front door was open.

The nausea gripped her and she decided to complete the hunt for her wayward crew after paying a visit to the restroom. She was already upstairs, so she headed toward the rear of the expansive outer office toward the washroom located in her private suite.

Tee heard her crew before she actually saw them. Robust laughter poured from the heavy maple door left ajar. The 17 members of her staff had taken up residence in her office. They all appeared quite comfy as they languished in the living area or around the impressive wood grain bar that sat catty corner near the furthermost walls.

Making herself at home behind Tee's desk, was office manager Vera Earl. Looking even more at home from his spot along the desk's edge, was Mercuri Nikolaides.

***

Princess Holland believed there was a huge benefit to reading in print. Reading in print ensured things got read. For her, anyway. Logging in for an online read- while convenient- kept things too neat. Prin needed the in-your-face reminder of an actual newspaper lying around and keeping things messy.

In the otherwise plush splendor of her Knob Hill condo, such a thing would be hard to overlook. She had given specific instructions to her cleaning crew that the papers were never to be touched. It would be her job to toss them once they'd been thoroughly scoured.

It wasn't the goings on of the Vegas scene that had her subscribing to several of its local papers. Nor was it nostalgia for the place she and her best friends had decided on to begin their college careers, that had her keeping subscriptions.

Hmph, college... Prin dropped the last two editions of the Vegas Herald to the beveled glass coffee table. Her expression was grim- the look in her uncommon blues was flat and haunted.

College had been the plan. Vegas had been the destination for obvious reasons- sun, fun, Las Vegas. What more could they want? Boy were they idiots. The plan had gone relatively well for a while, but had soon been waylaid by brutal reality for she and her friends.

Their lives hadn't gone off the rails following one disastrous night six years ago. They'd been off the rails long before that night. Hell, it was why that bitch Dorinda Patterson had swooped in like a vulture sniffing fresh meat.

Even after fate had dealt them a backhand, she, Tee, LuCarolyn and Berrill had dug in determined to make it. They applied to college as was the plan before it all went to hell. Correction- before everything went *more* to hell than it already had. College had proven to be a comedy of errors. Money; not too huge a problem when their adventure was in its infancy, became one in a big, ugly and unexpected way. When they were at their lowest, there was the divine Ms. Patterson to sink them lower.

Oh it wasn't her fault, Prin mused. Patterson was just a businesswoman out to make a deal. She hadn't forced them- no one had. They'd gone into it all with their eyes wide open and had seen-done things they would never forget.

Now, there she was, scouring a Vegas paper in hopes of finding a nugget, just a morsel that could set it all in motion again. She'd been on the verge of giving up her daily hunt through the headlines when she found it. It was there, so subtly placed, probably a rookie reporter's first piece. The story of a missing hooker wedged between an ad for a car dealership and an electronics store. Prin noted that it was clearly not a breaking news piece that got the press drooling, but it was enough to tell her that her obsession of the last six years had been worth the headache.

The piece hadn't mentioned Dorinda Patterson by name, but it didn't need to. The hooker had gone missing from Diversion, Patterson's brothel. Prin had ripped through the paper every day since, but there had been nothing aside from a quote by a sheriff's deputy saying they had no reason to suspect foul play. An official search would not be opened.

Prin thought of the rookie reporter and almost felt sorry that he'd been on the receiving end of a call from a concerned working girl. Sorry kid, didn't you know missing hooker stories are a dime a dozen in Vegas? And yet...it had been enough for Prin to consider the possibility of a connection.

She tuned out the quiet, monotone voice that told her she was being an idiot. What could a missing hooker have to do with the situation she and her friends had gotten themselves into all those years ago? Chances were, it had very little to do with it. Prin needed for that to not be the case. She needed that story to link back to that night. She didn't want it to be over. Not yet. Not before she'd had the chance to prove she was more than a useless piece of confection that had stood by one deadly night and lived up to all that her name implied. Princess- looking on from her place of protection while others bled for her.

***

"Alright, everybody out! The lady this gentleman really came to see has finally arrived."

Tee could hear Vera's voice- all authoritative and brooking no argument, but the words sounded muffled as though her ears were stuffed with cotton. That wasn't the case of course. Her ears were simply flooded by the sound of her rampant heartbeat. Meanwhile, her eyes were all but glued to the man smiling coolly at her from across the room.

Tee sensed her hearing returning to normal once Mercuri released her from the potent stream of his golden gaze. He was tracking it across the other women in the room and Tee could hear her employees giving their goodbyes as they took their time heading out. The women had apparently been encouraged to use his nickname. They all tacked it on to their goodbyes along with a wave, giggle, handshake or a combination of all three.

Tee followed the all-girl parade with express disbelief glittering in her dark eyes. Her no-nonsense crew was not known for falling to pieces when a man visited. Then again, visits from men as striking and blatantly male as Mercuri Nikolaides were few and depressingly far between.

Vera Earl; a full figured seventy year old beauty, was last to stroll by Mercuri. "Now don't you be a stranger, cute thing," she ordered.

"That won't happen," Mercuri's words carried laughter. "I take lunch offers seriously. I'll be back to collect on the one you promised. so long as Mr. Earl doesn't mind."

"Ah honey, don't worry about him," Vera waved her perfectly manicured nails in the air. "All I have to do to keep him in line is bribe him with a doggie bag and... other things."

The new friends dissolved in a bit of raucous laughter. Vera was taking Mercuri's hand once they'd both sobered and told him how nice it was to meet him. Mercuri returned the sentiment to Vera and then went back to intently observing her boss.

"You're welcome," Vera's steps slowed as she approached Tee. "Didn't think you'd forgive us for letting that leave before you got here."

Tee watched Vera sashay from the room and close the door. She took a second to collect herself before turning back to her guest.

"I'm sorry," she sighed, watching confusion bloom on his distractingly gorgeous face.

"There's no need to apologize, Tee," Mercuri shook his head. "I don't think I've ever met an office staff who made me feel so welcome."

"I'm sure," she muttered the words while making her way toward her desk. Though her team was usually a professional bunch, she wouldn't think of coming down on them for forgetting themselves. What was a woman to do, especially when what could be mistaken for nothing other than eye candy arrived in a tailored masterpiece of a suit?

The tawny colored fabric of the three piece did more than accentuate the breadth of his shoulders and chest. It somehow emphasized the feline allure of his gaze. Additionally, the suit's color gave the richness of his copper-toned skin a deeper and more vibrant contrast against the blue black of his thick hair.

No... she couldn't blame her staff for their reaction at all.

Those extraordinary eyes of his were cool and fixed and Tee conjured a question to ask before he guessed the path her thoughts had taken. Something told her he'd already done that, yet she forged ahead with starting the conversation. "Did you change your mind about the house?" She asked, savoring the shiver kissing her spine when he laughed.

"Still on the fence," his eyes were taking a lazy downward scan of her body then, "think you can change my mind?"

Arousal, potent and surprising at once daggered through Tee. She found herself clearing her throat to muffle a moan that had laid claim to her voice box. What the hell? Mortified, she fully expected her brain to issue some explanation for her inappropriate reaction to the simply query.

"Maybe you don't need your mind changed," she despised the breathy quality to her words, but she'd at least found words to utter while silently ordering herself to get a grip.

Mercuri shook his head when he smiled and re-engaged his lengthy scan of Tee's body. "Do you make a habit of trying to talk people out of hiring you?"

It was her turn to smile and shake her head then. Veering from her desk, Tee moved for the bar instead. Lightly, she noted that her earlier nausea had mysteriously vanished.

"It's not that," she told him. "A person's home is their world or, at least, it *should* be. Some people have exactly what they want- no enhancements required." Considering that, she continue her stroll to the bar.

Mercuri capitalized on the opportunity she presented in turning for the brief walk across the room. His gaze adopted a fixed intensity that had the potential to unsettle. Though that was rarely his intention, such intensity was unavoidable when his fascination was peaked.

The little molasses dark beauty with the hypnotic and haunted eyes, had him inarguably fascinated. He hadn't even sensed her trying. He tilted his head while attempting to take in every nuance of her stride. He was determined not to overlook a single aspect, from the sway of round hips beneath the violet dress that adored a full derriere and ample breasts to the shapely legs that were beautifully appealing on creatively sculpted pumps.

It was no longer a question of whether he wanted her. Hell, had he even taken time to question that? Doubtful. He'd known he wanted her almost from the second she'd come into view on the Brassels' stairway landing.

The question- *questions*- he'd assumed there would be several from this point out. The most prevalent being, what would it take to have her? Did she want to be had? Would he be able to let go of her when the time came?

The time would come, he knew. It always did. In spite of the money, power and influence he now held, the simple yet significant things of life had continued to evade. Until now, he'd been content to allow it.

"Maybe your world is exactly the way you need it."

He heard her speaking again and his brow quirked over the utter inaccuracy of her words. He thought better of admitting that to her just then. "Would you mind confirming that once you've seen my place for yourself?" he asked instead.

Though her earlier queasiness had fled, Tee still felt the need to use the bar for support. As a matter of principle, she refused to admit the man's presence was an intoxication.

"When would you like to make that happen?" Leaning into the bar, she stubbornly ignored the arousal now winding its way through her.

"Can we do it now?" Mercuri kept his expression schooled, but inwardly adored the surprise claiming her small face. "Your staff told me you were free the rest of the day when I told them I didn't have an appointment."

Tee felt her mouth tense, but she wasn't sure whether to be aggravated or grateful over her staff being so informative with a guest they'd never met. In the end, she cast it off as yet another of their tireless matchmaking efforts.

"Well then," fanning her arms at her sides, she gave a resolved shrug.

Mercuri finally abandoned his spot on the desk and stood. "Well then," he looked curiously to her office door and nodded. "You can bring Vera if I make you nervous."

If he made her nervous? Was he serious? Still, she managed an easy shake of her head. "I believe *your* nervousness would be in question if Vera came along."

"What about Mr. Earl?" he played along with the teasing.

"The man's a teddy bear," her smile was easy. "But when he's not, Vera just bribes him with food and... other things."

Tee's poke at Vera's earlier remark sent Mercuri laughing again. Again, she felt her spine singing in response.

~CHAPTER 6~

They took separate cars from the office. Not by choice. Well... not by Mercuri's choice. He'd offered to drive them both and told Tee it was no problem to drive her back anywhere she wanted to go. She'd refused, firmly decided on driving herself and relying on her GPS to get her there.

Mercuri offered no argument. He was just glad she'd accepted his offer to see the house. He could've cared less about the house. She could've been on her way to suggesting he repaint the entire place pink and cover it in sparkles and he doubted he would have cared. As long as it meant she would be there with him.

God where had all this come from? She wasn't the first beauty- tiny or otherwise- to catch his eye. She certainly wasn't the first black woman he'd taken to his bed or even fantasized about taking to bed. That she was haunted though...that nudged at him. Haunted- yes he'd caught that right away. As a man with his own share of ghosts, he recognized someone in that state when he saw them.

He checked the rearview of his F150, not really expecting to see the luxurious, navy blue crossover she drove. Chances were, the GPS would take her in another direction anyway.

What the hell are you doin', Merc? The question had been floating around the back of his mind and he'd been doing his best to avoid it. What he'd done was to invite a woman he very much wanted to know more about, to his home. That it was under the guise of him seeking her opinions for improving his home, was beside the point.

She might not think so. She might think it was exactly the point and then so much for getting to know her better. He checked the rearview mirror and smiled. He'd worry about ethics later.

~~~

They arrived within seconds of each other. Tee followed Mercuri who stopped at a small stone cottage she assumed housed his security personnel. She told herself there was no turning back now and watched as Mercuri spoke with the two men inside the construction. Soon, he was sending her a wave from his truck's driver's side window to beckon that she follow.

She got no frustrated vibes from him when she'd insisted on driving her car to his place. That she'd even accepted his offer was a big step all its own. Moreover, she'd sensed that he'd somehow understood that she needed to get there under her own steam. That had her reflecting on what she'd already sensed about him. He'd lived a life where the need often rose to shed the easy manner he gave off. Was it possible that he sensed she too had led such a life?

Whatever the reason, Tee was happy that Mercuri hadn't made a big deal of it. She was happier still that she'd accepted his offer. She never accepted. Men made their offers anyway. Whatever scars she still carried from that night, hadn't been ones that kept men from making their offers. Until that day, she'd refused them all.

Eventually, Tee was chalking it all up to plain 'ol sexual frustration. Sexual madness was perhaps better phrasing in light of the man she'd just met. Not accepting his offer for a ride had been about her own trauma-induced anxieties yes, but there'd been more to it.

She'd felt loopy, drugged, too... mellow from the moment she walked into her office and found him there. The sensation wasn't an uncomfortable one. Rather... it was as she'd observed earlier. It was intoxicating. *He* was intoxicating and though the looks were... godlike, it all went so far beyond them. That she couldn't actually put words to what 'it' was, merely enhanced the intoxication.

Oh what the hell are you doing here, Tee? Given the way she felt, she'd be asking him to show her to his bedroom the second she cleared the front door.

Mercuri left the muscular black truck and was opening Tee's side door after she'd parked alongside him on a horseshoe driveway of the same black brick that constructed the expansive house awaiting her inspection. He held the driver's door, but stepped behind it, once she left the shiny Infiniti as though he meant to give her as much space as he could.

"Thank you," her words were soft as her gaze swept the environment. "This is gorgeous, Mercuri."

He took a sweep of the grounds as well. "Thanks. Any homey touches you see out here are the work of my landscapers. No input from me."

"Well they do an amazing job," she studied the professionally kept lawn that rolled in a sea of sun drenched green.

Trees were abundant. They offered an array of shady spots from which to enjoy the view of stunning blue sky above. There were vibrant sprays of water from a boldly sculpted fountain centered inside the horseshoe drive. A bird's unexpected call succeeded in drawing Tee's focus from the landscape and she offered her host a lazy, satisfied shrug.

"It's like a dream," she said.

"Hope you feel that way when you see the inside," He pushed the car door shut.

Laughing then, Tee looked toward the dark dwelling they approached. The structure managed to give off an air of intimidation and yet there was something undeniably welcoming.

Boxes, fashioned of some unfinished dark brown wood, housed neat rows of plump yellow tulips along the outer window sills. The front door was a towering, wide rectangle of the same untreated wood as the flower boxes. It loomed behind a tinted glass door.

What had to be the biggest welcome mat she'd ever seen, lay against the long curve of brick steps below the porch. A huge yellow tulip on a backdrop of black, offered a remarkable contrast.

"Flower lover?" She was awed by the hint of embarrassment that flashed across his face.

"Sentimental reasons."

"How long have you lived here?" She asked, understanding that there was no more he wanted to add to the solemn explanation.

"Almost six years," he said.

"Have you ever had designers inside before?"

"I have," he almost groaned the words, "they were eight of the longest weeks of my life. I'm hoping once you're inside, you can tell me some of my torment was worth it."

"Well let's see," she headed for the house, but paused on her way up the wide steps. The extraordinary welcome mat was affixed to the steps, keeping it perfectly showcased despite the traffic it may have endured.

Mercuri watched as he cleared the top step and could no longer resist touching her. "People tend to trip here," he took her arm.

"Thanks," she studied the breadth of his hand on her arm. It was broad enough to encircle the entire width of the limb with room left over.

He pulled open the glass door, and then held it open for Tee to precede him once he'd unlocked the towering wood door behind it.

Tee couldn't resist brushing her fingers across the unusual door to see if it was as rough as it appeared. To her delight, it only appeared that way and had apparently been treated to give it a healthy buff shine making it smooth to the touch.

Mercuri followed her every move and could feel himself smiling over her sheer delight with the front door.

Tee moved on through the sumptuous foyer with its walls of gleaming light brown wood and rose blush marble flooring. Her gaze was drawn upward to the heavy dark pine beams that supported the ceiling. Spotlights tucked along the beams and showered the room in pale light that seemed to make the space gleam.

"Do you entertain here a lot?" Her voice was hushed.

"Not really. My friends say it's a shame with a place like this."

"They're right. I'm sure the woman in your life hates it too," she said the words before she could stop herself and was glad her back faced him then. She used the opportunity to roll her eyes at herself over the obvious probe into his relationship status.

"A place like this is made for lots of people," she went on in an attempt to gloss over the slip.

"I guess the woman in my life would agree if there was one," his voice was soft, reflective. "The only people I really care about spending time with here are my friends."

"I can relate to that," she was saying as she turned into a den that looked to be half the size of a football field. "Mercuri this place is unreal."

Her voice maintained its hushed tone. Tee had been in the midst of many exquisite homes, though few struck her as this one did. Everything was tasteful, understated and boasted relaxation and welcome. She'd expected a glamorous showpiece-what she got was the essence of a home. She hadn't seen many places that balanced those aspects so equally.

The den remained true to the home's tasteful, understated design of rich woods and glowing marbles. Long, overstuffed sand colored sofas and deep armchairs could have held five of her they were that enormous. A black staircase spiraled at the back of the room and could have appeared harsh were it not for the golden wood planks that offset the dark metal casing. Fleece blankets rested across the arms of each chair that also carried pillows of varying shapes and sizes. Splashes of bold colors mingled among a wider array of softer tones. Additional pillows and blankets puffed out of a grand white oak case near glass double doors overlooking a black tiled terrace.

Mercuri watched the appraisal from his spot on a beige Ottoman that flanked a set of easy chairs. "Give it to me straight," he said when she'd completed her turn around the room.

"I believe your money was well spent. The torture you endured was worth it."

"Thank you God for small favors," he clenched a triumphant fist and then eyed her with playful skepticism. "You know, most folks have to train before they can make it through a tour of this place. You up for seeing more?"

"Are you kidding?" She almost gushed and then reigned in more composure. "I'd love to see more." She kept her tone cool and measured.

Mercuri got to his feet and looked down at her. "I'm not anal about folks walking over my rugs in their shoes, but you're welcomed to take those off. My floors can be pretty unforgiving."

Tee gave a baleful look to the stunning neckbreakers she wore. "If you can endure torture, so can I."

His laughter seemed to echo across the room and up through the high beamed ceiling. The appealing sound of his laughter was becoming more familiar to Tee with every outburst. Still, she adored the sensation it sent up her spine. She wasn't in any hurry to overcome it.

~~~

Mercuri's home, reminiscent of a Tuscan inspired villa, held Tee in a state of wonder as she followed him through its casual, warm elegance. Earth toned walls brought out the subtle designs in the hand woven comforters and rugs found in the bedrooms. She could have easily imagined herself curling up in any of the six inviting chambers and drifting into a week long slumber.

"Is your tea alright?"

She gave a quiet smile as his query tugged her from a mesmerized study of the steep hills rolling beyond the glass wall of the den. She found his voice to be something of a paradox, clear and heavy but with a recognizable softness.

The paradox related not only to his voice, but to the man himself. His fierce features and warrior's build made it easy for her to see him on a battlefield- not so easy to see him as a host amid the quiet beauty of his home. He was so not what she'd expected at first sight.

"The tea's great," she raised the mug of the raspberry blend. "You didn't have to go to the trouble, though."

"Where's the trouble?" His big hands spread in a show of playful bewilderment. "You took time out of your day to share your opinion of my house. The tea was definitely no trouble." Mock uncertainty took hold of his expression next.

"Guess I should've asked if you charge for your consultations, huh?"

"Well didn't you find out all that from the Brassels?" she teased.

"Didn't ask. Guess I should have before I came demanding a consult. Doesn't speak very highly of me, does it?"

"I wouldn't worry about it," she smiled down into the vibrant depths of the liquid. "They spoke very highly of you. That's enough for me."

"You asked about me?" Curiosity was ablaze in his evocative eyes.

"It um...just came up," Tee ordered herself to maintain eye contact. She watched him nod, lean forward to study the backs of his hands and couldn't help but wonder what he thought of her admission.

"So would you take the job if you found my house in dire need?" He shifted the topic.

Again, Tee indulged in another survey of the splendid room. "It'd be a change of pace for me, but the house is so impressive. I'd love to work here. If it were in dire need," she qualified.

"What do you mean 'change of pace'?" His gaze had narrowed, bringing the thick sleek brows close.

Tee leaned forward then to set her mug to the big stone slab of a coffee table that was supported by a massive iron frame. "My residential clients are always couples- older couples. I've um... never worked on the home of a-" she broke off when a barrage of adjectives flooded her mind. *Sexy, smoldering, irresistible, intoxicating...*

"Single man," she forced out.

Mercuri resisted smiling though he enjoyed the small fissure he saw in her controlled demeanor.

Tee reached for the mug again, needing something to do with her hands. "There's an intimacy to what I do," her voice went softer then. "It's not just a single consult, but a series of experiences that help me put context to what I think the house could use."

"And how do you go about getting these experiences?" He smiled a little then.

"It uh- requires I spend lots of nights in the space."

"Ah."

She shrugged weakly, realizing that he saw where she was headed. "It's not a necessity, though. I've reworked lots of corporate spaces and I couldn't spend the night inside them to get my mojo working."

"But your mojo works best that way."

Again, she shrugged, the gesture holding a trace of pleasurable guilt. "It's why I have so much fun doing the houses. I feel like there's a real part of me in the finished work. A good part," she cleared her throat a bit on the admission.

"I commend your dedication. Not many people care that much these days."

Her smile was a modest one. "The corporate is my job. The residential is my passion."

"Guess that's how I feel about my job as well."

"Oh no," mortification claimed her dark lovely face then, "I'm so sorry, you've got things to do and I'm just going on-"

"Tee no, no I asked you here, remember?" He raised a hand to wave off her concern.

"I can't even guess what you must've had to give up to devote most of your day to this."

"Not as much as you're probably thinking. I had an early meeting on the same end of town as your office. When I got there I was sure you wouldn't have time for me. I only stopped by to leave a message with your receptionist-"

"And found yourself dragged upstairs to be grilled and drooled over."

His rich laughter filled the room again. "I might enjoy socializing more if all my experiences were as nice."

"You dislike socializing?" She sipped her tea, patiently waiting on his response.

Smirking faintly, Mercuri regarded the coffee table and the juice he'd opted for instead of tea. "I'm not the best at it," he confessed.

Intrigue and a fair amount of disbelief gripped her. "I wouldn't think you'd have to be good at it. Not in a situation like the one in my office. I doubt many women would hold your less than stellar socializing skills against you."

"Thanks for saying that, Tee."

"I'm sure you don't have those problems in business either," she said when the following silence held a bit too long. "It's obvious you're a success." Her dark, unfathomable eyes skimmed the beams of the ceiling.

"Business is my passion. Socializing...isn't."

Tee recognized his play on her earlier declaration. "So you're a homebody?"

His gaze skimmed the room then too. "Isn't it obvious?"

He was right, she thought. The warmth and welcome prevalent in the house was authentic. It was clear that living happened there, not just existing.

"It's obvious you've got some talent for socializing," she insisted.

"My friends are the talented ones," elbows braced to his knees, Mercuri bowed his head.

Tee inclined her head a bit to get a better view of his expression. "So you're just the wizard behind the curtain sending out your subjects to do your bidding?" She hoped he'd laugh and was pleased when the sound once again graced her ears.

"I wouldn't put it that way, but my friends are also my business partners. I had the idea- they were key in helping me implement it. Did Steve and Denise tell you about my business?"

"Denise said you're in shipping- told me she and Steve are clients. Mercuri Fleets?" She watched him nod. "Fitting. You share your name with the God of Speed. Guess that's what makes you such a success."

"Nah...besides, my name is spelled differently," he grinned when she snapped her fingers. "Truth is, I wouldn't be such a success if it weren't for Pope."

"Pope...Apos...Apostolou," she smiled when he gave her a thumbs up for pronunciation. "He's their neighbor, right? Steve's and Denise's?"

"That's a recent thing," Mercuri rubbed his thumb across a crisp, shirt cuff. "Long after he helped me start my business- we were friends long before that. The guy can talk people into anything- definitely someone you'd want on your side."

"Sounds like you love him a lot."

Mercuri sighed over the observation. Emotion fueled the gesture and the look in his eyes. "I've got four brothers," he told her, "We don't share blood, but I'd give my life for theirs any day."

His words warmed her and Tee nodded her agreement. "I've got three sisters," she said. "We don't share blood, but I'd give my life for theirs any day."

His expression mirrored approval. "Sounds like we're lucky people."

"We're very lucky people." Something had Tee checking her watch then and muttering a curse. "One of my sisters is gonna kick my ass if I'm late getting to Malibu. I'm spending the weekend with her."

Mercuri tried and failed to ignore the tense flex of muscle along his jaw. Malibu was a six hour drive. Not far, but not as close as she was right then.

"I should let you salvage something from your day, anyway," Tee was pushing to her feet.

Reluctantly, Mercuri followed suit. All the while, he wondered whether he'd see her again. He could tell her he'd call, but what would be the point? She'd already said his house wasn't in need of her services. Besides, as she'd pointed out, he was a single man. He wouldn't dare lie and say that he'd... behave with her sleeping under his roof.

A promise to call would be for purely personal reasons. Reasons that might lead to the simple, significant things of life.

Idiot. Silently, he berated himself. He was too complicated for anything that went beyond a night, remember?

He watched her round the sofa to precede him from the den. His purposeful scan of her curvy, petite frame resumed and his palm actually tingled as though the nerve endings were working to send messages to his brain for him to stop her. *You're too complicated for anything that goes beyond a night.*

Tee made her way back through the house in much the same fashion she had upon her arrival. Like a kid, she angled her head up, back and around intent on taking in the magnificent place she'd probably not see again.

Approaching the big, unusual door, she treated herself to another brush from her fingers along its smoothed weathered looking surface. Resolved, she pulled the door open only to have it promptly shut before she could move past it. Mercuri's hand rested several inches above her head. Tee spared a moment to study it, before turning. Half a second later, her back was against the door she'd just admired.

He had taken her off her feet, positioned her to a more accommodating level for his height. She was slight enough that he could hold her there sealed between himself and the door. His hands were free to roam her lush thighs, tugging them apart, angling them near his hips to accommodate his wide frame.

Tee hadn't expected the whimper that surged from her throat, but the reaction was no surprise. She discovered that all that… size belonged to him. Having it pressed do deliciously against her, was a treat to be savored.

Mercuri situated himself deftly and claimed Tee's mouth soon after. Her whimper became a gasp that gave his tongue ample room to plunder as it claimed. His fingers on her thighs began a sensual massage that he used to spread her wider.

Tee was rocking her hips in a mindless trek for enjoyment. Her moans flowed consistently and unrestrained. Tentatively, her tongue tangled with his and the crushing, lusty kiss became slower, more intense. She curled her fingers loosely around his jacket lapels. Moments later, her short French-tipped nails made the ascent to his nape and grazed the crisp darkness tapered there. Soon, she was tunneling into the dark forest of his hair, luxuriating in sensation and the discovery that it was as lustrous as it appeared.

Mercuri continued to ravage her mouth. He abandoned her tongue frequently, preferring to stroke her teeth or the roof of her mouth before fully engaging the kiss again.

Tee fisted her hands in his hair and gave herself over to the effects of the erotic assault on her mouth. Her moans entwined with whimpers, her hips rocked in suggestive frenzy and she rubbed her breasts across his chest as they heaved and threatened to overspill the bodice and lacy bra cups.

Mercuri retreated from the door and took Tee with him. She had no complaints, nor resistance and locked her legs at his waist. Moments later, her back was hitting the door again and he was setting her down. For a time, their labored breaths mingled in the foyer. Confusion was at its height over the sudden change in situation- over the situation itself.

She couldn't meet his gaze, but felt its thrilling potency just the same. Her legs were water, but she managed to turn, feebly hunt for the door knob and make her way out.

~CHAPTER 7~

Malibu, California~

"And then what?" LuCarolyn Young's eyes resembled two honey-colored moons as she leaned forward to spread her hands. The silence had lingered a bit too long for her liking.

"Then nothing," Tee kept her eyes fixed on the surf where frothy waves crashed with stunning grace. "I left."

"Did he come after you?"

The hopeful query had Tee sucking her teeth. "No," she threw an eyeroll in her friend's direction. "This isn't one of those romantic comedies you produce, Lu."

Disappointed by the culmination of the story that had the makings of a very sexy vignette, LuCarolyn flopped back against her chaise.

"Don't get pissy with me, Tee," Deflated, LuCarolyn hid long legs; the color of milk chocolate, beneath the folds of the coral lounge dress that she'd spread about her in a flourish. "You were the one who came out here looking like stress warmed over and with this fantastical story-"

"It's true."

"About this...hunk kissing you senseless in his Sonoma mansion. True, you say? I say 'bull'."

"Lu-"

"You haven't let a guy touch you in six years. None of us have." LuCarolyn grumbled out the last.

"Exactly. So why would I lie about it now?" Tee turned her back on LuCarolyn's staggering panoramic view of the Pacific.

Toying with a coarse flowing lock of her hair, LuCarolyn appeared to consider the argument. "So who is he?" She was then of the opinion that her friend's words had merit.

"I already told you," Tee smoothed a hand across the onyx waves capping her head.

"Mercuri Niko...laides," LuCarolyn recalled the story. "Lay? Or Lie?"

"Lie," Tee clarified the pronunciation. "Niko-*lai*-des."

"What is that? Greek?"

"I think."

LuCarolyn whistled. "Hell, I should've said Greek god instead of hunk."

Tee gave into a smile. "You wouldn't have been exaggerating if you did."

"This one got to you, didn't he?" Some of LuCarolyn's trademark playfulness had vanished.

"And what are the odds of that happening?" Tee was curious to hear LuCarolyn's point of view then. "I just met him two days ago for crying out loud."

"Things like that tend to happen when you're not expecting it." LuCarolyn gave a frail shrug. "At least that's what I've heard."

"But that's not what this was," Tee grimaced over the summation. "It wasn't a love connection, it was just..."

"Lust." LuCarolyn supplied.

Somehow, the label didn't fit as far as Tee was concerned. She didn't want to mull it over then though. Luckily, LuCarolyn was talking again.

"I say 'go for it'. You've denied yourself too long."

"I have, huh?" Tee's brow furrowed as she folded her arms beneath her breasts. "So you're ready to take your own advice?" She challenged.

"Well," LuCarolyn straightened, taking on a prim stance. "As I've yet to meet a Greek god, my answer would have to be no."

Laughter followed and soon Tee was joining Lu on the marina blue cushions of a bamboo framed chaise. She helped herself to the brew sitting on the glass table nearest the lounge.

"So what now?" LuCarolyn asked once she and Tee had shared a few sips from the bottle.

"Mmm...what do you mean?" Tee allowed the mellow vibes stirred by the setting sun and rolling waves, to work their magic on her nerves.

"Well hell, are you gonna call him?"

Stunned skepticism sparkled in Tee's dark eyes then. "What for?"

"Hell Tee, to goddamn ask if he'll finish what he started."

"I can't do that," she wouldn't admit that the idea alone sent pleasure streaking.

LuCarolyn was frowning harshly. "Why the hell not? It's time to put six years ago behind us."

"Us."

Again, LuCarolyn shrugged. "I'd be willing to give it a try if it was worth it."

"And no one's been 'worth it' to you in six years?"

"Not like this," there was no trace of the playful in LuCarolyn's honey-toned eyes. "Not like what I see on your face right now."

Tee rolled her eyes back to the surf. "There's nothing on my face."

"He shook you."

LuCarolyn's knowing tone, the truth in her words, sent a shiver whisking along Tee's skin. She was right. He had. He definitely had.

"I'm not done with it, Lu," she admitted, "Six years ago, My...Greek god isn't the only thing shaking me. There're parts of that night I'm still dealing with."

"Ah Tee," LuCarolyn half turned on the chaise to rub a concerned hand across Tee's thigh. "Honey we're all still dealing with it whether we can admit it or not. But that doesn't mean we can't grab hold to good if it sees fit to pay us a visit and how often over the last six years has good like this happened?" She bumped a shoulder with Tee. "So I ask again, what now?"

"Dammit Lu, what do you want me to say?"

"Well are you gonna call him or what? Shit, go see him. I'm pretty sure you could find your way back to that mansion of his." LuCarolyn gasped suddenly, her luminous gaze narrowing on her friend's face. "You want to," she continued to stare and muttered a stunned curse. "You didn't want him to stop today, did you?"

"Jesus, Lu!" Tee pushed off the lounge to stalk over to the glass barrier of the second story patio.

"Admit it to yourself at least and then go after him please." LuCarolyn chose another chilled beer from the mini fridge in the barbeque nook.

"You're the closest any of us has come to sex in six years," LuCarolyn raised her bottle in toast. "Take this one for the team as we're all in dire need of new material for our masturbation fantasies."

Just like that, Tee's minor outrage transitioned to amusement. Laughter resonated across the private stretch of beach.

***

Mykonos, Greece~

Slayte Miltiades didn't mind being labeled a playboy. He was actually quite proud to wear the moniker as opposed to all the others he'd worn during the course of his 31 years.

Unlike the others, *playboy* was a label he'd had an exceptional amount of fun earning. Fun, he thought of whenever he looked out over the ancient, exquisite town he now called home. Well...*home* was with his friends, but this would do nicely in the interim. It'd do quite nicely indeed.

Slayte looked out from his lofty position along the elevated villa he kept. The sultry curve of his mouth set into a smile that hinted of approval and the acknowledgement of something accomplished. The rich beauty and elegance of his lush accommodations and native land, was beyond stunning. Still, it was the contentment Slayte treasured most. He and his friends-his brothers- were alive. Aside from walking away with their lives, contentment was a gift they hadn't even bothered to pray for.

That had been six years ago and Slayte had spent every day adding miles to the distance between the life he'd bled through to the one he was cultivating. Whoever said living well was the best revenge, didn't lie.

Morning was on the horizon, but Slayte didn't stay to watch the sun's ascent. Instead, he padded barefoot from the terrace on the top floor of the multi-leveled villa of powder white stone and into the greatroom. He could lounge there most days until lunchtime.

Dropping onto a massive recliner, he grinned while thoughts surged of two of his four closest friends in the world. Mercuri and Pope worked hard enough for them all to live well for the rest of their lives and then some. Alas, the two were happiest when they were working which suited Slayte just fine. Of the five of them, Mercuri and Pope were best with money. Slayte was fine with letting them handle his investments while he immersed himself in travel and women. Truthfully speaking, it was really only the travel he preferred immersing himself in. Women, he lost himself in only for the satisfaction they provided. Afterwards, he preferred to have them vanish like mist once he was sated.

Slayte thought of the two in his bedroom that were sleeping him off. He could only hope they'd take the hint and make themselves scarce when they woke to find him gone. His men would soothe any ruffled feathers and see them home. Both, were tasks Slayte greatly appreciated his staff for. Most mornings, he was still trying to ward off the effects of too much ouzo and tequila from the night before.

Such was the case that morning. Still, Slayte kept to his regular routine of settling down with a read through of news from the States. Though his usual method was scouring the net, he kept a healthy print stash on hand for mornings such as these. Hangovers and internet searching didn't pair well.

With the snow white fabric of the chair pampering his back, Slayte eased in for a good old fashioned newspaper read. He'd enjoyed the indulgence for almost half an hour when he came across a story that stirred his interest.

A national morning news show was being featured for a story they had run on a small town hero firefighter. That particular story was old news. What was making waves then, was the discovery of the fireman's body along with that of his wife and two sons- ages 3 and 5- murdered. Their bodies had been found in a storage shed outside their home. The family had been missing for two weeks before anyone thought to look in the shed.

Slayte shook his head over the waste of life. Reflex had him clenching a fist as his deep-set violet eyes studied the faces of the family smiling out at him from the paper's photo. He read the caption beneath and frowned.

"Charles Lapis. Lapis…" A twinge of discomfort vibrated along his temple. Slayte shook off the sensation and tried to focus. *Lapis…God, why does that name-*

Rapid knocking on the door, stunted his fuzzy memory.

"Slay…? Slay, baby come back to bed…"

"You won't regret it…"

His bedmates were awake and Slayte regretted selecting the previous night for being the one to treat himself to two new enticements. His regulars understood he wasn't one for making morning- or evening-small talk.

"Slay…?"

With a soft, yet vicious curse, Slayte grabbed the cordless from the wall shelf and hit the button that engaged a member of his housestaff.

"Get rid of them," he instructed whoever answered and then fixed on the paper again. Nothing popped, except another hit of hangover pain.

"Fuck," wrenching the paper aside, Slayte shoved off the chair in hopes of scrounging up relief for his aching head. For the moment, the story of the firefighter and his family was forgotten.

***

Prin got to Malibu around 1am that morning. The long weekend sleepover had been planned for months. She let herself in the house, surprised to find her friends already conked out. Locating her usual room, she made quick work of tossing her bags into the nearest corner. Then, she was shedding her clothes and diving beneath the bed's welcoming covers.

~~~

Morning found the women outdoors on the beach and snuggled beneath luxurious fleece blankets on the lounges surrounding a blazing fire pit. Conversation was stifled for the moment as Tee and Prin filled their plates. A small yet hearty buffet was set on a short glass table near the pit.

LuCarolyn arrived decked out in another chic lounge dress, this one of a powder blue that matched the gorgeous morning sky overhead. "Bear should be here by lunchtime," she announced.

Tee and Prin traded knowing smiles. "You mean dinnertime." They spoke at once. Berrill Clayton was notorious for her tardiness.

LuCarolyn laughed. She took her place around the pit and helped herself to breakfast.

Prin was settled back on her lounge. The cornflower blue of her stare seemed more vivid as she studied her friends. "I was gonna save this 'til we were all together but I don't think I can."

LuCarolyn sent a look to Tee. "If she's about to tell us she's got a Greek god, I'm slapping somebody."

"What?" Prin frowned.

Tee was already shaking her head. "Nothing. Go ahead, Prin."

Prin needed a quick sip of coffee before she continued. "You guys know how I um...get those papers from Vegas?" she pursed her lips when her friends slouched in their lounges and groaned.

"I think it's finally paid off," Prin ignored the reactions. "I found a story on a missing hooker-"

"Prin jeez, why do you keeping torturing yourself-"

"Would you stop and listen?" Prin daggered a glare toward LuCarolyn. "The hooker was Dorinda Patterson."

Smiles and laughter fleeing, Tee and LuCarolyn exchanged placid looks.

"How do you know this?" Tee's usual cool, had returned.

"The paper," Prin rolled her eyes, sighed. "Not exactly the paper. The paper only said there was a missing hooker from Diversion and the cops had no plans to start a search."

"So how-?"

"I called the brothel."

LuCarolyn closed her eyes on the answer she'd dreaded receiving to her question. "Prin..." her voice was a low whine.

"Honey why won't you let this go?" Tee asked.

"Have you let it go, Tee?" Prin's eyes flashed blue flame. "Have any of us truly let that night go? We've all come so far now- I went back to my folks, made peace, got my millions. You've got a successful design business. Lu's production company is a force to be reckoned with and Bear's making a mint with that gun range of hers…" she shook her head, "but who among us wasn't changed in some pretty unsavory ways because of that night?"

For a time, there were only the sights and sounds of the refreshing environment to offer a response.

"What'd you find?" LuCarolyn asked.

"Her girls said they came back to the house that night and found it a mess," Prin forked up a breakfast potato but only studied it. "It was the kind of mess that told them something over the top had gone on there. Dorinda gave them the night off so nothing was scheduled."

"That they knew of," Tee chimed in around the strawberry she nibbled. "Let's not forget Dorinda has a thing for farming out certain jobs."

Prin inclined her head, sending a cascade of wavy blonde across her shoulder. "Only one job that I know of resembles what Dorinda's girls told me they found that night."

Her strawberry an afterthought then, Tee directed her pitch gaze toward the calm waters beyond the beach.

"Dorinda wasn't there, but her room was messier than the others," Prin went on. "They found blood and… indications that someone had been tied down to the bed."

The skepticism in Tee's gaze had mixed with memory and regret. LuCarolyn sighed a curse and rested back against her lounge to turn a haunted stare toward the water.

"I'm sorry for bringing down the mood. Just thought you guys should know," Prin tried for an encouraging smile then. "It could all be a coincidence. There's been no backlash from that night. It's been six years, anyway. For the thing at Dorinda's to have anything to do with that night does seem a little farfetched."

"She could've underestimated a client," LuCarolyn pulled her stare from the water. "Maybe she got caught out there with a new one who showed his true colors."

Silence lingered and Tee knew her friends were waiting on her to make the final call as to whether this merited their attention. "It could all be a fantastic coincidence," she set down the fruit-laden saucer. "But we agreed to never make a decision unless we were all four in agreement and since Bear's not here…I say we wait 'til she is to get her opinion. If she agrees we take a deeper look, then we do it. Agreed?"

Tee extended a hand to Prin, one to LuCarolyn. She smiled when both women accepted and squeezed her hands.

"Agreed," they said.

~CHAPTER 8~

"What the hell is up with you?" Pope spread his hands and gave the man on the other side of the door, the benefit of his strongest glare.

Mercuri reciprocated with a strong glare of his own. "Why didn't you use your key?"

"I've been calling since yesterday afternoon," Pope strolled into the foyer when Mercuri moved from the door. "I'm pretty sure there's no room left for voice mail as I left a message every time I tried your cell. Tried calling here with no luck and finally broke down and called the security house. When they told me you hadn't left since arriving with 'the lady' and that the lady didn't stay very long... I got concerned. I didn't just want to bust in, though- hence, ringing the bell."

Mercuri was already on his way back through the house. "Thanks for caring," he called over his shoulder.

Again, Pope spread his hands. "What the hell happened?"

"What shouldn't have," Mercuri grumbled out the reply while reclaiming a controller and his spot on the den sofa where he'd been embroiled in a fierce game of *WarCraft*.

Pope watched the battling resume on the mounted 75" screen above the hearth. "Wanna talk about it?" he asked.

"I don't," Mercuri followed up the decision with a fierce oath as the gaming move he'd executed was foiled by an enemy.

"How about we head over to The Rascal for lunch?" Pope sat on an opposing sofa and suggested his favorite restaurant. He felt a glimmer of hope when Mercuri smiled.

"Thousands of restaurants in the city and that's the only one you ever choose," Mercuri's bright eyes were still fixed on the television screen.

"It's the best," Pope declared.

"It's a madhouse," Mercuri said of the eatery that was popular with everyone from finance geeks to film executives.

"Because it's the best," Pope insisted, then shrugged. "So? How 'bout it?"

"No."

The flat refusal had Pope cursing fiercely then too. Still, he held his frustration at bay with admirable willpower and reached for the unfinished popcorn in a neglected glass bowl on the floor.

"It might help to talk," Pope took his time selecting choice kernels from the bowl.

"It won't."

Smirking, Pope kept his deep-set sapphires fixed on the bowl. "Am I correct to assume you sitting here slacking off has to do with the lovely and tiny Ms. Shaw?" He crunched on a handful of the corn.

"I won't bother pointing out that slacking off is allowed on Saturdays, but yes you could assume that." Mercuri grinned when his next move resulted in the annihilation of his opponent. Satisfied, he tossed the controller and rested back on the sofa.

"She mad at you?" Pope continued to pluck through the popcorn.

"If she's smart, she is. And she's very smart."

Pope paused over the bowl then. "Well goddamn man, what the fuck happened?"

"I kissed her."

"Ah man," Pope bowed his head, using a hand to keep glossy waves of shoulder length black from his face. "A kiss? That's nothing you-wait-" he set the bowl to the coffee table. "Was this like a brotherly kiss or-"

"No way in hell."

"Well shit, Merc," Pope slumped back on the sofa, "that's not the end of the world. What'd she say before she left?"

Mercuri responded with a hard laugh and massaged the heels of his hands into his eyes. "She didn't say a damn thing. Not that I could blame her. The moment didn't call for lots of conversation," he jerked a hand through hair that was a mass of tousled onyx.

"Lighten up, man. I seriously doubt she'd hate you for one steamy kiss. She came out here to see you, didn't she?"

"She came out here to see the house. To see if it should be redecorated."

Pope winced. "I still think you're bein' too hard on yourself."

"I don't." Leaning forward, Mercuri rested elbows to knees and linked his fingers between them. "She never should've come out here. I never should've asked, but she did what any polite person would when they meet another seemingly polite person- they trust them. Until that person shows them who they really are."

"Bein' too hard on yourself..." Pope sang the phrase that time.

Mercuri left the sofa to prowl his den. "She accepted my offer to come out here. Her first day back in town after another job. She had to have a ton of stuff to clear from her desk, but she came here anyway believing all I wanted was her opinion on the house. I almost did it," he slid Pope a sly grin across his shoulder.

"I almost let her go. Her hand was on the doorknob. I pushed the door shut and put her back against it instead. If she had asked me to let her go, I-"

"Stop. That's not the kind of guy you are."

"But she didn't know that. I could've done anything to her out here."

Impatience had Pope's aquamarine gaze darkening to navy. "You're starting to piss me off," his voice adopted its trademark soft roar.

"You have no idea what was going through my mind while I had her on that door."

"I can guess well enough, but that's not the point. You're not the kind of asshole to take a woman who doesn't want to be taken," Pope reclined on his sofa. "Besides, I'm pretty sure she didn't get to be a grown woman without learning to take care of herself."

Mercuri was making another turn around the spacious room. "She put herself in an awful position coming out here with me like that."

Pope was reaching for the popcorn again. "She came out here because she saw a decent guy looking to have his home redecorated."

"Which I lied to her about."

"To steal a kiss, jeez, get over yourself."

Mercuri regarded his old friend with cold scrutiny. "It amazes me how you can turn on and off your ability to forget what we were before we made a play at being civilized."

"It's not a play," Pope's voice was tight. "I may not be so quick to believe our *new money* would get us choice seats at our local country club, but the rest of it- the animals we were- are all back in the past where they'll stay. We aren't those assholes anymore, Merc. Folks might not be so willing to believe that if they knew the whole truth, but I thought that you- with all you've accomplished- I thought you got that better than the rest of us."

Mercuri settled back to the sofa, scrubbed his hands over his face. "I thought I did too."

Pope gave his friend a long look as sympathy fought back the agitation that had taken possession of his face. "She really got to you, didn't she?"

"She really did." Mercuri confessed without hesitation. "It's scary how fast she did."

"I've heard that's how love at first sight works." Pope sighed at the eyeroll he received. "If you're that concerned about her state of mind, go see her. Why not?" He tacked on when Mercuri started shaking his head.

"The next visit is on her."

"And you're good with that?"

"I'm good with that."

Pope gave Mercuri the benefit of an incredulous stare and then he shrugged. "Okay. Dumb, but okay." He stood, dropped a punishing clap to Mercuri's shoulder on his way past. "If you need me, I'll be raiding your fridge."

Mercuri continued to brood. Moments later, he was embroiled in another gaming battle.

***

Memphis, Tennessee~

"We did right to put Harris on this."

Jake Grodins and Brody Alberts exchanged looks they thought were passive enough. The other two men in the room deciphered them all too clearly.

Lorne Grodins shared a look with his oldest friend and business partner Nathan Alberts.

"You think we made a mistake sending Harris?" Lorne Grodins asked his son.

Jake mussed his hair, a shock of silver blonde that lay in slashes across his brow. "Not a mistake, exactly." Jake leaned forward in the tall, cream leather wing chair he'd chosen. "Harris is a good man, but he's always had this beef with Merc. It blinds him."

"You agree with that Brody?" Nathan Alberts closely regarded his son.

"I think he's been acting a little hasty and I don't think it's wise to get Merc's suspicions up," Brody Alberts' shrug resembled a shudder. "It's like poking a stick at a sleeping dragon."

"A sleeping four-headed dragon," Jake chimed in.

Brody nodded. "They're bound to hear about what happened to Patch and the rest."

"And our...Greek contingent still frightens you?" The hint of an ill-humored smile tugged Nathan Alberts' mouth.

Brody seemed to bristle over the slight. "They don't frighten us-"

"We just don't see the point in getting them riled up before we know for sure they've got a part in this," Jake tacked on before Brody could add to his father's taunt. "Mercuri's some big shipping mogul now and the others are living their lives. Some have families."

"Had families," Brody served the reminder. The gleam in his light brown eyes was a grim one.

"Was that a problem for you?" Lorne shifted a probing glare between the younger men. "They took members of *your* families, after all. Or have these long years helped you forget that?"

They hadn't forgotten. Brody's and Jake's vengeance ran deeper than their fathers could guess at. There were however, other things at stake- information that could either strengthen or obliterate the organization they one day intended to command. Retrieving it was the highest priority. Revenge was a luxury they would enjoy later and at great length.

"We haven't forgotten Pop," Jake bolted from his chair and began to pace. "But like you said, it's been a lot of years. Why would Merc and the others lay low with what they've got on us?"

"Maybe because they're of a mind that we're defeated and they see no reason to beat us further into the ground," Lorne Grodins advised his son. "They know when to wage war or grant mercy. It's what makes them such excellent soldiers."

Jake turned as if to head back to his chair, but it was only so his father wouldn't see the eyeroll he gave into over the man's insight.

Brody saw his friend's reaction clearly enough, but gave no indication that he had. "We just don't think it's wise to get suspicions up on Merc's end before we see the Roya angle through," he said.

Nathan Alberts stroked the neat, dark goatee he sported and considered. "You don't believe it was necessary to see someone connected with Mercuri in order to get information on Roya's location?"

"Seeing Patroclus Kostas was unnecessary," Brody insisted with a slashing wave. "He didn't have any information we didn't already know. Harris used this assignment to feed into his hatred for Mercuri. In the end, he only wanted two things- to torture those guys and to know if the takedown at Roya's place was set up by Mercuri.

Patch did confess that before he died," Brody continued, his eyes fixed on the fist he clenched and unclenched. "*He* was the one Harris wanted- the reason we tracked down the others… to get Patch's location. Him being part of Merc's… Greek contingent, Harris knew Patch's death would hit Mercuri hard. He fed off that knowledge. Six years being ordered to keep a lid on it, has only given his hatred time to fester. If we don't locate what we got into this for, that hatred might blow us out of the water. There may be no coming back from it this time."

"Did Patterson give up Roya's whereabouts?" Lorne Grodins asked once he too had taken several moments for consideration.

"She had a phone number. We're running it now to get a location," Jake told his father.

"You think she told you the truth?" Nathan asked.

Brody's grim eye-gleam returned. "Oh yeah," he sighed, recalling Grant Zubin's retelling of his encounter with the Vegas madam.

Nathan walked to his side of the ballroom sized corner office with its eye catching view of the Hernando de Soto Bridge. "Perhaps the visits to Kostas and the rest were mistakes, but what's done can't be undone," he turned to bring an index finger down on the desk.

"The Venezuelan incident crippled us," he went on. "If Mercuri and the rest have indeed just been living their lives, then that's a lucky break for us. It's given us time to replenish our forces and to mend important friendships that were broken after what happened to The Ten."

"But the rekindling of those friendships hasn't come without a cost," Lorne chimed in the caution from his place behind the polished pine bar that seemed to span one long wall. "That cost rests in what was taken from the slaughter inside that penthouse," he reminded them. "Now, as you've both said. Harris has a beef with Merc. That could play into our favor as well."

Jake and Brody passed looks across the room.

"How Pop?" Jake asked with a mystified shrug.

"If Mercuri's overall plan included sending those girls there to take out The Ten and secure what was taken, then the deaths of Patch and the others might get us a reaction. I'm confident we'll catch it if Mercuri makes a move that involves what we're looking for."

"And what if Merc's got nothing to do with what was taken?" Jake asked. "What if all this was just about him and those other cocksuckers wanting out of the business?"

Nathan was already nodding in consideration of the possibility. "Then, so much the better for us, because then it all comes down to the efforts of a greedy pimp who saw himself clever enough to use a few hookers to run a blackmail scheme."

"Do you really buy that, dad?" Doubt had pushed in alongside Brody's grim look. "There was no record of those girls entering or even leaving the hotel. They may've taken the discs- convenient given they had access to the control room. But afterwards? Them heading out? The security cameras were still rolling. It's just too much of a stretch to buy that they were savvy enough to pull or wipe that feed if we're to believe they were just hookers running a scam for their pimp."

"This was a professional job," Jake said.

"So you *are* sure it was Mercuri?" Lorne probed.

"Maybe." Brody raised a beefy shoulder. "Maybe someone else entirely."

"But not Roya?" Nathan grinned. "Guys, we know your egos won't allow you to admit this, but our odds are much better against the likes of Enrique Roya than Mercuri Nikolaides. Roya's a coward. We get our hands on him, he'll spill everything he has on how our property walked out of that room."

***

"Thanks for the bail-out, man." Ethan Scales' voice was emotion-filled as he extended a hand to shake with Mercuri.

Following the gesture, Ethan's stone gray eyes scanned the executive board room which was clearing of personnel on hand for the meeting.

"I don't know how we would've come out of this if you hadn't stepped in to take over-"

"Credit for that goes to Rand," Mercuri stopped his old friend's grateful spiel. "He's the one who called me, remember? A call you could've made."

Ethan grinned in spite of himself and nodded. "It's that reporter's nosiness that had him stepping in, in the first place, I guess," he spoke of their mutual friend Randall Caffrey a well-known journalist who had once fought alongside Ethan and Mercuri for the GAN.

"You know what a procrastinator I've always been, Merc. I'm grateful though. Very."

"It's only my name on the lease, E. The business is still yours to run as you and your people see fit."

Ethan's cement-colored eyes narrowed then with playful intent. "How'd you get to be so rich, being so decent?"

Mercuri threw back his head to release a savory blast of laughter. "It's a gift!"

Ethan laughed then as well. "Well, I'm glad it's a gift you don't mind sharing," he clapped Mercuri's back as they both rose to their feet.

The men parted ways then and Mercuri took time to observe the executives filing out of the staid boardroom. What were the odds that he would've been remotely associated with a business that built hospitals?

Chuckling inwardly, Mercuri made his way from the room. He nodded to those he passed or stopped to take part in brief chats. Once he'd cleared the fray, his thoughts rolled back to his talk with Pope over the weekend. *They weren't those guys anymore,* Pope had said.

Mercuri thought he knew that. In times like this, closing deals and making connections, he thought he was absolutely certain of it. Then... the most unexpected things occurred that had him second guessing everything he thought he knew.

His steps slowed as he neared the elevator bay. On the other side of the long corridor of maple paneled cars, was an auditorium.

What were the odds of finding Etienne Shaw waiting there?

She wasn't exactly waiting, though. Mercuri realized once he stood in the broad entryway of the space that was otherwise empty. Relaxing there, in a leaning stance against the entryway, Mercuri watched Tee leave the chair she'd occupied on a long row- one of several that went far back into the vast, darkly paneled area. Intrigued, he watched as she selected another chair along the same row. She appeared to change her mind on that one and moved to a spot four rows back.

Realization took root then as Mercuri moved farther into the room. "So today we're redesigning corporate spaces."

The rich, rumble of words, had Tee dropping back into the seat she was about to leave. "Mercuri," she straightened, hands resting along the arms of the navy Captain's chair she occupied.

He moved toward the seating, appreciating her surprise at seeing him and the smile he could just glimpse on her small, exquisite face. "You working?" He leaned against the wall of the aisle nearest the seat she'd selected.

Tee got to her feet slowly, but made no move to leave the row. "The owners are looking to soften the place, wanted to get my take on it." Her eyes swept his imposing length. "What um, what are you doing here?"

"I own the place," he was standing near enough that he could glimpse the mild distress take shape on her face. The look told him all he needed to know. Bracing off the wall, he began a slow walk back to the entryway.

"It's a name only thing," he spoke to her over his shoulder. When he was halfway to the exit, his steps slowed to a halt. "You don't have to worry about me showing up here everyday. I doubt I'll ever have to come back here again."

Tee left her row when he resumed his walk. "Mercuri?" When he turned, she found she couldn't move further than the seating aisle.

"I don't sleep with my clients, Mercuri."

He felt the wicked dance of a muscle along his jaw. Bowing his head, he eased both hands into his trouser pockets to hide suddenly clenching fists. "That's good to know," he managed the words on an easy sigh, "considering your clients are married couples in their sixties."

She smiled and bowed her head then too. "I don't sleep with any of my clients, Mercuri. Married or otherwise."

"I got it the first time," traces of temper sparked in his exotic gaze then and he turned to leave.

"Mercuri."

His steps halted again, but he didn't turn to face her. "What is it, Tee?"

"Why didn't you-?" Uncertainty had her words in a choke hold. Needing support, she rested her hand on the wall.

Curiosity outweighing temper, he turned.

"Why didn't you do more?" She asked.

Surprise had its way with his expression then. Slowly, he retraced his steps to the aisle.

Tee kept her place near the wall. She shifted to rest flush against it, when he invaded her personal space.

Leaning down, Mercuri brought his unusual gaze level with her eyes. Her alluring black pumps with plum piping, made the task somewhat easier. "Did you want me to do more?"

"I-"

"Honesty, Tee."

Intoxication at its height then, she swallowed, managed a nod and then a quiet "Yes". She was able to breathe the word, but any other movement was virtually impossible when he set himself against her. One hand, he set a few inches above her head on the wall. The other rested near her hip.

Tee commanded herself not to moan, but arousal peaked so sharp and quickly that she feared the sound would present itself soon enough. There was no strength in her hands which hung limp at her sides.

The brown flecked, golden pools of his eyes glinted with a fire that demanded her attention. When he released her from the potency of his stare, it was so he could caress her earlobe with the tip of his nose. Then, barely touching her skin, he trailed it down the line of her neck.

"I make you jumpy, don't I?"

Her lashes were seconds from fluttering all the way down over her eyes when she heard his question, felt his breath soft and warm on her skin. "No Mercuri, you-"

"You're curious too, though. Despite being a little intimidated. Is that right?" He raised his head to pin her once more with his riveting eyes.

She couldn't even work up the desire to conjure a response. Of course, her only response would've been 'yes'.

Mercuri didn't press for a reply. "Be sure, Sprite." He smirked with understated wickedness when he felt her bristle in response to the slur referencing her height.

"Be sure you want this. Want me." He lifted the hand at her hip to prop her chin on the curve of his fingers when she would've looked away. "Be sure you want me to finish this." Muscle flexed dangerously along his jaw again. He wouldn't hope that any part of this was a start instead of a finish. Not yet.

"Be sure," he saw fit to caution her a fourth time. "I don't hear so well when I'm… enjoying things. I may not hear you telling me to stop if you change your mind halfway through. Do you understand?"

She nodded, finding his expression to be an expectant, encouraging one that harbored a more intense element. "Yes," her voice was hushed.

"I'll let you get back to work." The hand propping up her chin, moved to cup her cheek briefly. Then, he was leaving.

Tee watched him go. She waited until he'd cleared the doorway, before she groped her way back to a row of seating. She settled into the first chair she found.

~CHAPTER 9~

Burlingame, California~

Emotion that could be described as nothing other than pure malice radiated from Berrill Clayton's mocha eyes. Her expressive, almond shaped stare slid over the speaker box set in the middle of a gleaming clawfoot desk. The surface teemed with an abundance of catalogs showcasing the latest in assault weaponry and other firearm paraphernalia.

"All businesses benefit from the support of their local communities Ms. Clayton. Yours is no exception."

On the other side of the big desk, Berrill's two assistants exchanged woeful looks. Silent prayers ascended for their boss to go easy on the lawyer they conferenced with.

Prayers went unanswered.

Berrill smiled in a manner familiar to those who knew her well. She enjoyed opportunities to eviscerate anyone who thought to approach her with an air of superiority.

"Well thanks for that education Mr. Lehman," Berrill's voice was deceptively cool. "Senator Morrow has selected a very passionate man as his newest campaign manager. I absolutely despised the last fool he put on the job."

The speaker box erupted with the sounds of Jerome Lehman, Esq. clearing his throat. "The last manager was Rich Lehman, my brother."

"Well you're doing a far more superior job than your idiot brother ever bothered to try-"

"Ms. Clayton-!"

"And while I appreciate the superior job you're doing for the Senator," Berrill steamrolled over the campaign manager's outrage while her assistants held their palms to their foreheads. "It's unwise to call my place of business and seek to advise me in matters related to a business you know absolutely nothing about."

"Ms. Clayton I'll have you know I come from a long line of gun range enthusiasts."

"How nice for you. Tell me, Mr. Lehman, did I own any of those ranges your... enthusiasts frequented?"

"Well I-uh-no."

"Then again, I'd say it's unwise for you to call my place of business and advise me on matters you know nothing about. Your idiot brother should've told you I get a little pissy when I deal with know it alls. Now back to the unsolicited advice you saw fit to share. You were actually quite right in your summation. Businesses *do* benefit from the support of their local communities. Especially not for profit businesses, like local community centers that offer afterschool programs to help keep kids off the streets and out of trouble. They benefit a helluva lot from such support."

"Ms. Clayton-"

"Businesses like the ones, local community officials; such as those who make up the good Senator's constituency, turn their backs on every chance they get- even during those all important election years when every politician on the ballot is visiting as many black churches as they can find. Even *then*, Senator Christopher Morrow's constituents turn their backs on such businesses."

Silence held the other end of the speaker. Berrill observed her short manicure while she waited.

"I'll relay your feelings to the Senator," Lehman said at last.

Berrill continued to study her nails. "You do that," she said.

"Ms. Clayton, I understand your frustration, but please know that the Senator is currently working to secure additional funding for-"

"Save it, Lehman. You'll find no votes coming from me or my staff." Berrill reached over to lift the phone receiver and gave it a hard slam back to its cradle, effectively cutting the connection. Next, she was pointing a finger at her two assistants.

"You're fired if you throw a vote to him or any town official who supports him. Pass it along." Frustrated, Berrill gathered up the locks of glossy black that hit her back and drew them into a messy ponytail.

"Because of that bastard sending his parade of aides and constituents out here to soften me up," she grumbled, "I missed out on a long weekend with my girls and I really could've used the time off."

Berrill's business, Bear Arms offered everything from basic target practice sessions to elaborate weekend shooting retreats for serious gun lovers. The establishment's upcoming event, promised to be more successful than the three preceding it. For months, Berrill had been immersed in planning meetings with her 120 member staff.

Much of that planning involved trimming the list of interested participants, down to the agreed upon 100 guests. Senator Christopher Morrow had instituted a whole other campaign to ensure invites for he and his associates. While Berrill had hated missing out on her weekend, it had been worth it to sit through the Morrow camp's excessive presentations, just to turn them down.

Shaun Oates mussed his hair, a fuzzy cap of auburn curls and gave his boss a companionable smile. "Like you said, it's coming up on an election year," Shaun shrugged. "The Senator loves his photo-ops."

"Damn right," Mike Hough agreed, "Your weekend shooting soirees draw big names, which can translate into big donations for the Distinguished Gentleman."

Berrill snorted. "Distinguished, my ass. Maybe I *should* invite him," she tapped a perfectly curved nail to the perfect curve of her mouth. "Those soirees *do* draw big names that translate into big donations- donations that benefit the businesses he and his supporters turn a blind eye to," she reared back in her wide desk chair and considered. "Maybe seeing some of that decency will have some of it rubbing off on him."

Mike's broad gleaming grin was an appealing contrast against his dark skin. He gave Shaun a look. "So boss uh, does that mean we should send the man an invite?"

"Hell no." She pushed back from her desk and smiled in appreciation of the men's laughter. "Now, if you gentlemen will excuse me, I'm gonna try reaching out to my girls and see if they'll let me treat them to some fancy lunch to make up for standing them up last weekend."

Mike and Shaun stood, prepared to give their boss her privacy when the desk phone rang.

"I got it," Berrill waved off the men while pushing in for the call. "This is Bear."

"Berrill Clayton?"

"You got her."

"The Berrill Clayton who worked for Diversion House in Las Vegas, Nevada?"

Slowly, Berrill reclaimed her desk chair. "Who the fuck is this?"

"Someone you and your friends will want to listen to, Ms. Clayton."

***

One Week Later~

David Sentry nodded his satisfaction as he browsed the pages in hand. "Very good," he shuffled through the legal sized white sheets set against the backing of pale blue card stock. "We appreciate the quick turnaround Merc, but we have no problem with you taking the weekend to review the contracts."

"My people and I went over them more than a few times. We're satisfied. They've already gone back and forth between our legal departments several times," Mercuri gave a casual shrug of one shoulder. "I think we're all as satisfied as we're going to be."

Again, Sentry nodded and extended his hand for shaking. A round of handshakes then commenced around the table with the others who had taken part in the lunch meeting.

"Next round's on me!" Sentry waved for the server.

The announcement met with cheers of approval in the hotel's heavily patronized restaurant- one of three that it boasted. Mercuri didn't begrudge the round of drinks, but he didn't plan on celebrating too long.

He had a far more appealing plan in mind for the rest of his day- his weekend.

He'd never in his life dealt with any feelings remotely related to nerves. Etienne Shaw, small yet potent, had changed that in the span of a day. He'd done his part, warning her of what she could expect if she was sure that a night in his bed was what she wanted.

It had been close to a week and she'd yet to make any indication that she'd changed her mind. Mercuri had worked diligently to clear his calendar so that his time would be hers. No woman had ever turned him into a sap and this one… This one, he'd allowed to do that and more, with pathetic ease. He didn't resent it at all.

The waiter arrived to take drink orders and, while Mercuri gave his, he saw her. Just like that, she was there in the line of his gaze. She was being led up the back spiral staircase where he knew a bank of meeting rooms were housed. Following close beside her, was a tall beauty who made Etienne look even smaller. This, in spite of the pumps Tee sported with a snug frock that adored her curvaceous frame.

Mercuri gave his drink order, and then told the waiter he needed one more thing.

~~~

LuCarolyn let out a long whistle the second the double white oak doors closed behind the host who had led them. She threw a wave to Berrill who poured a drink from the bar that snaked along a far wall. "This elaborate setup, your way of making up for stiffing us last weekend?" LuCarolyn taunted.

"It was supposed to be," weariness held Berrill's words as she added a splash of soda to her vodka.

"Alright Bear," Prin, already seated at the elegantly set round table, raised her hands expectantly, "we're all here now. Could you please spill whatever's got you acting so funky?"

"What's up?" Tee's voice was soft, slow. She moved into the room and set her tote to an embroidered black chair- one of four that provided a stark, lovely contrast against the all white environment.

"I got a call a few days ago from a man who claimed to work for Enrique Roya." Berrill sipped her drink and walked the wide space behind the bar.

Prin straightened noticeably in her chair. Her stirring blues had ignited with a fire that she directed towards LuCarolyn and Tee.

"He said he was calling as a favor to Mr. Roya who wants to be sure we're keeping our guard up. When I asked why Mr. Roya hadn't called himself-"

"Dammit Bear why'd you admit you knew him?"

"He already knew I did, Lu." Berrill's tone was cool, almost monotone. "The first thing he asked was if I was the Berrill Clayton who worked for Diversion House in Las Vegas."

Prin left her chair then. "Coincidence," she whispered to LuCarolyn and Tee.

"What else did he want, Bear?" Tee claimed her spot at the beautifully set table.

Berrill helped herself to more drink first. "Wanted to make sure we were keeping it safe, said Mr. Roya was concerned about it-*more* concerned in light of what he now fears has happened to Dorinda." She eyed her friends warily. "He wants us to consider letting him secure-"

"Bullshit to that," LuCarolyn stalked the elegant sunlit room, the long, scalloped hem of her casual cream dress complimented her ankles and clear, thin-heeled sandals.

But for the hand she dragged through her lengthy hair, Berrill appeared much calmer than her friend. Resolved, she shared the rest of the details from the conversation that had haunted her for almost a week.

"The guy said Roya didn't make the call himself because he's too busy relocating again. Seems he isn't at all happy about the state of upheaval his and his family's lives have been in since our serious lack of judgement in Vegas."

"We should've never brought them into this." LuCarolyn's pacing gained determination. "We should've never told him or Dorinda-"

"What choice did we have?" Prin blurted. "They already knew we were there. All it would've taken was for someone to ask about us. Do you really think Roya would've helped to protect our identities had there not been something in it for him?"

No one in the room had a comeback. They knew Prin spoke the truth. Tee's calm on that fateful night had played in everyone's favor when she'd had the forethought to look for anything that could have identified them. The cameras they'd uncovered in each room fed to a state of the art control room of sorts off from the master bedroom suite. The girls took every disc they could find, including a cache of blank discs waiting to be used. Once everything was shoved into a bag they'd located, they wrapped themselves in robes and turned their backs on the destruction they were responsible for.

"Prin's right," Berrill drained her glass. "None of us knew what the fuck we were doing. We'd have been as good as dead or in jail had we taken that shit to the cops that night. Telling Dorinda and Roya what we'd done had been our best move. Our only move," Berrill indicated her point with the raised glass.

"Lest we forget," she continued, "The lives we now lead, what we've been able to accomplish, got started from a very healthy payoff courtesy of Mr. Enrique Roya."

"Exactly." Prin gave a prompt nod, while she was still strolling the room. "Who knows what happened to Dorinda Patterson and you two wanted to cast it off as coincidence," she glowered at LuCarolyn and Tee both seated at the table.

"Aw, save it Prin," LuCarolyn rolled her eyes. "The lives *we* lead wouldn't have been possible without Roya-without Tee- is more accurate. In the end, all *you* had to do was run home to beg Mommy and Daddy for-"

"Lu. No." Tee didn't raise her voice, but her words carried all the same. "We aren't going to do that. We aren't ever going to do that," she said.

LuCarolyn bowed her head, kept it so for several seconds. Then, she was tugging back the coarse locks that bounced at her shoulders like an onyx cloud. Quickly, she closed the distance to Prin and drew her into a fierce hug.

Prin reciprocated the strength of the embrace.

"Forgive me," LuCarolyn squeezed her friend tighter when she felt her nod.

"It's already forgotten," Prin whispered.

"So what do we do now?" LuCarolyn asked once she and Prin broke from their embrace.

"Was that all this guy said when he called?" Tee asked Berrill.

"Roya's nervous," Berrill headed back to the bar for a refill on her drink. "He got word that Dorinda couldn't be reached. She's not even returning *his* calls."

"If she's in trouble, he could be concerned she might say anything to get herself out of it," LuCarolyn mused, resuming her pacing. "She could give him up or us for that matter," LuCarolyn followed up her observation with a hissed curse. "All this for sex tapes of some old assholes who are already in their graves."

"Some very important assholes given what we all now know about some of our... friends from that night," Berrill cautioned. "Dead or alive, maintaining the images they wore for the public, is key. However much seed money Roya gave us, it's nothing compared to the payoffs he's gotten over the years because of what turned up missing at that hotel."

Berrill studied the vodka on the bar and considered a refill. "It's never been in his possession and he's made nearly a killing off the mere threat of exposing it."

"Alright," LuCarolyn challenged with her nod, "so what do we do now?"

"Roya wants what we took because he's worried whoever suddenly has a renewed interest in it might track him down," Berrill theorized, having decided against a refill on the vodka. "With it in hand, he could threaten to use it to get them to back off. Without it, whoever's behind this may feel he was blowing smoke and kill him for the hell of it."

"Just because he doesn't have it in hand doesn't mean he can't get his hands on it," LuCarolyn argued, leaning against a far wall.

"They may not care," Berrill took her place at the table.

"So what are you saying?" Prin returned to the table and waited on Berrill's response.

"Whether Roya has it or not isn't the point. He's dead anyway," Berrill said. "They'll kill him for vengeance sake over what happened to their people," her flawless brow quirked. "What concerns me is what he'll say to save his own ass."

"Like giving us up," LuCarolyn guessed.

Berrill shrugged. "If he thinks it'll buy him some time," she shrugged again. "But if he outs us and he's got all the goods in hand..."

"Where does that leave us?" Prin slouched against the back of her chair.

There was a knock on the dining room door- the waiter inquiring about the orders. The meeting room allowed for occupants to call their selections in to the waitstaff. The women had yet to do so.

For a time, normalcy ensued as they placed orders from the establishment's popular seafood menu. Typical fashion, had LuCarolyn flirting outrageously with the waiter. The display raised everyone's spirits and had the server blushing wildly. When he left to put in the food requests, the heightened mood left with him.

"I say we hold on to our leverage," Berrill answered the question posed before the waiter's arrival. "Anybody comes looking for trouble, we put every bit of it out there- reputations be damned."

Silence carried in the room as everyone considered the ramifications of the bold suggestion.

"Fuck it," LuCarolyn whispered fiercely. "I make my living in Hollywood. Something like this will only make me more successful."

"If my folks disown me again, at least I'll have my advance from the book deal," Prin mused with a sly grin defining her stunning features.

"Don't sweat it," LuCarolyn soothed amidst her friend's laughter. "I'll buy the movie rights."

"A thing like this will only bring more business my way," Berrill said as the laughter tumbled in more riotously. "'Come shoot your guns and see a fallen woman while you're at it' What more could a man want? Tee?" She called for her quiet friend's input once the laughter had eased.

Tee clasped her hands over her place setting. "Sounds like we're all in agreement," she smiled.

A quick round of celebratory applause ensued. LuCarolyn and Prin decided more drinks were in order and headed for the bar. Berrill followed, all the while wondering if she was the only one who noticed that Tee didn't seem agreeable to their idea at all.

~CHAPTER 10~

The bulk of the heavy conversation had passed by the time the ladies' lunch orders had arrived. Conversation hit more enjoyable topics when talk of another girls' weekend was in the air. Feelings were unanimous that another trip was definitely in order and soon.

By the time all the wine, lobster rolls, shrimp salad and seafood linguine had been consumed, the group was of a mind that they had settled a wealth of issues. Lingering discussion filtered out from the meeting room as the women took their leave.

Lingering discussion filtered out among Berrill, Prin and LuCarolyn. Tee had lost her ability to pretend that the overarching topic, hashed out that afternoon, wasn't occupying the majority of her thoughts. First to exit the room, she was strolling a little ahead of her friends, when she heard her name.

"Ms. Shaw?"

Tee saw the waiter from that day approaching her and she smiled. The young Asian man reciprocated the gesture while passing her an envelope.

"From the gentleman," he said.

Her smile reflected confusion, but the waiter only supplied a polite nod as he retreated into a side corridor. Tee could hear her friend's voices lifting as they got closer, but she was too curious to resist tearing into the envelope. What she found there was a plastic card emblazoned with the hotel's logo. The strip along the back distinguished it as a room key. There was a note card inside the envelope as well.

1812 -M.N.

Tee halted her steps when she felt dangerously close to teetering on her high heels.

"You comin' Tee?" Prin's voice resounded as she and the others caught up.

"I uh," Tee held the envelope and its contents out of sight along her side. "I need to make a few calls before I head out- some clients in the area," she explained.

Her friends said their goodbyes. Tee set off to find an elevator.

~~~

The certainty in her steps lost momentum and confidence once she stepped onto the 18th floor of the hotel. The establishment was a coolly, lovely structure, well deserving of its 5-star status and staggering nightly rates. Nevertheless, Tee couldn't help but be reminded of the only other night she'd visited a hotel for the purpose of sex. It was the thought that had her steps halting as she lost herself in the graceful design of the smoky brown carpet accentuated by swirls of black. The design was understated, yet potent. She smiled then, an approving one that had nothing to do with the deep carpet along the wide corridor or the hotel's overall appeal. Understated yet potent. That summed up Mercuri Nikolaides perfectly.

His name inside her head, motivated her steps. Soon, she was approaching double doors finished in some glossy dark wood that contrasted warmly against the cream toned walls of the hallway. She was brushing her fingers across the small, brass-plated oval denoting the suite's number and she recalled his words of caution.

'Be sure, Sprite… I don't hear so well once I'm enjoying things…'

That warning should've had her demons roaring for her to get out of there as fast as her high heels could carry her. Instead, the precaution had another unexpected effect on the voices of her demons. It silenced them.

She raised her hand to knock and then remembered the key.

The locks clicked softly once the green light approved admittance. Tee hesitated in the doorway for just a second or two. A beckoning aroma invited her entry as it wafted to envelope her in a cool fragrance.

Her dark, questioning gaze skimmed the suite's gracious living area awash in lamplight of the lowest setting. She tilted her head then, the sound of voices having captured her ear when she took the short staircase off the living room.

The voices seemed to grow louder, but struck her as somehow muted the further she went along the hall at the top of the stairs. Turning into the room at the end of it, she understood why.

Mercuri relaxed on a bed that spanned almost the entire rear wall of the room. Massive pillows lined the base of the tall headframe cushioned in fabric of the same smoky brown as the carpeting. His close cropped hair, usually tamed away from his face, lay in a tousle of inky black slashes across his brow. The effect softened his breathtaking features while somehow maintaining the ferocity they boasted.

The sleeves of a silver gray shirt rolled at his elbows to reveal forearms packed with muscle. The shirt hung outside steel blue trousers and was open to partially display a sleek, superb chest and a defined abdomen that looked too perfectly sculpted to be real.

One of the powerfully corded forearms rested casually over a raised knee where he held a remote. A mounted flatscreen showcased highlights of a boxing match from the night before. His brilliant eyes slid from the screen to Tee in the doorway and he smiled. The gesture caused her heart to thud in her throat, yet she managed an equally riveting smile.

"I just got your note," she waved the envelope.

Mercuri shut off the TV and; still reclining against the headframe, nodded toward his bare feet. "Thought taking off my shoes would make me less intimidating."

Her eyes were fixed on his chest and he followed the line of her stare.

"Thought taking everything off would make me too forward."

She laughed. "Understood." Silently, she noted that the man would never be able to pass himself off as less intimidating regardless of the effort he made.

"How'd you find me?" She asked.

"Had a meeting in one of the restaurants. I saw you going up to one of the meeting rooms," he inclined his head in a playful manner, "thought I'd take a chance." His gaze narrowed when he saw her expression make the quick change from easy to stressed. "Bad meeting?" he asked.

Her low sigh served as an ill-humored laugh. "A bad meeting is one thing. A bad meeting with friends, is a whole other animal."

"Ah," forearm still resting across his knee, Mercuri propped a fist to his chin and sighed as well. "Bad meetings with friends... I've had my share of those. Wanna talk about it?"

Smiling easier then, Tee waved the room key in his direction. "You didn't ask me here to talk."

"But you need to, right?"

Incapable of denial, her smile quivered with the lone nod she gave.

"Here," Straightening, Mercuri directed her over with a wave. When she moved to approach, he shook his head. "If *I* can be less intimidating, so can you."

Tee followed the pointed look he was sending her pumps. Smiling, she braced a hand on the cream Queen Anne chair she stood closest too and wiggled out of the alluring heels.

Mercuri deliberately scanned her body beneath his extraordinary gaze. The dress she wore was of some lightweight fabric that hugged her upper body while it flared at her hips in a way that was both prim and chic. He adored the appeal she unintentionally exuded upon settling to her natural height. Satisfied, he lifted a hand to encourage her approach.

He locked on to her wrist once she was close enough and directed her to rest back against the inside of his raised calf. Resuming his recline, Mercuri rested against the headframe and waited.

"How do you make peace with the fact that you got your friends into a situation they wouldn't be in if it weren't for you deciding you knew what was best?" she asked.

"Mmm," Mercuri inhaled deeply, her query stirring his own regrets. "Tough one, though surprisingly one I can relate to."

It *was* surprising and Tee left her post against his calf to angle toward him on the bed. Expectant and curious, she watched him.

"I've been trying to figure an answer to that one for years," he said, "just when I think I've got it figured-found a way to justify it-there's a voice telling me I'm full of shit."

99

"Even though you're such a success," she pointed out.

He grinned though his expression was grim. "That's often how I justify it. Sometimes, you see a way to something better and you want to take those you love along with you to claim it."

Tee felt driven to nod. Even so, she couldn't fully agree that the *way* she'd selected on that long ago night had been a better one.

"Usually the better way is one that'll come back to haunt you."

Jolted by the way he'd perceived her thoughts, Tee scooted to her knees. "Was it worth it, though? Whether you've been haunted by it or not? Was it worth it for where you came out to on the other side?"

"I think so," he nodded and the wide, appealing curve of his mouth softened as some of the grimness eased. "How about for you?"

Tee studied her hands, brushing a thumb over the lines of one palm. "I'm trying to believe it was." Her words tumbled out in a shudder.

Concern had Mercuri frowning when he noticed her dark eyes glistening with unshed tears. "Hey," snagging her wrist again, he tugged her the brief distance down the bed toward him. Gathering her close, he settled back to the head of the broad bed with her tucked under his arm. She lay her head on his shoulder and he pressed a hard kiss to her hair. He was smiling again as the scent of green apples wafted from her dark cap of waves.

"Can I help?" He pampered her arm with slow, methodical rubs.

Tee snuggled her head into the crook of his neck then. "You are," turning her face into his neck, she breathed in the clean scent of soap clinging to his skin. The simple aroma triggered something soothing and had her burrowing in closer.

The quiet hum of the central air stirring through vents, was the only interruption of the silence between them. Tee was lulled by the sound and the serenity of their conversation on the heels of such an exhausting one with her friends.

It wasn't long before Mercuri realized she'd drifted off. The feel of her resting trustingly in his arms, roused a new kind of contentment- one that lulled him into his own restful doze.

~~~

She woke with an easy sigh. She usually woke with a jerk. Tee noted that silently when her lashes fluttered apart. Still bleary-eyed, she tried to bring her gaze into focus. She fixed on her hand. Her fingers were lazily entwined with the collar of the open shirt brushing her cheek.

She considered...yes, the jerkish start that usually ushered in her waking moments was a feeling she was all too familiar with. But this... there was no jarring effect; instead she emerged from her sleep as though gently roused from rest that had been altogether peaceful.

She wouldn't admit that it was all due to the man she rested against, though she knew it had to be true. He'd slumbered off as well, Tee realized upon lifting her head from his shoulder. She studied Mercuri's features relaxed in sleep. God where had he come from? *Why* had he come? Was there more to this than where they were right now? Briefly, she gave an appreciative scan of the elegant room before returning to the sleeping giant next to her. Did she care? She asked herself.

The answer to that was an emphatic no, Tee thought. Her eyes wandered across his bold, brutally devastating face and she felt the telltale stirring at her core. The sensation was one she was all too familiar with and; until now, unfortunate enough to have to endure with no reprieve. She wanted this reprieve, even if there was to be nothing more to it than a quick release from the distractions of sexual need. She wanted it- wanted him.

Eyes drifting away from his face then, Tee returned to where her fingers toyed with his shirt. They were skirting the buttons and subtly drawing back the material to reveal more of his chest. She regarded him with the same appreciation she had the room, but in a manner that was far more approving.

Curious about what the shirt hid, she outlined the curve of one pec beneath her thumbnail. She bit down on her bottom lip, adrenaline beginning its slow stir as she grazed the bulging curve. A minute flex of the toned muscle beneath the rich, copper-toned hue of his skin, sent her eyes back to his face. Relief pooled when she saw he hadn't awakened. They were sharing a bed, but for him to wake and find her fondling him beneath his clothes would be... beyond mortifying. Deliciously naughty, but mortifying.

Satisfied that she hadn't awakened him, Tee continued her investigation. Now, her fingers charted an undeterred path to the abs that had fascinated her from the moment she'd glimpsed them beneath his open shirt. Her eyes hadn't deceived her. The compact, sinewy slabs were perfectly sculpted and; as her deliberate touch proved, very real.

Now, heat bloomed alongside the telltale stirring below her waist. Tee got lost in her appraisal of the formidable physique beneath her fingertips. Her thumbnail skirted his naval and she smiled at the slow, consistent rise and fall of his abdomen against her palm as he breathed.

Her gaze travelled lower to the dark gleaming buckle of his leather belt. She was seriously entertaining the idea of continuing her exploration when his throat cleared ever so softly. She discovered that delicious naughtiness had nothing on the mortification she felt once her eyes made the difficult climb to meet his.

Mercuri appeared content and well-rested, though his unforgettable eyes sparkled with a mix of amusement and something... basic and far less amused.

Tee revisited her acknowledgement of him as a sleeping giant. The acknowledgment warranted tweaking. It was well known that it was unwise to wake a sleeping giant. Oh how she hoped there would be consequences.

"Is it my turn now?" He asked.

She pushed up on the bed, tucked her legs beneath her. "I guess that's fair," she said.

It wouldn't be, Mercuri thought, knowing the smile he shared then was just as he'd intended it to be-unreadable.

Fair, as *she* meant it, would indicate that he intended to follow along the lines she'd initiated. She hadn't taken him out of his clothes. He'd awakened the moment she shifted against him. He remembered that her touch had been tentative at best while he lay there feigning sleep for her benefit and his pleasure.

No, Mercuri thought, his 'turn' wouldn't be fair at all.

~CHAPTER 11~

His tug at the hem of her dress was enough to indicate that he wanted her out of it. The item was a simple, emerald green number that flared just below her knees and matched the intricate piping of the pumps she'd worn. Gathering the hem, Tee drew the garment up and over her head.

Mercuri gave the impression that he was wholly relaxed while he lay there watching her. Such couldn't be farther from the truth. He wanted out of his clothes almost as much as he wanted her out of hers. He knew teasing wasn't her intention as she stripped for him, but the unhurried ascent of the soft cotton frock did that and more.

His body temperature had risen far beyond its usual sultry heights. He had her the instant she'd tugged the dress over her head and was then moving to smooth a hand across her naturally wavy hair. He lifted her, settling her to straddle his lap. Satisfied for the moment, he indulged in a closer inspection of her curvy, petite frame. First with his eyes- the uncommon golden orbs wandered over the pear-green bra that lovingly cupped cleavage more ample than he'd originally guessed. Her rich, molasses dark coloring doused her evenly from head to toe and was as flawless on her small, captivating face as it was over the rest of her.

Quickly, the need to add touch to sight had Mercuri massaging her hips where he still kept her snug against him. A wisp of pear-green lace covered her there and he slipped inside the seam to test the suppleness beneath. He studied her fingers resting lightly against his ribs and took the time to appreciate and approve of all the distinct differences between them. Curiosity had him firming his hold at her waist while he adjusted her position astride him. The move aligned her lace covered sex with his trouser clad one. Her mouth, full and X-ratedly kissable, parted a fraction. He spied her pupils dilating in response to what he put her in contact with. His smile defined as he savored the look of her.

For Tee, arousal was no longer just a tell-tale stirring. It was a full blown insistent and frustrating reminder of the need she wanted him to tend. Missed sensations erupted from his sex nudging hers. His sex didn't merely nudged though. 'Nudge' was such an...inept descriptor for the organ that felt wondrously thick and thoroughly capable against her.

Mercuri indulged in the exquisite image she cast, her hips faintly rocking on the assumption of what she wished to experience.

Too soon, Tee was feeling all the indications of what promised to be climax at its best. She was on her back before she could experience it. Lashes fluttering madly, her dark eyes widened to dazzling onyx pools before she took in the picture that eclipsed all else.

He'd turned the tables, parting her thighs to accommodate his body between them.

"None of that now," he whispered in reaction to her attempt at climaxing without him. "Not just yet," he muttered.

Arching her hips, Tee sought just a measure of the sweet pleasure his sex against hers had brought.

"Not yet," he murmured, propping her chin on his finger to ready her for his kiss.

It wasn't the thunderous claiming he'd treated her to the first time he'd taken her mouth. This kiss was a more patient invasion that assaulted her as erotically as before. The same lengthy, deep lunges that detailed their previous kiss, encompassed this one. As his tongue thrust, rubbed and coaxed, Tee felt her panties go damp-same as the first time he kissed her.

The similarities ended there. He took her mouth relentlessly, but stopped mid thrust to suckle her lush lips. Her hands, so intent on exploring his body earlier, could only rest against the satiny caramel colored comforter at her back. Her fingers curved weakly into the material as they were incapable of doing much more.

The suckling transitioned to outlining, with the tip of his persuasive tongue tracing the shapely, parted petals of her mouth. Tee emitted the most infectious combination of gasps, moans and pleas.

Mercuri returned to sample more of her mouth and picked up on more guttural sounds joining in the sensual medley. His own? The sound of his own responses was a novel experience. He was used to eliciting such responses, emitting them... when was the last time *that* happened? Whatever the timeframe, it certainly hadn't been summoned by the simple act of kissing.

Tee eventually regained the use of her hands. She gripped the tails of Mercuri's shirt, still hanging open and providing something of a shelter for her body as he caged her beneath his warrior's physique. Languidly, she splayed her fingers wide across his chest cupping one of the flexing pecs and taking great delight in the sensation of the hard muscle filling her palm. She used her thumbnail to lightly scrape at his nipple and felt her heart lurch when his vocal responses took on a more animalistic tinge.

She was once again toying with the lapels of his shirt, curving her fingers around the material and then skimming across until she was stroking the bare flesh of his forearms revealed below the rolled sleeves. Down she stroked, moaning throatily into his mouth when her hands met his closed fists. They were pressed on either side of her hips, deep into the mattress. Tee gripped his wrists and tugged, indicating that she wanted to feel him- all of him against her.

Finally, Mercuri broke the kiss. "I weigh a ton."

"You don't."

"It'll feel like it. Trust me."

"Please Mercuri," boldly, she cupped the erection ruthlessly straining the zipper of his trousers.

He groaned his appreciation over the unexpected and pleasurable caress. Succumbing to its effects, he brought himself down over her seconds later. Her thighs were toned, supple and he gripped them in a fashion that was both commanding and tender.

Keeping her open, he drew her snug into him. Hiding his face in the side of her neck, he commended another round of the mock thrusts that had almost brought Tee to climax before. His hands weren't still either and moments later, she was moaning to a new sensation. Mercuri's sleek, excellent chest was bare next to hers once he'd undone her bra and slipped it from her shoulders.

He dragged a kiss across the delicate curve of her jaw when her velvety soft breasts met his chest. The mounds crushed into him, resulting in an almost drugging effect on his hormones. Starving for her then, he took one of the ebony orbs in a loose grasp and watched the nipple firm from his thumb's slow caress. As she writhed beneath him, sobbing out moans, he turned his attention to the other waiting breast. The nipple beaded against his tongue when it circled the licorice dark nub.

Tee was caught up in a mindless whirlwind of sensation as Mercuri tirelessly sucked and fondled her nipples. His hand planted in the center of her back, kept her arched, her body at his mercy. She couldn't remember when such enjoyment had been hers for the taking. She didn't care. It was hers for the taking now and she intended to take all. Mild disappointment wedged into her subconscious however when he abandoned the nipple he'd coaxed into a plump, erect jewel. Her disappointment faded into anticipation as she reacted to his fingers skirting along her curves until they were again curving into the seam of her panties.

Again, she was lost in the thrill of him dividing his attention between her breasts. She shivered when he left one nipple glistening wet and chilled by the circulating air when he moved on to the other. She luxuriated in the onslaught of sensation, compounded when she plunged her fingers into the dense forest of his blue black hair. The longer inches on the top shielded his forehead then, giving him a relaxed look that made him appear no less fierce.

Tee heard the sound of tearing fabric, but barely reacted to the sound that signified the destruction of her underwear. It seemed to her that his focus was in feasting on her breasts. Eagerly, he sucked at her, kissing his way over and beneath her weighty breasts and using his nose to outline the blackberry cloud of her areola. Then, she felt his thumb tracing the seam of her sex and realized how wrong she was.

Mercuri dipped his thumb inside her core to test her size and she reacted as he'd expected. Her resulting gasp confirmed pleasure, hinted at pain. He used his ring finger and smiled when her reaction confirmed more delight than discomfort.

She gave herself over to the savory caress without hesitation. Her hands weakened again. Bonelessly, they rested near her head as she arched up to take what he wanted to give.

Mercuri's enviably long lashes settled over his eyes. Arousal, and the need to quench it, had him completely ensnared. Carefully, he used his finger to sample her core. He could only imagine how the tight bundling of muscles there would feel when they were squeezing his dick. His hormones had ceased their frenzied dance in demand for appeasement and were then doggedly clawing at his willpower, He ignored the demands tormenting him- he couldn't rush this. Taking her would require a finesse that commanded patience. While no man in his right mind would take issue with her fit, he wanted her to enjoy everything he planned to do with her.

Just then, Tee had no issue with his treatment. She would've taken no offense were his treatment more demanding. To prove that point, she locked her hands over his wrist and arched up to take all of his gently exploring finger.

Mercuri let her have her way just shy of five seconds, before withdrawing to the sound of her agonized sob. He abandoned her breasts then, to kiss his way down her body. Lustier intentions were on his mind. Her hips pistoned off the bed, when she felt his nose skimming the seam of her sex. Mercuri firmed his hold on her hips, bringing her back down upon the decadent tangle of covers.

She fisted the linens and felt well out of her mind from the sensation hitting her from every angle. She felt him gliding his nose along her folds. There was the wondrous thrust of his tongue then. It was strong enough to fill and stretch her to the point that she felt the unmistakable pressure of orgasm slap at her once again.

It was the reaction Mercuri had hoped for. He knew she would take him much easier, if she were dripping wet for him. Besides, he found her scent to be a heady one. A faintly fruity fragrance teased his nostrils and taste buds as he plundered her body.

Her quiet sounds of pleasure hummed constantly on the air. Her legs were draped carelessly across his magnificent shoulders, upper thighs loosely cradled in his hands while he feasted. Her intimate muscles clenched and released his tongue in heated anticipation. She wanted more than his skillful tongue, but... not yet. The promise of orgasm was asserting itself and she was eager for it to have its way.

The slide and rotation of his tongue brought her to a shattering climax. The intensity of it almost blinded Mercuri to the demands of his own need. She was so controlled, he thought. So self-composed. To see that persona collapse and know that he'd been solely responsible... Would this moment, this one time with her be enough for him? Casting the unwanted thought from his mind, he drove his tongue harder, faster, deeper inside her. The flood of her moisture against his tongue was thoroughly appreciated and he didn't stop until the volume of her breathy cries had lowered.

She lay writhing atop covers that were almost completely off the bed. Mercuri could've taken pity on her then, allowed her to come down off what she'd just experienced. He didn't. While she lay there quivering, he left the bed, stripped and took time to set their protection in place.

Tee had only a few seconds between the time she saw Mercuri applying the condom and the time he was returning to the bed, to appreciate his build below the waist. He didn't cover her, but instead braced his weight to the fist he'd pressed into the mattress.

Guiding the erection that jutted stiff, Mercuri took her in a compelling lunge that buried him mercilessly deep. He didn't wait to take in her reaction, he was too preoccupied by his own. Her grip on his shaft was painfully sweet. She had resumed the ego-stroking cries she'd uttered when he'd pleasured her with his tongue. He barely had to move for sensation to flood thickly, consuming him in a pounding array of sex-saturated waves.

Weakly, Tee met his faint thrusts. When he traded them for a round of stronger rotations inside the moisture-rich well of her sex, she submitted to another shocking peak of gratification. Mercuri leaned in to nuzzle into another kiss and she purred from the flavor of her body on his tongue. Linking her arms about his neck, she proceeded to drink him in with sultry laziness.

He could sense from her manner that she was practically fulfilled for the moment. He didn't mind her going over without him. He planned to have lots of time to catch up. Still, she received him, matching his measured stretching glides with the most provocative arches and twists of her hips.

He wanted to hold his own climax at bay. Orgasm would slay him soon-savagely and repetitively during the course of the long night he intended to have with her. Now, he wanted only this, this generous give and take as mutual pleasure hummed between them. He sensed- hoped she needed that to last as much as he did.

~CHAPTER 12~

Tee wasn't jarred from her sleep. Rather, she floated into waking with a contented sigh-a testament to a night well spent. Regrettably, the night had to end though to make way for morning.

The early hours found her gingerly making her way from the bed. She and Mercuri had all but pummeled it in into a mass of disjointed wood during their long afternoon and evening together. She had no idea of the time. She only hoped it was early enough so that the hotel would still be blessedly quiet and its halls relatively untraveled. Her watch had disappeared some place inside the room. It was likely amid the folds of linens tangled on the floor or hanging from their tucked spaces beneath the covers of the heavy mattress.

I can do without it, she thought not wanting to wake Mercuri.

She considered her panties, which had also gone missing in the night. Not that they'd do her much good anyway. Recalling how they'd been massacred, Tee had to stifle a moan over the sensation stirred by the lusty memory.

She had no qualifying adjectives or metaphors to describe what had taken place between them there. Only now, she had no idea what, if anything, was to happen next. Would they see each other again? It didn't take much to realize their worlds didn't normally orbit the same sun.

She wanted to see him again. She really did. In six years, she had known little in the way of contentment. She endured- that's what she did. She kept anger and upset at bay outside a fortress of control.

Mercuri Nikolaides had rendered that fortress to rubble with little more than an embrace. With him, she hadn't needed the fortress. The upset and the anger were mere wisps of memory- ones she could regard as figments of her imagination. It felt so good and she wanted to experience those feelings again. It was appropriate to say that those feelings went well beyond contentment.

Tee smoothed her hands along the sides of her dress and studied the bed where Mercuri still rested. The linens that weren't on the floor, twisted appealingly about his big, powerful limbs. Temptation surged and told her that leaving was a mistake when all she wanted was more of him. Giving a critical sigh, she went to slip into her shoes.

"So I guess this means 'no' to breakfast?"

She whirled and Mercuri had to admire the graceful pirouette she completed on the killer pumps. Eyeing the provocative stems, had regret streaking through him then. He wished he hadn't asked her to take them off before joining him in the bed. Next time, he thought. There would be a next time.

Graceful pirouette notwithstanding, Tee stood there gaping. She had only looked away for a few seconds while slipping into the shoes. Mercuri-relaxed against the towering headframe, arms folded across his gorgeous chest, appeared as though he'd been that way for hours. How a man his size moved with such effortless ease, was beyond her.

"I was trying not to wake you," her voice sounded hushed in the room.

"Obviously," he said.

Tee couldn't tell if he was really as cool as he seemed or secretly pissed with her for leaving. Before she could scrounge up an excuse to explain herself, he was speaking.

"You okay?"

She replied to his query with an easy nod, easier smile. "I am," silently she noted that the delicious ache of sore muscles was nothing a long soak in her tub wouldn't fix.

"So I'll see you later then?" His bright, assessing eyes wandered suggestively down the length of her.

The particular query gave her pause. Did he mean that literally or was it an afterthought as one might say, 'Take care'?

"Sounds good," she decided to keep her confusion to herself. Turning then, she continued her determined journey toward the room's open entryway. She stopped, bracing her hand on the doorframe when she turned back to him.

"Thank you for this," she bowed her head suddenly, cheeks burning over lustful memories.

Mercuri kept his expression closed, though he couldn't help but relish the adorable affect that embarrassment had on her small, lovely face.

Clearing her throat, Tee forced eye contact again. "Thanks for letting me drone on about friendship drama."

"We've all been there, Sprite and you're welcome."

She lingered in the doorway a moment longer. "Okay um, so I'll see you later," she said in a whimsical manner that clearly relayed her doubt that she would.

Mercuri watched her go, waited for the sound of the main door closing, before he replied. "Count on it, Ms. Shaw."

***

Golden, British Columbia~

"The boss won't appreciate us rousting him out of the wilderness, Chief."

Ben Weis waved off the warning that his young officer tried to make sound playful. "He won't mind so much when he finds out why."

Lamar Tilson didn't look too convinced if the shift of his olive colored gaze from the front of the room back to his chief, was any hint. "I've worked here for four years, Sir and I've never seen the man appreciate being called off a hunt."

"That's because you've only worked here four years," Ben settled deeper into the wide brown leather chair he occupied. It was one of many that furnished the immense, maple paneled great room.

"He'll want to know this, kid. Trust me."

Nodding, Lamar tried to accept the outlook of his experienced supervisor.

Ben, meanwhile, rested his head back and propped his feet on a matching Ottoman. He didn't fault Lamar for being on edge or skeptical.

112

Rutger Eliades, was not someone a sane man would want to rile. That was a fact even when Rutger wasn't partaking of his passion for hunting. In Golden, British Columbia, such a passion was common. For Rutger Eliades however, it was religion. Golden, was a place that epitomized rugged, outdoor living. It was the place Rutger had called home for almost six years and Ben Weis had done the same.

Ben had known Rutger since the old days when everything, including their next breaths were uncertain. The old days, Ben mused as he was coaxed into serenity by the room with its panelled walls, gleaming hardwoods and plate windows that showcased the wilderness beyond.

Ben knew his serenity would last at least until the man of the house returned. Sure enough, a teasing grimace tugged his mouth when the roar of gravel under truck tires reached his ears. Yep, Rut was gonna be pissed, alright. It wouldn't last long, not when he understood why the officers had brought him back. Ben's grimace wasn't quite so teasing then.

The storm began as most do, with a whisper. Rutger Eliades entered his home quietly enough. The officers, members of his security team, had only informed him that the chief needed to see him. They'd offered no additional detail and Rutger knew they wouldn't regardless of whether they'd known any. Rutger may've signed their paychecks, but the men took their orders from Ben Weis.

Such was the way Rutger wanted it, after all. He depended on those he trusted most to handle the things he had no interest in, but were no less vital to his life running smoothly.

Rutger located his security chief relaxing near a huge hearth- one of two- in the sweeping great room. The sensation of flexing muscle ignited along his jaw and Rutger's deep-set bourbon colored eyes narrowed to lethal slits. "What the fuck, Ben?"

Ben, still relaxed in the chair, only raised a hand toward a round clawfoot table of rich maple. It flanked one of the big chairs in the room.

The muscle flexed more wickedly along Rutger's jaw. "Goddamn you, Ben, if you're running one of your pranks," he muttered but chose to stifle the remainder of his rage. For the moment.

Moving to the table as instructed, he found two newspapers. Rutger felt his chest tighten with a new kind of rage as he scanned the headlines.

***

113

Las Vegas, Nevada~

Officer Nolan Booker often wondered if the shit beat he walked was a sign-part of the dues he had to pay before the lights, sights and sounds of Vegas were more a part of his working hours.

For now, his time consisted of dismal treks along the property surrounding the airport. It was his first night on the stroll. He'd been on the outskirts of Old Vegas prior to that. Booker didn't know what was funnier- that his three years on the force hadn't gotten him a better assignment in the rotation or the fact that he'd been walking a beat for 3 years.

Things could be worse, he thought, grateful that he at least had a partner to keep the loneliness at bay. Unfortunately Officer Tab Montgomery was away on maternity leave.

"Lucky lady," Booker sighed, thinking he might start advocating for expectant fathers to be eligible for the leave. He decided to discuss the matter with his wife when he got home. After all, he should *be* an expectant father before he went around advocating for them, right?

Grinning, Booker stopped to watch a departing plane making its final turn along a far off runway. He continued his stroll while periodically observing the plane gaining speed. He was looking over to check out the takeoff when he stumbled, losing his footing and flashlight when he encountered something in his path.

Cursing viciously, Booker rubbed his side where he'd landed in the dirt and brush. He saw the butt of the flashlight nearby. Reaching for it, his eyes strayed to the beam of light streaming from its single eye. Booker froze.

There, in the path of the white beam, was the image of a face framed by curly ringlets of hair. Bangs brushed the forehead. It was a beauty of a face in spite of the streaks across it. Booker took the streaks for dirt and slowly pushed to his feet. Carefully, he reached for the flashlight and kept it trained toward the face. Advancing, he slowly turned the light from the face to the body it was attached to.

His first instinct was to scream- his second to wretch. He quelled both urges. He may have been walking a beat, but he wasn't some green faced rookie, Booker reminded himself. He drew the light back up to the face and knew the dark streaks across it had to be blood.

Aside from the flashlight, his vision was understandably impaired given the night. He could tell, once the light slid over the body, that it had been relentlessly trampled. In that moment, Booker was grateful for the shadow blocking the naked corpse. He was sure he didn't want to see; by the light of day, the extent of the damage done to the woman's body.

Drawing on whatever remained of his courage, Booker moved in for a closer look. His need to wretch returned with violent insistence.

Savage scrapes marred the woman's leg from thigh to ankle. They spelled out a single phrase:

WHERE IS IT?

PART II

*You can't break the rules until
you know how to play the game.
-Rickie Lee Jones*

~CHAPTER 13~

Loriler Village was a shopping haven that catered to tastes ranging from the simple to the most decadent. The landscaping and architecture whispered money, status and Olde English charm. Still, the overall feeling was one of warmth and intimacy.

People visited Loriler as much for its shopping as they did to enjoy simpler things. Visitors gathered to read, jog, walk or just to sit on its sprawling lawns. The village also served as the residence for many of the city's professionals. Two bedroom condos with terraces overlooking the activity below, were constructed above many of the village shops. Instead of appearing crowded, the look was cozy and old world quaint amidst 21st century advancement.

Loriler had been Tee's home for four years. She'd been in love with the area since she and her friends had abandoned the lights and sounds of Vegas to set their sights farther west.

While LuCarolyn, Berrill and Princess had opted for more spacious digs, Tee's selection criteria was of a different ilk. She didn't mind that her choice wasn't as sweeping in size as the others. It was the noise- the life- that she craved. She believed she'd go crazy with unending quiet and privacy.

Privacy and quiet were too reminiscent. The penthouse had been private and quiet. Once The Ten had drifted off all sex-sated and slushy drunk, Tee had lay awake trying to wipe her mind of the night's events.

There was no unending quiet in the place she now called home. After 11pm, Loriler Village catered to the interests of night owls. Posh clubs and bistros kept the area lively until the smallest hours of morning. By then, whatever quiet there was had been enhanced by birdsong and the breakfast staff opening the diner downstairs.

For Tee, it was heaven. She could count on signs of life no matter the time of day. She especially appreciated it on those days when the office got to be a little too much and she decided to call it a day early.

Days like today, she thought as she finger combed her hair still damp from the shower. She'd hopped in shortly after arriving home from the office. The day had been heavily overcast which made her want out of her office even sooner.

The shower had helped to settle her somewhat. She dressed in a sporty, denim-colored sweatshirt dress that stopped just above the knee. Barefoot, she moved around drying her hair with one hand while setting out the work she'd brought home to finish. Before settling in with work, she went to open the wine she'd put in to chill before the shower. Dinner would be in an hour. She had already called down to the diner to confirm her usual table would be free.

The apartment ran to artsy chic, in a dark caramel and gold color scheme. Framed opera posters decorated the cream walls. The furnishings were cushy sofas and scoop chairs with matching footstools. Short, round end tables with hand carved doors were used to store part of an impressive DVD collection. The rest were stored on the room's built in bookshelves. Everything was hospitable, unpretentious and Tee couldn't have imagined herself living anywhere else.

Except maybe...Mercuri Nikolaides' Sonoma mansion.

Bursting into quick laughter, Tee shook her head and focused on the work she'd brought home. Vera would be proud, she thought, taking a sip of the wine while she settled into the recliner near one of the towering lamps that bathed the room in soft gold.

Vera had pretty much kicked her out of the office that afternoon when she caught Tee doodling Mercuri's name during their staff meeting.

"Idiot," the memory had Tee rapping her knuckles to her forehead. She was resigning herself to finishing all the work in hand when the doorbell rang.

"I'm trying, Vera," she grumbled, pushing herself out of the soft, dark chocolate chair. Ingrained caution had her stopping a few inches from the door. She had no peephole on the door, but she knew it wasn't any of her girls. They all had keys to each other's places.

"Yes?" She inquired of the visitor.

"Tee. It's Mercuri."

Surprise had her stepping back a few more inches. Several weighty seconds ticked by with her looking down at the gleaming hardwoods beneath her bare feet. Then, before the surprise could render her totally immobile, she crept to the door, opened it to Mercuri.

He didn't look at all pleased. "You're very fearless." His voice was low, controlled.

"Maybe I'm just trusting," she gave a lazy shrug.

"Both could get you in trouble," his expression remained grim. "I could've been anyone, Tee."

Still at ease, though touched by his concern, she gave him an understanding look. "I knew you were who you said you were," his voice was quite unmistakable but she decided to keep that to herself. To thwart the argument still lurking in his eyes, she stepped aside to encourage him through the front door. She watched him angle his frame slightly to clear the space and looked away to hide her smile.

Questions abounded nevertheless and she took her time closing the door while putting them together inside her head. Mercuri it seemed, had already guessed at one of them.

"Vera told me where to find you," he explained when she turned from the door. His smile issued a playful challenge. "We did say we'd see each other later, right?"

Tee refused to give into her own smile begging for release. She could tell that he knew she hadn't counted on him holding true to that plan.

Mercuri didn't wait on her response, but turned and began a slow walk to observe his surroundings. "Given the way Vera rattled off your address, I think she suspects that there's more going on than me wanting my place redone."

"Yeah," Tee managed not to grind her teeth and hoped her savvy assistant hadn't mentioned the name doodling. "Vera and her intuition,"

119

she noticed Mercuri watching her more expectantly then. "I decided to work from home this afternoon."

"How's that going?" He asked, though it was apparent that his interest lay more in his appraisal of her.

Tee resisted the urge to fidget, when his bright eyes fixed on her bare feet before slowly working their way up her legs. "I just got started," she managed before a sudden stab of arousal had her clearing her throat on a moan. The man was walking enticement; she thought and tried hard not to gawk at the gorgeous sight he made in the salt and pepper trousers and pearl gray shirt.

"Could I uh, get you anything?" She headed for the kitchen and the wine she'd left open to breathe on the counter. She had no sooner cleared the entryway when she found herself on the counter.

There was no time for surprise, only more arousal. Mercuri's divinely sculpted mouth latched onto her earlobe and he sucked with an intensity that could've been painful were it not so serenely pleasurable. He cradled her ample bottom, lifting her slightly while his talented fingers and thumbs eased into her panties and tugged them away with little effort. Tee assisted, wiggling the garment down and off her calves and ankles.

Mercuri traded his suckle of her ear to latch onto the zipper tab of her dress. Once the material parted, he muttered an appreciative curse at finding her nude beneath.

Tee arched into a rigid bow, one hand hidden in the forest of Mercuri's hair, the other braced behind her on the counter for support. Her nipples were treated to his ravenous feasting while he made quick work of undoing his belt and trousers. Her gasps and cries were all that filled the air for a time. Her position on the counter put her at a prime height for him to take her easily and he did. Mingled sounds colored the air then with Mercuri lifting her into every thrust. He groaned richly as sensation seized and all but had him losing strength in his legs as his sex was massaged and bathed inside hers.

Elation ensnared Tee as well. Desire invaded as her walls were deliciously stretched and thoroughly invaded. She cursed in appreciation as well when orgasmic tremors began to claw at the edge of her reason. She willed them back, not ready for an end to the relentless advance and retreat of his erection sliding back and forth, slow and thick adding layer upon layer of pleasure until she came apart shattering and clutched in a whirlwind of sensation.

She needn't have worried about that being the end of things. Mercuri lost his composure moments later and took all of a few seconds to regain it.

"Where's your bed?" He roughly demanded, while one-arming her from the counter.

Tee managed a weak wave toward the vicinity of her bedroom where the scene vigorously replayed.

***

Esperance, Australia~

"Here's a hint for future reference, Zoo, you never kill the goose before it lays the golden egg."

Grim amusement curved Grant Zubin's mouth as he rubbed down the already gleaming blade of the knife he handled. He smoothed a white cloth between the jagged edges with an almost affectionate intensity.

"Do I have permission to question *your* methods now?" Zubin asked.

Harris Van Deer shoved at the edge of an Ottoman with the toe of his boot. He and Zubin had headed back to the inn they had secured inside the town limits. The information Dorinda Patterson had shared-which had done nothing to spare her life- had been a phone number. The earlier passes through their in-house software had turned up nothing-either the line had been disconnected or Patterson had led them on a wild goose chase with a phony number.

With nothing more to go on, they ran the line again and hit paydirt. It was a landline located in the Australian seaside town of Esperance. Harris and Zubin had returned to relax at the inn while their men kept watch.

Patterson's lead had panned out. Unfortunately the lead was to what appeared to be an abandoned chalet tucked into a remote lagoon. Esperance was a beach lover's oasis with idyllic nooks for all sorts of outdoor interests. Sadly, the appeal of the pristine beaches and turquoise waters, along with an array of art galleries, B&Bs and golfing courses, were of little interest to the brooding colleagues.

"She led us to a goddamn decoy and because of you we can't even go back to question her." Harris shoved up from the armchair that matched the Ottoman and began to storm the corner of the airy lobby he and Zubin had taken possession of.

"You didn't have much to say about that when I was in there getting the information, did you?" Zubin was still fixed on wiping the knife blade as he spoke.

"That's because you told me you'd gotten it all," Harris sneered.

"You saw what I did to her," Zubin's voice held matter of fact coldness. He grinned when Harris only responded with a look. "Take it easy, man. No whore is that loyal to her pimp. Any holding out she did was out of thinking she'd make her way out alive and be rewarded for keeping her mouth shut. When she understood that wasn't going to happen, she gave up what she had hoping *that'd* be her way out."

Harris studied Zubin at length happily cleaning his knife and thoroughly confident in his reasoning. "There is a third possibility and one I think is more plausible," Harris marveled over Zubin's pompous air when the man looked up in total bewilderment.

"Say you're right," Harris leaned back on the glossy snakeskin boots he sported, "Say she did accept that she was on her way out. But what if- for a final 'fuck you'- she decided to play you for the overconfident idiot you are and gave you some shit piece of info to send you and the rest of us running around like assholes looking for her boss in some shack he abandoned decades ago."

The possibility evidently niggled at Grant Zubin's iced-edged demeanor. In less than a minute, he was coming out of his chair with such momentum, he sent the furnishing skidding back several inches.

Harris remained unperturbed, even when Zubin lunged to take hold of his collar. He held the knife's blade turned outward and in range of Harris's jugular.

"Let's not forget the overconfident idiot *you've* been playing these last few months, partner," Zubin snarled the words while flexing his fingers on the hilt of the knife as though he were more than ready to wield it. "How long do you think it'll be before that bullshit with Patch comes back to haunt us?"

Unmindful of the blade at his throat, Harris wrenched free of Zubin's hold. "Patch would've died anyway," his voice rasped. "It was part of the plan, part of the steps we all agreed on."

"Yes, it was part of the plan, yes it was part of the steps we all agreed on but it wasn't to happen until much later. Well after we were back on the winning side of the game."

"The plan was to keep Merc and the others relaxed," Zubin went on while Harris began another brooding pace around the room. "They were supposed to keep livin' their cushy lives while we made our moves in the background until the odds were back in our favor." Zubin used the blade's tip to point. "You better hope your inability to keep that personal shit on the backburner doesn't bite a chunk out of all our asses. We get Merc and the rest on us before we're ready and-"

"That fear I hear in your voice, Zoo?"

The jolting coldness of Grant Zubin's strange, metallic blue gaze, held unflinchingly for a long moment. "I only want two things in life," he breathed the words, "to live like the fat, rich pricks we've been slaving for all our lives and to rip the hearts out of the ones who made their own plans and left the rest of us to sloth through the aftermath.

I want it in that order, Harris. The only way to get the first, is to track down that pimp fucker Roya. Anyone gets in the way of that and they can get in line for what Roya, Merc and the rest of those punk sons of bitches are in line for."

Static fizzled into the tense air at the sounds of their names coming through. Harris grabbed his two-way from the coffee table where he'd placed it after he and Zubin had assumed control of the lobby.

"Come in, Jack," Harris ordered.

"We got movement at the chalet."

"How much movement, Jack?" Zubin was speaking into his two-way then.

"A moving truck, nothing major." Jack Rylance reported. "Recon proved the place was already furnished."

"Do you have eyes on Roya?" Harris asked.

"Roger that.

The confirmation had Harris and Zubin trading glances that confirmed, for the moment, their disagreement was tabled.

***

The Food Place Diner satisfied the needs of all its patrons. Whether it was for breakfast, lunch, dinner or just a snack before a show, the spot was adored for the homemade touch that flavored its creations. The only complaint the diner ever received was that it didn't stay open long enough.

Owner Zeke Baylis appreciated the love, but held firm to the diner's hours of operation from 5am-1am. In Zeke's opinion, it took at least four good hours of sleep to fuel up to prepare such fine cuisine.

The diner's floor plan catered to patrons who found food prep to be a spectator sport. The open, state of the art kitchen was boldly outfitted with chrome finished equipment done in brilliant emerald green trimmed in gleaming black. The place allowed for customer seating along the bar skirting the entire area. For those content with the mere aroma of food in the air, cozy tables dotting an emerald and black checkered floor. Wide booths hugged the walls. Lamps, glowing gold, hung low from thick gold toned chains. The place had an upscale appeal that was distinctly homey.

If Zeke's appreciation for his customers skimmed levels of adoration, then the man was absolutely over the moon for the customer who resided above his establishment.

Tee's preferred table was a booth in a far corner that; in her opinion, offered the best vantage point from which to view the greatest portion of village activity. The trouble with booth seating was that it wasn't the most comfortable place to be if you were around 6'7 and weighed over 270lbs.

Luckily, Zeke Baylis could relate. Big, blonde and jovial at 6'4 and 250lbs, Zeke knew the man walking in with his favorite customer that night would have a devil of a time fitting into the booth she favored.

Indeed, Mercuri was already eyeing the booth with dark skepticism when Zeke and two of his waiters arrived. The two servers carried a large Chesterfield chair between them and set it down at the end of the table. Grinning, Mercuri turned to offer Zeke a hand and his thanks.

"Gotta look out for a fellow big man," Zeka leaned down to accept the kiss Tee pressed to his cheek.

"Looking out, my eye. You're just a big 'ol softie," she grumbled playfully.

Smiling, Zeke shrugged. "Never a problem for my favorite tenant."

Tee laughed. "I'm your *only* tenant!"

"I've got three teenage sons at home, remember? Trust me, *you're* my favorite tenant."

Laughter followed and then Tee was raising a hand as she prepared for introductions. "Zeke Baylis, Mercuri Nikolaides. Mercuri, Zeke's the owner here," she explained.

Again, Mercuri extended a hand to shake. "Good to meet you."

"Same here," Zeke's big, round face beamed with an approving smile.

A server arrived with menus then and Zeke clapped Mercuri's shoulder before waving him into the chair.

"You two enjoy your food," Zeke urged, before taking his leave.

"How long have you lived here?" Mercuri asked as he settled down.

"About four years," Tee folded her small frame into the booth.

Mercuri's vivid stare was approving as he assessed the diner's atmosphere. He'd asked to come along earlier when Tee told him she had a table waiting. This, after they woke from a nap following the explosive session of sex they'd enjoyed not long after his arrival in her apartment.

The approval in Mercuri's exotic gaze curbed a little as he took in the activity beyond the booth windows. "Noisy."

"I prefer it."

Something in the way she said it, had him studying her with a curiosity that also hinted of understanding. It also told him that she wasn't interested in defending her decision.

A smiling server arrived to take their orders- water and Jasmine tea for Etienne. Apple juice for Mercuri. The young woman zoomed off with the orders, leaving quiet hanging between her guests at her departure.

Tee feigned greater interest in her menu, though she knew she'd order her usual meal for that time of night-homemade chicken noodle and a roast turkey sandwich. Finally, she pushed aside the menu and asked Mercuri the question that still nagged.

"Why'd you come see me?" When his brow quirked in response, she smiled and shook her head before rephrasing.

"Why'd you stop by the office to see me?"

Though he'd understood her perfectly, Mercuri nodded as if she'd clarified things. "Part of it was so I could return your watch."

She saw him reach into the deep front pocket on his shirt and produce the delicate silver timepiece.

"Found it tangled in the sheets when I got up," he handed her the watch and then brought his fingers to his brow as he enjoyed the sight of her trying and failing to keep her expression unreadable.

"Part of it?" She slipped the watch over her wrist.

"The rest was about me calling your bluff," he waited patiently for her eyes to meet his. "I know you didn't think we'd see each other again after last night. Was I right? Fair's fair, Sprite. I answered your question," he said when she offered no reply.

The server returned with their drinks before she could. Tee put in her request for the soup and sandwich while Mercuri went for a much heavier order of a ribeye and steak fries.

"You're right," she gave in once he'd settled back to regard her with an expectant unwavering look.

"Thanks," Satisfied, he turned to study the lively streets beyond the window. "I should get Vera a little gift while I'm out here. If it weren't for her telling me where you live...none of this would've been possible."

"I'd be careful with Vera if I were you," Tee blew across the surface of the fragrant Jasmine blend filling her cup. "She's determined to see me married off before she retires."

"Is that right?" Mercuri didn't know which surprised him more, that someone actually thought him worthy husband material or that the idea of being married actually pleased him.

"Yeah, she's got it all planned," Tee didn't appear to notice the effect her words had on the man seated to her right. "Mr. Earl will give me away. They've got four sons, no daughters, so he's never had the chance to do that."

Considering, Mercuri sipped his juice. "Wouldn't your own dad want to be the one to do that?"

"No. No, he wouldn't."

For the second time that night, Mercuri found himself regarding her demeanor and word usage. Again, he caught the tone in her voice that confirmed she wasn't interested in giving explanations.

"I should probably get going after we eat," he said once quiet held between them for a full minute.

She was all smiles again. "Is that your way of hinting for an invite back up to my apartment?" she teased.

Mercuri drew a thumb around the mouth of his glass. "If I wanted back up, I'd just ask."

"Ah," she merely watched him, waited and heard herself actually giggle when she saw him flush beneath the rich copper of his complexion.

"I'd like an invite back up to your apartment," he said at last.

Sighing woefully, Tee pretended to hedge over her reply. "I don't know...my place is very small and I don't have a big... Chesterfield to accommodate your size."

"That's true," he propped an elbow to the table and massaged his neck. "But I enjoy small places and you accommodate my size just fine."

Tee had to laugh then. Mercuri joined in, though his humor gave way to a more sobering emotion soon after.

"Tee um," uneasiness had the sleek dark lines of his brows meeting. "Before...I should apologize for not thinking to use... protection," he winced a little over the word.

Her smile harbored understanding and she nodded. "Thank you I- I'm on the pill though and I'm tested twice a year."

"Twice a year. Impressive," inclining his head, he shrugged. "I can only claim to testing once a year."

"That's acceptable."

"Acceptable enough for an invite back to your place?"

"Mr. Nikolaides do you ever give up?"

"No."

"Ah...not until you get what you want, right?"

"Not even then. Getting what's wanted is only half the job."

"I see," she nodded as though mesmerized by the feral beauty of his stare. "And the other half?" She managed to ask.

"Keeping it, Ms. Shaw. Keeping it."

~CHAPTER 14~

Morning found Tee waiting on a fragrant French blend to finish its slow drip into her coffee mug. The device had just signaled a tiny beep of completion when she heard a key twisting in her front door lock. Leaning on the counter, she decided to wait and see which of her girls had decided to use her key that morning.

Berrill Clayton walked in with all the authority of a woman used to being in charge even when she was in someone else's home.

Tee took her mug from its compartment on the beverage device. Then, staying out of sight, she observed as Berrill made her way from the living room to the short bedroom corridor. Hearing the woman's gasp was a priceless moment for Tee. Strolling to the bedroom doorway, she found that her tough, confident friend appeared to be in a state of sensual shock as her eyes roamed the bed in helpless fascination.

Leaning against the doorframe, Tee blew across the steaming surface of the coffee. "See something you like?" She asked.

"Fucking absolutely," Berrill's eyes never left the bed where Mercuri slept. "How'd you find it?" Her luminous mocha browns greedily absorbed the man, naked but for the sheets seductively tangled around a trim waist, perfect ass and massive thighs.

"It's a long story."

"And I'm sure a pun was very much intended," Berrill's smile relayed intense delight. Yet, something pensive captured her expression then. She spent a few additional moments observing the divine specimen between the sheets and then looked to her friend.

"Tee."

Tee heard the question all too clearly in the lone pronunciation of her name. "I promise to tell you about it next time we're all together." She cringed a little. "Lunch the other day didn't seem like the best time."

Berrill rolled her eyes. "Amen to that." She treated herself to another lingering look at the bed and sighed. "Lunch the other day is actually what I came to talk about."

"What about it?" Tee pushed away from the doorframe then.

Berrill was already fixated on the bed once more. Her eyes literally feasted on the candy there while she toyed with a coarse, lone curl that hung from the low chignon she wore.

"Bear." Tee spoke softly for Mercuri's benefit, firmly for her distracted friend's.

Berrill reluctantly tugged her gaze away for a second time. "We should probably go somewhere..."

"Breakfast at the diner?"

"What about?" Berrill looked to the bed again. "Your friend."

Tee went to her desk, a construction of glossy golden wood. Setting down her mug, she grabbed one of the colorful index cards from a sectional box in the corner and began to write.

Berrill gave up her post next to the bed and went to peer across Tee's shoulder. "'Quick breakfast with a friend downstairs'," she recited the note, "'Stay if you can. Help yourself to anything'. Mmm...now isn't that sweet and smart?" She crooned, nudging Tee's arm with her own. "I wouldn't want that leaving my bed too soon either."

"Shut up," Tee hissed albeit playfully. Folding the card in half, she went to put it on a pillow near Mercuri's head.

Berrill followed Tee around the side of the bed and was able to glimpse Mercuri's face half hidden in a pillow. "God Tee, he's gorgeous and...big," she regarded the note skeptically. "Aren't you afraid he'll roll over and crush that?"

129

Tee was already shaking her head. "He doesn't seem to move much once he dozes off. Sleeps pretty hard."

"Mmm!" Berrill gave a saucy shiver and sultry wink. "Does he do everything hard?"

"Shut it!" Tee paired her hissed order with a shove to Berrill's side.

"You know you'll need a bigger bed if you plan to keep entertaining a guy that size? Think of all he could do to you with more room-"

"Dammit Bear!" Tee was all but dragging the woman from the room then and fighting desperately to stifle her laughter.

The front door was closing a minute later. His face still half hidden in a pillow, Mercuri smiled.

~~~

Tee watched, grim-faced while Bear prepped her coffee. The women had just put in orders for bagels and fruit. Bear gave a start when she looked up and found Tee glaring. Abandoning her china cup of the fragrant blend, she regarded her friend squarely.

"What the hell was up with you the other day?"

Tee settled back on the booth's black leather finish. She didn't attempt to school her expression- didn't attempt to convince Bear that she'd misjudged her mood.

"What is it?" Bear leaned close to whisper.

"None of this would be necessary if I hadn't started this, B."

A storm brewed in the smoky mocha depths of Berrill's eyes. "You didn't start anything."

"I slit a man's throat like I was cutting a sandwich in half."

"You didn't-!" Berrill stopped short and cast a quick look around to see if they had captured unwanted attention.

"You didn't start anything. Those slimy pricks did."

"They paid for sex, B. We were there to provide it."

Berrill moved back against the booth seat's soft dark leather as well. "We weren't there to provide what they were doing to Prin."

Tee clasped suddenly chilled hands around her warm cup.

"Remember that, Tee? Remember what we walked in on? Chains on the bed. Blood on the sheets, that had to be hers? What that cum stain was doing to her, remember that?"

"I remember, Bear," Tee snapped.

"Then please don't sit there and tell me you started this. If anything, you finished it."

"Doesn't sound like it's finished," Tee pushed away her cup having lost her taste for the brew. "This is a nightmare we've all spent the last six years trying to wake up from and we still haven't."

Berrill's expression turned smug. "Sounds like you're waking up just fine."

"That probably won't last a month," Reconsidering the coffee, Tee reached for her mug and sipped.

"Is that what you're hoping for?"

"I don't know what I'm hoping for. I just don't want to get my hopes too high and have to retask my reality when it ends," as though the idea made her shiver, Tee rubbed her arms briskly on the sleeves of her Lakers sweatshirt. "It's taken me long enough to get through my nights without screaming, B. I can't go back to that."

"That might not happen, you know?" Berrill found Tee's sneaker shod foot beneath the table and nudged it with the toe of her boot. "I haven't seen a guy in your apartment in over six years and definitely not one who's stayed the night, or white *or* one you've told to 'help himself to anything', the next morning."

"I'm just being polite."

"You're just being a woman whose acting interested in living again."

Conversation ceased when the server returned with their orders.

"Are you sure this is the way we want to handle this?" Tee probed once the waitress had gone. "Airing everybody's dirty laundry, including our own?"

"Are you worried about what Mercuri will think?" Berrill recalled the intriguing name she'd pried out of Tee when they first arrived at the diner. She then focused on slathering whipped cream cheese to her bagel.

"I'm worried about us," Tee's reply was like stone and came without hesitation. "I don't want to get bloody again, Bear. I could stand most anything but that, but you know I'd do it in a heartbeat if I had to." Silently, she debated the idea, wondering how she'd stand Mercuri having a front row seat to the bloody actions that'd had a hand in the creation of her dirty laundry.

Berrill let any nagging retorts slide and the discussion eased into light-hearted chatter over the tasty breakfast. Tee continually evaded

Berrill's attempts to pry out more details regarding her unexpected bed partner. When Berrill practically begged for her to at least provide Mercuri's last name, Tee caved and wasn't at all surprised when the chat focused on Mercuri's 'Greek God' status.

~~~

Mercuri remained in Tee's bed for about ten minutes after she'd left her apartment. He was no longer pretending to be asleep. Instead, he relaxed against the pillow-lined headboard and observed his surroundings. He found that the artsy appeal of the space complimented its owner in the warm colors, gold lighting and plush rugs that lay over gleaming hardwoods.

A person could be quite content there, he thought while leaning over to take a closer look at a picture on the nightstand. Tee beamed into the camera. She stood in front of an operatic poster for *Don Giovanni*. In her hands, she held two tickets. Mercuri smiled, loving the happy light in her dark eyes. He returned the picture and saw there was another poster for the same opera framed above the nightstand.

Her favorite? He wondered, though it was hard to tell. The apartment's artwork ran to the framed posters. Works such as *Faust, The Magic Flute, Aida* and a host of others were featured in custom framework throughout the apartment.

He'd left the bed, snagging the sheet and securing it at his waist. It didn't slip his notice that there were no indications of additional family. The pictures decorating the home were of Tee alone or with her three friends. They were her only family. It was a statement Mercuri understood all too well.

~~~

Back at her apartment, Tee expected to find Mercuri still asleep… or gone. She found him in her kitchen helping himself to orange juice. She couldn't help but feel a little sorry for Berrill then. The woman would've fully appreciated the statement Mercuri made wearing nothing but the sheet she had admired him in earlier. The wrinkled peach colored linen hung low where he'd knotted it at his lean waist. It accentuated not only his complexion, but the array of chiseled abdominals that flexed as he moved.

Tee tried exceptionally hard not to gawk and lose herself in memory over how he'd felt next to her all night. She failed at the task with exceptional ease.

Mercuri saw her hovering near the door and smiled. "You said I could help myself."

"You got my note."

"I saw it," he gave a minute shake of his head. "No need to read it, when you friend did that for me so nicely."

Bear, Tee seethed in silence. "You weren't supposed to hear that. I'm sorry."

"Nothing to apologize for," he grimaced and added a wave. "It's fine."

"No, it's not," she moved toward the kitchen, unconscious of his bright eyes trailing her steadily as she tugged off her lightweight sweatshirt to reveal the snug tank beneath it. Black, capris of the same sweatshirt fabric rounded out her morning wear.

"She stood over you while you were asleep-*supposed* to be asleep," she qualified when he grinned, "and sized you up like you were a slab of beef she was planning to devour." Silently, Tee admitted she'd behaved no better. She'd joined in and done pathetically little to reign in her friend.

"My friends- we all have keys to each other's places," Tee explained.

"I was honestly not offended or upset in any way," he smiled on the memory. "It's the same with my friends. We've all got access to each other's places. If I ever get you back out to my house though, you won't have to worry about them standing around and sizing you up. They know they'd be seriously jeopardizing their health if they did."

She spotted the teasing light in his eyes as hers narrowed. "But they're your brothers. You'd die for them, remember?"

"I would," he nodded, "but we're close enough to understand that some things cancel out all bets." The teasing left his gaze then. "When do you have to go?" he asked.

"Not for a while. I'm happy you stayed."

"You asked me to."

"Do you always do what you're asked?"

"If it benefits me or if the request comes from someone I don't think I can say 'no' to."

"You don't think you can say 'no' to me?"

133

"I don't think so," again his eyes commenced a sweep of her body. "Ask me something," he said once she'd rounded the counter into the kitchen.

"Pick me up," she said once she was within his reach.

Mercuri hooked a finger into the waistband of her capris. "Technically you've just given me an order instead of asking a question."

"Is that a problem?"

"Apparently not," he was hoisting her high against the broad muscular wall of his chest. His vivid eyes were hooded, giving him a countenance that would've made him appear utterly dangerous were it not for his locks of tousled black. They shielded his forehead to temper the dangerous with boyish endearment.

"What now?" He asked.

"Kiss-"

He did so before she could complete the command. His tongue took full possession of her mouth to force wavering moans past her lips when he began to thrust.

"What next?" He asked in the midst of teasing her tongue with his.

"Bed."

He treated her to another deep thrust from his tongue that would've been powerful enough to drive her head back, had Tee not countered with equal intensity.

Obliging her command without argument, Mercuri made his way from the kitchen. Tee wanted to feel her chest bare next to his and tugged off the tank top she wore. Her C-cups were full, yet firm enough to allow her to go braless when she wished. She felt the low rumble of approval vibrate deep in his excellent chest and was thrilled she'd made the decision. Brazenly, she pressed herself harder against him, sank her fingers in his hair and reveled in how secure she felt with her bottom being cradled in his wide palms.

Mercuri retraced his steps to the back of the apartment, the sheet trailing the floor majestically behind him. In the bedroom, he tossed her down to the mattress. "I just took a guess that'd be your next question- excuse me- order."

"I'm about all question and ordered out," her dark eyes blazed with something bold and wanton. "Could you take it from here?"

"Happy to," he proceeded to kiss her out of the rest of her clothes.

Content, Tee relished the feel of him. He was a man of contradictions. His body was rigid, unyielding, unconquerable yet despite its beautiful ferocity, his hold was gently persuasive- tender in many regards. He was a man fully aware of his power and gifted with an innate sense of how, when and to what degree it should be used. Her pants and undies whispered across the carpet upon contact. They were followed soon after by the sheet when he jerked it free of his waist.

He kissed his way back up her body, lips cruising the dips and curves doused in flawless licorice. Those succulently sculpted lips rooted to a puckered nipple which he treated to intermittent bouts of suckling and bathing with his tongue. His fingertips skimmed the generous curve of her ass while Tee hiccupped gasps and sighed appreciative cries into the otherwise quiet room.

Those fingers of his caressed the smooth waxed triangle at the apex of her thighs and when the tip of his thumb caressed her clit, she spasmed at the sheer elation funneling inside her. He fondled her there without mercy, using his middle finger to tease open the seam of her sex.

Mercuri was shifting his attention to her other breast; dipping two thick fingers into her drenched core, when her gasps and cries mingled with sounds that were far from elated. His head whipped up and the danger, his expression had only hinted of earlier, was then fixed and heated.

"I'm hurting you," he spoke with conviction, the matter settled in his mind.

"No, Mercuri I-no-"

He interrupted her denials with another gentle yet filling plunge of his finger into her sex.

"You were saying?" He watched her wince, felt her tense.

"Alright, so it's been awhile since I've had two steady nights of sex," *and never from a dick like yours,* she added silently, almost moaning from the punch of pleasure the thought roused.

He nodded as if to accept the explanation. Then, easing back he began to get her settled beneath the covers.

"Mercuri?" Confusion had her bottomless gaze flaring. "What-?"

"Rest."

She couldn't help it then, she pouted. "So much for doing what I ask."

"I also said I do what benefits me." He cupped her jaw, holding firm until she looked at him. "Hurting you doesn't benefit me, Tee."

135

"But I want to," she smoothed both hands over his waist.

"So do I," his smile was as soft as the look in his jolting tawny eyes. His words were softer, "But I want you to enjoy it too." His gaze sharpened when he spied her reaction to his words. There was the haunted look he could always spot lurking just under the expressions she used to mask it.

His hand firmed on her jaw again. "Why do I feel that, between the two of us, I'm the only one who cares about that?"

His hold may've been firm, but not so much that she couldn't easily free herself. "The door will lock behind you." She said.

Unfazed, he grinned. "If that's you telling me to go, that doesn't benefit me either."

Still feeling stubborn, Tee refused to answer.

The sight of her battling to hold onto control was an absolute treat for Mercuri. Leaning close, he trailed his nose along her jaw and the curve of high cheekbones.

"Or could it be you've only got use for me when it involves my dick?" he accused.

She bristled, still refusing to answer. Talk of his dick kept the arousal punching violently however.

He gestured with a quiet 'tsking' sound. "That hurts, Sprite. Guess we're even, huh?" He saw the faint twitch of her lush mouth betraying a smile.

"Such a shame," his nose coursed the line of her neck, stopping to nuzzle the base of her throat and across her collarbone. "I've got so much more to offer than my dick," he murmured.

As his gaze was downcast, Tee didn't mind what her expression revealed. She pushed her head deeper into a pillow and delighted in the sweet sensation of his mouth on her skin.

"So much more," he quietly promised her while easing back the covers he'd just tucked in. Circling a nipple with his nose, he moved to the underside of her breast and then down her torso to outline her naval.

The simple caress had Tee snuggling deeper into the bed and even relaxing enough to feel drowsiness tempt her. Drowsiness became an afterthought and her eyes rolled back in her head when his tongue generously filled the heart of her.

Slow, exploring plunges massaged away whatever pain remained. Her hips arched and rolled while her inner muscles repeatedly clenched and released his tongue. Too soon, he was taking her with bolder lunges that had orgasm cresting. She shattered on a wave of piercing pleasure and could feel the proof of her release oozing to coat his still thrusting tongue.

Mercuri loved her until he could feel the waning effects of her climax. Tenderly, he withdrew, kissed his way back up her body and was pleased to find her sleeping when his gaze settled to her face. He tucked the covers in again and left her to her rest.

~CHAPTER 15~

Wilmington, Vermont~ 2 weeks later

People always told Pope Apostolou he'd been aptly named. Many thought 'Pope' had to be a nickname given that it suited him so well. The name was all his though, and he was often pleased by the fact that his closest friends felt they could count on him for sage advice or just an ear to listen. There were however, times when he felt the sheer burden of it.

Times like these, Pope thought, taking in the bland view from the open blinds of the office where he'd been waiting just shy of 15 minutes. The call to come there hadn't set well, especially when he knew what had prompted it.

Next of kin. Pope rolled his eyes away from the remarkable sights of natural beauty beyond the window. He'd recalled when he and his friends had all laughed over that shit. Just a formality. It'd been a required field to complete on forms for homeowner's and life insurance policies and such. The things that had become parts of their new lives as upstanding citizens.

Again, Pope rolled his eyes, sending enviably long lashes of inky black fluttering down over a gaze the color of a tropical sea. How ironic, he thought. To live one's life in a way that taunted death and to have death show when it was no longer being taunted.

"God Patch, what'd you get yourself into out here?" Pope muttered, turning as the sound of approaching footsteps caught his ear. A man he pegged to be in his late fifties entered the room through a thick, wooden door a few shades lighter than the paneling of the office.

"Mr. Apostolou," the man greeted with an outstretched hand.

"Sheriff," Pope accepted the shake.

"Gerard Deese. Good to meet you." The Sheriff said and then turned to acknowledge the young, pretty woman who waited in the office doorway. "That'll be all, Kelly."

The young brunette nodded, but her green doe-eyed gaze was fixed on the visitor she'd led to the Sheriff's office some 15 minutes prior. When Deese stepped behind his desk and began to clear his throat, Kelly made herself scarce.

"My niece," Deese explained.

"Very efficient," Pope said.

Deese grinned. "Your compliment is appreciated, but misplaced Mr. Apostolou. My niece is a cheaper alternative to someone more experienced. A measure of nepotism is one of the things you can get away with at a small town station, I suppose. Did she at least offer you coffee?"

Pope grinned, bringing life to the flash of a singular dimple. "She did. I declined."

"Good decision." Deese grinned then too. "Have a seat."

With a wave, the Sheriff offered Pope one of the standard office chairs before his desk. Deese's assessing brown stare scraped over the seating and then to his guest who easily dwarfed his own 6'2. Deese wagered the man's weight was well within the range of 270 to 280. With those guesses as to height and weight, the Sheriff doubted standard seating would be appropriate.

Deese jerked a thumb toward a worn, but more substantial looking leather sofa hugging the wall closest to the door. Satisfied once Pope took the sofa, the Sheriff opted for the wide deep chair of similar wear that flanked it.

"Thank you for coming, Mr. Apostolou. I appreciate how difficult this is. I'm sorry for your loss."

139

"Thank you, Sheriff. What can you tell me?"

The Sheriff grimaced. "Not much, I'm afraid," his tone was quiet. "We've already done the official identification."

Gaze narrowing, Pope sensed the difficulty the man was having. "You can speak frankly, Sheriff. When we...served together, Patch and I saw things, did things that would sicken a man with the strongest stomach."

Deese observed the man on the sofa and didn't doubt his words one iota. While his niece had most likely been mesmerized by their visitor's movie star looks, Deese saw a man with great potential to be lethal.

"Pat was a friend of mine too, Mr. Apostolou," Deese shared. "We took a few fishing and camping trips together. My friends and I welcomed him into our circle early on. He was easy to like." Deese leaned over to rest his elbows to his wide knees.

"You're right," Pope mimicked the man's position.

"No one had seen him in town for several days, but that was nothing strange. He had a...lady friend in a neighboring town so it wasn't a big deal for him to take time out to spend with her.

After ten days, folks started asking questions. Small town like this, unorthodox stuff tends to stand out. Papers were piling up on his porch, mail filling the box, stuff like that. I wasn't on edge 'til Bud Tilson at the town limits gas station teased about Pat runnin' off with those fancy friends of his that came through. We joked about him leaving us country bumpkins in the dust."

The rich ultramarine of Pope's stare seemed to darken from its already deep hue and he straightened on the sofa. "Fancy friends," he was unmindful of his voice skirting the edge of a growl.

Deese didn't seem to have taken offense. "That's actually why I wanted to meet with you in person. As I said, Pat was a friend- we had to ID him from his dentals. Whoever got to him, messed him up pretty bad. This was personal-not the random drifter type shit we tend to see around these parts. We're gonna find who did this, but you knew him long before we did. Can you think of anyone from the past who might've had a personal beef to settle?"

Pope believed he would have laughed were grief not blooming thick and hot inside his chest. "Sheriff, Patch and I had a long, complex history. I'm afraid there may've been several *anyones* with a beef to settle."

"Beef enough to kill?"

Pope's voice was an unmistakable growl then. "I'm afraid so, Sheriff."

***

Esperance, Australia~

Harris and Zubin waited an additional week following the alert of Roya's arrival at the remote chalet. The man had arrived with a sultan's share of employees. There had been no sign of the rest of Roya's extended family, however.

Brody Alberts and Jake Grodins had encouraged a bit more wait time and an additional three days eeked past. By then, Harris and Zubin decided that enough was enough. They descended on the Roya home which was still in a state of move-in chaos. No matter, as the business at hand required no rolling out of the proverbial red carpet and least of all meticulous surroundings.

'Business' involved 48 hours of questioning the man of the house. When he stubbornly refused to cooperate, the next 24 hours were devoted to the 'questioning' of his staff. Roya broke, but not in the manner his interrogators expected.

~~~

"All these years later and you two are still errand boys for a group of old perverted farts," Roya managed a snarl, despite the pain it must have produced given the bloodied and bruised mouth that should have made speaking an agonizing task.

"Why is that, I wonder?" Roya continued, "Why didn't you jump ship along with the rest? Nikolaides could tell you I reward those who save my life very well."

Across the room and out of direct line of the bloodletting, Brody and Jake exchanged a look.

Grant Zubin did his own share of snarling then. "We don't need a payoff from a pimp."

Roya laughed, though it clearly cost him to do so. Aside from his abused face, his torso had suffered a great deal beneath the boots of his torturers. Every breath sent pain piercing his chest like a stabbing knife

<center>141</center>

and he was certain he'd suffered more than one bruised or perhaps cracked rib.

"Idiots!" he persevered. "Who do you think you've been working for all these years? The Grodins Alberts Network is built on a foundation of the very profession that seems so detestable to you."

"Tell us what you know about that night, goddammit!" Harris hissed.

Roya appeared unfazed. "And then what? You'll let me go?" His pained laughter returned.

"Maybe we'll just kill you fast," Zubin sneered, flexing a hand around the hilt of his favorite knife for emphasis.

"Go ahead," Roya snarled, "I don't have what you're looking for."

"But you know where it is," Harris stated as opposed to questioning.

"I know," Roya spoke with relish. Whatever tension the pain had etched across his face, eased. In its place was something akin to contentment.

"And though I assume you boys have lots more in store for me before I meet my death, I'll never tell you."

"We could kill your staff slowly and right before your eyes."

Roya sighed, some of his tension returning in response to Zubin's promise. "My employees- *these* particular employees knew what demands could be made of them when they joined my organization. Why exactly do you think I'm not here alone? You didn't infiltrate my home as easily as you'd planned. My staff took out quite a few of your men as I recall." A smile ghosted across his battered lips. "They'll consider it an honor to die in my service. They're loyal. You two know about that? Loyalty? Isn't it why you're running all over the globe, trying to track me down and making all sorts of mistakes along the way in your blind pursuits? Loyalty to your employers- working to do whatever it takes to get what they crave."

"What do you mean? Mistakes?" Harris asked.

"Messing up your fine clothes and shoes," Roya paused his musing to hawk a stream of blood and saliva to Zubin's shoe. "All this and you were right in the States with someone who knew it all," he continued while Zubin raged over his defiled boot.

"You killed Dorinda." Roya followed the accusation with a tight smile. "Oh yes, even with all my travels, I still make time to keep up with current events. She knew everything and out of haste or mere stupidity, you killed her. That you're here tells me she didn't betray the confidences we swore to uphold."

Zubin bristled, noticing the look Harris sent him. Though the look was unreadable, Zubin saw the accusation clear enough. "All this to protect some hookers," he muttered.

"It was the landline, wasn't it?" Roya countered. "That's what she gave up when the fear got the best of her. We swore to take what we knew to our graves even if it meant one giving up the other. She gave me up instead of giving you the rest."

"Why?" Harris hissed again. Roya's serene mood in the face of his death, his inexplicable loyalty to protecting something that didn't even concern him, unsettled him. "All this to hold onto your blackmail leverage, Roya? So you can pass the baton to your family?"

"My family has nothing to do with this- *wants* nothing to do with this. Knowing they're protected makes accepting my fate easy."

Again, looks passed between the four men in the room. If Roya's family was being protected, there was little doubt who he'd tapped for the job.

"Listen old man," Zubin bolted close to his quarry once more, "we don't give a shit about some sex tapes, but the people we work for do. Give us what we want so we can end this," urgency swam amidst the madness that usually commanded his steel blue gaze.

"My God…" Roya's coffee brown stare flared with a similar urgency and understanding. "You do realize, my boy, that penthouse wasn't the only place filmed in that hotel?" He shook his head as though answering his own question. "Ha! This feels better than I thought it would! You're being played for a fool." His booming voice grew hushed then. "I wonder if you'd be working so hard to track down those discs if you knew what was on them-"

"Son of a bitch!" Harris exploded when Zubin lunged forward to open Roya's throat with his knife.

Brody and Jake rushed forward, wearing identical expressions of horror as they watched the flow of crimson glide in a slow, gruesome stream from Roya's neck. The man's head bowed as though in slow motion.

"What the hell, man?!" Jake Grodins gaped.

"He wasn't gonna talk." Zubin turned away. "This was a waste of our time," he wiped the gored blade across a swath of linen covering a chair. His calm returned as seamlessly as his rage had flared.

"That wasn't your call to make," Brody walked the room, relentlessly pulling his fingers through his hair.

"Dammit, we should've been-"

"Let it go, Jake," Harris flicked one last glance across Roya's corpse. "Zoo's right. He was never gonna talk. Let's get the fuck out of here."

Harris Van Deer left his colleagues staring after him as he strode from the room.

~CHAPTER 16~

An unexpectedly quiet Friday afternoon found Tee, Berrill, LuCarolyn and Prin in Tee's office gorging themselves on gooey pizza, sweet iced tea and chardonnay. Finding themselves all in the area, the friends decided to meet up and take a stab at making up for their fiasco of a lunch a few weeks earlier.

Tee had been the only member of the group to clarify that she didn't think lunch was a complete fiasco. Of course, she'd been factoring her own 'after lunch' activities into her outlook. With over half the pizza demolished and the expected 'catching up' chatter out of the way, talk had turned to those 'after lunch' activities.

Berrill, LuCarolyn and Prin were quick to inform Tee that they'd been painfully patient in waiting on details about her affair that was approaching the one month mark.

~~~

"Wait a minute," Prin sliced the air with one perfectly manicured hand. "We aren't talking about Mercuri Nikolaides of Mercuri Fleets, are we?"

"Could there possibly be more than one person in the world with a name like that, P?" Berrill queried, her tone playfully dry.

Conceding the logic, Prin resumed her prone position on the sofa. "And you met him at a party?" She drew on information covered at the onset of the discussion.

Tee, sitting crossed legged on her office floor, decided to spend her time clearing out old papers from a cluttered cabinet. "He was there with a friend who knew my clients that were giving the party."

"Guy friend?" Bear asked.

"Oh yeah," Tee winked.

"Sexy?" LuCarolyn queried.

Tee let her lashes flutter. "Oh yeah."

"But only one?" The natural pout of LuCarolyn's mouth adopted more of a downturn as her disappointment took shape.

Shrugging absently, Tee studied the pages she held before deciding they were garbage worthy and tossing them into a nearby box. "Mercuri told me he's got four friends who are like his brothers. Says he'd die for them."

Berrill whistled.

"Four, huh?" LuCarolyn nodded slowly. "I'd say that's more than enough to go around."

Prin snorted, "Count me out," she leaned over to help herself to another swallow from a glass cooler.

"Aw Prin, don't be that way," LuCarolyn crooned.

"You guys haven't even seen Mercuri *or* his friends," Prin pointed out.

"*I* have," Berrill argued. "And if his friends are half as sensational looking as he is, you may not want to take yourself out of the running just yet, P."

Prin only rolled her eyes and returned her attention to the TV that had been droning while talking and eating had commenced.

"So Bear, what's your take on Tee's Greek God?" LuCarolyn was asking.

"Well," Berrill gave a theatrical sigh, "What I saw of his face was stunning, but still not enough to give any real details. My best details relate to his naked body in her bed."

Tee shook her head and was on the verge of laughter when LuCarolyn swooned. The woman sat on her knees and draped her upper half over the side of the chair she occupied.

Berrill, who rarely raved over men, did so with relish. "He's got to be at least six-seven. Two sixty, two seventy-easy."

LuCarolyn replied with an appreciative grunt and appeared to melt down into her chair.

"He was sleeping on his stomach, so I didn't get a good look at the abs, but the shoulders…" Berrill shook her head as though she were in awe.

"Massive?" LuCarolyn prompted.

"Mmm," Berrill gave a firm, singular nod. "I'll bet he just eclipses Tee when he's got her on her back."

"Jesus," LuCarolyn closed her eyes to savor the image.

"You guys really need to stop before you go into convulsions," Tee advised while her friends dissolved into wild laughter.

"Would you guys hush?!" Prin's outburst rendered silence among the others.

Berrill was first to recover and sucked her teeth. "Aw Prin, don't be so-"

"Listen." Prin was sitting up on the sofa then with the remote toward the TV. She raised the volume.

Tee, Berrill and LuCarolyn turned disinterested looks toward the television. Dorinda Patterson's image flashed on the screen and disinterest turned to haunted amazement.

"…the body of the Vegas madam was found on property along the outskirts of the airport. Official reports are still sketchy, but Patterson appears to have been the victim of a severe beating and brutal sexual assault. Officials are confirming that they are treating the death as a homicide. The body appeared to show signs of mutilation that hinted of a message, but authorities will neither confirm nor deny at this time. Reporting live, this is-"

Knocking echoed in the room and caused the women to jump in response. Tee found Mercuri filling the doorway and she couldn't be certain if the sensation pooling her insides was relief or nerves.

"I'm sorry," Mercuri hiked a thumb over his shoulder, "Vera wasn't at her desk."

Tee felt herself gulping and had to mentally command herself to speak. "It's alright," she managed a wave to beckon him into the office.

"Mercuri, these are my friends LuCarolyn Young, Berrill Clayton and Prin Holland, guys this is Mercuri Nikolaides."

LuCarolyn and Berrill abandoned their seats. Prin threw Mercuri a wave from where she stood across the room, her cellphone pressed to her ear. Tee remained where she was as well. She wasn't altogether sure that her legs would support her if she tried to leave the floor.

LuCarolyn and Berrill had recovered faster and were already shaking hands with Mercuri.

"Tee's told me a lot about you guys," he was saying.

"It's such a shame we can't say the same," Berrill sent a glare across the room. "Getting details out of Tee is like pulling teeth."

"We hope you've got time to start changing that, Mercuri?" LuCarolyn kept hold of his hand once she'd shaken it and was leading him to the sofa Prin had vacated to make her call.

"Guys...don't," Tee managed a firmer wave then to dissuade her friends.

Berrill held onto the cuff of the olive toned jacket Mercuri wore with a black shirt open at his collar. Together, she and LuCarolyn guided him to the sofa.

"Guys…"

"It's alright, Tee, I don't mind," Mercuri's voice soothed in tandem with his smile.

LuCarolyn and Berrill paused to fix their friend with looks far less soothing. "See? Hush." They ordered in perfect unison.

Mercuri's laughter filled the room and; resigned, Tee watched the scene play out. Berrill sat to one side of Mercuri while LuCarolyn; legs tucked beneath her, sat on the other. Prin had even finished her call and came to join them. She took a seat on one of the cushy tanned swivel chairs facing the cream sofa.

"You're Mercuri Nikolaides of Mercuri Fleets, aren't you?" She asked.

"That's right," Nodding, Mercuri offered a polite, easy smile.

"My parents are clients- Holland Furniture."

Again, Mercuri nodded. That time, he closed his eyes as though he were tapping into memory. "They ship tons of desks. Their specialty, right?"

From her vantage point on the floor, Tee could tell Prin was both surprised and impressed.

Her blue eyes cool yet intrigued, Prin smiled. "It's rare for the top dog to know all the little people," she said.

Mercuri spread his big hands and inclined his head a fraction. "Your family's far from that, but a smart businessman makes it his mission to know who keeps him working."

"Very true," Prin shifted a look to Tee that said 'well done'.

"Tee says your place in Sonoma is amazing," LuCarolyn continued the Q&A.

"Thank you," he grinned and then winced playfully. "I think it's a little too amazing since I can't get her to improve on it for me."

"Well see, now I'm jealous. She found everything in the world wrong with my place when she came to put her two cents in."

Mercuri chuckled when Tee shrugged in a non-verbal but clear confirmation of LuCarolyn's complaint. His bright eyes lingered on her where she sat cross legged and content on the floor. She was completely adorable, undeniably sexy and Mercuri knew he was done convincing himself that he wouldn't be hooked on the combination-the woman- for a very long time.

He resisted the urge to clench a fist, the need to have her in his hands sent the nerve endings tingling across his palms. Realizing he was still under scrutiny, he turned his focus to Berrill. "Tee says you own a gun ranch in Burlingame?"

"Are you into guns, Mercuri?" Prin asked before Berrill could reply.

Nonplussed, he smiled. "Once, but not for a long time now."

Prin's phone chimed with an incoming call, but she took time to reciprocate Mercuri's smile and nod in approval of his response. She checked her phone and her cool expression appeared to heat. "I'm sorry guys I need to take this outside."

Prin stood and; as etiquette dictated, Mercuri followed suit. On the sofa, LuCarolyn and Berrill traded delighted and approving smiles.

Prin moved closer to extend a hand. "It was nice meeting you Mercuri."

"Same here," he said.

"We should be hitting the road too," Berrill said as she and LuCarolyn pushed off the sofa. Again, they each took one of Mercuri's hands, squeezed.

"Nice to finally meet you Mercuri," Berrill said.

"Very nice," LuCarolyn added, "and thanks for helping our girl to loosen up. She's way too serious. Bye Tee," she sang, "We'll make sure the front door is locked behind us," she added the promise while floating from the office after Berrill and Prin.

Alone in the room with Tee, Mercuri let his laughter ring out again. "Your friends are very… outspoken."

Tee grunted a laugh, tossing papers into the trashbox. "I won't argue if you speak your mind and say 'nosey'," she accepted the hand he offered to help her to her feet.

"You're lucky to have them," he said.

"Thanks," Tee found that Mercuri's offer to help her stand was only so he could lift her off her feet instead.

He kissed her, the gesture holding a famished intensity as his tongue thrust tirelessly, rotated languidly. "Hi," he said when he finally withdrew to let her breathe.

"Hi," her voice quaked as she angled her jaw to allow his nose ample room to skim the curve.

"Where is everybody?" He asked.

She enjoyed the substantial rumble of his voice vibrating through her. "If we're between projects, on Fridays, I let everyone set their own schedules. Some work half days, some take the day off."

"Nice," Mercuri was returning to the sofa with Tee in tow. "Sounds like you're a good boss," he brought her down to straddle his lap.

Playful modesty tempered her shrug. "People tend to turn out better work for bosses who treat them fairly and pamper them generously."

Mercuri was already nodding. "My employees could tell you I feel the same."

She beamed. "Sounds like your employees are very lucky too-" her observation ended on a breathy moan when his mouth found her earlobe and suckled patiently.

Arousal throbbed heavily at her core and Tee rocked her hips slowly-all the while inclining her head to enjoy more of the attention he gave her ear. Her hands tunneled through his hair while his found their way inside the plum colored tennis jumper she sported.

"Are you free tonight?" he murmured against her ear when he cupped her breast.

"I can be," she was all but breathless. "Who's asking?" she panted.

The guy who's in love with you, he wanted to say. "I am," he told her instead.

"Well then," she shivered in total approval of the thumb he dragged across the nipple pressing for release against her bra. Impatiently, she slid her fingers from his hair to unhook the straining front clasp of the lacy garment.

He stopped her, taking her wrists and holding them to the small of her back. *Later,* he told himself. He had plans for them. If she came out of her clothes now, those plans would never take shape.

Tee knew any real resistance on her part would have broken his grip. Breaking his grip was the last thing she wanted to do. His hand over her wrists was added stimuli that set her pulse to a frenzied rhythm. Her breasts, crushed into the dense wall of his defined chest, ached with a need to be more than crushed.

She was seconds away from begging for more, when he put her on her back. He didn't follow her down though and with impatience swelling again, she reached for his jacket lapel and tugged.

Mercuri took the demanding hand and kissed the back of it. "I'll see you later, alright?"

"Why later?" Disappointment surged in her pitch stare.

"So you can get home. Get ready for me. I don't want to wait when I get there."

"Well why can't we just-"

Mercuri cut her off with a kiss to which Tee happily submitted. Fingers curling into his shirt collar, she made a play to keep him close. Her panties dampened steadily the longer his tongue stroked- advancing and retreating at an insanely slow glide. Tee couldn't help but compare it to the manner in which he'd claimed her so completely during the past weeks of their relationship.

"Please stay," she begged at last.

"Later," he graced her with a final deep thrust of his tongue before rising to leave her craving him on the sofa.

"Be ready by six," he didn't look back as he called the order over his shoulder.

She lay there delighting in the memory of him against her. The rough, yet soothing quality of his tongue massaging hers as they kissed, his hands as powerful as they were gentle...

Tee was on the verge of swooning, when she gasped and sat straight up on the sofa. She realized he'd never told her where they were going. Smiling coyly, she noted that it looked like he'd have to wait when he got to her place after all. She'd be sure to make the inconvenience worth it.

Satisfied, she mentally ordered herself from the sofa then. A glance at the TV had her moves slowing again as thoughts emerged- memory seized- these not nearly as delightful.

"Who did this to you, Dorinda?" She asked. "And why?"

~CHAPTER 17~

"How about we stop off for drinks and dish some more about Tee's yum yum?" LuCarolyn suggested as she and her friends headed for their cars across the street from the office building.

"I'm game. Prin?" Berrill rolled her eyes when she saw the woman still on her phone. "P?" She waved Prin off when the woman raised a finger to request patience.

"He's somethin' else, huh?" LuCarolyn's amber gaze was soft with consideration as she studied the building across the street.

"Yeah," some of Berrill's agitation with Prin, seemed to ease when she too looked to the building. "Tee's very lucky."

"If anyone deserves it, it's her," LuCarolyn noted.

The women were nearing Prin's sporty Lexus. LuCarolyn leaned against the hood. "Hope some of that luck rubs off on me," she gave a quick belt of laughter at the look Berrill shot her. "Don't even *try* telling me you wouldn't enjoy a little of that? Having a guy over the moon like that for you like Mercuri clearly is for our girl?"

"I'm happy for Tee," Berrill lifted a hand to attest to her sincerity. "I just think my days have passed of being attached to a guy, distracted over what he thinks about me, having to compromise and see things from his point of view? Forget it."

Horror flared in LuCarolyn's light eyes. "Jeez, I was just speaking in terms of amazing sex."

Berrill's expression cleared as she too appeared to consider that aspect. "Well... if that's a certainty then maybe..."

The women dissolved into laughter then.

"I'm sure that's a definite certainty," LuCarolyn sighed moments later.

Berrill's mocha stare followed the path of her friend's gaze to the office front as Mercuri left. "I'd say you're right."

"What do you think his friends are like?" LuCarolyn asked, smiling when she heard Berrill's snort. "Guys like that usually travel in packs, B." She theorized.

Again, Berrill snorted, rolled her eyes. "Right. With our luck, Mercuri's probably the only one of that caliber in the bunch. The rest are all probably smaller than Tee."

Laughter flooded uproariously between the women then.

"Finally!" Berrill called when she spied Prin putting away her phone. "Lu suggested drinks-P?" She snapped her fingers to get LuCarolyn's attention when she noticed Prin's stricken expression. Soon both she and LuCarolyn were crowding Prin. Their expressions demanded answers.

"Dorinda's girls," Prin swallowed, her light honey colored skin carried a pale, waxy tint. "A lot of them have cops for clients. They say the news report was accurate enough. The um...mutilation was on her leg. It was a message like they said on TV."

"A message..." Berrill made a rolling motion with her hand to encourage more information.

"'Where is it'? That's what it said."

"Ah, Jesus," LuCarolyn moaned, pressing her hands to her cheeks while reclaiming her leaning stance against the car.

"I don't guess we can deny anymore that this is not about us."

LuCarolyn shook her head. "It's been six years and who knows what Dorinda got herself into-"

"Lu." Berrill's tone was a soft but effective silencer. "Even you have to admit that'd be one hell of a coincidence. For me, it's a coincidence too big to be overlooked."

"So what now?" LuCarolyn sighed.

"Dorinda obviously didn't say anything about us," Berrill began to walk a path in front of the car. "She's been missing for weeks- we'd have heard something by now if she had."

In an attempt to stop her fidgeting, LuCarolyn folded her arms across the front of the flowing pale, blue frock that billowed against an inviting afternoon breeze. "What could anyone want with sex tapes when all the folks they could do any real damage to are dead? I mean, let's face it- big name powerhouses or not, paying for sex is not *that* big of a scandal."

"Do we tell her?" Prin was looking towards Tee's office building then.

"No…" Berrill shook her head, sighed. "It's Friday. She and Mercuri are sure to have plans for the weekend. Let her enjoy herself. Like Lu said, it's been six years. Three more days won't hurt."

***

Rutger Eliades, Pope Apostolou and Slayte Miltiades arrived at Mercuri's house that evening only to find that their host had left for parts unknown. According to Mercuri's staff, their boss said not to expect him back until the top of the week. Maybe.

"Is it business shit he didn't tell them about?" Rutger asked when he and the others gathered in the kitchen.

Mercuri's house was the standard meeting place whenever everyone came to town. No hotels for his friends, Mercuri had purchased such a large outlay to accommodate them all comfortably. They could enjoy their space without having to travel so far to spend time together when the fates aligned to put them all in the same country. Pope rarely used the place he kept in Pacifica, California. He preferred to stay with Mercuri whenever he was in-state.

"I seriously doubt it's business," Pope said.

Having known each other all their lives, it wasn't hard for either of the other two men in the kitchen to detect the hint of playful sarcasm in Pope's voice.

Slayte's violet eyes shifted to Rutger who stood near the stainless steel refrigerator. Then, he was moving closer to Pope seated at the kitchen island.

"Somethin' you wanna tell us, Po?"

Pope faked heightened interest in the built in tablet on the glazed brick island. "Do I need to spell it out for you *that* much?" he murmured.

155

"Hell yeah!" Slayte and Rutger responded in unison.

"We know Merc occasionally takes a piece to bed, but for an entire weekend?" Rutger mused.

"Maybe longer," Slayte added, recalled what information security had given.

"He met somebody," Pope was still focused on the tablet.

"That's obvious, Po," Rutger's bourbon colored gaze smoldered then like molten caramel.

Pope finally left the tablet alone and went to lean against the high backed barstool he'd occupied. "I've never seen anything like this. You guys know how he is?" Pope watched his friends nod and then shook his head. "All that's out the window when she's in the room or on his mind."

Slayte whistled. "We talkin' about the same Mercuri Nikolaides? Poker-faced, scary observant, cool as ice?"

Pope was already nodding while dragging a hand through the loose ebony waves that fell just below his jawline. "That's the one," he grinned.

Dazedly, Rutger retrieved a bottled water from the fridge. "What's she like?" He asked.

Approval had Pope's grin broadening. "Gorgeous as hell, built with curves for days, black."

Grinning then too, Slayte and Rutger nodded. "Nice," again they spoke as one.

"You haven't heard it all yet. She's tiny," Pope explained. "Five-two, five-three. *Maybe.*"

Again, Slayte whistled.

"Mercuri always did like the little ones," Rutger considered, "but she's got to be the smallest yet."

"And that's just the physical side. Whatever else there is, it's all got our guy acting like a kid with his first girlfriend."

"Hell," Rutger breathed the curse, "does she have any friends?"

Pope breathed out an oath of his own then. "Haven't been able to get Merc alone long enough to grab any details. If he's not working, he's gone missing- chances are with her. Now..." a stony element claimed his expression, "the time for easy conversations may be past us."

Following suit, Slayte's and Rutger's striking features grew taut with stony stress as well.

"I take it all of us showing up here like this is no coincidence?" Rutger queried.

"I came across a story," Slayte left the island to pace the kitchen, "hero fireman and his family found shot to death and stashed in a storage shed in their yard."

"Corky," Pope guessed, having uncovered the story during the additional investigative work he'd put in following his trip to Vermont.

Slayte dragged fingers through his glossy dark forest of curls and tugged until he winced. "Fuck me, I couldn't lock in on the poor bastard's name when I saw the story." Muttering another obscenity, he leaned over the sink and splashed water into his face from the tap.

"They killed the kids. Tortured Corky and his wife," Slayte continued after taking another hit of cold water to his face. "There'd been evidence his wife was sexually assaulted."

"Slimy shits," Rutger sneered, rubbing a hand briskly across the whiskers that further darkened his bronzed complexion. "I found a story about Les and Jose," he referenced their old acquaintances Les Rollins and Jose Arroyo.

"Both went missing within two weeks of each other in their respective towns. Both were found beaten to death."

"You're sure?" Pope frowned at Rutger.

"Read the stories myself," Rutger rubbed the bridge of his nose. "Very detailed pieces with pictures and everything."

"What made you check up on them?" Slayte asked.

"Hunting trip. We get together for one every now and then."

Pope and Slayte only nodded. Both understood their friend's dedication to and obsession with the sport.

"When they didn't show, I didn't question it, but when I called about rescheduling and they didn't get back to me...I had Ben try tracking them down. He came through."

"That's Ben," Slayte smiled, recognizing the name of fellow GAN alum and Rutger's security chief Ben Weis. "He could probably track down signs of intelligent life on Mars if they put him on the job."

"What brought *you* here?" Rutger's eyes were fixed on Pope.

"Something neither of you will want to hear until you've had more to drink than water."

"What's up, Po?" Slayte insisted.

Sizing up his friends, Pope knew they wouldn't be put off for long. "They got Patch too."

"That can't be," Rutger's voice was like jagged stone.

"I just came from Vermont at the request of the Sheriff's office. Patch had me down as next of kin, remember?"

"Are they sure? Did you see the body?" Slayte's violet stare gleamed with disbelief.

"They'd already ID'd it- he had a girlfriend next town over."

"Christ…" Rutger walked the perimeter of the kitchen, head bowed.

"Was it an accident?" Slayte asked.

"This was no accident," Pope caught Rutger's eye then. "I've got pictures too. Connections with the State investigative bureau. They got me in- got me the crime scene photos. Ones that won't ever make it to the papers."

"Let's see 'em," Rutger demanded.

Pope eyed his friend warily. "You stickin' with your water?"

"Until we get to the bar."

Smirking grimly, Pope led the way from the kitchen.

~~~

"This was overkill," Slayte said. His and Rutger's gazes were flat as they viewed the autopsy and crime scene photos Pope had brought along to Mercuri's cherry paneled bar room.

"This was personal," Rutger observed.

"The organization?" Slayte considered.

Rutger shook his head. "After all this time? Who the fuck's left? The old men?"

Pope went to help himself to another mug of the Red lager on tap at the bar. "Either them or Brody and Jake."

"Spineless," Slayte muttered. "They wouldn't have the guts to dirty their hands with somethin' like this."

"Not when they've got others to muck through the shit for them," Rutger added.

"Harris and Zoo," Pope's vivid blues narrowed at his guess of Harris Van Deer and Grant Zubin.

"Overkill is Zoo's specialty and we all know how Harris feels about us." Slayte studied the contents of his whiskey as though he'd find more answers lurking there.

"Going after Patch like this, it was bound to get back to us," Rutger turned away from the pictures and reached for his gin. "Why give us a heads up that he was on his way to settle a score?"

"Maybe there's more to it," Slayte threw back the rest of his drink, grimaced appreciatively over the burn.

Rutger headed to the bar for a refill. "When do you guys want to start digging into this?" He called over his shoulder.

Pope lifted a brow. "Haven't we already?"

"So how long before we call Merc?"

"Ah, let him have his fun," From the bar, Rutger waved off Slayte's question. "It ain't everyday Mercuri Nikolaides falls in love."

"That's why he should know about this now," Pope decided. "These asswipes could be anywhere. *Anywhere* being near his girl. He'll rip our hearts out if he finds out we knew all this and didn't come to him."

Grim-faced, Slayte and Rutger nodded.

Pope reached for his phone.

~CHAPTER 18~

"Well this answers my question," Tee said when she opened her door to Mercuri around five to six that evening. Her gaze was undoubtedly flattering in the way it scanned Mercuri's imposing frame clad in a bespoke tuxedo that made him more breathtaking than usual.

She looked down at the sheer peach nightshirt she wore and sighed. "Sorry for not being dressed yet."

"No complaints," he angled himself inside, closed the door at his back.

"So where are we going?" Her voice seemed hushed in wonder.

In response, Mercuri slipped an arm about her waist and tugged her back against him. "Have I told you how much I like your artwork?"

"Uh...well...no, but thank you," smiling curiously, her dark eyes scanned the array of framed operatic posters adorning her walls. *Carmen, The Barber of Seville, Tosca, La Traviata* and more occupied prime positioning.

"So why didn't you suggest anything for my walls? I've hardly got anything up."

"Art's different," Tee shivered content and secure wrapped up as she was. "It's not everyone's thing and it pays to know the client better before making a suggestion for it."

"Didn't realize there was a science behind it," he murmured, more interested in inhaling the green apple fragrance of her hair than with making conversation.

"Well, it's intimate," Tee went on, "selections should be made or at least approved on by the person or people who live where the art's going."

"Well since I don't trust myself to pick anything other than 'Dogs At Cards', I guess I need to wait until I've got someone to share my home. I'll leave it all to her-happily."

She felt his arms flex once about her as he made the declaration. Twin sensations of anticipation and uncertainty began to take shape. "I should get dressed," lightly she patted his arm. "You know, you still haven't told me where we're going."

He propped his chin to the top of her hair. "I saw that poster in your room above a picture of you holding tickets."

Tee laughed. The memory eased some of her uncertainty and she rested her head back on his chest. "Don Giovanni. Prin got tickets after I went on and on about wanting to see it. We couldn't even pay Lu and Bear to go."

"I knew they were smart women." His savory jab, had Tee poking a punishing elbow into his gut.

"*Anyway*, it was just the two of us- a really fun night." She blinked, and then turned in Mercuri's arms. "What did you do?"

A cool smile emerged before his reply. "I got tickets to Don Gio-"

She was wiggling in his arms before he could finish.

"Guess this means you're happy," Mercuri let her go in order to watch her turning as she jumped in place. Leaning back on the door, he propped a fist beneath his chin and delighted in the look of her tiny polished toes sinking into the rug as she bounced. He took so much delight in the sight of her that he began to seriously reconsider them going out.

"Oh shit, shit," she raised her hands defensively. "I'm so sorry for not being dressed. I'll only take a minute."

"It's alright," Mercuri's voice was as soothing as Tee's was frantic. "We've got time. The show doesn't start 'til midnight."

"Wow," the awestruck look returned to her eyes, "a midnight opera." Something in her expression sobered and had her closing the slight distance between them. Squeezing Mercuri's forearm, she tugged urging him to lean down as she stood on her toes. When he was near enough, she put a lingering kiss to his jaw. "Thank you."

Before she could step back, he was scooping her up and treating her to a more demonstrative kiss.

"Your clothes-"

"Fuck them," his voice was a soft roar as he settled next to the door, keeping her ass cradled in his wide palms. She was naked beneath the shirt and his fingers slightly grazed her sex the higher the shirt eased up her thighs. He launched a pleasurable assault on her earlobe and then down the slope of her neck. Following a slow, wet nibble along her collarbone, he worked his way back up.

Tee pampered her palms, smoothing them across the luxurious fabric of his tux. Somehow, she denied herself the indulgence of letting her fingers sink into his hair. "I should go dress-"

He reclaimed her mouth for another overwhelming kiss and Tee gave up the argument. She was sliding into delicious acceptance of obliging whatever he wanted, when he ended the kiss, set her to her feet.

"Go on," he dropped a kiss to her temple and forehead, then turned her into the direction of her room.

Mercuri watched her go and, alone in the living room, he rested on the front door again. He marveled then over how absolutely she'd gotten to him. She'd gotten to him to the point that there was no doubting he was in love with her. He fought against the smile that the thought would have brought to his mouth. He knew the smile would've only been a precursor to him following her into the bedroom and then... to hell with the opera.

Before he lost that battle completely, Mercuri felt his phone vibrating against an inside pocket of the tux. Fishing it out, he turned it over with intentions of activating the silencer. He saw Pope's name on the faceplate.

With a knowing smile, he proceeded to silence the mobile. "Later," he sighed.

***

Los Angeles, California~

Dinner was first on the evening's agenda. Tee was glad. Following the shock of flying into L.A. on one of Mercuri's company jets, she was certain that a hearty meal would be required to keep her from submitting to the shock of more surprises.

Their restaurant of choice was a surprise all its own. The Douglass, was a mass of private dining suites arranged in a circular design along the continuous top floor wall of the scraper where it resided. Each room had a parlor like feel with intimate round tables and plush seating. Small lamps decorated the dining and end tables and provided most of the room's illumination. The lighting was soft enough so as not to wash out the stunning view of the city beyond the windows. The food was even more stunning with choice cuts of beef and fresh caught seafood.

Tee was enjoying the starlit view beyond the tall windows when Mercuri gathered her back against him.

"So how am I doing?" he asked.

Briefly, she closed her eyes, rolled her head on his chest. "I don't think I'm skilled enough to properly compliment you."

"That's doubtful," silently, he noted that her dress was compliment enough.

The designer cut was a one piece creation of chocolate cashmere that molded her nonstop curves and enhanced her already flawless complexion. The collar was high, fashioned like a choker at her neck. The deep side split stopped midway at a lush thigh.

Mercuri kept his hands at her arms and resisted the urge to skim them down the length of her. Doing that would certainly result in them using their private dining room for much more than dining.

Luckily, protocol intervened and the server arrived for introductions and to collect drink and appetizer requests. The service was exceptional. Mercuri and Tee were having their drinks with a warm porcelain platter of shrimp puffs, less than ten minutes after the waiter's departure with the orders.

"You live very well, Mr. Nikolaides." Tee raised her champagne flute in mock toast.

He nodded, though his expression didn't express total agreement. "I always thought so. I'm not so sure now. My friends say I don't live enough," he tacked on the last before a question followed the curious look she gave at his prior confession.

"Seems I'm not the only one with friends who give it to them straight," Tee sipped more of the crisp champagne.

"My friends live for that shit," he grinned then inclined his head fractionally. "They aren't always off the mark about me, but if you ever expect me to admit to saying that in front of them, I'll deny it."

"Same holds true for me if the situation ever comes up."

Mercuri plucked another shrimp puff off the platter and followed it with a healthy swig of his Guinness. "So how'd you guys meet?" he asked.

"Prin's parents," she nodded when he seemed surprised. "We were all fresh out of high school and in need of jobs. Prin's folks always hired big for the summer. Prin even worked- the Hollands had her learning the ropes from the ground up. We were all assigned to the same department and… the rest is history."

"So from V.A. to Cali, that's some hike, Tee."

"Yeah…" she selected another puff but only nibbled at it absently.

They had put in entree orders during the waiter's prior visit. Silence hadn't quite blanketed the room when he returned with their meal. Whatever unrest Mercuri's observation had caused, was soon being replaced by distinct delight over the plump broiled scallop Tee popped into her mouth.

She moaned, hung her head for a second while savoring the taste. "If our night ends right here, it'd be the best I've ever had."

Mercuri's chuckle had his devastating eyes narrowing beautifully. "I hope we'll have the chance for more."

Tee chased her seafood with another swallow of the fine champagne and almost purred her satisfaction that time. "How's your steak?" she asked, noticing that he was just watching her.

Instead of answering, Mercuri only leaned forward to cut into the 24 oz. T-bone majestically displayed on an enormous platter.

"So how'd you meet *your* friends?" Tee asked.

Mercuri savored his bite of steak and smiled. "We weren't exactly… introduced when we met. We couldn't even talk when we met."

Delighted, Tee laughed. "So you all grew up together?" She asked, pleased and intrigued when he nodded. "That's hard to believe. It's quite an achievement keeping a friendship together for that long."

Mercuri shook his head while cutting off another sizable portion from the mammoth steak. "Tee that's a fact that often keeps me in a state of disbelief as well."

She heard the teasing chord in his voice and laughed again.
***

The evening of surprises continued. Mercuri had not only gotten tickets to her favorite opera, he'd gotten them to a showing that was to be performed in one of the country's newest opera houses. Though it was among the country's smaller houses, The Haven promised those patrons fortunate enough to secure one of its pricey tickets, a theatrical experience unlike any other.

The establishment was a study in grandeur. The lobby was resplendent with marble columns, gilt framed murals of amazing scope and detail with stately round eggshell sofas, high-backed benches, settees and wing chairs finished in sumptuous suede. Engraved railings and hand carved bannisters gleamed of rich maple with bronze adornments and piping that all seemed more brilliant offset against the sea of plush crimson colored carpeting throughout.

Despite the jaw dropping splendor, perhaps The Haven's most unique aspect were the midnight showings it reserved to premiere operas upon the production company's arrival in the city. Regardless of where the show was to be performed in town, a stop to The Haven was fast becoming the norm for the most anticipated events.

Mercuri kept a hand to the small of Tee's back as they worked their way through the dense, well-dressed crowd. The late hour was apparently no deterrent; moreover it seemed an inducement if the swollen crowd was any sort of proof.

Mercuri's focus wasn't on the massive crowd they'd soon be joining inside the auditorium or the magnificence of the facility. Instead, he was transfixed by the woman at his side. Eyes alight with excitement and anticipation, Tee seemed to be absorbing the beauty and creative air that charged the place like an electric current. She wasn't ashamed to let her awe show. Her head tilted up and back, her lips parted to utter hushed sounds of approval as they moved deeper into the house.

Again, Mercuri focused on his hand lying flat at her spine. He had to send himself more than one mental order not to use it to haul her up against him. He couldn't say that he'd ever met another who actually wore their rejuvenation so well synced with their control. On Etienne Shaw it was like an article of clothing. Even with that distinctive air of freedom following her like mist, she kept her control in check. Her uncanny ability to keep all that calm and composure managed inside such a small package, had him beyond captivated.

Mercuri was so captivated that he almost let Tee lead him the wrong way toward the semicircular rows of crimson steps leading up to the auditorium's entrance. She had taken his hand and was squeezing excitedly as she tugged him along on her eager tour.

Carefully, he turned the tables. Giving her hand a few brisk pumps, he indicated their change of direction with a slight jerk of his head when she looked his way. Soon, they were in route to the attendees podium, one of several across the expansive lobby. They were seen to within moments of their arrival. Mercuri gave his name and an attendant- one of four manning the station- escorted them through the lobby.

A bit more subdued then, Tee's excitement was still peaked as they followed the dark suited attendant to a quiet bay of elevators.

"Where does this go?" She whispered up to Mercuri when she noticed the majority of the elevator traffic collecting in other bays.

The attendant answered instead of Mercuri. "This car will transport you directly into your private box, Miss." Smiling and with a gracious sweep of his hand, the attendant waved them toward the opening maple panels. "Enjoy your evening," he bade them.

Ensconced in the pampering quiet of the black upholstered car, Tee squeezed Mercuri's hand in both of hers and smirked up at him.

"So you *are* an opera lover."

He smiled, but didn't look down. "Not even on my best day, Miss Shaw."

"You've got a private box."

He looked down at her then, immobilizing her beneath the feline allure of his extraordinary eyes. "That's because *you're* the opera lover."

The car panels glided apart before Tee could either question or process his point. Once again, she was suspended in the state of wonder that had gripped her since their arrival at the grand establishment.

"Wow," she breathed, leaving the car to be enveloped in another level of exquisite luxury. She had heard of The Haven's...regalness, but had yet to visit. Tonight's trip had definitely been worth the wait.

Her pumps sank into rich carpeting the color of an aged merlot. The box; intimately designed to accommodate two, was complete with inviting seating, and small tables for programs, opera glasses or other paraphernalia as well as a serving console for any refreshments from The Haven's box seating menu. She all but floated into the space, smoothing her hands lovingly across the chairs occupying the box. The sleek dark gray fabric of the seats gave wondrously beneath her touch and she imagined what it would feel like to be relaxed in such a place while enjoying her favorite opera.

Though identically upholstered, the chairs bore distinct differences. Tee was sure that the wide, comfortable looking wingback was hers, while the much wider and less elegant easy chair with matching Ottoman, was Mercuri's.

Delight sent another shiver along her back when she moved to the box's glossy dark wood barrier and took in the view of the auditorium below. Even from where she stood, she could tell that the seating there appeared as sleek and inviting as those in the lofty boxes. It was an expanse of cool elegance upon a sea of merlot carpeting.

Her eyes wandered up into the highest tiers of the house where ropes, pulleys and more advanced devices existed to operate the mechanized stages and set equipment. From there, her gaze drifted down to scan the long, circular row of private boxes.

"Wow," she stepped back when velvet drapes the same tone as the carpet, slid closed to obscure her view. Looking over, she saw Mercuri's hand near the panel she assumed controlled the drapes.

"You said 'wow' already," he murmured against her skin where his mouth pressed the spot behind her ear.

Tee felt the drugging, intoxicated sensation she'd come to expect whenever he was near and she let herself float on the moment.

"I'm having trouble coming up with more words," smiling lazily, she let her head rest back on him.

"That's not a problem," his hand at her hip, roamed up to cup her breast.

"Mercuri," her voice carried caution, "this is about to get started."

"Damn straight," he spoke while tending her earlobe.

The painfully sweet suckle would've caused her to gasp. Instead, she moaned when his thumb began a slow affecting rub across the nipple well hidden beneath her dress. In an attempt to prevent or to encourage, Tee wasn't sure which, she put her hands over his. She'd forgotten about his free hand which he'd insinuated inside the slit on her dress and hooked around her thigh bared above the lacy black top of her garter secured hose.

167

Mercuri caressed the silken dark flesh he found there and smiled when she moaned her approval. His thumb outlined the impression of her clit beneath her panties and he heard her beg him to wait, even as her hips arched in anticipation of more. He chose not to listen and claimed her thigh with his free hand, hooking around the limb and lifting her back against him.

Tee felt them retreating from the curtains and then descending as Mercuri lowered them to his easy chair.

"Mercuri…please wait-" the request hesitated on her gasp when she squeezed his wrist in a weak attempt to stop his fingers from probing beyond the edge of her panties. He'd set her calf over the arm of the chair- the move giving him more room to explore.

Desperate then, she squeezed his wrist insistently. "Please don't. Mercuri…I-I can't sit through the opera with my panties wet." She felt his big body shake then with laughter summoned by her admission. Weakly, she poked an elbow into his ribs.

"That's all you had to say," he whispered while putting a kiss to her neck. He joined in softly when she began to laugh at herself.

~~~

Mozart's *Don Giovanni* was the tale of a talented and flamboyant 18th century artist whose true passion was the seduction of women. Whether the women consented or not, it made no difference to the villain. When fate intervenes to encourage him to repent, the Don refuses and has to suffer the consequences of his decision.

Though an evening at the opera had not yet made his 'must do' list of outings, Mercuri admitted the story wasn't half bad. Tee was quite obviously in a state of bliss. She sat with perfect posture, rapt by the performance. Only when the story reached its most critical heights, did she abandon her perfect carriage to lean against the box ledge. Arms folded, chin resting on the backs of her hands, she appeared to be inhaling the unfolding drama. When Act One concluded and the thirty minute interval commenced, Mercuri watched as she resumed her strict posture. Her head bowed as though she were replaying the act in her mind.

"How often do you get to the opera?" Mercuri asked her and, for a moment, wasn't sure whether she'd heard him.

Tee remained silent, her head still bowed. Her eyes were fixed on her hands folded in her lap.

Concerned, Mercuri pushed out of his relaxed position on the chair to watch her closer. He lifted a brow when she finally-slowly-looked his way. Additional seconds passed before the vacant look left her expression and she graced him with a one shoulder shrug and smile.

"I don't get to the opera nearly enough," she smiled out over the chatting audience then, "and I never get out like this. I sit down there with the masses. Never up here with royalty."

He watched her hand resting casually across the chair arm. Taking it, he turned her palm face up and slid his thumb across it as he spoke. "You should change that," he said.

Sensations flooding at once, Tee smoothly tugged her hand free and fixed him with a look that said she knew what he was doing.

Acknowledging his guilt, Mercuri shrugged and grinned with a boyish guile. "Your friend Prin is royalty, isn't she?" He sparked new conversation. "Her family's company dates back to the Reconstruction. I'll bet her seats were up here with the elite."

Tee smiled, but the gesture didn't quite reach amusement or approval. "We were all on a budget then."

"So why this one?" He asked, having read the sadness in her response. He tilted his head toward the stage when she looked his way. "Why Don Giovanni?" He watched, newly fascinated by her expression change. This one, far more visceral than the last.

"Bad guy gets his in the end. Who doesn't love that?"

She punctuated her reasoning with another half-hearted shrug, but Mercuri saw her fists clench. He decided to follow up his query with another probe to see how deeply her emotions ran.

"So you've got something against playboys?" He asked.

"No," she regarded the stage with malice pooling her ebony stare, "I've got something against monsters."

~CHAPTER 19~

The Haven offered more than a splendid operatic experience, it also offered splendid lodgings. Patrons could secure hotel accommodations when they booked performance tickets. Haven Manor provided the same majestic style as its neighboring house. All rooms, immense, two-level suites, boasted balconies that overlooked the Haven Opera gold lit and brilliant against the equally brilliant Los Angeles backdrop.

Tee was as staggered as she'd been upon entering the opera. Unlike before, she didn't have the opportunity to indulge in a lengthy admiration of the suite with its bold color scheme in shades of plum, midnight blue and hunter green.

Mercuri had other ideas that skirted a tour of the accommodations. He felt he'd exercised more patience than he thought himself capable of. Tee had forbid any contact through the duration of the second act. Knowing the suite awaited them was the only thing that kept him from brooding- too much.

He gave her time to marvel over the room while he pulled out of the bow tie and tuxedo jacket. He partly unbuttoned his shirt and then she was his.

The staggering sensation Tee felt then wasn't due to approval of her surroundings, but the unexpected treat of Mercuri's hand hooked over her thigh so that he could haul her back against him in continuation of what they'd started in the private box.

There was no need for her to request touring the gorgeous suite before they did... anything else. He wouldn't allow it, not when he'd abided by her wishes to view the opera without so much as holding hands, Tee thought. She could feel the famished urgency in his touch. "Mercuri..." she sighed then only in appreciation of his touch.

Mercuri thought he was about to hear more urgings that he wait, same as the ones he'd endured from her over the course of their long evening.

"I don't want to hear it, Tee."

His tone was harsh, yet she laughed in understanding that he *had* misunderstood. Her laughter melded into a wavery, delighted moan once his hands disappeared into her dress split. There, he launched a pursuit which progressed until his fingers were inside her panties.

His mouth was insistent at the base of her neck where he bathed her skin with brush strokes paired with lingering kisses. She worked her bottom against the crotch of his pants and his hand slid from her breast then to smother her hip. He kept her firm on his lap so that he could savor what she roused.

Tee could barely lift her head and soon abandoned the effort. She let it rest back on his shoulder and took great pleasure in his skillful tongue that was then intermittently bathing her ear. His fingers had pushed inside her panties and spent several torturous moments sliding along the moistened seam of her sex.

Ever so slightly, she began to buck her hips, yearning to have him fill her. She had one hand deep in the rich silk of his midnight hair, the other she clasped over his wrist squeezing subtly to relay her desires.

Mercuri had no intention or ability to resist- not when he too had struggled with keeping his desires on simmer for the better part of the night. His ears and ego hummed to the sound of her breathy cries mingled with his name on her tongue when he used his middle and ring fingers to take her.

Tee bit down on her bottom lip then. She relished the intrusion of the long, thick digits turning her breathy cries into low, quaking moans as sensation consumed her. The hand at her hip began to roam, smoothing along her torso and stomach, squeezing at her thigh with faint persistence.

"How the hell do I get you out of this thing?" he snapped.

"Under my arm," she threw back hastily, far more concerned with what his other hand was doing.

He located the gold zipper tab beneath her arm and had it tugged past her hip in no time. Greedily, he plundered beneath the material to reclaim the breast he'd fondled. In response, Tee's gasps and moans swirled with words of encouragement.

Mercuri craved her taste and sustained himself through a harsher suckling of her earlobe and the satiny skin beneath it. He treated her breast to a few slow squeezes and then his middle finger slipped inside a lacy bra cup to stroke a pebbled nipple.

Sensation rendered Tee almost insane with need. Nerve endings fired rapidly at the nipple he molested. She wiggled her bottom against his substantial erection, while using her tight inner muscles to clutch his fingers that relentlessly probed and rotated inside her.

"Mercuri...no..." she groaned when he abandoned her nipple.

Her disappointment was short-lived, turning to anticipation when she realized his fingers were cruising down toward the waistband of her panties. Sensation flared then like a live wire inside her when the very tip of his ring finger skimmed her clit and subjected the nub to a succession of rotations. The pressure of climax was an aching throb that primed her for explosion. Instead, disappointment once again reared its head when the spectacular rubs and plunges ceased. She could feel his fingers curling into her panties and understood his plans.

"I have to wear these," she cautioned.

"You won't need them. Trust me."

"I have to walk out of here, remember?"

"I'll carry you."

She heard the unapologetic rip of the material and felt the tattered garment slide away shortly after. Elation pooled anew when his hands smoothed over her torso and waist to cover her mound once more. He pleasured her with another round of dual fondling before he deprived her of one hand in order to free himself of his trousers.

Tee could feel her heart's steady climb into her throat then. Mercuri resituated the folds of her gown to expose the part of her he demanded access to. Taking her hips, he lifted her and settled her deliberately. The move was beautifully erotic in its execution.

172

The incomparable pleasure of being stretched and filled to such an extent, was an almost painfully sweet occurrence. It was fast becoming an addiction for her. Tee was happy to let him take full control, not only in setting her down, but in guiding her movements to suit his preference.

The cry leaving her lips then was sharp and emotion-filled as moisture oozed from her sex to glide along the wide obstruction that drove high and steady inside her.

Mercuri guided her moves with one hand to Tee's hip, the other was drawn to her clit. Her intimate moisture flowed at a steadier pace then and he quite clearly approved. He rested his forehead to her shoulder and muttered soft, satisfied words to that effect each time she sheathed him.

She'd orgasmed on multiple occasions and he treasured the vice like capability of her inner muscles when they gripped his shaft like a fist. She was so saturated from such a loss of control that he could easily imagine his dick drenched in a solid coating of shimmery white.

Once her climax had marginally eased, he resumed his thrusts with a ruthless intensity that propelled her into the clutches of renewed arousal. Tee submitted without complaint.

They spent two hours in the living room before the need for more space took them into the bedroom. Following another lengthy, lusty session atop a decadent Emperor-sized bed, they didn't fall into exhausted sleep but lay there sated. Sometime later, Mercuri drew the covers over them, gathered Tee closer to his chest and they continued to enjoy a companionable silence.

~~~

"Remember that flower on my welcome mat?"

"Yeah," Tee pushed a hand against his side to use for leverage. Bracing herself, she propped on her elbow to look down at him. "The yellow tulip," her dark eyes narrowed with interest.

Mercuri nodded, dragging his fingertips across the back of her hand where it rested on his chest. "They were my mother's favorite."

Something inside her seized. "Were?"

His gaze was like stone. "I think it's 'were'."

"Mercuri…" Her whisper held sadness for him. "I'm sorry."

He offered a quick smile that didn't affect the stony gaze. "It was a long time ago, it's nothing I can remember- nothing I witnessed.

173

Sometimes I can barely remember what she looked like. Most of the time, those damn flowers are the only memory I can pull into my head."

Keeping a corner of the sheet at her chest, she pushed up to sit. "What do you remember?"

"I told you I've known my friends since before any of us could talk?" For a moment, his gaze softened as he followed her nod. Distracted then, he brushed the back of his hand along her cheek before returning to his troubling memories.

"Our mothers knew each other before any of us were born. They all came from Greece and for some reason settled in Texas." He rolled his eyes then as if that reality were a source of irritation.

"Texas...We left when we were kids, but one of my friends still has his accent. Can you believe that?" He shook his head on the pillow as thoughts of Slayte emerged. "I guess it didn't matter where they landed as long as they got their new life," he said.

Tee watched the hand that had so tenderly skimmed her cheek moments earlier, curve into a foreboding fist. She covered it with her hands and squeezed.

Mercuri's resulting smile held traces of gratitude. The story was one he rarely told-never told. He wanted to tell her.

"What about your dad?" She regarded the clenched fist and wondered if his father was the reason for it.

"Never knew him," his voice was quiet. "None of us knew them. Not then. Pope and Rutger... they found out later. But they were never around when we were small and our mothers never talked about them."

"What happened?" Tee expected his expression to grow darker. Instead it brightened.

"We had good lives, actually. I can remember it, vaguely but... I think I had a really good childhood. We all did. Our mothers managed to provide for us very well," the lightness of his expression began to dim.

"I was nine maybe ten when that changed. We were taken- all of us. Our mothers were there. They were smiling," his hand unclenched, re-clenched. "There're times when I can't remember what she looks like, but her smile- it's like I can always see it." He moved a massive shoulder in a semblance of a shrug. "Maybe I'm just remembering the way I felt when I saw it."

Tee nodded. She could relate. She could totally relate.

"Anyway… they were smiling and telling us that it was fine. After that, we were going with the people who came for us. I never saw my mother again."

"I'm sorry, Mercuri," she gave his hand another squeeze. "Where did they take you? The people who came for you?"

"A military school in Oregon."

"Your mothers allowed that?" Her eyes stretched.

"Tradition is a big thing where I come from," he could tell by her reaction then that she most likely figured it was something related to his heritage. He couldn't tell her that there no choice in the matter. That part of the story would only trigger his anger and that was a part of himself he never wanted her to see.

"I keep the tulip as a reminder," he said.

Tee rubbed his arm, "Of your mom."

"I keep it to remind myself that there was a time when my life actually made sense."

The symbolism of the tulip story was more than a reminder to Mercuri of a time when his life made sense. It was a reminder of a time when he'd been surrounded by everyone he loved. He'd had his friends, his mother and the sublime emotion only beloved family could inspire. Not since then had he experienced such feelings- that everything was as it should be. Not since then… and then he'd met Etienne Shaw.

Never had he confessed love to any woman. There had been no need, for the emotion hadn't stirred. He wasn't worried, believing when the time came he'd have no issue saying the words. He was in love with Tee- of that he was sure. Still, *knowing* that hadn't done a damn thing to ease his terror and he'd needed the tulip story to bolster his confidence.

His story was a heartbreaking one and Tee's ached for him. Scooting closer, she enveloped him in a hug. "There was a time when my life made sense too," her voice was a shudder. "I wish I'd had something as symbolic as a beautiful flower to help me remember it. I guess there's just too much ugliness in the way for me to get back to it."

Hands going to her arms, Mercuri eased her back to look into her captivating dark face. Though he'd grown accustomed to the anguish that often took residence in her eyes, it disturbed him just the same whenever he glimpsed it. His feelings for her now were too defined to allow her troubled expressions and demeanor to go unquestioned. He waited for her eyes to meet his. When they did, he knew he wouldn't have to ask for explanation.

"I lost both my parents at thirteen. It was a car accident. Drunk driver-my father." She admitted derisively.

"They were coming home from a party- they'd been drinking. The outcome would've been the same regardless of who'd been behind the wheel. My parents were great, but they did love their parties."

"I'm sorry, babe," he smoothed a hand along her arm, squeezed her elbow.

Tee appreciated the gesture, but scorn continued to harden her face. "I was angry with them for a long time. It kind of overshadowed the whole grief process."

"What happened?" He would've done anything to ease the hurt he watched slip in to replace the hardness on her face.

"I went to live with my aunt and uncle in Louisville, Kentucky," she gave a quick shrug, even quicker smile. "Life didn't make much sense to me after that."

He released her arm, feeling the urge to draw a fist. He had a fine idea of how things had gone senseless. Imagining her defenseless, afraid, alone… The anger he didn't want her to see, threatened to make an appearance.

"Is your uncle still alive?" He asked.

The question made her smile-a genuine smile. "It wasn't him, Mercuri." She knew what he was asking- and why. "He and my aunt were good people. Churchgoers, but they were rather naive in the way they blindly followed."

His hands were on her arms again, flexing infinitesimally as he gave her the slightest shake. "Who hurt you?" he softly demanded.

"Members were taught to be obedient and that expectation went double for the kids. If you were... chosen to spend the weekend at the pastor's house-"

"Jesus…" Mercuri dragged a hand up the side of his face and back through his hair.

"I was told that I had to atone, that I had to be made new," her eyes were fixed on the bed. "The pastor was the only one who could help me battle the evil residing in me- the evil that took my parents. The accident was my fault, you see?" She looked at him then. "I'd never know happiness until I vanquished it. It could've reached out to take my aunt and uncle next, you know?" She burrowed her hands in the sheet she'd tucked beneath her arms.

"I stayed 'til high school was done. At first, I bought the bullshit they fed me. I wised up finally, but I knew I wouldn't be much use to myself if I didn't at least have a diploma. Between school and taking every job I could find, I stayed too busy to accept many of the pastor's weekend invites."

"Christ," Mercuri slammed his head back into one of the generous pillows bunched along the upholstered headboard. He then flashed Tee a fierce look that appeared more lethal given the natural, animalistic intensity of his eyes.

"Please tell me the son of a bitch is alive and give me your blessing to kill him."

His words had her smile returning easier that time. "I don't know if he's alive- I don't care. I've made peace with it, Mercuri."

He watched her, looking past- *trying* to look past her physical appeal to what lay beneath. Yes, he recognized a tortured soul when he saw one and he could tell she meant what she said. At any rate, he couldn't help but to wonder if she'd let go of her past because she had later found something uglier to replace it.

"Thank you for telling me," his voice was a few decibels above a whisper.

Tee shook her head. "I can't believe I did. I'm sorry I- for overshadowing your story."

"If I hadn't told mine, you wouldn't have shared yours. So we're even." He gathered her close, dropped a hard kiss to the top of her head.

"Sounds like we had some pretty shitty childhoods," she said.

"Agreed," he put another kiss to her head. "But we started out knowing love. That's more than most have. It's gotta count for something."

"I hope so," Tee burrowed into him, drawing strength from his intoxicating ability. "I hope so," she murmured.

~CHAPTER 20~

They spent all of Saturday in bed. The fact that it'd rained throughout the day, aided a great deal in helping them make the decision to do so.

Mercuri was convinced that he finally knew what heaven was like. Even so, being a good host meant making sure his guest was having as much fun as he was. Tee found his thoughtfulness admirable, but couldn't have been more surprised when he asked if she wanted to go out.

"Not even if it was the sunniest day on record," she said, "besides, we don't have any clothes."

With a snap of his fingers, Mercuri habitually knocked his head back against the headboard and winced. "That's right," he muttered as though he'd forgotten. Earlier he'd sent their things down to the hotel dry cleaners.

"And I think we'd be kind of overdressed for a walk around the grounds even if we had them," Tee shrugged. "When you think about it, this is the only place we can be."

He could not and would not argue her reasoning, not when he had her straddling his waist- right where he wanted her. Heaven indeed, he relished the sight of her bare to his gaze and his for the taking. Possessively, he roamed her thighs- first with his eyes and then with his hands until his thumbs met at their juncture. Next, he executed a teasing assault on her naval. His expression sharpened suddenly, growing more defined with the serious air claiming it.

"Thank you," he stroked the curve of her bottom when she frowned, "for telling me about your childhood. I know it wasn't easy."

"I keep thinking I shouldn't have. I've only ever told it to my friends- never to a man."

"You can trust me to keep your confidence, Tee."

"I know," she shook her head. "It's not that only…" *Only*, she thought, there was something about him that made her want to share things about herself that she didn't ever want to think about. How was that possible?

"Most guys would've already had me back in San Francisco tucked in my apartment with an 'it's been nice knowing you, but girls with baggage really aren't my thing'."

"As incredible to look at as you are, I'd think you've captivated enough men to know that most of us are idiots."

Her brows rose as though he'd proffered a novel observation. "I kind of figured that, but didn't want to rush to judgement."

"It's sound judgement. Trust me. Not many of us are worth wasting your time with."

"But you are? Uh-worth wasting my time with?"

"Course I am," he grinned when she began to laugh. "But it wouldn't be a waste," to emphasize the boast, he nudged her with a semi-hard but undeniable erection.

She feigned disinterest. "Is that all it does?" her tease lilted into a gasp when he raised up to topple her from his lap and onto her back.

"How quickly they forget," hand beneath her back, he lifted her effortlessly and placed her in the middle of the enormous and well-used bed.

"I need constant reminders, you know?" Laughter accented her words.

"I see," Mercuri dipped his head, his nose outlining her breast while his hair pampered her skin like mink. "Run of the mill reminders?" he suckled a pouting nipple and chuckled while she moaned and squirmed. "Or the special kind?" he drew her snug against a powerful erection, smiling as he watched her lashes settle in reaction to the contact.

"The special-special kind'll do…" she was already rocking her hips in anticipation.

"Those are the best," he said and set out to prove that his opinion was fact.

***

Saturday passed in a wave of lusty bliss. Mercuri found himself doing something he would've believed quite impossible had he not been there to witness himself doing it. He could say; without ego ever entering into it, that he was a lot to take. Following their fourth straight hour of sex that day, he didn't know who was more stunned when he suggested Tee get some rest.

He'd dozed off for a few, but woke in the wee hours of Sunday morning to find her still unconscious. Taking advantage of the moment, he watched her sleep and replayed what had been spoken between them. He hadn't said the words he'd intended to share that weekend, but words had been spoken that revealed so much more.

If a person was very blessed or extremely lucky, they lived the whole of their lives believing monsters only existed in horror movies and books. The knowledge that they were all too real, changed a person forever.

The 'senseless' events in Tee's life had undoubtedly changed her. Was her sometimes haunted and withdrawn manner, a result of that time? He wondered. Were there additional tragedies in her life that were responsible for the fixed, vacant expression that frequently claimed her lovely features? Were the monsters in the past she'd spoken of, the only ones she'd ever encountered? If she knew of the 'senseless' events in his life, would he be categorized as a monster in her eyes?

Swearing quietly, he decided to leave her to her rest. After dropping a kiss to the tapered dark waves at her nape, he walked naked from the room. The suite was still dark in the wake of pre-dawn light. Mercuri took in the view of the opera house that remained a golden lit beacon throughout the night. Slowly, his gaze moved beyond the structure to the view of the golden lit city in the distance.

His stomach muscles twinged, another reminder that morning was present. Mercuri spared another few moments for the view and then went to seek out the eating nook located in a shadowed corner of the living room. He decided to wait until Tee woke to order room service.

His wallet, keys and mobile waited on a credenza near the nook. Curiosity getting the better of him, he detoured to the credenza and grabbed his phone. The vibrations of incoming calls and notifications would become an irritation he'd soon resent, so he didn't bother to take the phone out of silent mode when he'd programmed it before leaving Tee's apartment that Friday evening. He already knew he was sure to find Pope's name occupying the majority of missed calls among his contacts.

The smirk coming to his patiently sculpted mouth proved just that when he dragged a thumb along the screen to find his friend had called over ten times in the past 34 hours. Muttering his second curse of the morning, Mercuri decided to make time during the day to return the calls. For Pope's sake, he prayed the man hadn't been calling to waste his time.

Shaking his head, Mercuri scrolled past Pope's name to see who else may've attempted contact. He found nothing of real surprise until the name Roya scrolled to the center of the screen. Roya. Eduardo not Enrique. The son? Mercuri scrolled his mental directory for the name, but came up empty. He and his friends had only done business with the senior Roya.

What the hell did Junior want? Again, the word 'monster' came to mind and Mercuri felt his jaw clench in response. He and his friends had definitely owned that moniker. For a time, they'd worn it with pride. They were doing bad things, but bad things for right reasons. The ends justified the means, by any means necessary and all the other phrases that polished the bad with a gloss of good.

It was all bullshit. The ends were never justified when they were meant to benefit the unworthy. They had spent their lives toiling for an organization that epitomized the word.

Operative word 'spent' past tense. They were done. *He* was done. He'd return the call. He owed that much at least to the son of the man who had bankrolled his life. He owed that much and no more.

As Tee was still asleep, he decided to go on and get the matter over with. That Roya had called from an identifiable line could have meant the issue was a simple one. Maybe the man was organizing a surprise birthday party for his dad and wanted to make sure he was free. Grinning over the improbability, Mercuri sent the call through and waited. The line was ringing before he considered the time difference. If Eduardo Roya was on the West Coast, Mercuri hoped he was an early riser.

"Mr. Nikolaides, you're as direct as my father said." Eduardo Roya's voice was light, all perfectly rolled Rs and melodic resonance. "I know we've never spoken, but I appreciate you taking time to return my call."

"You've got me curious."

"Then I won't prolong this. My father is dead Mr. Nikolaides. It was...unexpected."

Mercuri read through the lines well enough. 'Unexpected' translated into murdered. "My condolences," he said and waited.

"Thank you. Mr. Nikolaides I was hoping we might schedule a meeting at your earliest convenience. Yours and your associates'."

Curiosity mounted along with a fair amount of suspicion then. "I'm out of town for the weekend," Mercuri shared.

"I'm in San Francisco," Roya returned. "Closing out business my father has here. I'm staying not far from your company headquarters. I'll be here all week. Longer if need be."

Mercuri's suspicion surpassed curiosity then. "I'd have to check with the others."

"I understand. I'll wait to hear back from you regarding a suitable time. I'll take whatever you can spare, Mr. Nikolaides. Seeing you is my only concern."

Mercuri knew Roya couldn't afford to be less vague. Such things shouldn't be discussed by phone, he knew. "Expect my call tomorrow," he said and broke the connection.

He studied the faceplate long after it had gone dark and then he was murmuring his third curse of the morning. It was best not to waste what time there was before it was time to return to the real world. He set the phone back to the credenza, not really caring if the force he used shattered the device.

He went back to the bedroom where his mood hovered between approval and irritation when he found Tee still asleep. The emotion was selfish. He knew she needed her rest, but having her to talk to was perhaps the only cure for his approaching anger.

Choosing to exercise consideration, he settled back onto the bed. The superior mattress didn't so much as shudder, he noted grudgingly. She remained undisturbed. His spirits did manage to lift somewhat when she shifted, turning from her stomach to her side. She wasn't waking though, merely settling into a more comfortable position, Mercuri realized. Still, his upset almost totally receded when she shifted again to move steadily toward him until she was burrowing into his side.

Mercuri discovered that talking to her wasn't the only cure for his upset. Being able to put his hands on her worked just fine.

Gently, he tugged her closer until her head was resting in the crook of his shoulder. He planted a kiss to the top of her head and let his lips linger on her dark, cottony soft waves.

"I'm in love with you," he said to himself and the room. Tee didn't stir.

He held her close for another hour at least- taking solace in her nearness. When her shifting resumed, Mercuri convinced himself that she was waking and thought it couldn't hurt to offer her a little encouragement.

Besides, he was awake. Fully. Having her so close was a strong reminder of that. Slowly, he set her back next to one of the king pillows that littered the bed like clouds. He heard her sigh when the back of his hand brushed a nipple. He watched, fascinated by the sight of the nub firming.

Unable and unwilling to resist, he dipped his head and used his tongue to lightly encircle it. Soon, he was capturing the firm tip in a wet, lazy suckle. A voice scolded him- *lightly* scolded him- for taking such advantage. Again, Mercuri convinced himself that he could have backed off if only he hadn't treated himself to a bit more fondling and felt her folds slick with moisture.

Done with being considerate, he intensified his feasting at her breasts. Patiently, he divided his attention between both. His hand at the small of her back kept her close, crushing the mound he devoured deeper into his mouth. His hand at her sex launched an indulgent exploration of her saturated core.

Sensation flooded Tee's semi-conscious mind. Reality or fantasy, all she knew was that long, thick fingers were the cause. They slid high, rotated leisurely, retreated and then repeated the action. She woke up moaning, gasping and rocking her hips. By then, Mercuri's head had replaced his fingers and he was using his energetic tongue to take her into elation. Slow, plundering strokes roused a wondrous friction that stole her breath. Her hands sank deeper, disappearing into the dark forest of his hair.

"Mercuri…" Weak, she loosely fisted his thick locks as she rode his tongue. "Please let me come…" her sleepy plea roused a chuckle she felt rumble through him before she actually heard it.

Mercuri abided, taking her more vigorously then. He chose not to prolong the wait for her first climax of the day. It wouldn't be her last.

~CHAPTER 21~

Tee could recall the rest of her weekend in rich detail. She recalled the sweetness swirling during the aftermath when Mercuri took her home and spent the night. She recalled kissing him goodbye that morning.

What she hadn't been able to recall with quite as much detail was the act of *walking* through any of it. Floating, yes that's what she'd done. What she was still doing. The mere memory of the past 2½ days was enough to keep her footsteps light as air.

That was a lofty accomplishment on a Monday. As it was a workday, she put in the necessary appearance at the office. There were meetings regarding upcoming proposals in need of review for potential eShaw projects. Tee handled it all in a manner befitting the head of a respected design company. By lunchtime however, she was all played out and decided to call it a day.

Too mellow for the office, but still too restless to head home, Tee took the half hour drive from San Francisco to Burlingame. Soon, she was pulling up to the eclipsing pine gates of Bear Arms.

Tee figured Berrill would be working, but took the eastern road that led deeper into the ranch and Bear's home. While Tee preferred to keep her living spaces more confined, the airy open majesty of the ranch never failed to leave her breathless. It was a sprawling piece of real estate that spanned at least sixty acres.

The gun range portion of the property provided generous spacing for indoor and outdoor target practice. Defensive firearm use training was popular with law enforcement professionals across the state. Still, others preferred to try their luck with skeet shooting and the in-season hunting parties that drew big game hunters from across the country.

Berrill's home spanned at least 10,000 square feet of the 60,000 acres. The Spanish-styled estate was a work of astounding architecture. A jaw-dropping atrium opened into an immense portrait-lined corridor of white brick supported by stone columns leading the way into a dwelling that was both immaculate and surprisingly homey. Recessed lighting poured on golden illumination as did the tall lamps with their wide, ornate vases.

Tee had let herself inside and was soon greeted by one of the members of the small housestaff Bear employed. Jean Kearney escorted Tee to a sunken living room just off the main corridor. The tall, stately woman made a discreet exit through a side panel in the room after informing Tee that she'd let Berrill know she was there.

Tee urged the woman to take her time and she meant it. It was never a hardship relaxing at Bear's. A long L-shaped sofa with chaise sectionals accounted for the front room's main seating. Springy burgundy and tan accent pillows of varying shapes and sizes decoratively cluttered the furnishing set atop a plush carpet of gold, rust and tan. Glossy hardwoods shone around the edges of the carpet. They were more widely displayed as one looked from the vast seating area to the coffee and wet bar across the room.

Tee was in heaven as she inhaled the hint of ground coffee beans that lightly fragranced the room. She was stretched out on one of the chaises when Berrill arrived.

"Well, well look at you all relaxed." The lady of the house waltzed in grinning gaily and exuding her usual air of self-certainty.

"I asked Jean to tell you not to rush," Tee kept her eyes closed.

"Girl please," Berrill waved that off. "It's not every day I get to see you fresh off a long, relaxing weekend with the likes of Mercuri Nikolaides."

Berrill took a seat at the end of the chaise Tee occupied and squeezed her foot-bared as Tee had kicked off her shoes. Berrill's gay grin turned slightly wicked as she fixed her friend with a measuring look.

"I said 'relaxing', but could it be you're exhausted after being kept on your back the entire weekend?"

"Oh Bear," Eyes remaining closed, Tee settled deeper into the pillows cushioning her. "Mercuri's a creative guy-he found other places to put me besides my back." She made eye contact with Berrill then and soon the two of them were dissolving into unrestrained laughter.

"Wait," Berrill gave a resounding clap. "Let me get a drink and get out of these shoes," she gestured to her worn brown leather hiking boots, "then I want *all* the details."

"A lady never tells," Tee heaved a delighted sigh.

Berrill snorted. "She does when the circumstances are extreme and her best friends in the world are living vicariously through her experiences."

"That wouldn't be the case if you took any one of the many offers you're always getting from the gorgeous, rugged types who parade in and out of this place for their shooting weekends."

Sucking her teeth that time instead of snorting, Berrill tugged off her shoes and then sprinted to the wet bar. "Those potential offers can go one place only- it's not like you and Mercuri." She took a bottle of her preferred Dos Equis.

"What?" Berrill queried Tee's look and stopped short of returning to the sofa. "Did you want something from the bar?"

"What do you mean? Me and Mercuri?"

Berrill swigged from the bottle, rolled her eyes. "Hell Tee. Love. Stop." She ordered when Tee gaped.

"That's crazy." Tee looked far removed from relaxed then. "Bear, people need to know each other before that happens and please don't throw 'love at first sight' in my face."

"Alright then," One hand propped to her hip, Berrill regarded her bottle. "I'll admit it may be more about lust than love. You're coming off a six year sex hiatus and he's...hell, look at him..." As if overheated, Berrill tossed back another swig of the brew. Sobering some, she joined Tee on the sofa.

"But that was then and this is now."

Tee was the one to snort that time. "*Now* is only about a month later, B."

"Mmm...and as I recall, you didn't expect to be seeing him *this* long, right?"

"The sex is quite good," Tee meant it as a tease, hoping Berrill would smile. She didn't. "Alright, alright we're enjoying each other," she caved. "What's wrong with that?"

"There's nothing wrong with that, except I think you know it's more than that." Berrill leaned forward on her part of the sectional. "I saw the way he looked at you."

Tee waved a hand. "Good sex."

"Okay." Shrugging, Berrill relaxed back on the sofa and happily imbibed.

"It can't be more than that, Bear." Weak strains of misery began to work into Tee's gaze.

"Can't? Or you won't let it be?"

"Do you know what he did for me this weekend?" Tee asked, once the silence following Berrill's question held in the lofty room for a time.

At her friend's saucy look, Tee shook her head and smiled. "Besides that."

"I can't imagine."

"We went to the opera. He got tickets to Don Giovanni- private box at The Haven and everything."

"Whoa...I'm no opera nut, but even *I've* heard of that place. Tickets in aren't easy to come by. I won't even guess how hard it was to snag a private box. He sounds like a keeper, Tee."

"He is and not because of the opera or any of that. There's...I don't know, B...something good about him. It's like he wants me to see beyond the obvious- the danger, the intimidation factor, the 'this is so not a guy to come across in a dark alley'."

"Amen," Berrill said over a quick laugh.

Tee gave a quick laugh as well. "He's not trying to buy me, he just-just has a way of tuning in to what's up with me."

"Does that frighten you?"

"No," Tee answered quickly, yet honestly. "But it does surprise me. Especially from a man like him. I mean, intimidating or not, he doesn't have to do any of this to get a woman into bed."

"Maybe it's about more than that for him," Berrill shifted her empty bottle between her hands. "Maybe it's about more than that for him- with you."

Thoroughly tempted by the faint smell of the roasted coffee beans; or just needing something to do with her hands, Tee scooted from the chaise and went to prep a mug of the brew at the bar.

"Maybe he's just a pushover for the controlled, composed type," Berrill continued her musing, "maybe he sees past all that to the caring, sweet woman beneath."

Tee set a tall, glazed mug on the beverage plate of the coffee dispenser and waited. "I told him about my parents."

The quiet admission had understanding pooling in Bear's milk chocolate stare. "How'd he take it?"

Tee smiled on the memory. "Wanted to know if there was anyone I'd give him my blessing to kill."

"See?!" Berrill's laughter exploded in a gleeful surge. Her high, glossy ponytail swung energetically about the perfect oval of her face. "I mean, could the guy be anymore perfect?" Sighing her contentment, she rested back on the sofa and crossed her legs at the ankles. "Just keep me posted on the wedding date. You guys can have the reception here," she moved her feet merrily back and forth along the edge of the chaise and hummed.

The dispenser gave its tiny completion beep, but Tee only stared into her cup's murky contents. "It can't go there, B."

"I know, I know," Bear rolled her head against the chaise. "Gotta get to know each other first and all that-"

"It can *never* go there, B."

"Why?" Berrill straightened then, her brow furrowing in surprise and suspicion. She shoved up from the chaise when Tee's responding look confirmed what she'd suspected. For a while, Berrill studied her now empty beer bottle and then she shook her head slowly as if the effort was some great feat.

"You know, Tee, of the four of us, I thought- no, no I *knew* you were the smartest," Berrill began a slow walk of the room.

"You were the one who thought things through most thoroughly- who left no detail uninvestigated. I never thought there would be a day when I'd look at you and see an idiot."

"B-"

"No Tee. That night," Berrill stopped. She tossed away her bottle, into the wastebasket she passed, with a bit more force than needed. "That night changed us. All of us. Maybe the changes weren't good ones, but they allowed us to function and thrive afterwards. Out of

189

the four of us, I'd say you've thrived the best. That control, that... composure of yours, it's allowed you to form and run one helluva business and be a lady while you're doing it and not some hard-assed alpha girl bitch."

Tee; forgetting her own woes for a time, studied her friend with mounting concern. "Bear, you're not-"

"I am. Yeah Tee I am and the thing is, I wouldn't change anything about that. See, the hard-assed alpha girl bitch is who *I* had to become to thrive. I *had* to become her. I don't think I had a choice in the matter." Still walking the room, Bear began to study her hands as though they carried some secret she was obsessed with uncovering.

"I don't think I had a choice in the matter," she said. "I think she was always there somewhere inside me, covered up under all that weakness that kept me from protecting the people I loved."

Memory had Tee bristling then. She knew her old friend had ghosts of her own that the night six years ago had helped her to triumph over.

"You were a kid then, B," Tee kept the reminder soft.

"Well," Berrill's lip curled tensely, "this is about who I am now- and I'm not the sort men fall in love with. Oh, they're intrigued, challenged, aroused even, but love? The kind of love that leads to all the good things in life that we tell ourselves we don't need but secretly wish for?" She shook her head, her smile less tense and more solemn. "Men don't develop that kind of love for girls like me. I don't think there's a man who could handle what I am enough to fall in love with me. You've got a chance at that, Tee. You've found a way to control your darkness. I let my darkness control *me*. *You* have a guy who I strongly suspect will fall in love with you if he hasn't already. You'd be an idiot to walk away from that before you see what it could become."

"I know what it could become, B." Tee snapped, smoothing a shaking hand over her brow before focusing on prepping her coffee. "I know what it could become," her tone was a disheartened one.

Berrill blinked then. Discovery had her crossing the hardwoods to the coffee bar where she took a seat on one of the wrought iron high stools there. "You're in love with him, aren't you?"

Tee gave a quirky toss of her head, just managed a quirky smile. "Like you said, I'm not an idiot. But I can't ask him to accept this, Bear. What happened that night- my part in it," she shook her head defiantly. "He doesn't deserved to deal with that kind of baggage. Relationships are hard enough without all that and this is way beyond the usual sort of drama."

"Well hell, Tee, why tell him?" Berrill spread her hands across the bar top, incredulity stoking her gaze.

Tee appeared just as incredulous. "Are you serious? How much longer do you think we'll keep a lid on this after what happened to Dorinda?"

Berrill seemed to go ashen beneath her dewy caramel brown complexion. She looked down at the hands she'd unconsciously clenched into fists.

"Her death was no accident, Bear," Absently Tee sipped at the coffee, too distracted to appreciate the creamy hazelnut when it coated the back of her throat. "It was a message and it won't be long until whoever killed her delivers another."

"They already have." Berrill cringed when she looked into Tee's frowning face.

***

Patroclus Kostas had suffered unrelenting brutality before he'd met his death. The crime scene photos presented the images of that suffering in excruciating detail. Facial recognition had been impossible as there wasn't much of a face left to identify.

'Overkill' was the unanimous opinion and Mercuri had to agree as he shuffled through the glossy 8x10 color prints. The violence depicted was nothing he hadn't seen before. Hell, he thought, it was nothing short of the kind of brutality he was capable of and had, on occasion, been responsible for. Nevertheless, seeing the results of such depravity displayed on the face of a close friend- a man he'd considered a brother-scorched the desensitized wall he'd erected to hold his prior bad acts at bay.

Mercuri found that the brutality had also been deemed 'personal' in the eyes of his friends when he saw them that day. He'd arrived home that morning from Tee's to find that his three remaining best friends in the world had already made themselves at home while they'd awaited his return.

He'd had to endure light ribbing for coming home in a tux, but such was to be expected. He hadn't minded. He'd bought his home for the purpose of spending time with his friends, after all. Still, he would've enjoyed a little while on his own to mentally recap certain aspects of his best weekend on record. One look at his friends' faces told him that such indulgences would have to be reserved for another time.

"You guys think this was Harris and Zubin?" Mercuri faced the den's massive hearth while shuffling through the crime photos.

"It's Zoo's style. I should know," Slayte's confirmation was grim in tone as dark memories surfaced of his ill-conceived acquaintance with Grant Zubin.

"Harris would've savored this too," Rutger massaged his whiskered jaw while reclining on the far end of the den's longest sofa. "He swore he'd get back at us for betraying him the way he thinks we did," he sighed his frustration.

"Why the fuck now after six goddamn years?" Pope's quiet roar underscored his question.

Slayte, Rutger and Mercuri observed their friend with a mixture of mild surprise and approval. Pope Apostolou preferred to display his rage through deed instead of word. It was rare for the man to lend heated verbal insight to his emotion. The outburst, though slight said much about his level of frustration.

"Did the Vermont sheriff have any leads?" Mercuri asked.

"Not a thing," Pope's roar melded with a snarl, "and that fact was only another clue about where this attack came from."

"So why now?" Mercuri reiterated the relevant query. "It's not like we've been hiding."

"But we have been living and very well." Rutger pointed out.

Slayte released a rip of laughter into the room. "Only *you* would think 'very well' meant livin' out in the wilderness hunting squirrel."

Despite the morose circumstances, soft laughter followed the observation.

"Don't knock it," Rutger advised once he too had enjoyed some of the stress relieving laughter.

Soon though, all eyes had returned to the gruesome photo array strewn across the big coffee table.

"It *is* personal." Certainty flavored Mercuri's voice as his striking eyes crawled over the prints in loathsome disdain.

"That your own personal perception, Merc?" Rutger asked.

"That and a conversation with Eduardo Roya."

Looks traded between Pope, Slayte and Rutger. Pope frowned as if confused.

"Did you say 'Eduardo'?"

"That's the son, right?" Slayte noted.

"He called to say his father was dead," Mercuri told them.

"Fuck," Rutger leaned forward while sliding his fingers through the close crop of curls adorning his head.

"And what else?" Pope asked.

Mercuri shrugged. "Not much. He was pretty vague. Wants to meet in person."

"What do you think he wants?" Slayte was watching Mercuri closely.

Mercuri tracked his gaze back to Patroclus Kostas' brutalized image on the photos. "I think he wants revenge for his father."

"Understandable." Pope said as the others nodded.

"It's also understandable why he'd come to us for it," Slayte chimed in.

"Hold on," Rutger leaned back against the sofa and fixed his friends with disbelieving looks. "Are we seriously discussing this like we're gonna go out and get it for him if he does?"

Slayte took a seat on the sofa as well. "He might feel like we owe him."

"If we owe anyone, it's his father," Pope said. "And all *he* did was pay us back for saving his life."

"Maybe junior feels differently," Slayte countered.

Nodding, Pope shrugged. "Guess we'll find out."

"I told him I'd call once we were in agreement about the meet. Sounds like we are."

"We'll talk to him." Pope answered Mercuri's unspoken question, but looked to Slayte and Rutger for confirmation which they gave in the forms of slow nods. When Mercuri only shrugged his consent, Pope's bright eyes narrowed.

"What?" Pope moved closer. "What the fuck aren't you tellin' us, Merc?"

Mercuri sent Pope a look, amused but for the thin layer of malice glossed over it. "I hate how you do that."

Pope graced his friend with a smile that intensified the jolting ultramarine of his eyes when they narrowed in humor. "Don't hate me because I'm perceptive or smarter than the rest of you. Besides, you idiots aren't that hard to read."

"I'll give you something hard to read," Rutger murmured from the sofa where he rested back with his eyes closed.

Pope snorted. "My guess is it would be a very short story."

"Still above *your* comprehension level," Rutger gave Pope the benefit of his deepset gaze then.

"Guys," Slayte groaned, "it's too early in the day to sit through a conversation about your pathetically short dicks. Besides, Merc's got the floor and I'd like to know what he's not tellin' us too."

Again, Mercuri looked to Pope. "Don't you already know?"

Pope grinned, recognizing the tease. "I don't, but somehow the name Etienne Shaw keeps coming to mind."

Whatever playfulness that may've been lurking in Mercuri's vivid stare, turned over to pensiveness. "I've got no idea what Eduardo Roya wants to talk to us about, what he expects of us or if this thing with Patch stems from old beef with Harris and Zubin. All I know is I can't be involved in it." He let the decision hold on the quiet air for a few seconds before he continued.

"I'll support you however I can, you guys know you can toss ideas off me, I'll give my input and help you strategize only…I can't…physically put myself in it."

"Jesus Merc…have you told her how you feel?" Pope's query held on a stunned whisper.

Mercuri paced the den in his bare feet. He'd traded the dapper tux for sweats and a faded Nirvana T-shirt. The more comfortable attire did nothing to ease the apprehension tightening his chest.

"That's what this weekend was for and I blew it," he clenched a fist as he walked, "I just couldn't find a way to say it and I want to. I want to say it so much," he brought the fist up against his open palm. "It's like I'm afraid and what the fuck?" Harsh laughter colored his sigh. "How the fuck can I be afraid to do something like that after all the shit I've done?"

Standing then, Rutger raised his hands in defensive mode. "I've got no idea what it's like to tell a woman I love her, but I'm sure it's something that occurs on a whole other realm from any of the shit we've pulled in the past. A realm that's a helluva lot scarier."

"Agreed," Slayte gave an approving wave. "Gotta be hard putting yourself out there like that, not knowing if she feels the same or if she'll think you're a sap for feeling something she doesn't."

"Do you know that for sure?" Pope watched Mercuri draw a hand through his hair.

"I don't know. I know how she reacts to me when we're together but that's just-"

"Sex." The others chimed in, grinning when Mercuri chuckled.

"Thought you losers would think I was an idiot for wanting to tell a woman I'm in love with her," Mercuri admitted when his chuckles subsided.

"Oh the idiot factor remains whether you're in love or not," Slayte said matter-of-factly and received a pillow to his grinning face for the slight. Sobering, he put the pillow behind his back and straightened on the sofa. "Jokes, aside Merc. This is love. From what I've heard, you never know when it'll punch you in the face. When it does, there's not a damn thing to do but to go with it." His violet eyes filled with a sage wisdom. "Some say a punch like that is one of the best feelings there is. I think we'd all be lying if we didn't say we weren't all a little curious to know what that's like."

"Still feels like I'm leavin' you guys in a lurch." Mercuri folded his arms over his chest, gaze hooded as he studied the others. "I'm the one who set this shit in motion six years ago. Now it's revving up again and I'm saying to hell with it."

"I'm confused about how that leaves us in a lurch?" Appearing bewildered, Rutger folded his arms across his own exceptional chest. "Sure we could use that cannon of a right hook you've got, but you make it sound like you're leaving us to clean up your mess."

Mercuri raised his hands, let them fall to his sides. "How is it not like that, Rut?"

"Are you serious?" Pope's query was a whisper. "Did you really think you were skilled enough to talk over one hundred men into revoking their service to an organization many of them had been part of since they were kids? You're good, Merc, but a feat like that means a certain level of desire had to be present in the hearts of the ones you were trying to sway.

Every one of us who followed you, wanted that freedom you said could be real and not just some carrot those cocksuckers used to sweeten the pot when they got the urge." Pope scanned the room, Slayte and Rutger. "We all wanted this, Merc," he said, "Now whether we were too lazy, too uncertain or hell, just too plain scared to go after it- it doesn't matter. You didn't *start* anything. You only got us to see that something we all wanted was attainable. We love you for that and I, for one, can't think of a better reason to walk away from this insanity, than love."

"Agreed," Rutger; who stood closest to Mercuri, extended a hand to clasp as they hugged.

Slayte stood then as well. "I agree with everything, but the love part I-I'm just too afraid to say that."

In seconds, the deafening rumble of male laughter was soaring.

~CHAPTER 22~

Mercuri headed into his office headquarters early the following morning, leaving Pope to serve as travel host for their friends. It was no hardship. The four had few common interests which made their list of things to do relatively short.

As they all had a love for cars, horses, basketball and food, planning a day's agenda wasn't a nightmarish task. With the exception of Mercuri, no one else rose before 10am.

Pope, Rutger and Slayte met at the stables for a morning ride on the stallions from Mercuri's lucrative herd of breeding stock. Afterwards, a game of one on one was in order and played in the private court just off from the pool. Serious hunger pangs set in later and the guys opted to enjoy a meal out somewhere. As steak was an appropriate staple no matter the time of day, Pope treated his friends to lunch at one of his favorite restaurants.

~~~

The day didn't begin with quite as much ease for Tee. Following the afternoon with Berrill and the new details she'd shared regarding

Dorinda Patterson; and the state of her body when she was found, Tee was able to focus on little else.

Mercuri hadn't called and she was glad as he would have surely known all wasn't well the moment she answered the phone. She slept over at Berrill's where she kept a small wardrobe of clothes in the room designated for her use whenever she visited. She left word at the office, letting them know she'd be in after lunch. She and Berrill had decided that it was time to meet with LuCarolyn and Prin to lay down firm plans to confront whatever was in store.

~~~

Slayte had already taken his place at the table Pope had reserved in what had to be the city's most popular eatery. On his way into The Rascal, he'd noticed the lobby was spacious and comfortably designed. A good thing, as it was damned near packed with patrons hoping for a table during the busiest time of day.

The daily grind, he mused, overjoyed not to be part of it. Additionally, he was overjoyed to have a friend who could command such a reservation at the spur of the moment. They were seen to upon arrival. Apparently Pope had dined there and tipped well often enough to be recognized on sight.

Slayte was shown to the table while Pope and Rutger hit the men's room. Slayte was taking his seat and thanking the waiter for the menu, when he heard a woman nearby telling someone she was being seated and asking if she should order. He smiled, evidently Pope wasn't the only one capable of wrangling prime lunchtime seating. She breezed by him, the scent of her perfume wafting pleasantly beneath his nostrils in her wake. He was prepared to browse the menu, but instinct had him looking up to see if the woman was as pretty as the scent she wore. The menu was swiftly forgotten.

He had a thing for blondes. The leggy kind were especially appealing. Throw in an abundance of curves and he was all but drooling. The one his gaze followed across the dining room, as she spoke into her phone, had all his favorite attributes to be sure. She was far from the norm, though.

Rarely- *never*- had he found all his favorites encased in a package of picture perfect honey brown. He found that the unexpected shade of her complexion beautifully complimented that of her hair. He couldn't make out the shade of her eyes, but could tell that they were almond shaped orbs that enhanced the fresh appeal of her face. What he wouldn't give for a closer look.

A quick glance at the silver winking on his wrist had him judging whether there was time for an introduction before his friends arrived. Then, he remembered her call and that she was meeting someone. He opted to wait and see before he approached. If she were meeting a man, he couldn't say that would be enough to discourage him.

~~~

"We understand that scene took a lot out of you Floyd, but Scottie says we really need to re-shoot it. He wasn't happy with the light and he *is* the director…" LuCarolyn rolled her eyes and cursed herself for answering the phone without checking the faceplate first.

"We know stunts aren't in your contract Floyd…" She was scheduled to meet Floyd Chapin for drinks. Chapin lived in San Francisco and she'd only agreed to make the drive up from Malibu because of the last minute lunch request from her friends. It hadn't been necessary for Floyd to call but LuCarolyn had worked with enough high maintenance actors in her day to expect such aggravations.

"Look Floyd, I'm already late for another meeting. We'll finish talking over drinks-"

"Ah Lu," Floyd Chapin's smooth, syrupy voice coated the line, "can't we squeeze in dinner too?"

"We only agreed to drinks Floyd."

"Dinner might make me more agreeable, Lu…"

She bristled. "I'll take you up on dinner if you redo the scene."

"For dinner, I'll *consider* redoing the scene and I can give you a firm…yes if you stay for breakfast."

LuCarolyn waged a battle to resist the urge to kick out with one of her toothpick heels while she made a fast mental count to three. "Dinner at your place and then we'll see what happens." Disgusted, she ended the connection during Floyd's flowery goodbye. Quickly, she put through another call. "What a scab," she muttered, waiting for the call to connect.

"LuCarolyn Young's office, this is Rita Friedrich."

"Rita hey, it's me, listen I just got off the phone with that prick Floyd Chapin. He says he'll *consider* redoing the scene if I have dinner with him tonight. Staying through to breakfast will get me a firm yes."

199

"Ha! The yes is by far the *only* thing you can count on staying firm longer than two minutes."

"Damn right," LuCarolyn enjoyed a few seconds of robust laughter with her assistant. "Listen, I need you to call Scottie and tell him I need him there and have him bring his assistant with a release form for that douche to sigh. With any luck, the three of us will get out of there in time for the talented but obnoxious Mr. Chapin to enjoy a quiet dinner alone."

"On it."

"Thanks Ree, catch you later," LuCarolyn clicked off from the call, sighed her satisfaction.

"You should be careful with that."

Though the voice at her back may've spanned oceanic depths, LuCarolyn was accustomed to looking down or at most eye level when she spoke to men. It was a rare thing to look up at one and rarer still to look up at one while a pair of stilettos adorned her feet. Not only did she have to look up at this one, but had to retreat a step as his brawny frame unapologetically invaded her personal space.

"My phone?" She said in response to his prior observation.

Her query came across sounding dazed. Sadly, it was the best she could manage as her focus was on his face. God, what a face- aesthetically perfect and accentuated by a thick crop of close cut curls the color of crude oil. The chiseled bone structure included a powerful jaw beneath a rich, coppery complexion and dark close-cut whiskers. His eyes were the most unforgettable shade-like smooth bourbon.

"Promises," he was saying in that ocean deep voice of his. "One day you might meet a guy who'll make you keep them."

A voice was telling LuCarolyn to snap out of it and somehow she adhered. "He might find that I won't mind keeping them." She impressed herself by not retreating when he advanced another step.

"You may mind a great deal once you learn what he expects from you."

With that, he walked past her. LuCarolyn stood gaping for several seconds before she felt the phone vibrating in her hand. Remembering to check the faceplate that time, she gasped at the sight of Prin's name.

"On my way, on my way…"

"Jeez Lu, where the hell are you guys? Tee's here at the table. She said she got here with Bear and they met you on the way in. We chose this place because of you, remember?"

"Yeah, yeah…" LuCarolyn muttered, having made the suggestion because it was near the bar where she was to meet Chapin.

LuCarolyn headed for the main dining room and the trio of podiums where hosts waited to escort diners inside. "I had to stop off to take a call. Bear went up to the ladies' room," angling the phone away, she smiled at the host.

"I'm meeting friends," she said, her manner distracted as she scanned the area for the soft spoken giant with the whiskey colored eyes. He'd disappeared of course and she chalked it up as a testament to her rotten luck.

~~~

It was too late for Berrill to adhere to advice about being careful. With her phone anyway. She'd all but resorted to snarling during the call with her office managers who had just informed her of Senator Chris Morrow's latest attempt to gain an invite to the upcoming shooting soiree. The distinguished gentleman had decided to have his constituents reach out to Berrill on his behalf.

She had camped out in one of the upstairs lounges off from the men's and women's washrooms for the impromptu conference call with her assistants. Phones at Bear Arms had been ringing for much of the morning- all calls from soiree guests who were also Morrow supporters. Everyone wanted to know what they could do to convince Berrill to bend her staunch rules and open another space for the good senator.

"Boss wouldn't it be easier to just save yourself the grief and let the man win this one?" Shaun Oates asked.

"No it wouldn't be easier to let him win because then I'd have every gun enthusiast asshole senator or lobbyist in the country trying to horn in on my events when they're on the campaign trail."

"I agree with you, Boss," Mike Hough was next to chime in, "but with so many guests asking for him we may not have a choice."

"Well guys," Berrill left her spot on a black velvet settee where she'd settled in for the call. "Your input is duly noted and appreciated. Now why don't we handle some business that really matters? We've been so distracted by Morrow and his mess that we still haven't done anything about that property adjacent to the ranch. I need to know who owns it. I can't have another issue like last time. I want to secure ownership before the soiree. So get on it and I'll see you later. And guys? It'd be good for you not to call me again before I get there. Bye."

Berrill opened her mouth for a scream, but kept the actual gesture silent. "Why is it always on the days when I take time for myself?" She muttered.

She had enjoyed goofing off with Tee for what remained of the previous day. It hadn't been easy given what she'd had to share about Dorinda Patterson, but good spirits had eventually returned and Berrill had no interest in returning to work.

She had no interest returning that day either given the mess waiting on her there. Requiring an outlet for the agitation that was beginning to bubble like a noxious stew in her gut, she hurled her phone across the lounge area and winced at the tell-tale cracking sound it gave upon making contact with the wall. She was standing there glowering at the destruction when she noticed the shadow in her periphery. "Do you make a habit of spying on women in restrooms?" She asked.

Pope smiled, watching as the statuesque looker strode over to where she'd smashed her phone into the wall. Bracing off the curved frame of the entryway, he crossed into the space.

"Technically, it's not a restroom but a lounge," he said, "There's no door, so to say I'm spying... kinda harsh, don't you think?"

Berrill rolled her eyes, and picked up the pace to her smashed phone. "What is this? Men's 'Let's Piss Off Bear Day?'" She grumbled.

A hand at her wrist kept her back when she would have knelt for the mobile. Primed to lash out, Berrill had already opened her mouth to hurl insult when she took a good look at the latest man to aggravate her that day. He was kneeling to collect the mess she'd made of the phone and her eyes lingered on the jaw-length waves that covered his head like mounds of black felt. With a quick tilt of her head, her eyes greedily surveyed what she could while he was occupied.

His face was obscured by the magnificent waves of his hair. He was focused on putting the phone and its chipped fragments in one of the thick hand towels from the wide, wicker box on the counter. His face may've been obscured, but there was still lots more to greedily survey.

In helpless fascination, Berrill's gaze roamed his wide back. Christ, he was a big son of a bitch she mused. His hands were massive and made her phone appear miniscule against his palm. When he'd completed the clean up and stood, Berrill hoped he hadn't caught sight of her noticeable swallow. She couldn't do anything about the way her eyes stretched and raked his face and body. She could all but see herself gawking.

The time she would have spent marveling over his height, was instead spent marveling over his looks which were beautiful and sharply chiseled. Patience and a ton of good genes had gone into the creation standing-towering-before her.

And the bastard knew he was gorgeous, she thought when he took her hand and put the wrapped phone in her palm. He never took the brilliant blue green stare off her face and the sultry curve of his generous mouth was set in an all too knowing smile.

"How many of these do you go through in a week?" he asked.

"Three or four," Berrill kept her mocha stare fixed on his face and prayed she didn't look as dazed as she felt. She was glad to hear the playful nonchalance come through in her voice. She watched his smile define, narrowing his stunning gaze in a way that had her clearing her throat when a mortifying stab of arousal threatened a moan.

Pope kept his smile in place, though watching her intently would've suited him just fine. Watching her struggle to mask the emotions playing out on a seductively crafted face the tone of softened caramel was a fascinating endeavor and he had to force himself to remember where they were.

"Three or four, huh?" He closed his hand around hers. "Expensive habit."

"Good stress reliever," there was no forcing strength into her voice then.

He nodded. "There're others, you know?"

"All the best ones are taken."

"You should look a little harder." With that, he squeezed her hand and left the lounge.

Alone, Berrill groped for the counter. Leaning there, she tried to wrap her head around what had just happened.
~~~

Lunch got off to an intriguing start. Tee and Prin spent the first five or ten minutes trading looks with one another and then staring at LuCarolyn and Berrill who had been abnormally quiet since taking their seats at the table. Eventually, Tee and Prin were trading looks as well as shrugs. The women made silent decisions to let the weirdness play out.

That decision held until the waiter arrived. It was his second trip to the table. The first time none of the women acknowledged his presence. Tee ordered a soup and Caesar salad while Prin opted for heavier and ordered the seafood pasta salad.

"Lu?" Tee watched the woman staring at the table and toying with the handle of a dessert fork.

"Bear?" Prin nudged Berrill's elbow and gave her a start.

Berrill managed to open her menu but was clearly not reading anything on its laminated pages.

"Bring my friends the soup and salad too." Tee asked the waiter.

"What the hell is up with you two?" Prin demanded once the server had moved on. She gave Berrill another nudge.

"Huh?"

"What the hell?" Prin persisted at Berrill's absent response.

"Cute waiter at the table and no flirting from Lu?" Tee used her napkin to slap LuCarolyn's hand. She shook her head when LuCarolyn only watched her with vacant eyes.

"Is this about Dorinda?" Tee shifted a look across the table. "Bear told me how they found her body- what they found on it."

Being reminded of their reason for the lunch, pulled LuCarolyn and Berrill from their dream states.

"What are Dorinda's girls saying?" LuCarolyn asked.

Prin's expression didn't foreshadow positive news. "The girls are too busy trying to plot their next moves to care much about finding their dead madam's killer. Dorinda didn't own the house, so the girls may not be there much longer anyway."

"Are they having any other trouble?" Tee fidgeted with her silverware. "Someone looking to give out what they gave to Dorinda?"

"Not that I've heard," Prin reached for her water glass.

"Maybe this is just some random thing," LuCarolyn settled back heavily against her chair.

"I'd buy that, Lu, if only they hadn't left that message."

"It wasn't for us, Bear," Lu argued.

"It was to whoever has *it*. That's us, Lu," Tee picked up a dessert fork and used it to jab at the tablecloth.

"I've been thinking about that," Berrill leaned toward the table. "Maybe it's not such a good idea to be keeping it all in one place like we've been doing."

"What are you suggesting?"

The waiter returned before Tee got an answer. The blonde, with his sun-kissed surfer looks set fresh drinks to the table. For his trouble, he got a thank you paired with one of LuCarolyn's dazzling smiles.

"I'm suggesting we split it up," Berrill continued. "Each of us keeps our own...stuff."

Dazed expressions took hold of everyone's faces then.

"I don't want it near me," Prin shook her head.

The bag and its contents had shifted back and forth between Berrill and Tee for a long while. For the last three years, it had been secure under lock and key inside the steel vaults at Bear Arms.

"It could be a good idea," Tee said.

"Why?" The word was a fierce whisper on Prin's tongue.

"Honey, we don't know what Dorinda said to her killer before she died," Berrill softly issued the reminder. "She could've given up one or all of us. We should each have something to bargain with in the event of anyone coming after us."

With a shudder, Prin reached for the fresh cooler of Vodka provided by the waiter.

"It's a good idea." Supportively, LuCarolyn leaned over to squeeze Prin's wrist.

"I know and I-I get it, I just..." Prin flexed her hand on the cooler but decided against drinking from it. "I just thought having it all somewhere under lock and key, would pack a bigger punch- make it a bigger bargaining chip to deal with whoever might come to screw with us."

"We should all decide how best to use it," Berrill helped herself to one of the pumpernickel medallions the waiter had dropped off during his last trip to the table. "Or whether to use it at all," she added before popping a morsel of the bread into her mouth.

Curious looks circulated the table again.

"Or whether to use it at all," suspicion had Tee inclining her head.

"Bear?" LuCarolyn whispered.

Prin finally took a healthy swallow of her Vodka.

"We have to think about what sharing this could do to our lives, reputations and relationships." Bear spoke through her energetic chewing.

"Bear, if we don't share it, it's like we don't have it." Prin gestured with her glass. "Where's the security in that?"

205

Berrill shook her head. "It's a decision we have to make for ourselves. Right now Tee needs to think about-"

"No-"

"Mercuri-"

"Stop Bear," Tee shoved the fork she'd toyed with, causing it to clatter lightly against the other silverware in its proximity.

"You've got a real shot with him, Tee," Bear's eyes spewed a fierce fire. "If this shit comes out, it could ruin that."

"If this shit comes out and ruins that it wasn't worth my time in the first place." Looking to Prin, Tee extended a hand and squeezed tight when Prin latched on and gave a trembling, relieved smile.

"I got us into this, B. I'm damn well not turning tail to run now. We swore we'd see this through to the end. No matter what."

Without hesitation, Berrill took the hand Tee offered and squeezed. "Fuck," she muttered. "You're right. You're right, nothing's more important than that. What was I thinking?" She put a kiss to the back of Tee's hand before offering her free one to LuCarolyn.

LuCarolyn, who had already clasped hands with Prin, wasted no time making the circle complete. "This all feels really empowering guys, but I'm still scared shitless," she breathed once they'd held on for a time.

"You know, we could always pull in Roya," Tee suggested. "He's the only one who knows what we're up against." She watched as the others nodded.

"Does anybody know how to get in touch with him?" Berrill asked, then shrugged. "I kind of hung up on the guy who called me that day before I thought to get any contact info out of him. Sorry."

"I think Dorinda had something," Prin said, "Maybe there's something the girls could scrounge up in her files."

"Look into that," Tee said.

LuCarolyn sighed, appearing more optimistic. "Sounds like a plan."

"Just in time. Food's here," Berrill announced.

The waiter and the server assisting him, quickly handled the task of setting out the meal. Berrill and LuCarolyn appeared ready to dive in, but hesitated when they saw their dishes. Both women exchanged dazed looks and then studied the waiter curiously.

Tee and Prin melted into waves of laughter.

~~~

Lunch was a quiet affair for the three men across the dining room, but there were no complaints or questions. Slayte, Pope and Rutger barely noticed the quiet. Actually, they didn't notice the quiet at all. Each was more focused on other more private things. It was only when the waiter arrived to ask if they'd like dessert, that it became obvious that things were off.

Pope declined, as did Rutger. Slayte gave no response at all. His attention as well as his gaze was across the room. Pope and Rutger sent the waiter off for the check and then tried calling out to their friend to get his attention. Pope eventually resorted to using the drink menu to slap Slayte across the back of his head.

"Ow!" Attention thoroughly redirected, Slayte tugged a hand through his hair and scowled. "Seriously, Po?"

"What the hell's up with you?" Rutger whispered to Slayte, scowling as well.

Slayte offered a quick shake of his head. "It's nothing." Still, he couldn't keep his eyes from shifting across the room. As he was more aware then of being observed, his gaze quickly returned to the table.

Rutger and Pope were already angling their heads to see what held the other man so transfixed.

"I'll be damned," Pope whispered.

"What?" Slayte's head snapped up and he looked in the direction he'd been staring. Darkly, he suspected that Pope too had been captured by the loveliness of his blonde.

"What?" Slayte persisted, having giving himself a mental shake to clear his mind of the word 'his'.

Pope nodded once. "That's Merc's girl."

The lone phrase was enough to have both Rutger and Slayte looking on with piqued expressions of interest. Rutger's expression sharpened suddenly, as did Pope's. They'd each spotted the women they'd spoken to on their way into the dining room. The women who had been on their minds for most of lunch.

"The one with the boy cut, she's Merc's," Pope said, his voice soft.

Slayte whistled. "She *is* a gorgeous little thing."

"Damn right," Rutger relayed his agreement in a soft, captivated tone as well. "I see why Merc doesn't have time for us now."

"Well, at least you won't have to ask him if she's got any friends. Looks like she does." Slayte added.

207

"Looks like," Pope's voice held a distracted air then.

The waiter returned with the check as instructed, but his diners didn't plan on relinquishing their seats for quite some time.

~CHAPTER 23~

After lunch, Pope, Slayte and Rutger set out for Mercuri Fleets. The administrative headquarters was located in San Francisco. The actual fleet made port in Seattle, Washington while vessels for the eastern arm docked in Charleston, South Carolina.

The ride over from the restaurant was a silent one as was the trip up to Mercuri's office suite located on the 70th floor of the sleek scraper that claimed its place like a distinctive silver lance among the other highrises. Slayte, Pope and Rutger each claimed a wall of the spacious, maple paneled car that made its ascent to the president's wing.

"Think he could get us an introduction?" Rutger asked the question currently running through his friend's minds.

"It's not too much to ask," Slayte sighed.

"He's in love with the lady," Pope confirmed with a shrug. "We should know a little about the kind of people she calls friends, right?"

"Hey, that's right," Slayte sliced the air with an index finger. "And we're Merc's friends. Watching each other's backs is what we do."

"It's the mark of a true friend," Rutger added.

Laughter rose between the threesome as the car dinged to announce its arrival on the 70th floor. Lazily, the guys pushed out of their leaning stances on the walls and filed out of the elevator to take the short, private hallway that would lead directly into Mercuri's office and allow them to bypass the main corridor. No one was in much of a mood for the usual adoration and shameless fawning over they received from so many of the women on Mercuri's staff. Utmost on their minds was putting in requests to set them on the path to knowing Etienne Shaw's friends a little better.

Introduction requests and all other frivolous matters however, fled to the far reaches of the subconscious when the guys strode into Mercuri's office. He wasn't alone.

Mercuri didn't seem to mind the interruption and sent his friends an approving look from where he stood behind the sleek blackwood counter of a wall bar that stored what appeared to be every liquor known to man. To the far right of the counter, a dispenser showed an impressive number of brews on tap.

"Good timing, guys. We had a change in schedule. Looks like we can have our meeting earlier than we planned." Mercuri gestured toward the man near his desk.

"Pope Apostolou, Rutger Eliades and Slayte Miltiades, I'd like you to meet Eduardo Roya."

Though it wasn't the introduction they'd come to discuss, Pope, Slayte and Rutger were undoubtedly intrigued as they crossed the room to shake hands with the short, slender man who looked more like the son of a mild mannered accountant than a pimp for crime bosses.

Pope stepped forward and was first to shake hands. "Mercuri told us about your father. We're all very sorry."

"He also says you believe this was no accident," Rutger was next to step in and shake hands.

The hint of a smile came to Eduardo Roya's long, dark face. "It was no accident Mr. Eliades, it was the GAN."

Pope slanted a look to Mercuri who was downing the shot of tequila he'd poured.

"That's quite an accusation," Slayte noted while shaking Roya's hand.

"Truth usually is." Roya said.

"May we ask what led you to that truth?"

Roya gave Rutger the benefit of a level stare. "Harris Van Deer and Grant Zubin killed my father. They've been running jobs for the last several months under orders from Lorne Grodins and Nathan Alberts. Jobs, as I understand, include visits to several of your friends as well."

"Where're you getting your information?"

"My apologies Mr. Apostolou, but I'd be inconveniencing my sources to say."

"So why'd you come to us with this?" Slayte asked.

Roya's smile was serene. "I believe we want the same thing."

"Revenge." Mercuri held the tequila bottle poised to refill his glass.

"I was angry about my father but this isn't just about him. None of you were to be approached until all other avenues had been explored, according to my sources. What happened to Patroclus Kostas was personal."

"So why not have your sources get you your revenge?" Rutger chose his seat in one of the big black leather wing chairs before Mercuri's desk.

Roya paced before a matching sofa as he spoke. "It wouldn't be convenient for them as close as they are to The Network, but you…" he spread his hands accommodatingly.

"We don't do business that way anymore." Pope's voice was little more than the agitated growl when he brushed past Mercuri on his way behind the bar.

"I mean no disrespect, gentlemen," Roya showed the first strains of unease as Pope's temper seared the room. "I'm sure you all realize that business can be handled without a gun if the right ammunition is used."

"None of that will bring Patch back." Following his second shot of tequila, Mercuri reclaimed the spot behind his desk.

"True words, Mr. Nikolaides but you four aren't so civilized that it wouldn't eat at you to realize his death was just a means to an end."

"To what end?"

Roya directed slow steps toward the bar where Pope had stated his question. "A whore by the name of Dorinda Patterson," he replied.

"Doesn't ring a bell." Rutger said.

"Well," Roya chose a seat on one of the wide blackwood stools at the bar. "If Kostas had used that line *before* the GAN's raid on my father's compound in Venezuela, he might've been believed, but given the way it all played…" again, he spread his hands in the same accommodating manner. "It stands to reason that you all were acquainted," he finished.

"We all?" Slayte queried.

Roya inclined his head, smiling wryly. "You did know why that raid was necessary, correct?"

"The deaths of The Ten." Mercuri reared back in the desk chair that was the same make and color as the two wingbacks it faced.

"Mmm…" Roya gave a reverent nod. "Yes, The Ten...and then you warned my father while Kostas was here in the States to complete his mission to take down Grodins and Alberts."

"The deaths of The Ten had nothing to do with what we'd planned for Grodins and Alberts."

Roya willed himself against shivering beneath the chill of Pope Apostolou's growl of a voice. "It's a shame your former employers didn't see it that way." He managed, encouraged to move on when Pope appeared to consider his words.

"They've had six years to rebuild." From his stool, Roya made eye contact with each of the men. "Six years to rebuild and to scour the pieces of that night and label you all as the common denominator," he left the barstool then to resume pacing.

"They know you've got an army of your own now. They don't want to risk riling you before they exhaust all other avenues that might lead to recovering their property."

"We don't have an army," Mercuri studied the fist he'd drawn instead of the man who'd spoken.

Amusement loomed on Roya's dark face. "Seriously, Mr. Nikolaides? Every man you gave a way out to that night, would return to your side in a heartbeat if you called him. You can believe your ex-employers are aware of that. They aren't back to full steam yet and won't risk you making that call if they can find a quieter way to get back what was taken."

"What exactly was taken?" Slayte had joined Pope behind the bar and was filling a tall mug with one of the brews on tap. He looked up in time to see the gleam in Roya's eye as the man looked upon the foam streaming the sides of the glass. Taking pity, Slayte raised the mug in offering.

"Discs," Roya smacked his lips in approval of the rich lager upon tasting it. "A bag of discs was taken from the penthouse on the night of the murders. According to my sources, there are things in that bag that can bring down a great many people."

"Merc? What?" Pope questioned the curious smile his friend sent to Roya.

Mercuri responded at first with a slow shake of his head. "I find Mr. Roya's sources very helpful. I'm just suspicious of anyone who knows that much and shares it with an outsider."

Roya responded with a mock toast of his mug. "I'm not as much of an outsider as you might think. You see once the GAN scoured all the pieces from that night, they decided Dorinda Patterson could lead them to my father and their property."

"Why would they think your father had it?" Rutger asked.

Eduardo Roya finished off his drink in one long, impressive swallow before he answered. "The group that killed The Ten was sent by him," he gave the other men the time, it took him to return his mug to the bar, to absorb the news.

"Now, in light of the way you all graciously saved his life, it stands to reason that all this was part of the same coup, right? My father didn't have the GAN's property but his mere knowledge of it and threats to share it besides, kept him alive and wealthy until those psychotics tortured and murdered him."

"How'd they find him?" Slayte leaned on the bar counter while sipping from his mug.

Roya had somewhat mellowed as he'd shared his story. The aggravations and upsets of the past few weeks-months-had been all but debilitating. The opportunity to talk it through, albeit with a fierce looking group of strangers, relieved a great deal of his burden. He leaned on the bar, hands disappeared in the deep pockets of his olive green trousers.

"Dorinda Patterson was a good earner for my father. More than that, she'd been loyal and my father considered loyalty a top commodity. She had no idea that he'd already began proceedings to have the deed to her house transferred to her name. Then he learned of her death… I was already scheduled to travel to Las Vegas to meet with her employees and discuss the property remaining for their use but- there was the news of my father."

Folding his arms over a thin chest, Roya stiffened against the bar. "Dorinda Patterson could have led them right to those discs when

213

they came for her. Chances were slim, but it just may've saved her life. Instead, she sent the bastards halfway around the world to my father."

Slayte waved faintly. "I don't see how that proved her loyalty to him."

"It was what they'd agreed to," Roya explained. "In my father's opinion, nothing was more important than those discs. His knowledge of them put him on level with the elite. Gave he and his family credibility, respectability- grudgingly yes, but Papa wasn't choosy.

That information back in the hands of the GAN was something he never wanted. He despised himself for having them as customers but they paid well and Pop never really saw any of the girls as people. Not until those four. If there was ever a chance that the discs' security was jeopardized, he and Dorinda Patterson were never to give up those discs or the girls. According to my father, Patterson never knew of the discs. He only told her he wanted the girls protected at all costs. Ms. Patterson gave those snakes-Harris and Zubin, the number to my father's portable landline. It was her only way of contacting him. My father gave it to all his top level employees. He didn't trust cellphones."

Roya rubbed the bridge of his nose where tension had formed. "Son of a bitch," the sighed phrase held a sad affection. "His paranoia got him in trouble anyway. The landline is contained inside a tiny box that can be transported from place to place. The type of line my father owned allowed people to call him and never really know where he was-the way it works with a cell phone only...not. The line could be programmed to give whatever location my father chose."

"Unless they've got the kind of technology to track it," Rutger shared. "The GAN could easily access technology like that."

Roya nodded his agreement. "We think Harris and Zubin didn't find him sooner because the box wasn't being used while in transit as Papa relocated. Most likely their early scans failed. They must've utilized that technology and re-scanned to get the hit in Australia and killed Patterson right after she gave over the number to make sure she didn't warn him."

Slayte snorted. "They'd have killed her anyway."

Roya nodded. "The fact that she'd gone to Papa with all this earned her a lot of points in his book. She and those girls could've profited obscenely from those recordings. Of course, my father knew she called him primarily out of fear and panic, but over the years she's proved how well she can keep a-"

214

"Hold on a minute," Rutger gave up his seat for a perch on the desk instead. "Are you telling us that The Ten were killed by hookers?"

"Well I-" Roya gave the men a curious frown. "I assumed you'd heard the story."

"We did," Slayte's grin served to sharpen his to-die-for features. "Hell, we thought those clowns were killed by professionals not *actual*...professionals."

Laughter rumbled between Slayte and Rutger. Mercuri and Pope couldn't resist grinning. Even Eduardo Roya's mouth twitched on the cusp of a smile.

"Sorry," Slayte lifted a hand, "it's just hard to believe hookers slaughtered ten men that way."

"It *is* sort of poetic justice," Mercuri's expression had made the shift back to grim.

Roya noticed a similar effect take place on the faces of the other men. Feeling more subdued then as well, he rubbed the tips of his fingers into suddenly tired eyes.

"From what I understand, those girls weren't hookers any more than we are. Papa said they were just four girls who got in over their heads. They wouldn't give up what they'd taken from that room, though. My father said when he met them he knew they'd probably never let any of it see daylight. They were just four girls scared out of their minds and alone but for each other," Roya relaxed back on the long sofa near the main office door.

"Papa tried to buy them off anyway, though. Told them he could give them enough money to disappear forever. They wouldn't go for it and, scared as they were, my dad was still smart enough not to push his luck with four women who'd just massacred ten men. But what they'd taken...it was gold. He viewed the discs and knew he could live the rest of his life in splendor off blackmail. The girls even got their hands on the security feeds- talk about gold." Roya threw back his head to express short, gleeful laughter.

"That footage showed everyone in or out of the place that night- not just The Ten but a number of big names who would have had a hard time explaining why they were socializing together."

"But the bastards are dead now."

"Legacies live on, Mr. Eliades. No one wanted what was on those discs to come out. The fact that those men would've even been

215

seen together socializing would've been enough to put their companies and, for several, their social standings in serious jeopardy."

"So if the girls weren't givin' up the goods, what'd your dad do?"

"He did what anyone with money would do, Mr. Apostolou, he threw money at it. Gave the girls enough to live on and exceptionally well. He counted on them squandering it, of course. No matter how smart they were, he'd seen enough young women to know that a taste of comfortable living would have them locked into him forever. He even told them to come back if they were ever in need of anything. He was confident the next visit would result in him gaining possession of those recordings before more funds were dispersed."

"But that didn't happen," Mercuri delivered the declaration from behind his desk.

Roya's nod was solemn, but amusement triggered his smile. "Women don't often surprise my father, but those four did. Instead of squandering the money, they grew it. From what I understand they're *still* growing it."

"Why didn't your dad just send someone after them to take it by force?" Pope rounded the bar to take one of the stools.

"I asked him," Roya shrugged. "I found out he rather admired them. They'd changed the rules of the game as cool as you please-brought down ten of the most powerful men in the world and no one ever saw them coming. My father never saw those recordings again after that first time, but he lived like a king because of them."

"You're right," Roya added, looking to Mercuri then, "I did come here for revenge. I believed it was something you'd want too, considering what was done to your friend. Beyond that," leaning forward on the sofa, he shrugged. "I can't believe it sits right with you knowing the GAN is trying to revitalize itself. You better than anyone know what they are. You know if those girls hadn't killed The Ten they would've been the ones slaughtered. It's what those… theme parties of theirs were for after all." His smile held a sardonic edge.

"Yeah, my father told me those stories too." Roya had noticed the way each man bristled over the mention. "Ask yourselves if it would be worth it to step back into this if it meant bringing them down with no chance of resurgence and in a way that wouldn't require bloodshed."

"Hmph. Spoken like a man who's never shed blood," Rutger mused.

Roya spread his hands, once again displaying the accommodating gesture. "I believe if you had those recordings- had them, used them, destroyed the GAN, and everyone associated with them, shedding blood would become irrelevant."

"You've led a very protected life, Mr. Roya. We're envious, aren't we fellas? I could almost kick you I'm so envious," Slayte's violet stare was as flat as his voice.

"In situations like this, bloodshed is always relevant." Pope's grin held its wolf-like potency. "Having those recordings, using them, won't suddenly make it irrelevant. There *will be* a desire for revenge. Whether for the events of that night six years ago or for the sheer audacity of returning to add insult to injury- it doesn't matter. Knowing you've felled your adversary is all that matters. That kind of single mindedness, it changes you. It strips away something vital- the thing that makes you civilized." Pope pushed out of the stool as though he'd suddenly found sitting to be detestable.

"My friends and I have had six years to find the civilized part of who we are and we're still works in progress. Our friend is dead and that's gonna claw at us for a long time- maybe forever. If there was a way we could save him, we'd be back on the inside in a heartbeat. You wouldn't have to be here trying to sell us on the job. As it stands, we can't save him and that would be the only reason...*relevant* enough for us to dive back into this madness." Apology shone in Pope's marine colored eyes. "You'll have to find another way to your revenge. We're sorry."

Roya nodded, but his overall demeanor didn't come off as solemn as the gesture indicated. "My father said you were good men. I see it's true. Your outlook is disappointing but I understand it. You were my best hope for making Van Deer and Zubin pay for what they did. Fortunately, revenge isn't the only way I can honor my father. He wanted those girls protected and the least I can do is work to uphold his wishes. If I can't encourage them to give over the discs, I can do my damndest to convince them to take the protection I can provide. Granted, you can't get much safer than a gun ranch, *but*," a quick, honest smile flashed across his mouth, "the least I can do is try."

With a refreshed sigh, Eduardo Roya straightened to his full 5'9. "Mr. Nikolaides I hope that I can trouble you for the use of the car that picked me up from the hotel."

"It's no trouble at all." Mercuri was standing from his desk chair. "I'll call down and have them assign you a driver for the duration of your stay."

"I'll be leaving day after tomorrow," Roya stepped forward, his hand extended for shaking. "It was good to meet you all finally."

"Sorry it had to be under these circumstances." Pope was first to shake the man's hand.

"As am I," Roya grinned. "Next time we'll have to make it a nicer visit. My father has properties that span the globe. When's the last time any of you had a vacation?" He asked and received roaring laughter in response.

"Fifty percent of our group have no trouble living lives of leisure." Slayte shared with sly confidence.

Pope was already shaking his head. "That's because the other fifty is busy working to make sure the leisurely fifty maintain their style of living."

There was more laughter and then Roya was reaching out to clasp hands with Mercuri.

"Thank you for what you did for my father."

Mercuri nodded. He gave Roya's hand a squeeze, but didn't let go when the man would have stepped back.

"Mr. Nikolaides?" Roya smiled curiously.

Mercuri's expression was like stone. "What did you mean, Roya? 'Safer than a gun ranch'?"

~CHAPTER 24~

The evening was cool, but a pleasant one weather wise. Tee left the front door swinging in her wake when she arrived home. It wasn't because the weather was so inviting, however, rather a testament to how brain dead she was.

Almost totally wiped, she kicked off her shoes and tossed her tote bag somewhere in the vicinity of the living room as she trudged toward the kitchen for sustenance. Her lunchtime meal of tomato bisque and Caesar salad had worn off long ago. What remained of her day, had consisted of proofing design analysis plans, timelines and budget proposals for the four potential projects her firm currently had under consideration.

Tee was certain her team could handle all the jobs without issue. Deciding where to fit them on the calendar was where the headache started to come in. Design analyses, timelines and budgets all required close scrutiny if the best decision was to be reached.

She'd worked through late afternoon into evening even as her eyes crossed over all the data that passed over her desk. When she began to zone out and snap at everyone who knocked on her office door, she decided it was time to call it a day- or night-as it were. It was approaching 9pm when she dragged herself into her apartment.

She'd put in late nights before, ones that surpassed the 9pm mark by four hours or more. That day had been different, she knew. Her exhaustion was a result of the draining conversation with her friends over a past she feared they would never outrun.

Unlike prior conversations, this one dealt with imminent factors that would bring the past back to their doorsteps on a vicious wave. They would have to reveal what was on those discs. Tee had already accepted that as a certainty. Threats would be unacceptable then- it would have to be all or nothing.

Nothing. The word was a relentless loop inside her head. She couldn't help but acknowledge the other word on loop-Mercuri. Once those discs were revealed 'nothing' would exist between them. She couldn't let herself entertain the possibility that none of it would matter to him. She had taken part in the brutal murders of ten men. She would be seriously concerned if such a thing *didn't* matter to him.

She made it as far as the breakfast nook where she gave in to the demands of her tired legs and pulled herself onto one of the cushioned high backed stools dotting the counter.

Mercuri found her there with her head down ten minutes later. Somehow, he tapered off the quick slam of frustration that bolted through him in response to her carelessness. Kicking the front door shut, he went and retrieved her from the stool. He put her on the sofa instead of taking her to her room. The visit would be hard enough without having to have it near a bed.

Tee was shifting on the sofa within minutes of having been set down. Frowning over her change in location, she made the slow push to sit and blinked dazedly to get her bearings. When her vision focused and fixed on Mercuri at the stove, she gave a start.

"Stay where I put you, Tee." He didn't turn to give her the benefit of eye contact. "I found you asleep at the counter with the front door wide open."

Any budding desire she may've had to argue, made way then for mortification. Slumping back into the sofa, she rested her head on one of the plump, dark pillows there and let the sounds of Mercuri working in the kitchen coax her into some semblance of relaxation.

It didn't take long for the water to boil and soon the fragrance of steeping tea drifted into the living room. She smiled, upon recognizing the aroma but didn't open her eyes.

"I usually drink that kind in the mornings," she said.

"You need it now. We need to talk."

Inner warning shimmered and Tee sent him a curious look. She tried to gauge his mood by observing his stance. His broad back and powerful shoulders were straight as ever beneath the worsted fabric of his charcoal gray suitcoat. Even when he removed his coat and rolled the sleeves above his forearms, he gave off no clues. She'd have to wait until he turned to more accurately assess his attitude.

When Mercuri approached her with the mug of tea in hand, she found that his expression offered no more clues to his temper than his posture had.

"Tea for Tee," he said in observance of the elegant scrawling across the stout, glazed burgundy cup.

Shaking her head over the common joke, she accepted the mug with both hands. "My friends and their senses of humor."

Mercuri watched her inhale the contents before taking a slow, careful sip. His face remained impassive even when she smiled in approval of the brew. "Your friends know you well," he said.

"Better than anyone."

"So do mine. They're all I've got. All I ever thought I'd need."

Tee enjoyed the gentle glide of the brew coursing its way through her body. Patiently, she waited for the punch of caffeine and the energizing effects she knew she'd need if she hoped to get him to listen to her that night.

She was working to bolster her confidence to begin, when he suddenly relieved her of the cup, scooped her into his arms and settled them both to the sofa. Great, she kept her musing silent. How do you break up with a guy when he's got you on his lap? She wondered.

"Mercuri-"

"I'm in love with you, Tee."

She tried to close her mouth, but it was set on hanging open.

"I wanted to tell you over the weekend. Kept losing my nerve," he brought his knee-weakening gaze to her face. "I'm in love with you."

"Mercuri you-you can't."

"But I am."

"I'm not for you."

221

"You're all for me."

His simple response almost robbed her of more words. Almost. "It won't work. There're things you don't know-"

He propped an index finger beneath her chin, bringing an effective end to her tirade. "I know more than you think."

He was kissing her then and Tee could virtually feel her mind emptying of its doubts and fears. They were replaced by the intoxicating sensations that he alone could deliver.

Effortlessly, he set her neatly astride his lap. The flowing cotton of her powder blue dress slipped seductively from her thighs as her knees settled to either side of his hips. Tentatively, she stroked his chiseled cheekbones and the potent angle of his jaw. Their tongues tangled, dueled, retreated in a dance that was at times languid and probing or heated and desperate. The steamy advance and retreat of his tongue as it slid back and forth against hers, provided a sensational friction. The act coaxed movement from her hips and slowly she worked herself over the stiff ridge taking shape along his thigh. Soft, satisfied grunts proceeded the flex of his hands at her waist as he took charge of her movements.

"Mercuri-"

"Later."

She wanted to listen. How she wanted to listen. His kissable lips were nibbling their way along her jaw. He paused to treat her earlobe to a wet, hungry suckle before moving on, down the line of her neck. His tongue infrequently bathed her skin on the way to continuing his nibbling along her collarbone. He didn't ignore her breasts for long, their persistent heaving as her breathing raced, soon had him burying his devastating face in the deep valley and inhaling to his content.

Easing his hold at her hips, Mercuri indulged in the feel of her full bottom filling his palms. Every squeeze set her even more securely against the erection straining savagely beneath his zipper. He was smoothing back her dress hem, fingers roaming her thighs and curving around the seam of her panties, when Tee unexpectedly pushed out of his embrace.

"I can't see you anymore," she said when he looked ready to follow her to where she'd scooted to the other end of the couch. She saw the disbelief and hurt shift into place across his fierce features seconds before she pushed to her feet.

"It's all too fast Mercuri," she kept her back to him, "if you take a minute and think about it, you'd agree. There's a lot we don't know about each other."

"So tell me then."

She turned, disbelief taking charge of her face. "People... they...need time to learn about each other before they go around thinking they're in love."

Mercuri somehow managed to exude an intangible alertness even as he relaxed on the sofa. "What things do you think I need to learn, Tee?"

"All kinds-"

"Like?" He inclined his head just slightly then. "Is this racial?" he asked.

"What?" She gaped.

"Honest question," he leaned forward, grabbing the mug and helping himself to a sip of her tea. He grimaced over the taste. "What?" He looked up as though surprised to find her speechless and staring. "Was I just an experiment for you?"

"That's crazy."

"Is it? You wouldn't be concerned over what all your exes may say if they saw you on my arm?"

"Stop." She knew he was goading her and sent him a murderous glower. "Why are you making this so difficult?"

"The woman I'm in love with is telling me she can't see me anymore. Makes sense I'd want to know why."

"I've told you why."

"'All kinds of things', is no answer."

"It's the best I've got."

"It's a lie though, isn't it? There's really only one reason, isn't there?" He made himself stay rooted to the sofa when she turned her back again.

"One reason- a thousand. It doesn't matter. We can't continue this, Mercuri. It's not personal. I just-"

"Not personal?" He was behind her then-swiftly-suddenly. He made her face him and leaned down to put his face on level with hers. "I just told you I love you. You say you can't see me again and that's not personal?"

"I'm sorry," she could feel the unmistakable pressure of tears behind her eyes.

223

He muttered an obscenity and shook his head. "I don't want your apologies. I want the truth."

"Alright," her voice broke on the admission. "It is...one thing."

"Which is? Tee?" His hands went firm on her arms when she thinned her lips and stubbornly refused to answer.

"Mercuri don't, I-" her eyes were damp, "I can't-"

"You will."

"Just stop!" She shoved at his chest, anger funneling beneath helplessness when he didn't so much as budge beneath the contact. "What do you want me to tell you?"

"Goddammit," head bowed, his jaw clenched, not as much from anger as impatience. Reigning in emotion, he massaged her arms and forced his eyes to remain on hers.

"I want you to tell me about the night with The Ten."

Like something supernatural, her demeanor morphed from outrage to control. Mercuri found it quite fascinating to watch, but in that moment there was too much requiring his attention to spend time being dazzled. She was rigid in his arms. Had he not been holding her, he'd have wondered if she was breathing. Her eyes though, the brilliant dark orbs sparkled with questions he could easily decipher.

"My friends and I knew Enrique Roya. We just talked to his son. Roya's dead. His son told us that too." Mercuri saw the slightest fissure in her control as she took the hit his news delivered.

"The same people who killed Roya, killed Dorinda Patterson. Roya's son says she was the one who introduced you and your friends to his father."

Hearing Mercuri say Dorinda's name took away whatever strength that had surged into Tee's legs during her earlier outburst. His hold had eased on her shoulders and she moved to one of the armchairs in the living room. Folding herself into the chair, she locked her arms around her middle.

"Did you know her?" The question was barely a whisper.

"No," Mercuri kept his response nearly as soft. "Roya's son told us about her." He watched her absorb the news like a blow. She pressed the back of her hand to her mouth as though she was going to be sick. He could tell that it cost her.

Tee bit down the bile she could taste at the back of her throat. "How do you know Roya?" She asked.

"I helped save his life once."

She only nodded at first. "Mercuri you should go." She stated the words like a declaration after she was quiet for a long time.

He went to her then, kneeling next to the chair but not touching. "Roya says he wants to offer you and your friends' protection."

The idea made Tee smile. "His father obviously didn't tell him me and my friends know how to protect ourselves."

"He knew that. You and your friends did something a lot of people have been wanting to do for a long time."

She shuddered, averting her face. "We weren't trying to be heroes."

"I know that, Babe," he took her hand then and squeezed.

"No," smiling miserably she eased her hand free when his hold loosened. "No you don't. If you did, you wouldn't be here with tender words and you certainly wouldn't be telling me you love me. Mercuri please? I need you to go-" she began to shake her head when his hand latched onto hers and he squeezed.

He felt her tug out of reflex, but there was no escaping his hand on hers. He could've forced the issue, pressed his considerable advantage and refused to leave. Arrogance assured him there wouldn't have been a damn thing she could've done to stop him from staying. Love and consideration of her feelings though...they had him seeing how she was suffering. He wanted to give her whatever she thought she needed for it to ease. If that meant leaving her be, he could. He could give her that.

Once he had wondered whether he'd be able to let her go when the time came. It had come- all ugly and snarling and staking its place between them. Alongside arrogance, love and consideration however, there was more. There was certainty. Certainty that if he left her, that would be it. She'd never come to him, not after this.

Perhaps, if she had no idea that he knew the truth, she'd have been able to accept his declaration of love- content that he would never be the wiser. That couldn't have happened, he knew. She wouldn't have been able to live with herself if she thought she was deceiving him. How could she possibly *not* believe that he was in love with her? He could've laughed over the absurdity of her doubting that.

For him though, laughter would be a long time coming. He'd fallen in love with a poised, intelligent woman whose control had bewitched him almost as completely as her loveliness. And she expected him to just walk away?

"Mercuri please go."

225

It was as if her subconscious had picked up on his unspoken query. Drawing on the restraint he didn't know he had, he resolved himself to believing she would come to him. He could give her time to deal with the devastation he'd brought to her door that night.

He had to believe that once she'd processed it all, she would come to him. He had to believe that. It was the only way he'd make it out of the door.

Giving her hand one last squeeze, Mercuri pushed to stand and then he knelt again. He pulled her into a hard, fast kiss that crushed her mouth to his. He followed with a second hard, fast kiss to the top of her head. Determined then, he stood and went to the kitchen for his jacket where he'd tossed it over the counter.

He left without looking back. Not even when the soft sound of her weeping touched his ears.

PART III

"I fear all we have done is to awaken a sleeping giant and fill him with a terrible resolve."

-Said by Admiral Isoroku Yamamoto (So Yamamura) in the film "Tora! Tora! Tora!"

~CHAPTER 25~

Memphis, Tennessee~ 2 weeks later

The Marshall Club catered to a specific clientele. Membership or invitation by a member was required for entry. Use of the club's more exclusive facilities however such as its suites, private drink and dining rooms and spa areas, were only offered to members and a member was required to be present for guests to be granted access to the exclusive offerings.

      The Marshall didn't ban women, but the subtle messages regarding the club's philosophy on female members was strong enough to discourage the opposite sex from wanting to step foot inside… unless they were being paid to.

      It was a place that catered to men, their tastes and interests. The furnishings of buttery black leather were understated, tasteful and sat upon carpets the color of rich moss. Murals depicting epic medieval battles in addition to masks, helmets and shields adorned the glossy paneled walls and maintained reverent positioning in polished glass cases that stood upon stone pedestals. Medieval weaponry was also proudly displayed as many of the pieces were on loan from members who were avid collectors.

Brody Alberts and Jake Grodins had done nothing to earn their admittance. Legacy spoke volumes. The Alberts and Grodins names had their places upon the membership rosters since the club's inception. Blood rite had secured Brody's and Jake's places and they didn't mind giving the lessers among them a taste of how the other half lived. Especially when they-in their own subtle ways-were trying to make a statement and remind the lessers who was in charge.

"Could this be any bigger of a clusterfuck?" Jake threw back his fourth shot of whiskey and palmed the bottle with a loving touch.

"Given the track record we're laying I'd say that's a big 'hell yeah'." Brody concurred.

Jake raised his shot glass in toast. "Knew it wouldn't be a walk in the park, but this is ridiculous."

"Tell me about it!" Brody's laughter was fueled by harsh amusement. "I knew when the old men said they were putting their *best* on this, that it wouldn't be us. In our father's eyes putting us on it would've loused the mission up all to be damned...Wonder what they're sayin' now? Now that their... specimens have fallen flat on their perfect asses."

Zubin vaulted to his feet. He and Harris were making a statement of their own and had chosen their spots on the other side of the pool table in the wide lounge room. The space was soft lit by stout lamps on round, clawfoot tables of untreated maple. Such outings were nothing new to them. They had lived, worked, bled for the other half all their lives. They knew better than most when they were being put in their places.

"I got no time for your dickin' around, Brody. You got somethin' to say, say it," Zubin all but snarled.

"The situation's pretty obvious, Zoo," again Jake raised the whiskey glass in mock toast. "We're here. Our property isn't. I think that about sums it up."

"Plus the fact that we lost all leads to the property." Brody mimicked Jake's toast with his beer mug.

Zubin muttered something foul and began to pace.

"We haven't lost *all* leads," Harris informed his colleagues. "Some are just better hidden than others." He waited until he had the attention of every man in the room, including Zubin's. Intently, he studied the other men who had been summoned to watch Brody and Jake play their game of heir-apparent.

"You two were the first, last and only to see those women that night. What can you tell us about them?"

Luke Robb remained unruffled beneath Harris Van Deer's cool, probing stare. He'd told this story more times than he'd given his own name. It hadn't changed, but everyone knew how smart Van Deer was. The man could sniff out a lead from the slightest info if he heard or saw it enough. It was quite a talent and one Luke hadn't seen since the likes of Mercuri Nikolaides. Mercuri, Luke recalled, hadn't required as many replays as Harris.

"We picked up the girls from Dorinda Patterson's," Luke began on a sigh. "We didn't frisk them, sensors in the car would've picked up anything they may've been carrying-"

"Luke, Luke," Harris waved for silence, "What I meant was for you to describe them."

Luke could all but feel Caleb Stein's tension radiating in hot waves across the table they shared. Still, this was also part of the story he and his partner had told many times before. Though they had done everything to keep the girls' identities protected, there was always the chance they'd been noticed.

Four women who looked the way they did were always bound to draw attention. Therefore, he and Caleb had decided to be forthright in their descriptions. A good thing too, as a server who had delivered drinks that night had been questioned. The man had delivered a description that had corroborated Luke's and Caleb's recollections. Every good lie required some presence of truth, they'd decided.

"There were four of them," Luke began. "They were all black but different-different...shades. You know how they...look different."

Harris gave a conciliatory nod. "Yes, yes gotta love black girls, so devastating, so many different flavors- never a dull moment. What else?"

"One was tiny-short, but curvy, really built. So were the others," Luke qualified, "but they were way taller. Like Amazons-one had really light skin with blue eyes and blonde hair even. I remember that night... someone said they um- they couldn't wait to see if the blonde was a natural. They were all lookers." *And all too sweet to be there*, he tacked on silently.

"Tiny and built, huh?" Harris stroked the goatee fuzzed about his chin. "Sounds like the kind of woman preferred by a guy we all know and loathe. Gentlemen, I'd say we've exhausted all other avenues at our disposal. The time has finally come to pay a visit to an old friend."

***

It was a usual occurrence for Moira Kent to be found on the work floor on a Friday afternoon. Visitors were few and far between in the mornings, virtually non-existent by the afternoon and Moira adored her time to socialize.

What wasn't usual, was for Moira to leave the main floor reception area to provide visitors with a personal escort. When she arrived on the work floor that afternoon, no one questioned the woman or blamed her for the sudden change in protocol. No one could argue the fact that visitors like the ones she escorted that afternoon, were entitled to every aspect of the eShaw personal touch.

~~~

Friday afternoon found Tee hunched over her desk, elbows planted on the surface. Her short, clear-polished nails were dug into her temples as if that would do something to help her maintain focus. Her ability to concentrate had been in a state of consistent decline for the last week and a half.

During the last few days, it had become a joke. She hadn't even been able to focus on any of the complex discussions she'd had to endure among her friends over that time. For Tee, it had become impossible to take part in contributing to suggestions to ease their current unrest. She'd told them what had happened between her and Mercuri and had been grateful for their understanding.

Tee shook her head then to prevent thoughts of Mercuri from taking root- taking any *more* root than they already had. Working-*trying* to work- was the only thing that brought her any reprieve. Unfortunately, the charts and graphs she'd struggled through that day, weren't making the reprieve anything to boast about. The fierce pounding behind her eyes had become such a constant, she barely noticed it there now. Regardless, she didn't want to end the day with nothing accomplished.

Out of desperation, she dialed out to Vera in hopes of organizing an impromptu meeting. A get together with staff, who'd worked up the data, would be her best bet if she hoped to make sense of it all. They

<center>231</center>

were at full staff that Friday, given the work required when new projects were being considered.

"Vera?" Tee called out through her open office door when her assistant didn't answer. After waiting a beat, she pushed back from her desk and headed out.

Were the three men standing in the middle of her work floor not such a formidable looking bunch, they may have gone unnoticed given the way her staff had clustered around them like vines.

The three apparently had no qualms about being descended on by an office full of women. They chatted enthusiastically and graced the women with killer smiles. When one of them looked directly at her, Tee felt her heart lurch in a manner she was certain had to be normal for anyone- any woman- lucky enough to draw the attention of such a man.

Blinking suddenly, she realized she'd seen him before.

Vera was next to look Tee's way. Sending her boss a dazzling smile, she curved a hand over the jaw-dropping bicep of the visitor and began to lead him away from the group. The visitor's two, equally jaw-dropping associates, followed.

"Etienne, these gentlemen would like a moment," Vera's sauntering gait and the saucy look in her luminous gaze belied the formal tone she used.

The familiar visitor was already taking Tee's hand in a polite yet smothering hold. "Ms. Shaw, we've never been formally introduced. I'm Pope Apostolou; I'm a friend of Mercuri's."

The Aspen party she recalled once she'd endured the queasy wave that jolted through her stomach at the sound of Mercuri's name. She managed a nod and was thankful her smile proved easier to manage.

"Steve and Denise Brassells' party," she said.

"And you're the modifier," Pope smiled his approval of Tee's laughter before he turned to the men accompanying him.

"Slayte Miltiades and Rutger Eliades, also friends of Mercuri's."

"Ms. Shaw," Slayte moved in first to shake hands.

"It's good to meet you, Ms. Shaw," Rutger said when he moved close.

"Please call me Tee."

"Tee we apologize for dropping by unannounced but we hope you might spare us a minute."

Again, she felt the queasy wave work its way through her stomach. Pope hadn't spoken Mercuri's name that time, though the visit evidently concerned him. "Can we um, get you anything first?" She asked.

"Of course," Vera chimed in on the suggestion, "we were about to send out for lunch."

"Oh we don't want to impose-"

"Nonsense," Vera steamrolled Pope's response, "no imposition at all. We're doing Chinese fellas, what'll it be?"

As Vera was a hard woman to dissuade, the guys accepted the hospitality and made their requests. Once the matter was settled, Tee led them into her office. Behind closed doors, she let her concern show.

"Is he alright?" She asked.

Pope stepped close to take her hands, once again smothering them inside his own. "He's not in a good way."

Her eyes began to mist and she appeared to be on the verge of crumpling. Hands still covering hers, Pope led Tee to one of the chairs in the office living area. He took the end of the sofa nearest the chair.

Concerned as well, Slayte opted for a post directly before Tee on the sturdy coffee table. "Jeez... you're just as miserable as Merc is."

Rutger had gone to the bar and returned with a glass of water. He squeezed Tee's shoulder when she thanked him and he took a seat next to Pope on the sofa.

"I'm sorry," she blurted after drinking deeply from the glass. "I never meant to hurt him I- he didn't deserve that but there wasn't another way."

"Why would you say that, darlin'?" Slayte squeezed her hand once he'd relieved Tee of the glass.

"He said you all talked to Enrique Roya's son."

Pope nodded. "That's right, Tee."

She shook her head as if bewildered. "Then you know what I did, why I was there- what Dorinda Patterson was. What man could stomach a woman after that?"

"Tee we aren't here to pass judgement," Rutger leaned forward on the sofa when he chimed in. "We're the last folks in a position to do that. We can only tell you our friend loves you. He loves you in spite of what you think he should be disgusted by."

"He'll get over it," Tee sighed, looking down into her lap.

"Beggin' your pardon, Tee, but we'd have to disagree," Slayte sent a look to his friends before looking back at the small woman. "Mercuri has never told a woman he loves her. We've known each other all our lives- that was like a cardinal sin for us. 'Scuse us for sayin' but we don't expect him to get over you that easy."

"No one should have to deal with that sort of baggage," she muttered and looked to Rutger when he spoke.

"I don't know what it's like to be in love, Tee, but I'd guess that'd make baggage not so much of a burden- not when you're bearing it for the one you love."

"But he didn't deserve that," her dark eyes shone with pleading tears then.

"Tee, let me ask you something," Pope squeezed the hand he'd kept hold of since he and Tee had taken their seats. "Do you think ending things is going to magically have him shirking off this burden you think you're saddling him with? He's making himself sick over it."

"How? What's wrong with him?" Concern overshadowed her misery then.

"Well, for one, he's not sleeping," Slayte gave a defeated shrug, "not unless he drifts off for a few minutes during his marathon gaming sessions."

"He isn't eating much either," Pope added, "unless you count the junk he's been shoveling into his system between his gaming sessions."

"And he's scratched going to work, off his 'to do' list," Rutger shared, "Gaming sessions are taking precedence over that too."

"Luckily, the company runs like clockwork without him, but he'll snap soon Tee," Pope cautioned, squeezing her hand with a bit more insistence. "We've seen that happen before and we're here hoping you can stop it."

"You don't know what you're asking. What kind of woman I am-"

"Tee-"

"No Pope. You don't know what I did. Roya's son doesn't even know- not really. His father was the only one who saw it-saw what was recorded on those discs. What I did that night, if you'd...*seen* it... you wouldn't be here trying to encourage this between Mercuri and me."

"Well that's a shame Tee," Rutger relaxed back on his place on the sofa and stretched his long legs before him. "Since that's what we're here for. I guess we're all in for a very lively lunch."

~~~

Lunch was both lively and hearty. The conversation had turned progressively lighter due in part of Tee's doting staff. The 'doting' was of course reserved for the guests. Pope, Slayte and Rutger seemed quite appreciative to the glee of all.

"How did Mercuri find out about this?" Tee was asking once she and her guests were camped out in her office where they finished off the last of the shrimp lo mein and eggrolls. Tee sat behind her desk with the guys camped out around it.

"We never did give our real names to Enrique Roya," silently Tee mused that if a person gave out over a million dollars in seed money, it stood to reason that he'd damn well know who he was giving it to.

"Mercuri's mind is a fascinating place, Tee," Rutger marveled while breaking his last egg roll in half. "He figured it out before Roya Junior gave up your names. He was talking about offering you and your friends protection-saying he couldn't imagine anywhere safer than a gun ranch," he shrugged, spoke around the corner of egg roll he'd shoved into his mouth. "Apparently, Merc remembered something about one of your friends."

"Bear," Tee smiled at the blank looks sent her way by the devastating trio at her desk. "My friend Berrill Clayton owns a gun ranch in Burlingame."

Rutger straightened, the rest of the egg roll forgotten. "Not...Bear Arms?" He asked.

"Here we go," Slayte groaned and proceeded to finish off the rest of his lo Mein with gusto.

"That's right," Tee smiled while confirming the guess.

"Rutger's a hunting fanatic," Pope explained, "he's been suggesting-"

"And not lightly," Slayte interjected.

"A guy's weekend out there," Pope continued.

"Since the rest of us despise hunting," Slayte shuddered, slanting Tee a wink when she laughed, "his suggestions have fallen on deaf ears."

Again, Tee laughed as she watched Rutger who had happily returned to finishing his lunch. She enjoyed his easy acceptance of the good-natured ribbing. Mercuri was lucky to have them, she thought. The fierce, dangerous element that followed them like fine mist, didn't just pertain to their looks. She sensed it in their loyalty to Mercuri, knowing that without question, they would put themselves between him and anything that threatened him.

"Bear's place isn't just for hunters," Tee set aside her leftovers, "but for people in law enforcement who want to keep their marksmanship skills sharp in an environment that goes beyond their own training facilities. Even civilians who just have a love for guns enjoy the place. Her annual shooting soirees attract thousands, but are limited to about a hundred people. It's quite a place. I'm sure she'd be happy to set up a tour. She's always looking for new clientele."

"Is she uh, the blonde one?" Slayte quickly cleared his throat following the query. "Pope recognized you at lunch in The Rascal a few weeks ago with three other women," he explained.

Tee was already nodding in recollection of the date. "That'd be my friend Prin. Prin Holland."

"Prin Holland." Slayte quietly repeated the name.

"So Berrill owns the ranch?" Pope asked.

Again, Tee nodded. "LuCarolyn Young, my other friend, she's a film exec in L.A."

Rutger smiled, recalling the very interesting conversation he'd overheard between the woman and her colleagues.

"So is Prin short for Princess?" Slayte was asking.

"It is," Tee added a sly smile. "But you'd be putting your health at serious risk if you dare to call her that."

"If you ever meet her, *please* dare to call her that," Rutger urged his friend.

Tee laughed, recognizing how much she'd miss the gesture. Still, the men hadn't stopped by on a laughing matter.

"I'm sorry," her composure had returned.

Slayte was already waving off the apology. "Please don't, Tee. If Mercuri knew we'd come here and upset you, he'd kill us."

"Go see him, Tee," Pope's easily persuasive manner held an almost hypnotic intensity. "You're both miserable. Talking might get you past it- not in order to get back together or anything, but just to explain things, you know?"

"I do and you're right."

"Well then," as though he were satisfied by where the conversation had led them, Pope pushed to his feet. "Thanks for lunch. We'll let you get back to work."

Tee rounded her desk, intending to shake hands and found herself happily surprised when each of the towering three dropped a kiss to her cheek.

Pope was last to give his kiss and he put a key in Tee's hand when he straightened before her. "To Merc's place," he explained.

"Pope-no, I-"

"Stop." He simply folded her fingers down over her palm. "You know, some would call me a know it all."

"Amen," Rutger and Slayte called in unison from where they stood near the office door.

Pope's mouth twitched, but he continued smoothly. "I've got a strong feeling that you're about to be the lady of that fortress Merc calls a house. I'm just getting the jump on giving you what's yours." With that, he squeezed her hand, released it. "We'll see you soon."

When the office door closed behind her unexpected guests, Tee opened her hand and studied the key.

***

Blaring guitar riffs spiked up from the lower level of Mercuri's home. The entire basement floor of the space had been dedicated to an expansive gym/rec area that a man could disappear into for weeks on end and never have to surface. It was where one could find Mercuri if one had the desire or the courage to go looking for him.

The stirring riffs either drowned the clash of weights or the slaps of wrapped hands to the heavy bags along with the tell-tale grunts and quiet roars that accompanied every punch or lift. Only Mercuri knew that the grunts and roars weren't only a side effect of his workout.

He'd spent all of two days believing the bullshit he'd told himself about giving Tee time to come to him. As far as she was concerned, they were done, he guessed. The only thing worse than that was that he'd let her make the decision for both of them and without argument.

The electrifying guitar chords were all of a sudden nerve wracking instead of inspiring and he shut down the vintage Metallica piece.

He had walked away. That was the part that had him beating his punching bags to shit and lifting weights until his sweat poured and glistened like oil. He'd done nothing except to walk away. Walking away from a challenge was not what he did. Though he'd have to be the first to admit the Mercuri Nikolaides who didn't walk away and the one who had done just that two weeks ago, were very different men. He'd spent his unexpected vacation from the world, wondering whether he'd have shown Etienne Shaw the Mercuri Nikolaides he was trying very hard not to be then, if he'd had it to do all over again.

No. No he wouldn't have. That was the one thing he was absolutely sure of. Even when he'd been at his worst, he hadn't been the sort to hold a woman when she didn't want to be held. At least, he didn't *believe* he would be that sort. Such behavior didn't appeal to him.

Truth was, he'd never had a woman to walk away from him before. He'd always been the first to end an involvement when his lifestyle-or his ghosts-made themselves known in the worst ways. Where his situation with Tee was concerned, he should've been too fucking pissed with her anyway to have spent the last two weeks pining over her, but well...there he was.

Fuck that, the phrase resonated silently yet stonily inside his head. She could damn well think again if she thought he'd just let her go about her merry way all calm and satisfied in light of the selfless way she believed she'd set him free of all her insurmountable baggage.

It was then that he felt the first surges of clear-headedness sweep through the haze that had camped out over his brain for the last fourteen days. He refused to give those surges time to ebb though and made his way out of the gym. He covered the chrome stairs at a determined pace as he ascended from the basement level; and had not yet arrived on the first floor landing, when he sensed he wasn't alone.

~CHAPTER 26~

"Mercuri?"

The house was silent when Tee used the key to enter through the front door. Security had obviously been alerted to her arrival for they'd waved her on through the gate when she slowed her approach.

She wouldn't allow herself to get sidetracked by the beauty of the house as she strode through the rooms of the lower level. Touring wasn't on the agenda, but talking was.

Would he want to talk? She wondered. Pope, Slayte and Rutger meant well, but she had her own group of well meaning friends. How many times had Bear, Prin or Lu misread her mood towards a certain situation? Close as they were, there was always room for error.

The possibility that Mercuri's friends could've very well misjudged his mood, had her steps slowing as she moved through the kitchen and took the spiral iron staircase in the rear of the area. She'd just make a quick check of the rooms on the second floor to convince herself that she hadn't taken the coward's way out. Then, she'd hightail it outta there.

~~~

Mercuri followed the route Tee took through his home. Quiet as a panther, he stalked and kept issuing silent reminders that he not sigh in approval of her path. His bedroom was at the very end of a long, winding corridor. Its double doors were the only ones open on the floor. His steps slowed as she moved on ahead to where he wanted her. He made a pit stop in the upstairs den and used the tablet on the entertainment console to instruct his security not to disturb him and to park Ms. Shaw's car in the garage.

He liked the chic, yet confining pantsuit she wore that day. It would take a bit more finesse to get her out of it than he felt like exerting then. Chances were high that she'd need a change of clothes to wear out of there when he chose to let her go.

He revisited the conversation he'd posed to himself moments ago. Would he show Etienne Shaw the Mercuri Nikolaides he was trying very hard not to be if he had to do it all over again? Goddamn right he would.

~~~

"Mercuri?" Tee recognized the master suite immediately. It had not escaped her notice during the prior tour that she hadn't viewed the space. Given what had happened between them before she left, it was perhaps a good thing she hadn't seen the room.

They'd been dating a while, but he usually stayed at her place or took her somewhere- never there. It was a stunning area- vast and all male- intimidating. Perhaps it was why he'd never brought her up there. The colors were deep and accentuated the blackwood framing wide chairs and extra long sofas in the suite's living area. The colors ran to deep merlot, warm browns and woodsy greens against a backdrop of black.

An enormous flatscreen occupied the wallspace. A compact workout area claimed a far corner while a well-stocked food and beverage nook occupied the opposing space.

The blocky heels of her strappy sandals disappeared into luxurious chestnut brown carpeting as she took in the vaulted ceilings and framed portraits of ships adorned with the Mercuri Fleets emblem. She stopped to scan the portrait of an older ship. In the lower right corner of the frame, there was a magazine article featuring Mercuri. A picture of him next to the old ship in younger days was also featured in the article.

She recalled their discussion about art selection. She remembered his reaction when she'd said it had to be personal. The portrait she stood before then proved her point exactly.

Tee moved on, continuing her tour. There were no windows, save the glass double doors hidden behind gauzy dark drapes. The doors, she saw upon peering past the drapes, opened out to a huge terrace inlaid with the distinctive black brick. She found the room both alluring and exclusive. This was a place to hide.

It appeared he'd been spending quite a bit of his time there if the tangled state of his bed was any hint. The structure was immense- almost as wide as it was long- understandable in light of the body it was meant to support. There was a short row of stairs on the sides and at the foot of the bed that appeared as a recessed pool in the middle of the floor.

On easy steps, she skirted the area. It was clear that Mercuri wasn't there, but curiosity had her in its grips then. There were two, tall panels in the room. The first, opened into a master bath which was a creation of black tiles, glass and chrome fixtures.

She saw the tub and wanted to swoon. It was glossy black porcelain and appeared wholly capable of swallowing her. Tee adored it. Reluctantly, she moved on to investigate the mysteries behind the second panel. Sliding it back, she found the wardrobe-wardrobe *room*-more accurately. There had to be at least three or four rows of suits alone. The space was dimly lit by a trio of small lamps on a shelf that displayed an array of colognes. Beneath it, a glass case housed a collection of timepieces. Tee lost herself among the clothing racks, sliding her fingers over lapels, sleeves and pant legs.

"I should kill them for sending you here."

She moved only a little further down the row, before testing her ability to respond to his words. "They were worried about you," she said around the ball of nerves in her throat.

"They shouldn't have asked you to come here. They know the mood I'm in."

She turned then and treated herself to a scan of the relaxed yet lethal picture he made while leaning against the wall just inside the room. He wore only a pair of loose white sweatpants that hung low on his hips and accentuated his sleek, copper-toned complexion.

"They know you won't hurt me, Mercuri. I know it. They thought we could talk-"

"I'm not talking to you, Tee."

241

She felt the nerves swell in her throat then along with the unmistakeable pressure of tears behind her eyes. Fighting past both, she gave a succinct nod and headed for the wardrobe's panel. The way was blocked when he stepped in her path.

"I'm not letting you go either," his smile was easy and arrogant. "You should've thought about that before you walked through my door again."

She'd known that, hadn't she? She'd known he wouldn't let her go without...this. She'd at least suspected it, anticipated...hoped.

"Mercuri we need to talk," she said it to remind herself more than him.

"This was the only place I really wanted to show you when you were here before."

"Mercuri-" she clipped her words when he advanced, backing her up the way she'd come from the clothing racks.

"This is nice," he tugged the lapel of the tan short waist jacket of her suit. "I think you'll want to take it off if you plan on wearing it when I let you go."

"We should..." she bristled when her lashes stirred in reaction to his hand skimming her waist and then up to skim his thumb over her breast. "Should talk..."

"Not interested." He was unbuttoning her blouse then.

Tee felt herself going under, drenched beneath layers of sudden need. Still, she couldn't make herself forget-forget what he knew. Shaking her head, she retreated another step to escape his touch.

"How could you want this?" She retreated another step when he reached for her.

A powerful muscle began a wicked dance along his sculpted jaw. "*This* Tee, *this* is going to happen." He caught her to him easily then, jerking the blazer and underlying blouse from her shoulders.

She watched him with incredulous outrage filtering the beckoning dark of her gaze. His head was bowed as he focused on tugging her free of the sleeves. The blue black locks of his hair fell over his forehead and though she was enchanted by the boyish softening of his fierce features, she couldn't silence the question jockeying for prime positioning in her mind.

"How could you want me when you know what I am?"

His head lifted and the feline intensity of his gaze was razor sharp. He straightened- all 6'7 inches towering to eclipse her view of...everything.

"Look at me."

She found his order easy to follow as there was nothing else to see.

"Unless you want to sigh, moan or cry out my name, shut up." He saw temper blaze in her dark eyes and approved. Her anger set him at ease. Her helplessness broke his heart.

Quickly then, Tee lost what remained of her clothes. Mercuri yanked down her pants without taking time to loosen her belt or the trouser fastening. Luckily, none of the garments suffered rips or tears. She figured the same wouldn't hold true for her panties when his thumbs hooked into the stitched side seams. The hold was momentary, his fingers soon glided down her thighs.

Mercuri went to his knees before her as his touch drifted lower and Tee understood that he meant to relieve her of her sandals.

His moves were more agile then as he lifted her from the shoes and the mass of fabric pooled about them. She would've linked her legs at his waist, but that wasn't where he wanted them. Her pulse thundered when he set her astride his shoulders. She faced him...in theory. Her legs dangled against his bare back, her crotch perfectly positioned for his mouth.

Mercuri savored the advantage. He used his tongue to bathe her slow, lustily through the cotton fabric of her panties.

She clutched fistfuls of his hair for support. Then, pleasure was slamming into her and causing her eyes to roll back in her head. Her fingers, tight in his hair, eased to begin a slow, satisfying massage of his scalp. Gently, she bucked her hips, inner muscles flexing in hungry anticipation of his tongue. Moments later, she couldn't tell whether her damp panties were more a result of Mercuri's wicked caress or her own flowing need.

There was little time to consider the matter. They were back in the bedroom. Mercuri took the side steps down to the bed where he dumped Tee in the center without ceremony.

Once more, he hooked his thumbs around the sides of her panties before his striking golden eyes locked on her face in silent query. In consideration of her lingerie, Tee raised her hips to assist in their removal.

Her bra was next. He curved an index finger under the front stitching and gave a faint tug. "Take it off or consider it garbage."

She obliged without argument and was still slinking out of the black, cotton cups when he pounced. Seductive tremors worked their way throughout her body when he claimed one breast in a fierce suckle while his fingers ruthlessly assaulted the nipple he'd yet to feast upon.

Tee rolled her head on the crisp tangle of sheets, her cries were hitched uneven sounds that resembled hiccups and drove her breast deeper into his mouth as he devoured it. She found the guttural moans and grunts of approval that vibrated beneath the stone wall of his chest, to be an aphrodisiac all their own.

Mercuri used his free hand to skim its back along the toned line of her curvy molasses frame. He believed she would have arched right off the bed when he skimmed her clit, had he not smothered her thigh beneath his to keep her still. With her open to him then, he continued his assault. His middle finger stroked her slick seam while his thumb rotated the tight bundle of sensitized nerves above.

In a pleading fashion, Tee nudged her body against his fingers there. Laughter mingled with her gasp that time when he acquiesced and drove a finger deep. He explored her tirelessly then. Thick fingers- two drove into her then-claiming her greedily as his nose coursed the undersides of her plump breasts and the valley between. Her moans wavered when her hips nudged the erection she was sure neither of them could ignore much longer.

That was a certainty for Mercuri. He'd wanted time to enjoy her at length. Two weeks without her in his bed, without being inside her was a torture he didn't want to extend. Suffering a hard, swollen dick every morning and at various points throughout the day whenever she crossed his mind, had all but driven him insane. He'd been at his endurance limit when she'd arrived there unannounced.

Now, she was there, his name a litany on her full, kissable mouth and her dark, sensational body, ripe for his taking. He'd wanted to make it last. He'd have to make it last later.

Tee was on the verge of climax when she felt her body deprived of its delicious stimuli. The deprivation registered almost in tandem with the filling stretching pressure that only a well-built dick was capable of. Hers and Mercuri's satisfied verbal reactions became one and mingled with the tell-tale slaps of bodies at sex. The stiff, long slide of his erection against her intimate walls, stirred orgasm almost immediately.

She didn't want to go there without him, but feared the decision was about to be out of her hands.

Fortunately, Mercuri didn't seem to mind. He drove himself into her as though the pursuit and possession of supreme pleasure were his only goals. Satisfied they were of one accord, Tee let herself go. She abandoned her intense massage of his lower back and taut ass. By then, her hands were only capable of resting limp against the covers.

Mercuri had filled his mouth with her breast again and let out a sharp curse when he felt her coming on his dick. He resumed his greedy sucking, milking her breast in virtually the same manner she milked his cock. He emptied himself inside her, sprewing liquid jets of release while he was unapologetically slammed inside a torrent of rich sensation he had no desire to escape.

~~~

They didn't tumble into sleep afterwards. Instead, they lay there relaxed, replete in the decadent bed. Mercuri lay on his side, content with Tee resting next to him with her back to his chest. His bicep was an unyielding pillow beneath her head.

Tee lay there appreciating the way his hand smothered hers where it rested against the rumpled bottom sheet. Intermittently, his mouth moved across her shoulder in soft, slow glides. She couldn't help but wonder if heaven was any better.

Aside from the sounds of their co-mingled breaths, the room had been silent-companionably so. The need for conversation was not a pressing one and still, both knew there was so much more that needed to be said.

"Do you remember what I told you about my childhood?" Mercuri began the discussion, feeling her nod against his arm in response.

"I told you I had pretty much all I needed. What I didn't tell you was that my mother made a very good living as a prostitute." He waited a beat and then eased back when he felt her wiggle against him.

Tee moved to her back to stare up at him. Her small face was a study in disbelief.

Mercuri smiled, spying the questions filling her deep eyes. "It's true. Same goes for my friends," he said, "We didn't know that 'til years later, but it's true."

"Is that why you were taken?"

245

"Not exactly," his gaze faltered. "Our mothers were brought here from Greece by the same people who took us."

She pushed up to look at him then. It was early evening. The sun, that had been streaming through the glass doors of the terrace, had retreated. "What are you trying to tell me, Mercuri?"

"That my friends and our mothers spent our lives in the service of an organization known as the Network and it's got its hands into everything from healthcare to assassination. My friends and I were raised-trained to kill and we did so without question or hesitation." He let the admission loom in the silence for a while before he went on.

"The prostitution was a small, but very lucrative part- a necessity, if you will. For a specific group within the organization, it was vital because it allowed them to role play at things they'd have been blasted for in a world where they're regarded as our best, brightest and most esteemed."

"The Ten," Tee guessed with a knowing smirk. "What kinds of roles?" She asked, following his confirming nod.

Mercuri pushed up to sit then too, reclining against the long cushioned headframe teeming with an abundance of pillows.

"The Ten had a thing for theme parties," he said.

"What kinds of themes?" Tee felt her heart lurch.

Mercuri sensed his jaw clenching and could see that she had already puzzled out the nauseating truth.

"All kinds," he forged on, "from a Sheik being pleasured by his harem, to a professor issuing As to his worthiest students."

"Or a plantation owner visiting his slave quarters in the middle of the night," Tee supplied and then closed her eyes for a nod and a smile. "I'd wondered why they'd asked for only black girls that night."

Mercuri watched her shiver as the additional truth set in and she tugged the sheet over her chest. He hesitated to touch her, but knew he couldn't let her retreat into herself with that particular thought on her mind. He squeezed her hand where she clutched the sheet.

"I'm sorry, babe."

Tee shook her head, smiling at his hand over hers. "It's not your fault. You weren't there."

He withdrew his hand, fearing he'd crush hers as thoughts of what she must have experienced began to simmer beneath his temper.

"I'm sorry anyway, because I was glad-glad you'd been there. That night, horrific as it was for you, it opened the door for my plan to go to work."

"I don't understand."

"I knew Roya too, remember? What you and your friends did that night put the organization in uproar. It was deemed a hit and right away The Network was speculating on who was responsible. Of course, it could've been any number of people. The Ten have enemies everywhere."

Mercuri rested an arm across a raised knee, studied the fist he clenched and unclenched. "When the bodies were discovered, the organization went to work covering it up. For that group to be seen in *that* setting- together- it would've been a scandal that would have a ripple effect in the organization itself as well as in the varied realms they wielded their power. The organization is two-fold, you see?"

He held both hands parallel in example. "On one side they're responsible for accomplishments in medicine, technology, even education, but it's the underbelly that generates the funding for those accomplishments to thrive and funds like that don't come from dealing off the top of the deck."

"I know one of them was in the senate. Who else did we kill that night?"

"Tee-"

"Mercuri. Please."

He studied her at length, shaking his head when he saw that she wouldn't budge from the request. "Three senators, two drug lords, two nationally known pastors, the last three were rumored to hold high ranking positions within the intelligence community. The Ten always left room for at least three seats opened for those who made their living in that alphabet soup."

"God," Tee groaned into her hands.

"Yeah, it was a very big deal." Mercuri bowed his head to pinch at tension that had formed across the bridge of his nose. "The raid on Roya's place in Venezuela was as much about payback as it was about finding someone to pin blame on. There was really no clear cut evidence to go on aside from the server's description."

"Server?"

"I believe someone brought in drinks to you that night?"

Tee raked her fingers through her short waves and cursed.

247

"No one could make sense of why Roya would come up with such a wild plan, but it was all they had to go on."

"Well what happened during the raid? Roya wasn't killed then."

"No," Mercuri smiled albeit grimly, "That's where my plan came in. Roya was all anyone could talk about for the ten months leading up to the op. I'd already been subtly sharing my thoughts on our place in the organization- telling anyone who'd listen that we could no longer lie to ourselves that we were doing bad things for good reasons. They were talking about massacring his whole family- down to his servants' grandkids. My friends and I thought he might like to know that. He was very grateful for the headzup. Rewarded me and my friends very well for the tip. His generosity laid the foundation for my business."

Shaking her head then, Tee rested back near Mercuri against the headboard. "The man seemed to have a weakness for struggling entrepreneurs. My friends and I benefitted from the same generosity." She hid her face in her hands again, inhaling deeply. "Ours wasn't a payoff for saving his life, though. It was a bribe for helping his life veer in a new direction."

Mercuri took the hand Tee used to rub at the tension throbbing near her temples and he kissed the back of it. "The decision you made that night probably saved yours and your friends' lives."

"So I've been told," she sighed, looking at her hand hidden in his. "In some circles I'd be considered a hero. Hmph, I'm still having a hard time buying that one. Especially now that I know who it was we killed."

"Who are you grieving most about? The pastors?" He chuckled when she poked an elbow into his arm. "You know, there's a strong possibility one of The Ten could've been my father." He said, sobering and shaking his head when he saw the horror creep onto her face.

"No need for condolences, Tee. No need for the slightest condolences. Who my father is or was, is a mystery I have no interest in solving."

"What about your mother? Did you ever find out what happened to her?"

"All I know is she didn't stay where I left her. I looked into it- we all did and then..." his brow furrowed, "we just accepted that our mothers were better off not knowing what we'd become."

"Maybe she went back to Greece."

248

"And maybe not...those theme parties often resulted in fatalities."

"Mercuri..." tucking her legs beneath her, she faced him on the bed. "I'm so sorry for all this."

"Don't ever apologize to me again," the edge was sharper in his voice then. "Don't apologize to me and stop thinking you're unworthy because of that night." He rested his head back on the frame and scanned her with a heated and repetitive sweep of his eyes. "You astound me, Tee. Not just because you're smart as hell and sexy as fuck." He smiled when embarrassment had her averting her gaze.

"What you did that night, amazes me. Regardless of what you think of it, it's worthy of my respect. You accomplished something that I and a lot more like me wished we'd had the courage to do. At first, we were just too young and weak to do a damn thing and later...well later, The Network had tamed us- unleashing us only when it was to their benefit. When we finally had our chance to...escape, we took it.

We didn't think about cutting the head off the monster- we just wanted out. You and your friends may never have been there had me and my friends added that piece of business to our plan first."

She cupped his cheek, leaned close to brush her mouth across the lines marring his brow. "If you'd done that, we never would've met."

"Yeah," he tugged her astride his lap. "Yeah, that occurred to me." He kissed her deep and quick and then settled down with her, keeping her tucked against his chest.

The easy silence revisited and they were soundly asleep soon after.

~CHAPTER 27~

W eak beams of moonlight were filtering through the dark curtains when Tee woke a few hours later. She could hear Mercuri's steady breathing and make out his features relaxed in sleep thanks to the moon's faint illumination.

Secure in the knowledge that he was still resting deeply, she brought her lips to his jaw and brushed a kiss across its sharp angle. "I love you." She spoke the words into his skin. She could offer no more and no less than that.

She believed him when he said he admired her, was in awe of her for what she'd done. That would change though, wouldn't it? If he ever saw those discs...they would be over and fast.

The only thing she could be grateful for in that, was she wouldn't be at fault for telling him to go. He'd see the discs, see her...at work and go on his own. Would she show him? Love meant trust. Trust meant truth. He deserved the whole truth about that night, didn't he?

Certain and miserable, she gingerly worked her way out of his loosened embrace. Faint twinges of discomfort throbbed deep, an erotic reminder of the afternoon and evening. Her thoughts on a hot soak, she made her way to the bath eager to lose herself in the gargantuan tub. She kept the recessed lighting on dim, dousing the space in muted gold. The tub filled quietly and quickly, thanks to not one but three wide spouts that handled the job. There were none of the frills that she used for her own bath-the scented candles, oils and such but the tub was a treat all its own.

The back dipped into a recline with an indention for head support. A dark, rectangular pillow occupied the space and Tee imagined another lengthy doze wouldn't be far off. She noticed a tablet screen recessed into the wall next to the tub and recognized it as a music console. She resisted the temptation, not wanting to awaken Mercuri.

She shut off the water when it had risen to her preferred level. Tee sank into the liquid heat and kept her appreciative moans on low. She settled back and had experienced unadulterated joy for at least 10 minutes when the low lights were turned on full force.

"Mercuri! Dammit!" Hissing, she winced when the light exploded.

"Are you alright?" His query was simple, and he made no apology for the light.

"I'm fine, I'm fine except for..." she waved a hand toward the ceiling.

Understanding registered and he returned the lights to dim. "Sorry. I only use the tub when I pull a muscle."

"Mmm..." Tee purred while resuming her luxuriating. "It's got far more enjoyable uses, you know?"

"Are you really okay?" His deep voice was adorably soft in its uncertainty. "I know I was rough with you."

"I'm not complaining." Even in the dim lighting, she could tell he wasn't convinced and extended a hand. "Join me."

"Shower's my thing, Tee. I can show you a helluva time in the shower."

"I'll bet...so...you're saying the tub's too girly for you?" She giggled when her tease had him bounding over.

"Scoot."

She obliged, giggling still when he settled behind her in the tub. Water threatened to spill over the lip and Tee pulled the plug for a few seconds in order to bring the liquid to a more suitable level. Content, she rested back, in love with the feel of his broad sleek chest supporting her.

"This isn't bad," Mercuri said following a few delightfully silent moments of relaxation.

"Told you," Tee sighed.

"Course, I've never had company to share it with," his hands smoothed up over her torso to weigh her breasts.

"Hmph…"

"What? You don't believe me?"

"Were you being serious?"

"Sure I was."

"Okay…"

"Tee?"

"Hmm…?"

"I've never brought another woman here-aside from those aggravating interior designers. The day you came to check the place out…you were the first…the only."

She heard the somber sincerity in the quiet boom of his voice. "I believe you, Mercuri. *Technically*, your record still holds," she drawled in an attempt to bring an air of the playful back into the moment. "You didn't actually *bring* me here, though. I just kind of showed up."

"Guess I should rephrase then," he set his chin to the top of her head, "I never *wanted* another woman here."

She angled her head back to meet his exotic stare and arched up to take the kiss he leaned down to bestow. His hand left her breast, fingers walking down the trim line of her torso until they were cupping her sex, curling into the place that hungered for him. When his middle finger invaded and she tensed, he cursed her.

"Don't start," she murmured against his mouth, "it's been two weeks, remember? Only way to avoid a problem there is to tend it daily." She smiled when an appreciative rumble surged in his chest and vibrated through her.

"I think I can handle that." He kissed her again.

The act was wet, lusty and had Tee bracing to meet the force he put into it. Too soon, he was pulling back.

"We're gonna have to talk if you expect me to behave."

"Talk about what?" Tee settled a little deeper into the hot water when a shiver kissed her skin.

Mercuri rested his head back on the bath pillow. "Anything," his rich voice was like a soft roll of thunder. "So long as it keeps my mind off your body."

She smiled, enjoying his humor and the easy mood between them. She wanted it to last, but he had shared so much more with her by then. It was only right that she do the same.

"Mercuri?"

"Mmm...?"

"I need you to know that...that night it was the only job we ever did for Dorinda- the only *job* we ever did. Period. Prostitution wasn't a thing we made a living at. It wasn't even something we thought about making a living at even when our next meal wasn't promised."

"How'd you meet her?" His voice was still soft, but carried boldly in the bath.

"I made a run for it after high school." Relaxation continued to seep into her bones, despite the topic of conversation. "I wasn't thinking about anything except getting a job before my money ran out. I took the bus to Virginia. I'd heard of Holland Furniture. It was big where I lived. Prin's folks held a big hiring spree every summer. Their fall collections were huge and they needed lots of manpower to get ready.

All you needed was a clean background and a high school diploma. They even had housing if you were seventeen or over. They hired me and I met Bear, Lu and Prin soon after. I would've been okay with working there for the rest of my life. I think we all would've been, but just before the end of summer...something happened- something with Prin. We never found out what. She's never told us, but when she begged us to make the trip to Vegas we were all in."

"Why Vegas?" Mercuri smiled when Tee's melodic laughter lilted.

"We would daydream about living the life in Vegas- going to college there...we figured what could be better, but it was just joking around. Nothing more than a group of girls being silly. College was the real joke. None of us had the money for that and Prin... whatever happened that summer damaged something between she and her folks."

Tee sighed, thoughts of her friend claiming a heavier spot in her chest. "Anyway, she was the only one with any real money so when she went, so did we. We never let on to her that we weren't all that jazzed about going. We could see she needed it. 'Course it didn't take long to realize we were in over our heads. *Real* money only got you so far in Vegas. We managed to get jobs at the mall and that's where Berrill and LuCarolyn were approached by a girl who worked for Dorinda. She gave them an envelope stuffed with money just to meet with her.

Bear and Lu said they couldn't do anything without me and Prin. The girl said it was cool for us to come along. Dorinda didn't seem to mind that we had no experience-being hookers, I mean."

Mercuri massaged the muscles at his neck and grimaced. He wouldn't tell Tee that The Ten preferred their girls fresh.

"She even paid us an advance while we thought about it for a few weeks. If we decided not to go through with it, we'd just give the money back. The money she gave us just to meet her was ours though."

"Let me guess, you guys spent most of the advance 'think about it' money?"

"Yeah, we were stupid," Tee smirked. "We weren't even close to saying yes to that insanity, but the money was gone and we had no other way to pay it back and then the time came for us to...and we-we should've told Dorinda to go screw herself but we-we just kept heading closer toward it and then-then we were just-just there."

"You can't change it, Sprite," he kissed the top of her head.

"No," she shook her head on his chest, "but that doesn't mean I can embrace being called a hero, either. This wasn't an accomplishment, Mercuri. It's not worthy of awe or respect. Those men didn't force us to do anything we weren't there to do. How am I supposed to justify sentencing someone for something they hadn't done yet because the *odds* were in favor of them doing it eventually?"

"It happened all the time where I came from, Tee."

She couldn't resist a shudder. "You world was pretty scary," she said.

He gave a short, quiet laugh. "Sometimes it still is."

As the water was still toasty warm, they were in no rush to leave the serenity of the tub and spent almost an hour there before Mercuri released the water, dried them both and carried Tee back to bed. They were settled into another snug embrace, where sleep eventually reclaimed them.

***

Tee smiled when the wondrous aromas of fresh brewed coffee and bacon teased her nose. She remembered then that she hadn't eaten since lunch with Mercuri's friends the day before.

Smoothing her hands across the lake-sized bed, she searched for Mercuri and wasn't surprised when she covered nothing but crisp, disarrayed sheets. Given the bed's enormity, she knew he could have been there lounging, but something told her he was already up and about. Forcing open an eye and yawning, she pushed from the bed intending to search the house. She tucked herself into one of the fluffy gray bath sheets she found in the bathroom and followed her nose to the terrace.

There was Mercuri decked in a fresh pair of sweats and relaxing on a wide chaise lounge with charcoal gray cushions encased in a sturdy blackwood frame.

"Good morning," he appeared a picture of sexy contentment, his long legs crossed at the ankles while he sipped a glass of what looked to be orange juice.

Tee looked to the round, dining table nearest the entrance and saw silver covers over platters, along with a coffee carafe and juice pitcher.

"Did you cook?" She asked.

"Hey, I take my host duties seriously," he called from the lounge. Mock offence colored his voice. "Thought I'd have to take it back to the kitchen, you were sleeping so hard."

"You bed's as amazing as your tub," she beckoned him with a wave, "come eat."

"Already did. You go on."

Tee peeked beneath one of the silver covers, eyed the contents skeptically. "No way I can eat all this and since I hate to see food go to waste, you're gonna have to hunt down your appetite."

Mercuri didn't require much coaxing and joined her at the small table. She helped herself to coffee, fruit, potatoes and bacon while he dove into the eggs. The morning was serene and beautiful. The sun played peek a boo with the puffs of clouds and danced across the rolling green landscape that made up Mercuri's back yard. For a while, they simply enjoyed their breakfast and the scenery.

"Thank you," she was telling him later.

One of his breathtaking shoulders lifted in a shrug. "I take my host duties seriously, remember?"

"I don't mean that," she smiled. "I mean for telling me about your past-your mom. I know that couldn't have been easy. Thank you."

"I thought it'd help you to know you aren't the only one who had to live with nightmares." A sly element pooled his bright eyes then. "There was an ulterior motive behind me telling you." He waited for her eyes to meet his. "The day I came to see you about the visit from Eduardo Roya, he was on his way to see you and your friends to offer his protection as his father had."

"Wow," quick, soft laughter burst from her lips. "We'd just decided to reach out to his father for that very thing."

"I told Roya his services wouldn't be required. No one's more qualified to keep you safe than me, Tee," he clarified after enjoying her confusion for several moments.

"No." She was already shaking her head defiantly. "No-absolutely not."

"You'll lose if you fight me on this," his tone remained cool as he wolfed down the eggs.

"Why would you involve yourself in this?"

"Are you serious?" He marveled over the bewilderment in her eyes. "There are several reasons. Surely you can remember at least one?"

"You lead a multi-national corporation-"

"I'm in love with you, Tee." He quietly interjected the reminder. "Do you think that means I'd leave you to fend for yourself against a gang of assholes I know very well?"

She left the table to pace the terrace and Mercuri allowed his temper free reign over his face. He watched her processing his words and knew she wouldn't confess her love as openly as she had the night before when she thought he was sleeping.

He wouldn't force her to confess that while they were both conscious if she wasn't ready, but neither would he stand by wringing his hands while certain death crept up to her door. Inwardly, he considered the irony. The very reason he'd refused to follow his friends into a showdown with their former associates was the same reason he was now ready to lead the charge.

"You have a reputation-a good one," she tried.

"So do you," Mercuri threw back.

"What I've accomplished, Mercuri...it's only because of what my friends helped me pull off that night. I'd gladly give it up to save them."

"And what about you?"

She bristled at the challenge. "No need for us all to go down."

"Wow..." He sighed coolly, despite the fact that her attitude had his temper raging. "I never knew you were this self-righteous. Stupid and self-righteous."

"Stupid," she folded her arms over her chest heaving beneath the towel. "Last night I was smart as hell."

"Yeah," Mercuri helped himself to a strip of bacon. "Looks like my opinion could stand some reassessing."

Some part of her resistance eased. "I thought you would understand. You once told me you'd do anything to save your friends."

"I would and I'd hope they'd tell me a plan was bat shit crazy if I didn't have the sense to see it for myself and *especially*," he stressed before she could interrupt. "Especially if there was a better way."

The last stopped her impending outburst. "A better way," she said instead.

"You're going to give up the discs, aren't you?" He leaned back from the table. "Show everyone what went down that night?"

"If I have to."

"Cause you've just got nothing to lose, is that it?" Pissed as he was, he couldn't help but sit in amazement of her.

"I was the one who started this, Mercuri." She stepped to the table, stabbed its surface with the tip of her index finger. "That's not being self-righteous. That's fact. If this thing comes to us- seriously comes to us- it'll take more than us threatening to show those discs. It'll take action and there's no need for us all to go down in the process."

"Stupid, self-righteous *and* selfless. Your friends are lucky to have you."

Tee shed more of her abrasiveness and resumed her seat at the table. "I'm not so stupid that I'm not scared. I just don't see another way. *Another way*," it was her turn to stress words when he braced to speak. "A way that doesn't drag anyone else into this unnecessarily."

His exotic, riveting stare was flat, unreadable. "I love you. That makes this very necessary for me."

Elbow propped to the table, she gave him a mourning look and set her chin to her palm. "You're a sap," she shook her head. "A big one. You know that?"

Smiling tightly, Mercuri leaned over to pour out from the juice pitcher. "I've heard love does that to a guy."

"It's alright. I love you anyway."

He set down the pitcher, blinking incessantly as he watched her. "Say it again."

"I love you, Mercuri. But I-"

"Wait," he shook his head to urge her silence. "Don't follow that up by telling me I'll regret it."

"Okay…" she smiled as his fingers tangled with hers across the table. "How about this, then? You've got a woman who loves you and she's in a bucketful of trouble. What better plan is there for her to get out of it than putting her cards on the table and letting the chips fall?"

"Okay…" he laced his fingers between hers. "Let's take you out of this for a minute because, when you think about it, this plan of self-sacrifice only benefits you."

"You have something against self-sacrifice?"

He smiled. "No, but I may have something against what's being offered up in the sacrifice. Do you really think my former associates would be satisfied with only you? Do you think they wouldn't go after Bear, Prin and Lu anyway?" His hand tightened on hers before she could pull away.

"Because they would, you know?" Stony assurance held his words and expression. "I've spent my life in this, Tee. I know how the players think. They don't give a damn about the cause, only whether fighting for it will provide an opportunity to shed blood. That there's real vengeance involved and the possibility of recovering what's been stolen from them, only makes the opportunity sweeter. They won't be cheated out of that, Sprite."

"So what am I supposed to do?"

"Trust me." He squeezed her hand and gave it a tug that urged her from her chair and into his lap. "Trust me to handle this in such a way that by the time it's all over with, you'll swear it all happened to somebody else and you were just a spectator."

~CHAPTER 28~

Harris slammed his fist against the passenger side dash and summoned Zubin's laughter from where the man sat behind the wheel.

"Does that help?"

Harris sent his partner a black look. "Yes, when I can envision my fist connecting with Brody Alberts' face."

"You should try firing a few slugs into the closest tree," Zubin shrugged when Harris daggered him another look. "Works for me," he muttered.

"This is all kinds of fucked up," Harris could manage nothing more humorous than a smirk.

"Guess we all lost it there for a while, drinking from the revenge cup before it was time," Zubin set his head back on the rest.

"Revenge," Harris snorted. "It's all that had me accepting Lorne Grodins' and Nathan Alberts' offer to track down their shit."

"So you're only motivated by revenge and property recovery now, huh?"

"Fuck it. I stopped thinking that command of the assault teams would ever be mine, long ago."

"Well I, for one, think you were the best man for the job," Zubin tugged the cuffs of his jacket. "Besides me, that is."

Zubin's tease got a broader grin from Harris, but the solemn tint soon resurged in his weak tea colored gaze. "You're forgetting about Mercuri," he said.

"Fuck Mercuri, he pissed that away after the Venezuela job."

"You think so?" Harris almost laughed. "Because I bet everything I own that Mercuri could walk into the old guys' office with his hat in his hands tomorrow and ask for forgiveness and get it along with the command seat."

"Why do you beat yourself up about this? It's the way of the world, brother. The man who's the best at pretending he doesn't want it all, usually gets offered the keys to the kingdom."

"You're wrong, Zoo. It's the man who really *doesn't* want it who's *always* offered the keys to the kingdom. All Mercuri and the others wanted was out and I could've given it to them if they'd just waited. Just given me a little time to settle my position. Taking out Roya would've done that."

Harris slammed his fist to the dash. "Because of them, I not only missed out on Roya, but my chance to claim what I sold myself for. Now, here I am six years later and nothing's changed other than I'm now taking orders from idiot sons *and* their idiot fathers."

Zubin adjusted the lens on his rifle scope. The wicked playfulness that had colored his voice, was nonexistent when he spoke. "If we could figure out a way in there, all this disappointment will be for nothing."

Harris followed Zubin's scowl to the corner of the tall stone gates surrounding Mercuri's estate. They'd been parked since the pre-dawn hours, shielded behind a generous thicket of brush and trees. Sighing, Harris rested his head on the seatback. "The bastard's security is a monster, but I'd expect nothing less of him. There is one thing working in our favor, though."

"Do tell."

"If there's a way out, there's a way in. We just have to find it."

"That's an inspired concept my friend," Zubin's tone was playfully bland. "Any idea where we should start looking?"

Relaxing on the seat, Harris closed his eyes. "One usually presents itself. We're at his door now and we've come too far not to cross the threshold."

"Son of a bitch...you may be right."

Something in the man's tone, had Harris raising his head.

"What are the odds that the man of the house wasn't entertaining *that* sweet piece in his bed all night?" Zubin removed the rifle scope, passed it.

Harris peered through in time to see a navy Crossover model rolling past the intricately carved iron gates between gray stone columns.

"Dark and gorgeous just like Robb said," Zubin remarked of the woman he'd seen behind the wheel of the CUV. "Only thing we don't know is whether she's tiny and curvy," he licked his lips as though the idea of finding out held a tasty appeal.

Harris passed the scope back to Zubin. "What do you say we find out?"

Zubin returned the scope to its case with practiced efficiency. "Harris, my man, I thought you'd never ask."

***

Brody Alberts and Jake Grodins arrived downstairs from their suites at The Marshall Club within minutes of one another. That it was pushing noon, didn't matter much. Brody and Jake had continued to languish at The Marshall long after their associates had left for California.

Though no plan of action had been set, Harris and Zubin decided it was time to pay a visit to Mercuri. The two set off for a bit of recon to surveil Mercuri's moves and confirm locations of his closest friends. Zubin had his own crew and had already decided to use them to serve as relief staff during any stakeouts that would be required.

Luke Robb and Caleb Stein, happy to be let off the hook for such a mundane chore, set off for some R&R. Meanwhile, Brody and Jake enjoyed more time at their Memphis club.

The Marshall promptly saw to the needs of its guests which were most often needs of the most eccentric variety. Even still, there was only so much pampering a man could take before the walls started to close in. Brody and Jake were becoming impatient.

The two headed down for their daily constitutional which consisted of a whiskey lunch and cigars in their designated lounge room. They were heading for the elevator bay that would take them to that wing, when they were met by one of the club's hosts.

"Coyt," Jake greeted the dour-looking rail thin man.

"Sir," Coyt returned in reverent tones used by all the service staff when addressing club members and their guests. "Will you and the other gentlemen require a private attendant for your meeting this afternoon?"

Still rather bleary-eyed, Brody and Jake managed faint frowns for Coyt.

"Other gentlemen?" Brody queried.

"They're waiting in the lounge, Sir."

Jake chuckled suddenly, nudging Brody. "I think the rules are slipping, B."

Brody grinned. "Must be. I'll bet Zubin and the guys are getting a kick out of helping themselves to our scotch. No problem, it's about damn time they got back here to give us an update."

"Coyt, old man," playful condescension dripped from Jake's voice. "Isn't a member required for these *gentlemen* to have access?"

Coyt's reverent manner never wavered. "These gentlemen *are* members, Sir."

Sly condescension abated until it was nonexistent. Brody and Jake traded looks that betrayed urgency instead of amusement. Dismissing Coyt, they continued their march toward the elevators. Minutes later, they were in the lounge corridor and approaching the door carrying a small, chrome plate marked Grodins/Alberts.

Brody and Jake strode in, prepared to meet their fathers or some other revered members of the club. They found no one from that expected group, but did see that the spirits were indeed being enjoyed and that the gentlemen were, in fact, members.

"So much for recon," Brody grumbled.

"Well, well! Now it's a reunion!" Pope's grin was half-amused, half-lethal. He tossed back the brown liquor in the glass he held. The other hand gripped a stout bottle of Courvoisier.

"The fuck are you two doing here?" Brody demanded.

"I'm not feelin' the brotherly love here. Are you, Rut?" Pope looked to Rutger who was sniffing at the contents of a glass decanter.

"I'm not tryin' to feel anything from those shits," Rutger muttered.

"Would you stop sniffin' at the stuff and drink it already?" Pope snapped on a chuckle. "We need to get the good vibes goin'."

"Good to know there're some things your ungrateful asses won't throw back in your fathers' faces." Jake sneered.

Pope's teasing grin turned glacial. "*Your* fathers is right and if it were physically possible, I'd take The Marshall off its foundation and shove it up your fathers' shriveled asses."

"Why the fuck are you two here?" Brody rephrased his query.

"Your presence is required in California." Rutger said, following a swig directly from the glass decanter he held.

"We don't answer requests from traitors," Brody spat.

"That's good, because this is no request."

Jake slid a look to Brody following Pope's response. "Funny how they don't argue being called traitors."

"Being called a traitor by the likes of you is a compliment," Rutger's voice was pure gravel.

"Get out," Brody dismissed them with an eye roll.

"Still chaps your ass that we're members too, doesn't it?" Pope's teasing grin made an encore, but the chill in his eyes gave the marine depths an even frostier gleam. "Being blood relatives and all."

"Blood relatives!" Jake hissed. "You dare to call yourself that after what you both did to your own?"

"I can't speak for Rutger-"

"Please do," Rutger urged Pope, frowning at the decanter's contents before setting it aside to select another.

"Sharing blood with you, Brody, makes me want to vomit. Jake, ditto for Rut."

Rutger raised a new decanter in toast.

"The only thing that keeps the upchuck down is knowing how much it eats at you knowing that after everything I've done, including conspiring to help dear old dad take his final nap, even after *all* that," Pope shook his head as though he were truly perplexed by the reality, "the son of a bitch would give me anything-everything. You're a joke to him. My mother sold herself to him and still it's me he'd leave his life's work to."

"You're dead men!"

Pope applauded. "Thanks for getting us back on track, Jake. As I said, you two are wanted for a little chat in California. Now in our continued pursuit for brotherly love, you two can either walk out of here with your dignity or we can beat you to shit and carry you out. We'd be happy to make the choice for you."

"In the spirit of brotherly love," Rutger rubbed fist to palm as though he were already imagining the beating he was about to dish out.

***

"I don't like it, Tee."

Tee worked her fingers along the bridge of her nose. "Prin I'm going to need you to be a little more specific when there's so much about this not to like."

"Alright then," Prin sighed over the phone line. "I don't like any of it. Mercuri knowing Roya and everything about that night is bad enough. Drawing him into this any deeper...just doesn't seem right, you know?"

"I know that all too well Prin and I tried to talk him out of this but he wouldn't listen when I suggested we take Roya's offer instead of looking for outside security."

"Well that's understandable," Lu chimed in from her end of the line.

Tee was glad the woman couldn't see her rolling her eyes. She'd come into the office after driving home from Mercuri's for a change of clothes. She'd set up a conference call with her friends where she'd stunned them all with the details she hadn't previously shared when she'd discussed the conversation that had prefaced hers and Mercuri's two week hiatus.

LuCarolyn hadn't been stingy with her criticism of the way Tee had handled the situation. She thought Mercuri Nikolaides was nothing short of a dream, wanting to stick by Tee in spite of what he'd discovered.

"Men like that are harder to find than needles in haystacks," LuCarolyn's airy tone drifted through the speaker box again. "And given his level of experience, you'd be a fool not to accept his help. I'll tell you this, I feel a helluva lot safer with him on the job than Roya's son."

"Tee? It couldn't hurt to hear him out on the matter, could it?" Berrill's voice was uncommonly soft. "Lu's got a point. I'd feel better with Mercuri on it too and let's face it, we know him way better than Roya's son."

"Exactly." LuCarolyn tacked on.

"Tee, what else does Mercuri want to talk to us about?" Prin asked.

"He wasn't very clear on the rest, but he'd understand if you can't make it-"

The jumble of voices tumbling from the speaker interrupted the rest of Tee's response. No one was missing out on the chance to see Mercuri's house.

"Anyone ever tell you guys you're shallow?" She laughed. "Alright then, well you've all got the address and time so I'll see you then."

A round of goodbyes followed as the call wrapped up. Tee waited a beat once all the lines had disconnected and then she dialed out again.

"Tee?" Berrill's smoky tone filled the line. "Is this is butt dial?"

Tee managed shaky laughter. "No I meant to call. I um...Bear I need you to bring my disc when you come tonight."

"Yours? But he doesn't need-"

"Bear, *I* need it. Just bring it, will you?"

"Ah hell, Tee...you're really going to show it to him, aren't you?"

"I don't know, but I want it if I decide to."

"You know, I'm starting to think Lu's on to something about you being a fool."

"Well she's a little late with her assessment, isn't she? You've already accused me of being one on several occasions here recently."

"I keep hoping the accusations will help you snap out of it."

"I don't expect you to get it Bear. Maybe you will when you meet the man you want to give every part of yourself to. Especially your trust."

"I'm confident I'll never understand it then. No man's ever gonna get all that," Berrill vowed and silence held the line for a long while until she let out an anguished sigh. "I'll bring it tonight," she said.

~CHAPTER 29~

Mercuri was rounding the desk in his study and extending a hand to shake with the tall, rangy man who sat on the other side.

"I appreciate you freeing up some of your guys, Jay."

"Not a problem," James O'hara stood to take Mercuri's hand in a firm squeeze. "If we can't do a special job for the boss, who can we do it for?"

"Well I appreciate it anyway. I know how busy I keep you guys around here."

It was true that Mercuri knew that all too well. Boss or not, he hadn't gained respect and loyalty from his men by being a disinterested employer. He made a point of getting to know everyone on his immense employee roster. That included everyone from his top execs at Mercuri Fleets to the caretakers that kept his estate looking and running its best.

"Just let us know when we're needed and in the meantime I'll get started selecting guys for the job," James was saying.

"Sounds good. I expect to have more details in a few days."

"Alright, we'll talk then," James nodded then and turned to shake hands with Slayte who had joined him and Mercuri for the meeting.

"You sure we'll need Jay's guys on this?" Slayte asked when they were alone.

Mercuri took no offense to the question and grinned. "I'm sure. Tee's gonna keep me busy enough- *too* busy to keep an eye on her friends on my own...unless you're offering assistance?"

Amusement took hold and Slayte's violet gaze narrowed. "That's a job I'd leap at, but what I meant was whether you're sure they'll go for it? Some folks like to travel with an entourage, others guard their privacy like gold. They may not appreciate having a shadow, no matter how unobtrusive it is."

"They were going to hire Roya," Mercuri quietly reminded him.

"That's different."

"In what way?"

"He's not sleeping with one of them."

"Are you serious?" Laughter clouded the reply. "If anything, that'll give me the edge-they'd know I'm committed to protecting their friend."

"*Or* they could flat out think you bullied their friend into it which would have them despising you as well as your best friends whom they've yet to become acquainted with."

Understanding swirled in Mercuri's bright eyes and his laughter flowed at a soft, yet steady pace. "When'd you meet 'em?" He asked.

"That's just it. We *haven't* met them-only saw them from a distance. We don't need you getting on their bad sides before we at least have the chance to shake their hands."

Moving closer, Mercuri patted Slayte's cheek. "Trust me. Her friends love me. I'm actually counting on them to convince Tee to go along with this. It was all I could do to stop myself from locking her in here when she insisted on leaving this morning."

"Love you, huh?" Slayte's stare grew into a pronounced leer. "Enough to let you set them up with your closest friends?"

Mercuri faked a shudder. "What was it you said about getting on their bad sides? That'll do it quick."

A wide, sleek mobile began to gyrate across the surface of Mercuri's desk. "Saved by the bell," he muttered and was greeting Pope soon after. He put the phone on speaker for Slayte to listen in.

267

"We're back-brought guests."

The easy smile that had softened Mercuri's fierce features, transformed his mouth to a hard line that emphasized the unyielding set of his jaw. "We're on our way," he said.

"You think those clowns will have anything to tell us?" Slayte watched Mercuri shove the phone into a back jean's pocket once he'd disconnected from Pope.

"If they don't, they're gonna wish they did." Mercuri nodded to instruct Slayte to precede him out of the study.

***

"'Etienne Shaw specializes in interior design and is most known for her work with several well-known corporations and philanthropic organizations. Most recently, her work has introduced her to a string of residential endeavors for high powered political and entertainment figures.'"

Zubin smirked as he listened to Harris read from the dossier on Etienne Shaw. He didn't look up, but continued to pour over the file he held. "Entertainment figures, huh? Guess she met them through Ms. Young here. Says 'LuCarolyn Young's beauty is only matched by her tenacity and both have made her a powerhouse among Hollywood's elite."

"Did you already read up on Berrill Clayton too?" Harris asked.

"Hers was the first I read," Zubin shook his head. "I thought Bear Arms was owned by men."

Harris whistled as he thumbed through the rest of the Shaw file. "They've come a long way from hooking. Looks like the blonde went back to being a princess-living off her family's money."

"Yeah," Zubin agreed, though his manner was distracted. He'd returned to the file on Prin Holland and was studying the blue-eyed blonde with the uncommon dark honey complexion. "If they weren't so goddamn gorgeous, I'd be having second thoughts about them being wrapped up in this."

"Well it looks like we've pretty much confirmed it now." Harris mused.

"So what's next?" Zubin queried with a raised brow.

"The plan hasn't changed."

"So you still don't want to call in the rest of the guys?"

"Caleb and Luke wouldn't have the stomach for it," Harris predicted. "Brody and Jake could stomach it only after they'd exhausted all possibilities of getting what they need to secure their power over the GAN. Then they'd kill them just for robbing them of the opportunity. I'm all negotiated out, Zoo. I want Mercuri and his BFFs dead alongside their whores. I've got no interest in following any agendas that don't fall in line with that plan."

***

"Remind me never to get you guys pissed with me," Slayte eyed the two men who only remained upright in their seats thanks to the leather straps holding them there.

"Too late," Rutger mussed Slayte's unruly mop of onyx curls on his way past. "We feel that way about you all the time. It's just that we have a soft spot for the most clueless among us. In short, your ignorance saves you from our wrath."

"Aww...I love you too, man." Slayte nudged Rutger's shoulder with his own and joined him in laughter even as the sounds of Brody Alberts' and Jake Grodins' moans rolled through the air.

"Guess their ignorance didn't save them," Slayte sighed. "Or were they not among the most clueless?"

Rutger's whiskey toned stare went hard as gemstone. "You bet your ass they are, but they were worth making an exception for."

"I appreciate your restraint," Mercuri spoke from his spot on the other side of Slayte. It was clear that his friends hadn't forgotten the coveted art of torturing a man without leaving a mark.

Pope, who was walking behind Jake's and Brody's chairs, leaned down to drop resounding slaps to their cheeks in unison. "Could've bypassed the physical altogether," he said. "Unfortunately, Rut and I realized our mistakes too late. See, our beloved brothers here, thought that since we let them leave their pompous club with their heads held high, it meant they were still in charge. But we corrected that misunderstanding, didn't we guys?"

By then, Pope had his hands curved over the back of each man's neck. He pressed down hard, sending Brody's and Jake's heads bowing in forced nods.

"Did they tell you anything?" Mercuri asked through his laughter.

"We didn't ask anything," Pope said.

While Jake quietly brooded, Brody lashed out.

"Bastards!" He spat.

"I believe that's been established," Pope slapped the back of Brody's head. "We're interested in new information."

"We've got nothing to say," Jake found his voice then.

"Well that's just fine," Rutger had moved in position to stand over the men with his arms folded over his chest. "You've only got the use of your jaws because Mercuri wants to talk. If you choose not to…" he shrugged, "guess that means the bastards can start breakin' shit."

Jake shared a foul grin. "Big talk Rut while we're strapped to these fucking chairs."

Pope flipped open a switchblade and released the leather ties binding their prisoners' wrists.

"And outnumbered," Jake finished, still grinning foully.

"Oh well Slayte and I would be happy to leave you four to it, isn't that right Slay?"

"Right as rain."

"Fuck! Shit-wait!"

"Brody, goddammit!" Jake snarled.

"Screw that, Jake. It's a trap! How well do you think we'd do against them when we've spent all morning being tortured?"

Considering the argument and seeming relieved by its merit, Jake began to nod.

Pope began to chuckle. "Is it any surprise that your fathers think you're spineless sons of bitches?"

"I could give a fuck about what our fathers think!" Jake was back to snarling. "As far as we're concerned, the old fools are setting themselves up for the same nightmare they found themselves in six years ago."

"And yet you're runnin' around like fools looking for what? Some sex tapes?"

"You're an idiot, Pope. You're all idiots." Brody spat.

"So the girls *did* take more than their share?" Mercuri took the outburst as confirmation.

"Those bitches," Jake rolled his eyes, "this would've gone off without a hitch if it wasn't for them."

"So why wait six years for your revenge?" Mercuri asked.

"Revenge? That's what you think this is?" Brody's amusement seemed to override his irritation.

"So what?" Slayte's tone was incredulous. "The discs? Anything could've happened to them by now. They could've been destroyed, copied-"

"Save it, Slay!" Jake snorted, his eyes hate-filled. "Stop acting like you don't know exactly where that bag is."

"Why would we know?"

"Fuck you, Pope," Brody scooted to the edge of his chair. "You expect us to believe you guys don't know, when it was you who sent those sluts to The Ten."

"All that time we wasted following our fathers' orders not to confront you- going through the pimp and madam first."

"Patterson and Roya," Mercuri deciphered from Jake's lament.

"It was a dumb play," Brody stretched out his legs and shook his head. "Of course it was always of the utmost importance to the old men that you all be handled with kid gloves. The old fools just couldn't believe your betrayal encompassed so much. We went along with this bullshit because somehow they managed to mend so many of the friendships broken six years ago. Those friendships will be needed once we-"

Jake cleared his throat, which sent Mercuri and the others trading knowing looks.

"So they did take more than their share?" Discovery pooled Mercuri's rich voice. "You guys aren't after The Ten's home movies at all, are you?"

Brody and Jake kept their eyes on the warehouse floor.

Mercuri began to pace. "The discs would only cast shadows over The Ten's outside interests."

"Because the fact that they're a governing body for the GAN isn't known by anyone other than the GAN," Rutger chimed in as he too paced some distance from where the others were gathered.

"So if you weren't interested in the sex tapes, it must've been all those other discs from all those other cameras hidden all over that very special hotel." Mercuri's smile defined when he caught the quick exchange of gazes between Brody and Jake.

"That only leaves me with one last question, fellas. Where are Harris and Zubin?"

"Here," Jake relished giving Mercuri his answer. "These two can torture us for more information if you insist, Mercuri but Zoo and Harris stopped answering our calls over a week ago. All we know is that they've added a few more steps to our original plan."

"Lemme guess, it had to do with killing somebody and us?"

Jake's eyes narrowed with malice. "Still the grinnin' pretty boy, huh Slay?"

"Damn right-grinnin' even while I'm shovin' my fist down somebody's throat." Slayte's grin turned acidic. "Did you ever see that Jake? It was some shit to witness I promise you."

Jake swallowed, noticeably shaken but maintained enough of his resolve. "Missin' your days as one of Zubin's animals?" He accused.

"No, but that doesn't mean I've forgotten all I learned. Maybe you'd like a demonstration." Slayte advanced until Jake shrank back.

"Let 'em go," Mercuri instructed.

"Should we put somebody on them in case they run to the psychos?" Rutger asked.

Mercuri was already shaking his head. "No, they'll be back in Memphis by morning. Isn't that right, boys? Besides, they won't want to be anywhere close when we catch up to Harris and Zubin."

"Well Po, looks like our work here is done. I'm goin' to get a drink." Rutger made way for the warehouse exit without a look back.

"Sounds good to me," Pope followed suit.

"Hey you fucks! How are we supposed to get back?" Brody leapt from his seat along with Jake.

"Where are our phones?!" Jake demanded.

"Sons of bitches!" Brody called to the backs of their captors.

Jake kicked at one of the rickety chairs, sending it across the splintered floor. "I'm starting to think Harris and Zubin had the right idea. To hell with the package, I want Rutger dead."

"And you don't think I want Pope to suffer?" Brody rounded on his partner. "But this has to be about more than revenge for us."

Jake held the fist he'd clutched to his forehead and appeared to be reigning in emotion. "You're right, you're right. I know you're right Bro. But...fuck! They've just gotten away with so much already and as much as I hate his fucking guts, Slayte's right. How do we know there's still a package to recover? Anything could've happened to that case in six years. Our chances of recovering it are slim, but getting rid of our bastard brothers once and for all is a chance ripe for the taking."

Brody's face was a feral mask as he glared toward the building's rusted exit doors. "Jake, my friend, it would seem that the time has come for me to agree."

~CHAPTER 30~

"Well, well, well! Look at you, lookin' all Lady of the Manor!"

Tee rolled her eyes as she stepped back from Mercuri's distinctive front door. "Don't start that shit, B."

"Aww," Berrill took no offence and leaned down to squeeze Tee's cheeks.

"Don't be that way," Lu sighed. "You look like a tiny queen. That chiffon makes the dress, doesn't it guys?" She fluffed at the fabric of her friend's long, coolly chic frock.

Tee merely shook her head and waved the women inside.

"So don't you have anything to say?" Tee asked Prin who was last to enter.

Prin took time to size up her friend. Her blue gaze was cool and far more measuring than teasing. "I think you look happy. Seems Mercuri Nikolaides is good for you and because of that I'm willing to listen with an open mind to whatever he has to suggest tonight."

Tee gave into a trembling smile. "Thanks Prin," she pulled the woman down into a tight squeeze.

A teasing light had crept into Prin's radiant eyes by the time she straightened from the embrace. "Lu and Bear are right though, this dress is to die for."

"Jeez," Tee responded with a playful eye roll. "Can't a girl be comfortable?"

"Sure she can, when she's the queen," Bear was already moving beyond the foyer. "Guys, look at this place," she called.

Laughing softly, Tee pushed the front door shut. The graceful folds of the muumuu-styled dress billowed against an early evening breeze as the heavy wood swung shut.

While the flowing cut of Tee's floor length frock wasn't designed to emphasize the figure, it was no less flattering. The long sleeves puffed and cinched tightly at the elbows and wrists. Subtle shimmers of gold, beige and chestnut brown made the even molasses hue of her skin appear more illuminated in its flawlessness.

"There're drinks and canapes in the living room," Tee led the way while her friends oohed and ahhed behind her. The women turned, angling their heads up and back, looking from side to side in an attempt to see every elegant corner of the beautiful, warmly designed home.

"Help yourselves. Mercuri had some of his housestaff stay over to make sure you have a good visit." Tee watched, smiling brightly as LuCarolyn and Prin stood transfixed by the majestic view beyond the room's window wall built around the massive hearth.

Berrill studied the spectacular view for a time, before she turned to tug at Tee's sleeve. "Can we talk?" She asked when their eyes met.

Tee's smile died a little when she saw the distinctive bag she knew carried the discs. She nodded. "There's a small den off Mercuri's study."

Berrill went over to wave at the others. "We'll be back," she told LuCarolyn and Prin. The women had already helped themselves to champagne and were moving out to view more of the scenery from the terrace.

Tee led Berrill toward the front corridor and took it deeper into the house until they were passing the wide entryway leading to Mercuri's study. Beyond it was a small, cozy room furnished with a long sofa flanked by matching scoop chairs of a deep blue color. It all set atop an intricately designed throw rug, the same base color as the furniture. In the back of the room, stood a black mini fridge beneath a well-stocked hot beverage bar.

"I've got the security discs here," Berrill set the bag to one of the three small coffee tables along the sofa. Taking a seat, she waved one disc in the air. "This one's yours and I know I'm wasting my breath, but showing this to him in a bad idea. Men don't...they don't handle this kind of shit well, Tee. They're taught to share, but it's not a part of their DNA. It's not even part of their realm of comprehension when the sharing involves a woman they've all but tacked their last name on. To hell with the fact that all this happened before you ever knew he existed."

Tee moved past Berrill, snagging the disc on the way. She set it next to her tote bag and the disc case on the end table flanking the sofa. She then rubbed her fingers across the flowing material of her dress as though she were wiping away undesirable residue left behind by the disc.

"He's not tacking his last name to me, B."

"Seriously?" Berrill shifted her position on the sofa. "He's willing to throw over everything he's built over the last six years. Men don't make such sacrifices lightly."

"I know they don't," Tee sat when Berrill caught the edge of her dress and tugged. "I know he isn't," she insisted. "But don't you think he deserves to know who he's chucking it all for?"

"I'd say he *does* know. I'd say he does without all the color commentary. I'd say he could've asked to see everything-*all* the discs and not just the security footage if he cared so much about knowing." Berrill stood.

"I get why it matters to you, Tee-honesty is the best policy and all that, but I'd say there's been enough honesty. Any more is redundant." Berrill offered her hand, smiling when Tee accepted. Together, they left the den.

~~~

Tee and Berrill returned to the living room where they saw LuCarolyn and Prin still on the terrace. Mercuri was there with them. LuCarolyn and Prin appeared rapt with interest as they listened, watching Mercuri spread a hand out over the terrace ledge as though he were explaining something about the landscape.

"Guys like that don't come by often, Tee. We all know that terribly well," Berrill sent a wave when LuCarolyn saw her and Tee and then caught Prin's and Mercuri's attention.

"Mercuri offered us a tour of the grounds," LuCarolyn announced when they all stepped into the living room.

Mercuri greeted Berrill with a hug and hand squeeze, then went to stand before Tee. "You look right at home," he rubbed at the material of her dress. "It's a good look."

With that, he tugged Tee around in front of his chest and held her there secure against him. "Are you guys only here for the tour or are you willing to hear me out?"

Prin spread her hands, let them fall to her sides. "It's what we're here for," she said.

"We brought the discs you wanted," Berrill added.

Tee looked up at him then. "They're in the small den off from your study."

Mercuri planted a kiss to the top of Tee's head. The gesture had Tee looking everywhere but her friends' smiling faces as her cheeks burned.

"Tee can give you ladies the tour. So enjoy and I'll meet you back here soon," Mercuri eased his mouth across Tee's temple and cheek to her ear. "I love you," he whispered for only her to hear and then he took his leave.

Alone with her friends, Tee finally met their interested gazes. "Shut up and follow me."

Berrill, LuCarolyn and Prin shared knowing smiles as they followed orders.

~~~

The women arrived back in the living room in little over an hour's time. LuCarolyn, Prin and Berrill had kicked off their shoes before venturing to the second floor but they were in no way bored by the tour. Instead, they were like children given permission to roam a stunning castle.

Even still, they were delighted to sink into the plush, body hugging furnishings they found in the living room. They were there, fixed up with fresh champagne cocktails when Mercuri returned. Immediately, the ravings began and the women told Mercuri how in awe they were of his home.

"This place is too gorgeous and palatial to be lived in alone," Berrill's tone was playfully sly.

Tee snorted a laugh at her friend. "Look who's talking."

"You're right," Mercuri grinned, while Berrill rolled her eyes. "It's taken me a while to realize that," he made his way to Tee who had curled up in a wing chair that all but swallowed her. Determination honing his stride, he advanced until he was next to the chair and leaning down to capture her mouth in the most tender of kisses.

LuCarolyn, Prin and Berrill pretended to be fixated on their drinks.

Smoothly, Tee broke the contact and hid her face in Mercuri's chest. He leaned closer to whisper to her for the second time that evening. "Stay with me tonight."

"Mercuri…"

"My next kiss will make your friends uncomfortable."

"I'll stay."

He straightened then, leaving Tee to collect herself while he addressed her friends. "Roya junior was going to offer you his protection, but he's got no clue who he's dealing with."

"And you do." Prin said.

"I do," a tendon flexed in Mercuri's jaw. "I learned from the same teachers they did. Worked for them, slaughtered for them…told myself we were all doing bad things for good reasons. I lied to myself but I got my friends out. Saved Roya senior in the process, but unless you pull a weed out at the root, burn it and the hole it festers in, you're just leaving the door open for another to take its place."

"And you know how to do this?" LuCarolyn probed. "Find the weed, burn its root?"

"I do, but that's not what I'm planning. Instead of burning the hole it uses to push its place into the world, I want to destroy the place it seeks to find."

"How?" Berrill scooted toward the edge of the sofa.

"The discs," Prin guessed, "but *why* discs? Aren't they a little…antiquated? I mean, why trust saving them to a medium that can be stolen, copied or easily destroyed?"

"Because they wouldn't think anyone would be so bold as to steal from them," Mercuri said. "Those discs are a safer way as opposed to digital means that can be hacked, easily shared… doctored…"

"But…you-you're going to release them, aren't you?" Prin queried.

Mercuri's expression was answer enough.

"But they just show people going and coming," Tee said.

Mercuri nodded then. "People going and coming who shouldn't be in the same place-least of all, *that* place."

"It'll take me time to put this all together and I need to know you're all safe in the meantime. I'd prefer you stay here with me and Tee," Mercuri slanted Tee a look that was both arrogant and adorable, "but I'll need more than one night," he told the others.

"I know you've got lives that won't allow for that, so I hope you'll accept my protection detail instead."

Berrill cringed. "How much of a detail?"

"Two men-one car. They're exceptional. You won't even know they're there. I can give you a day to think about it."

"And after that?" Berrill asked.

"After that, I put them on you anyway," he shrugged. "I'm sorry ladies for the caveman tactics. All this is probably too much- they may have a vague idea what you look like but chances are strong they haven't identified you yet. I can't take that chance, though and it'd destroy Tee if anything happens to you. I can't have that." He sighed, rubbed his hands together. "I'll get out of here now, give you guys time to talk."

"We'll do it!"

Mercuri was halfway to the living room entryway when Prin called out.

"We'll do this, we'll accept your offer," she said.

"When will they start?" LuCarolyn asked.

"Tonight," Mercuri turned to fix the women with an unreadable look. "They'll be with you when you leave."

"Do you trust them?" Berrill asked.

"They earn their livings watching my back. I trust them with my life," he looked to Tee, "and the important things in it." He fixed the others with another look and nodded. "Thank you for going along with this. We'll talk soon." He left them then.

***

After the talk with the women, Mercuri returned to his study. He'd wrapped things up with a call to Randall Cafrey, a very old friend and the V.P. of Programming for the Feature News Network. Mercuri could only hope the man would climb on board once he'd considered his plan.

Mercuri found Tee much later when he ventured up to his bedroom. She was on the terrace and looked at ease, but he knew she was far from it. It had been a long day and he knew she had to be as wiped as he was. The meeting with Grodins and Alberts had been a lot of extra he could have done without, given the pain it brought to Pope and Rutger. His friends put up brave fronts, but he knew there was unresolved hurt there that ran deep.

Over the drinks that had followed the meet, they'd discussed strategy and firepower for the job or *jobs* ahead. Mercuri and Slayte tried to raise Pope's and Rutger's spirits, but feared they wouldn't succeed. Mercuri left Slayte in the city to continue the spirit-lifting so that he could return home for the meet with Tee and her friends.

He watched her then. He'd seen her friends off with their security detail in tow over half an hour earlier. Tee was leaning against the terrace ledge and he figured she could stand some spirit-lifting as well as rest. He went to her, saying nothing only scooping her into his arms and carrying her into the bedroom.

Tee had no arguments, content to curl her arms about his neck and tuck her face there securely.

He set her to the center of the bed and went about doffing his clothes while Tee did the same with her elegant frock. She wore only a wispy pair of white lace panties beneath.

"Mercuri are you sure about your men?"

"Shh...I'm sure about everything. You need to rest." With that said, he tucked them both beneath the covers.

Curled into him, she sighed. "I don't feel tired."

"You're tellin' me," he massaged the tension at the bridge of his nose, only because it took his mind off the tension at work below his waistline. Forgetting the tension below his waist was a useless intention when she pushed up to begin a slow, wet assault on his earlobe.

"Tee-"

"Please?"

He was at her mercy then and sighed. Tee climbed onto his lap and settled herself astride him. Going the extra mile to get settled, she snuggled in tight against him, rocking her hips to nudge her sex into the sensational rock solidness of his erection.

She nibbled and sucked at his earlobe, tiny moans rising with every slow glide her tongue made across his skin. Her attention to his ear kept time with her rolling hips. Mercuri brought his hands up and around to cup her generous bottom while angling his head to give her more access to his ear. Moments later, he was cupping one of her breasts and squeezing it greedily. Pleasure blooming, Tee covered his hand on her breast and rotated her tongue in his ear as her moan turned shaky.

"Mercuri," her voice was equally shaky when she suddenly pulled back. "I just wanted to thank you for-" She was on her back before she could finish expressing gratitude for what he'd done for her friends.

"Don't do that," he told her. His expression was like stone.

"Do what?" She reached up to rake back the ebony locks falling into his remarkable face.

He took her hand, kissed the back of it before pressing it to the bed. "You don't have to thank me. You never have to thank me and if you ever feel like you do- you absolutely never have to thank me like this," he took stock of their position in the bed before his extraordinary eyes returned to her face. "You're safe with me Etienne. I need you to know that."

"I know that," her voice was hushed but her words were firm.

Mercuri nodded, his gaze going flat. "Just so we're clear."

Tee's eyes had faltered more than once to the undeniable erection resting heavily along her thigh. "So um...does this mean we can't...?"

"Hell no," a killer smile took possession of his mouth. He kissed her then, his tongue going deep the instant their lips touched.

The kiss was at once demanding, probing, conquering. The force of it, drove her head deep into the mattress and she welcomed the force. The kiss wasn't a lengthy one though and she was unexpectedly flipped to her stomach shortly after it began. Again, she welcomed the force especially when his hand smoothed across her hip to curve around and cup her mound. His fingers surged high and he lifted her just slightly off the covers to ready her for taking his tongue from behind. His free hand surged as well until it held her breast firm.

Her body felt riddled by a mass of sensation consuming her from every angle. Her moans became whimpers that were muffled into the covers she writhed against. Her focus was divided between triple points of pleasure.

Mercuri's fingers at her breast rubbed and tweaked an ever firming nipple. At her core, they rotated over her clit to send the nub radiating with dazzling sensation. His tongue thrust slow and potently- filling her deliciously, spreading her just enough to take it and his fingers at once.

Tee cried her approval shamelessly into the disturbed sheets. Climax made its relentless stab when he took her upper thighs, brought

281

her in even closer and deepened his tongue's exploration in the process. She was quivering from the inside out as a shattering orgasm rocked through her.

Mercuri didn't relent even when he felt her strong inner muscles lock around his tongue, squeezing the organ like a vice. His dick twitched anew. It was already painfully extended and craving the tight sheath his tongue was enjoying the pleasure of. He groaned, feeling her come oozing warm, slow and thick.

Tee was gasping, sobbing, trying to catch her breath as she descended from her high. She was still struggling to breathe steady when he put her on her back and claimed her in one seamless flow of movement. Familiar orgasmic waves began to simmer fresh as the stiff, filling slides stimulated every one of her nerve endings.

Arms resting above her head, hoisted her breasts even more prominently. Fully tempted, Mercuri lavished a licorice dark nipple with a deliberate wet suckle while adding more heat to his thrusts. He released the erect bud, dragging a wet kiss over the ample rise of her bosom to the delicate line of her collarbone. He set his face there to breathe in her scent even as he expressed his satisfaction with soft, deeply affected groans.

The sounds held unmistakable traces of helplessness that filled Tee with triumph over the knowledge that she could drive such a man to such a state. When he gave her his tongue, she had the treat of tasting herself and summoned another climax in the process. She didn't link her arms around his neck, but gripped his wrists instead. Using his long, muscle packed arms for purchase, she met his plundering strokes with her own fire.

Mercuri's soft groans, mixed with her name on his lips and he took her vigorously, tirelessly. Tee lost track of how long he worked her with such erotic expertise. Instinct had her wanting to lock her legs around his back, but he prevented that by keeping her lush thighs spread wide to accommodate him. Her body arched in the throes of satisfaction and her breathing erupted in rapid pants.

For Mercuri, he believed he'd never get enough of her sobbing gasps and wavering moans. Those sounds and the allure of her body however, had his shaft tightening in the manner that forewarned his release. His hold on her limbs began to ease as his own climax took hold. He was emptying himself inside her moments later.

Aftershocks of their dual release gripped them both for a long time. Exhaustion returned like a creeping fog that swamped them until they were both happily submerged in restful sleep.

~CHAPTER 31~

Tee was attempting a graceful exit from bed in the wee hours of the morning when Mercuri's arm tightened about her waist. Gently, she turned and smiled when she saw that his eyes were still closed.

"Go back to sleep," she kissed his jaw, the corner of his eye and his temple. "Just gonna grab some more of my stuff from home. I'm running low on outfits."

Mercuri sighed, his big body shifting beneath the covers. "I'll go with you."

"I've got bodyguards, remember?" She put an index finger in the center of his broad chest. "I have to admit that they seem to be as good as you claim."

It was true- Tee felt none of the apprehension or invasion of privacy she'd expected from her shadow over the last few days. She'd tried unsuccessfully to seek them out, but as Mercuri had promised, it was as if they weren't there.

"They're damn good," Mercuri kept his eyes closed while issuing the boast. "Don't be gone long," he added.

"Yessir," Tee's response earned her the contact of his unique gaze.

"How'd you know that's my favorite answer in the world?"

She shrugged, loving the grin he gave her. "Just a guess."

He braced on an elbow and cupped her cheek then. His thumb stroked the fully kissable curve of her mouth. "Now, get out of here before I send somebody to clear out your place for you."

"I'm just going to grab a few more things," she laughed.

Mercuri looked as though he'd just recalled the detail and appeared none too happy about the fact.

"Mercuri?"

"I know that's all you're going to do," he could tell his expression had her curious and pulled her close for a quick kiss. He refused to let it become more than that even when his dick stirred with arousal.

"Go," he ordered, giving her a mock frown to move her along. Pushing up against the headframe, he watched her rush naked around his bedroom, gathering clothes and slipping into them. He had to close his eyes to ward off steadily brewing arousal.

Tee was ready in record time and returned to the bed to offer additional goodbyes. Hands splayed across the bulge of his pecs, she leaned in for another quick kiss.

"See you later."

"Not too much later."

She adored the brooding expression he gave. "I promise," she pressed another kiss to his mouth.

His expression remained grim as he watched her go, his mind on his 'clearing out her place' remark. He wasn't sure that he'd meant to say it, but he meant it just the same. He'd meant it.

Things were still so new between them. He didn't want to scare her, but he had to be upfront about what he wanted. Dismissing the thought for a while, he grabbed his mobile from the raised console above the headboard and took time to call down to inform his security team of Tee's departure.

He left the bed then and began a slow walk around the room. He knew, better than most, how uncertain and un-promised the future was. Wasting time wasn't a high point on his list. His brilliant eyes flecked with something pensive as he strode the bedroom's perimeter. He also knew Tee would do all she could to try and convince him that she wasn't for him. She'd count on those discs to do the trick. He'd perceived that as well.

The perception had grown stronger once he'd viewed the goddamn thing. The night before, he reached for the single disc on the den end table with intentions to view it. Too late, he realized it was one he hadn't been expected to see.

What he'd watched happening to her that night had him wanting to trash his own office. He was snared by an enraged desire to inflict destruction on a substitute for the scum who pawed and salivated over her like she was a piece of meat. Time dragged once the lurid scenes reached their end. The only activity in the room where she'd been...used, was the snoring slumbers of the satisfied Ten.

Then, the action resumed in a way he was sure The Ten never anticipated. The slaughter was as beautiful as it was savage. Watching it, had been the only thing capable of muting his anger. He was beyond awestruck as he watched her. She'd spent years despising herself and thinking herself unworthy of love and happiness. It made him love her all the more.

***

Kevin Jonas and Vince Folksom had been relatively silent since returning to the car from the cafe where they'd parked. Shopping wouldn't get underway for another couple of hours when the rest of the store opened at Loriler Village. Traffic just then however, was almost nonexistent.

As was customary during a stakeout, time was required to prep coffee and add any additional condiments to sandwiches. The time was usually conversation free. Usually.

"Pretty convenient, her living in the middle of a shopping village. A ritzy one at that."

Vince, still in the process of loading sugar packets into his coffee, merely grinned. "Convenient."

Kevin didn't mind and went on with his compliments. "She's quite a little beauty, huh?"

That comment generated a bit more of a response from Vince. "Merc always had supreme taste. Have you seen her friends?"

"Hell yes," Kevin knocked his head against the navy seat back, sending a healthy mop of auburn curls jolting in the process. "Why couldn't I have gotten *that* detail? Tee's a doll, but she's like looking through a window at candy you'll never get to have. Her friends on the other hand-"

"You're an idiot if you think they're single."

"If they aren't, then why aren't their men part of this security detail?" Kevin challenged with a snort. "If a woman like that was on my arm, I'd damn well be highly involved in making sure she was safe."

Vince slid a look to his partner across the gear console. "If a woman like that was on *your* arm, I'd have to check her sanity." Vince cleared his throat and obviously faked an attempt at being serious. "Seriously man, you're gonna make some woman very lucky one day. 'Course you'll have to find one who doesn't run screaming when she sees you."

The vehicle's interior warmed with laughter and then the sound of crumpling sandwich wrappers and napkins merged in as the men began to eat. Their sandwiches were from The Food Place Diner beneath Tee's apartment.

After being alerted that their subject was on her way out of Mercuri's, Kevin and Vince began the tail once she'd left the estate. They picked her up easily and were confident and experienced enough to know she had yet to spot them although she knew they'd be there. Once parked and settled in with their food, the guys figured they had between 30-45 minutes of rest time before they were on the move.

"He sounds serious about her, Mercuri does." Kevin noted as he chewed the monstrous roast beef and turkey sub.

"Hell yeah, he does." Vince glanced up through the lightly tinted windshield to Tee's place. His wide, deeply tanned face was a study in approval. "More serious than I've ever seen him and I've known him a long time."

Kevin grinned. "We both have and I don't know about you, but seeing the guy head over heels like this gives me hope for what I might find."

Vince tipped his coffee cup in toast. "You and me both, man."

"Vin?"

Vince had heard the quiet pop of pierced glass seconds before Kevin called to him. The man's voice hovered between faint surprise and confusion. Vince looked across the gear shift to his partner and saw Kevin's spilled coffee blending with the crimson stain spreading rapidly across the upper half of the beige shirt he wore. The man's dark blue eyes appeared more vivid against the pale skin draining of blood.

"Kev-" Vince heard additional sounds of popping glass and he could feel pinpricks of pain stabbing his shoulder and forearm. He could see Kevin's shirt ripping beneath the incoming gunfire.

Vince watched a silent bullet open his partner's throat a split second before pain exploded along the side of his head. Somehow, and he feared he would never know how, Vince found a way to fight past the excruciating torment. He fumbled his gun from its holster. His hands were slick with blood and made releasing the weapon a chore. Pain all but blinded him then.

Gun at the ready, he crashed through the passenger side door, working doggedly to aim his weapon. He made out the threatening figure just as a blood red haze blurred his vision.

Vince squeezed the automatic's trigger several times and believed a few of the shots may have hit his target. That was another of those things he feared he'd never know. Pain bloomed fresh, white hot and fatal.

Zubin dropped his aim. The gun hung limp at his side as he moved out of sight and dug for his phone.

"It's done," he said once the connection had been made.

"I owe you, Zoo," Harris' voice drifted over the line.

"You want me there?" Zubin asked.

"This one's mine, Zoo. Talk to you soon, alright?"

"Yeah," Zubin winced. The gun felt like lead in his slippery hand. "Yeah, talk to you soon." The connection ended and he gave a pained sigh while setting the gun to the hood of the car he'd used to follow the detail on Etienne Shaw.

"See you on the other side, my friend." Zubin leaned on the car as the warm ooze of his own blood had his shirt sticking to his skin. The wounds were deep, but he couldn't risk lingering there for too long. Any moment, the carnage in the parking lot would draw attention. He staggered, but made his way behind the wheel. The engine ignited after two failed attempts. Soon, he was fishtailing out of the narrow side lot.

***

Tee fought to open her eyes. When she achieved success, she immediately wished she hadn't. She had already picked up on a scent that was dark and moldy. Having a visual reference for the smell had her feeling even more nauseous.

A small sound of discomfort surged up from her throat and she could detect the bitter flavor of bile coating her palate. The sound replayed itself as she shifted on what she assumed was a chair.

Through the haze resting like a shroud over her brain, she could sense that she wasn't being secured to the chair. Still, she felt incapable of movement. Her arms felt leaden as they hung past the sides of the seat. She could see them coming into focus along with the wet, dingy flooring beneath her feet. Her memory was sketchy, but she recalled pushing her phone into her jeans before everything went black. Her body was so numb, she couldn't tell whether it was still there or not.

How did she get there? Experimentally, she tried to move her feet across the floor. Nothing. Her brain and her limbs were on different wavelengths and the messages weren't computing.

The moldy smell was getting stronger as was the cold. The place was freezing and she wore only a T-shirt and faded pair of denim capris with canvas shoes. Not the best attire for wherever the hell she was. Beneath that moldy aroma was the hint of something metallic. The space was poorly lit but she was able to battle against the nausea and dizziness to lift her head in hopes of making out more of her surroundings. Infrequently, she could detect slashes of something red and unmistakably garish on the floor and walls.

Desperate then, Tee worked to get her arms and legs moving. She tried to mutter words of encouragement, but only succeeded in producing harsh grunts.

"I'm sorry Ms. Shaw, I'm afraid that's not gonna do you much good."

***

"I appreciate you handling this and putting it all together so fast, Rand. I know coming within a hundred miles of this stuff is something you never planned on." Mercuri used the phone in his study. Seated on the corner of his desk, his body was rigid; his exotic gaze was cold and fixed. Randall Cafrey's soft laughter coming through the line jarred him from the morose stream of his thoughts.

"Are you serious here, Merc? Hell man, if it wasn't for you, I'd still be crawlin' through piss and shit runnin' ops for the GAN.

"Well I appreciate it anyway in light of what I'm asking you to do."

"I couldn't believe what you said when we talked a few days ago and now…" Randall whistled.

Mercuri grinned, envisioning his old friend scouring the feed from the security discs he'd sent over electronically following their conversation.

"This will be the biggest thing my people have sunk their teeth into in a long time, Merc. They're overdue. This is gonna run and run soon." Randall promised. "Just wanted to let you know we're a go. I'll be in touch soon, let you know when I'll send over the preview recording."

"Sounds good, Rand. I'll let you get to work." Mercuri signed off the call and was watching the view beyond the study windows when his head of security James O'Hara knocked on the open door and stepped inside.

Mercuri needed only a half a second of looking at the man, to sense all wasn't well.

James didn't waste time with pleasantries. "Kevin Jonas is dead. Vince Folksom is in bad shape. He'll probably be on his way out by night's end according to the doctor."

"Kevin and Vince."

James grimaced. "Yeah, it's Tee's detail-"

"Where is she?" Mercuri rounded the desk. He braced his hands on the surface as he was badly in need of support for his legs which had gone to water.

"She wasn't in her apartment," James reported. "They found Kev and Vince in the parking slip across from her building. Before they took him away, Vince gave a pretty good description of Zoo."

"Grant Zubin?" Mercuri demanded the strength back to his legs. It was no time to let worry-fear-get the better of him. "And Harris?" he asked.

"No sign of him," James sounded hopeful. "Her place didn't even look disturbed when my guys checked it out."

Mercuri breathed a curse. "They've got her."

"Well it looks like Vince got in a few lucky shots with Zoo. One of the detectives called to the scene is a friend. He says they found a blood trail that stopped near tire tracks. If he's wounded maybe he and Harris parted ways."

Mercuri was already headed behind his desk to feel beneath its glossy maple edge. On the other side of the wide room, a lengthy mural-lined wall retracted.

"I don't want the cops involved." He issued the order without looking at James.

The man shook his head. "They won't be. Far as they can tell, it looks like Vince and Kev were victims of a carjacking. Easy to believe considering the slick piece of eye candy they were driving. They're both licensed to carry, so everything's in order there. What's the play, Merc?" James watched his old friend disappear behind the wall he knew led to an immense artillery bunker.

"You're going to look for her," James guessed when his question went unanswered.

"Harris has her," Mercuri spoke as though to himself. "He won't kill her. He'll need her to draw me out. It's what he wants- what he's always wanted."

Neither man acknowledged the obvious. Both of them knew that Harris Van Deer was twisted enough to kill Tee before he ever alerted Mercuri to where she was. The mere fact that he'd taken her would be enough to ensure pursuit.

Mercuri started towards the fake wall again and hissed something vicious when his phone dinged persistently. Leaving off his trek, he went to grab the large mobile and activated the screen. The read-out focused and that time, his legs went to water along with the rest of him.

***

Tee stopped moving or rather, she ordered her brain to stop commanding her limbs to move. As her head was the only part of her capable of motion, she attempted to angle it in the direction of the male voice from the bottomless depths of what seemed to be a cavernous space.

She made a stab at using her own voice then. "What did you give me?" Her words were slurred and her tongue felt as heavy as her arms and legs.

Tee's captor had obviously understood. "It's something that'll make it hard to get those excellent curves moving anytime soon."

Despite her paralytic state, Tee felt a shiver kiss her skin. "Who are you?" She tried out her voice again.

"A friend," laughter followed the response and echoed in the space. "I suppose I should say- a friend of a friend."

291

Her heart seized. "Mercuri."

Laughter roared out again. "Beautiful and smart! Mercuri always did know how to pick 'em. That's right, love. Mercuri and I go way back."

"What's that got to do with me?"

"Why everything, Ms. Shaw. This whole thing got started with you and your whoring friends."

Tee grunted again, that time in disapproval of the light suddenly filtering the room.

"Ah yes," he said. "There's that surprise. Surely you didn't think Roya and the Patterson bitch are the only ones who knew your names. Still, I gotta hand it to you- you kept your secret a lot longer than anyone else ever has against us."

The man had switched on some high intensity flashlight and, as her vision focused, Tee had a better idea of where she was being held.

The garish red streaks she'd been too terrified to acknowledge as blood, were actually garish orange streaks-rust. The walls were curved outward, tall and of the same dingy hue as the floors. A ship?

"Who are you?" She scanned the area with fresh interest.

"I apologize again, Ms. Shaw," he laughed. "I'm Harris Van Deer. As I said, Mercuri is an old friend."

"I've met all of Mercuri's friends." Her anger stirred in tandem with a slight tingling sensation in her toes and fingertips.

Harris' smile reflected doubt. "I'm not sure that's accurate, Ms. Shaw. I doubt you met Patroclus Kostas unless you started seeing Mercuri before his death."

Tee felt the shiver dancing over her skin again as Harris strode the vast space. As though he were recounting a scene in some exciting movie he'd watched, he spoke on the tragedy of the death.

"Did you know there wasn't even enough of his face left to identify through dental records? The killer just stomped it out beneath the heel of his boot." For emphasis, Harris stomped a booted foot to the wet floor.

Tee felt her fingers flex in reaction. "Why was he killed?" She forced herself to speak, not because she feared her voice might fail, but because she feared she might share Patroclus Kostas' fate. Keeping Harris Van Deer talking, might give her time to think of a way to keep that from happening. Luckily, the man seemed to be in a mood to chat.

"Mercuri, Patroclus and the rest decided to change the rules. Change 'em regardless of what the rest of us thought, regardless of what the rest of us had done for security in a place we'd slaved for. Mercuri wanted his freedom, but freedom means different things to different people, Ms. Shaw. Mercuri went to live his life and made his fortune while the rest of us had to watch what we'd sacrificed our dignity- our sanity-for, get pissed away to nothing."

She could feel sensation returning to her legs, but then she was riveted by the passionate delivery of Van Deer's monologue. "You really hate him, don't you?"

"I really hate him." Harris confirmed the question without a second's hesitation. "If for nothing else than him keeping this-this testament, this fossil to honor himself," he gestured to the decaying ship, arms spread wide and high. "Do you know how many thousands of dollars he spends each month to park this thing in dry dock? A goddamn memento?"

"You disapprove of sentiment?"

"I disapprove of betrayal."

"You hate him because you don't understand him- don't get how he's done what he's done. What he's done to accomplish what he has."

"What about what I've done?! Did he tell you about that, Ms. Shaw?! Hell no, because he doesn't know-never bothered to ask. Didn't care that some of us had been plotting our own escapes-our own plans- to take the crown. He didn't care how much dignity some of us had to cast aside in pursuit of it. You and your friends killed The Ten for taking what you were there to provide. You think you were the first to want them dead? I wanted to pull their fucking hearts out through their fuckin throats every time I got tagged for one of their theme parties and had to act like I enjoyed those fat bastards slobbering and coming all over me. Oh I wanted them dead! But there was more I wanted and for that, the ends totally justified the means. It was there for the taking and then there was Mercuri with his magnanimous gesture promising fortune and freedom and fuck anybody else's plans."

Harris silenced and turned. His expression hinted of mild surprise when his bland stare locked on Tee's face as if he had forgotten she was there.

Tee wasn't sure her arms and legs were at full capacity. She certainly wasn't sure of their capability against the man who held her against her will. Van Deer didn't have Mercuri's bulk, but she knew it would be unwise to underestimate the man's rangy, leanly muscled build.

Sadly, she had no time to debate further. Harris Van Deer's surprise had shifted into something feral and cunning.

"That's the thing about plans," He said, "there's always somebody around to fuck 'em up."

Tee gave a silent curse when she felt her eyes widen. She knew Van Deer had seen her surprise, her fear. His smile confirmed it.

"You shouldn't worry, Ms. Shaw. Once Kostas accepted that worrying wouldn't save him, he settled into it and soon he was beyond feeling anything-even the pain."

"At least tell me what you're going to do," she tried to think fast when he stepped toward her.

Harris appeared to consider the request, before he shrugged. "What the hell...you see, Mercuri's tribute to his past," he gestured to the ship's interior again. "It's about to play a hefty role in his future. When they find you, beaten-dead from your injuries and starvation, they'll go looking for Mercuri."

Tee's curse hit the air then. Anger was suddenly outweighing her fear. "No one will believe he hurt me."

"Maybe not, but that's not really what this is about. I've been watching the two of you. I dare say my old friend is really in love." Harris began to pace the wet, rusted floor. The sound of his soles slapping puddles added an eerie accompaniment to his words.

"It's no surprise that he's successful with women, but I have the feeling there's more to this. There's obviously more to you. Perhaps he senses a kindred spirit- that killer instinct you both possess," he shrugged. "I guess you don't believe he's capable of such maliciousness?"

"I believe it very well," Tee didn't flinch on the admission. "I pray I have the chance to watch him put it in action when he finds you."

Harris' chuckle echoed in the ship's lofty rafters. "I'm afraid those prayers won't be answered as that sort of goes against the whole 'fucking up plans' thing," his expression sobered.

"My old friend's very attached to you. Now, whether you're it for him or he just wants to enjoy fucking you a while longer, you've got a very important place in his life right now. Hell, he's going to all the trouble of making sure you're safe- putting his best guys on you and all.

Too bad they're dead now- you don't find good help like that, every day."

Tee gasped then, past caring whether her fear showed.

"Anyway, watching him deal with losing something so important to him in a place so important to him…"

"You're insane," she breathed.

"I am! Quite!" His chuckle confirmed the admission more than his words did. "You're such a quick study Ms. Shaw. It's a shame our paths had to cross."

~CHAPTER 32~

"You're a goddamn idiot if you think we're gonna let you go in there on your own."

Mercuri was in no mood to smile, but he did when he looked to Rutger. He brought a hand down hard on the other man's shoulder and squeezed. "Harris wants it this way and I'm happy to oblige him."

"You sound just as crazy as the fool inside that monstrosity over there," Pope cast a black look toward the cargo ship in the distance.

Mercuri rounded the truck he'd taken to the shipyard. "I'm good with that," he muttered.

He had battled and triumphed against sudden weakness earlier. The world had all but dropped out from beneath him when he saw the GPS readout on his mobile. Twin emotions of satisfaction and horror pooled. He had invaded Tee's privacy like a battering ram when he fished through her bag the night he'd viewed the disc.

He'd been in search of her phone and got sidetracked by the dreaded disc instead. After watching it, he cast off his debates and followed through on his plans. Now, he celebrated the intrusion. The tracker he'd installed on her mobile had allowed him to pinpoint her location. He'd been alerted when the phone moved out of the specified range from Kevin Jonas' and Vince Folksom's phones.

Tee's phone wasn't in the hulking ship standing beneath the day's darkly overcast skies and looking glorious yet doomed across the yard. Instead, Mercuri and his men located it in the trunk of the sedan Harris had apparently used for transport.

Yes, he'd celebrated his foresight with the tracker, but the phone's recovery had terrified him to no end. Harris Van Deer's choice of location wasn't without symbolism- he wanted to send a message. Mercuri couldn't help but think of the message he'd sent with Patroclus' murder.

"At least think about what you're doin' man," Slayte was speaking up then. "You don't know who Harris has in there watchin' his back. Even if Zoo's off somewhere having his wounds tended, they're still travelin' with a lot of muscle."

"He wants me too much to let anyone else kill me," Mercuri opened the truck's tailgate.

"And Zoo?" Slayte dropped a hand to Mercuri's forearm before he could reach over the gate. "You forget I've got business in there, same as you."

"No Slay, not same as me. They haven't touched what's yours." Mercuri waited, smiling tightly when Slayte moved out of his way. He retrieved the gun, knife and ammunitions belts he'd stored in the steel box along the flatbed. Once they were secured to his waist and thighs, he brushed past his friends and left them with a few last words.

"Follow me in there and I'll kill you all."

~~~

"You're a coward," Tee spoke the words as if she'd just accepted the realization as fact.

Her words didn't seem to offend Harris. In fact, his mouth curved into a smile as his thin brows lifted.

"Anything else?" he asked.

"Yeah, you talk too much," she countered. "Clearly, the only way you can get anybody to listen to your sob story is to tie them to a chair or drug them." Carelessly, she inclined her head in a dismissive manner.

"So you were betrayed, mistreated- who hasn't been? At least some of us are lucky enough to realize it so we can get out of it. You chose to play along instead of fighting your way out. All for greed," she sneered, loathing clinging to the slow scan she took of his face and form. "I suppose next to that, being a coward isn't so bad."

She watched Harris' easy smile thin into a cold slash. He came toward her, but she remained undaunted. For the first time in six years, she didn't try to stifle the rabid creature that still laid in wait. This time, she embraced it.

"You hate Mercuri, because he didn't play the game-he broke it."

"And you think I don't know about breaking things, Ms. Shaw? I know all too well."

"So do I." He was close enough to receive the full impact of her heel meeting his crotch.

The feeling had returned to her limbs during his lengthy diatribe. Harris went to his knees, curving into himself as pain had its way with his genitals. Tee bolted from the chair, but Harris battled past his discomfort and grabbed her ankle before she could clear him. His clutch sent her to her hands and knees on the wet, rusty floor.

She turned his own move against him and used the foot he held to jam into his ribs. Harris howled, releasing her and she followed up with another kick. Like a flash, she was using her other foot to punish his jaw.

Even as pain had him writhing, Harris fumbled inside his jacket. Tee was on him then, fighting to get inside the jacket as well. She felt the bulge of a weapon and her adrenaline pulsed. The butt of the gun was coming free of the holster. His hand far outsized hers, but she managed to wedged her fingers through his and put in her own bid for possession.

Harris had managed to push up to an elbow and used the leverage that provided, to roll to his side facing Tee. She capitalized, that time it was a knee that punished Harris' genitals. The advantage allowed her to seize the gun, a vicious tug freeing it from the holster.

Tee celebrated Berrill's obsession with guns then and recalled her friend's relentless demands that she, LuCarolyn and Prin all learn to handle themselves. Backing up on her haunches, she checked the weapon's clip, snapping it back into place and then releasing the safety. Pushing to stand, she made a quick scan of the dark area in search of an exit. She considered making a grab for the flashlight, but couldn't risk it. Van Deer would be on his feet soon.

Squinting, she used as much of the light afforded to her and headed for a curved doorway at the farthest end of the area. She noticed the steel ladders built at intervals along the walls, but she wouldn't risk losing her hold on the gun while she made the climb.

She made a run for it instead. The doorway- what she hoped was the doorway or hatch or whatever the fuck it was called- seemed to get farther away the further she ran. The place was the size of three football fields it seemed. She was coming in range, when a shot rang out and stopped her cold.

"I'm not one of The Ten," Harris was on his feet and steadily aiming another gun. "Are we done playing now?"

She turned, braced. "Not yet," she aimed her gun and fired.

Harris' roar reverberated along with the gunfire, but Tee wasn't stopping to check that she'd hit her mark.

She offered a quick prayer of thanks then, discovering that it was a doorway she ran towards. Thanks to her captor, there was no need to work at lifting the lever- the hatch was already open.

It was like running with her eyes closed, she thought while taking the passageways. Tee only knew she'd reached the end of one when she hit the wall. The sound of metal clanging against metal, when the gun she'd secured made contact, was sure to give away her location. Still, she forged ahead, consistently slamming into walls and making awkward turns down new passageways.

Tee kept a death grip on the gun but she didn't run with it aimed straight ahead. Last thing she needed was to run up against an unexpected wall and kill herself when the weapon discharged. Splices of weak light began to infiltrate the darkness, giving her hope that her blind jog was carrying her toward an exit. It was early morning when she'd gotten home, but she had no idea how much time had passed since her trip into madness.

Her hopes tipped into despair when she hit the next wall. Despair meshed with terror, for this wall-massive and unyielding-pulsed with life. She poised herself to fight. She wouldn't entertain the thought that a takedown of this new adversary might very well kill her.

She had no time to put her fight plan into action. Hands covered her hips and she was being lifted higher against the chest she'd slammed into. Only then, did she remember the gun. Her shadowed opponent slipped it from her fingers like one might take balloons from a child. She fought anyway, using her fists and nails to claw.

In the midst of rage, there was peace seeking to claim her. She could hear soft, shushing sounds and a voice-an intoxicating one- that sent her fears draining.

"Babe, it's me, it's Mercuri. It's me, it's okay."

"Mercuri?" His name was a whisper on her lips. Her fists unfurled to smooth up over the chest she'd pummeled at seconds before.

"It's me. I've got you."

Tee settled into the contentment his words provided. Soon, she was shaking her head and fighting to ward off the serenity his presence instilled. "A man- there's a man back there- Harris-Harris Van-"

"Shh... I know, babe, I know." Mercuri realized he didn't want to hear her speak the name. He took her with him through the passageways, back the way he'd come.

Tee marveled at the seamless efficiency of his moves. "How are you seeing in this?" She hadn't felt any kind of night vision wear when her hands had roamed his face. Contentment shimmied through her once again when she heard him chuckle.

"I know this place like the back of my hand. It was my first ship."

She remembered then. "The picture-the picture in your room."

"Yeah...I'm a little sentimental about it," faint embarrassment hugged the admission.

"He-Harris-told me that's why he chose it."

Mercuri felt a muscle clench in his jaw until it ached. "Tee did he...did he do anything?"

"No," she answered straightaway, understanding. "No, I had to fight him to get away, but that was it."

"That's enough," his voice was granite.

"I took his gun, but he's got another."

Mercuri felt the urge to smile. "Good for him," he said. His long strides carried them out of the ship, through a series of passageways that took them to a hatch that opened several decks below the main. There, Tee was quickly shifted from Mercuri's arms to Rutger's.

"Get her the hell out of here." Mercuri turned on his heel.

"Wait! You-you're going back inside?" Desperation widened her dark eyes as she took a quick scan of her new surroundings. "You're going back in there alone?"

"I said get her out of here!" Mercuri called the order over his shoulder.

Tee began to squirm. It did her no good. "Rutger please," she smiled her gratitude when he set her to her feet, just as Mercuri returned to crowd her.

"Mercuri you can't-"

"I have to, Hon."

"Not like this," she shook her head but could tell his mind was already made. "At least take someone with you."

He smiled, his gaze made more brilliant given the gray tint to the environment. "I seriously doubt anybody here can watch my back better than you," he dragged a thumb down her cheek. "As much as I'd love to watch you kick the guy's ass, this is something I should've done a long time ago." Over her head, he nodded to Rutger who lifted Tee without hesitation.

"Mercuri!" Fists bracing against Rutger's chest, Tee strained to see past the man when he turned to carry her off. Mercuri didn't register her cries to him and didn't stop his journey back into the bowels of the ship.

~~~

His vision quickly adjusted once he was on the inside. It didn't much matter. The place was black as pitch, but it was as he'd told Tee, he knew it like the back of his hand. Mercuri's long strides ate up the length of the twisty passageways that wound deeper into the vessel. He'd freed a gun from the holster at his waist, but had no plans to use it. He wanted to take Harris apart with his own hands- no enhancements required.

The path Tee was on when she met him led from a storage compartment on the lowest deck. Chances were strong that Harris had moved on, but there was as good a place to start as any. He noticed the flicker of light as he neared the compartment area and took his steps with more caution then. Approaching the hatch, he ducked to enter and made his way toward a big flashlight perched on one of only a few crates in the immense space.

"How the fuck are you here?"

Mercuri turned, leaned on the crate. Harris saw the gun he carried, but made no effort to raise the one he held. Coolly, Mercuri set his weapon atop the crate. He made no move to relieve himself of the rest of the weapons on his person. The lone gun Harris brandished was by no means his only defense.

301

"You know what a control freak I am, Harris. I put a tracker on her phone. You should've searched her better."

Harris offered a lewd smile. "I decided to save that part for here. I was just getting to it when she had a flashback to the night she sold herself to The Ten. Thought she could take me down," he laughed then. "Can you imagine that? A little thing like her!"

"She took your gun, so yeah I can imagine it just fine."

Harris' lewd smile became a snarl. "Who would've thought it? The great Mercuri Nikolaides brought to his knees by a little whore."

Mercuri shook his head. "It's interesting to hear you use that word with such disgust, when you once whored yourself regularly for The Ten."

Harris had no time to mask the stricken wave that sharpened his features. "How...?"

Mercuri laughed, the sound harsh when it bounced off the metal. "Did you think I didn't know? That we all didn't know? You think it was me who ruined your chances for leading the GAN? It was you all along Harris. Nathan and Lorne weren't going to give that kind of power to the organization's in-house hooker-"

"You shut your mouth!" Harris aimed his gun then. "I was loyal to them-unlike you."

"They used you Harris. They used us all, just in different ways. What I did wasn't meant to take your future. It was meant to give you one."

"The magnanimous Mercuri!" Harris spread his arms in an exaggerated gesture. "They were willing to hand it all to you on a platter-things the rest of us had to sell ourselves just to be in the running for- and you gave them your ass to kiss. This is going to be such a pleasure," he cocked the gun.

"Then why not enjoy it?" Mercuri was close enough to reach for his own gun. Instead, he raised his hands in the universal gesture for surrender and moved away from the crate.

"The gun gets things over with so quick," he said. "I don't buy that you haven't thought about taking me down with your own hands. Or do I still frighten you?"

Harris hurled the gun and sent it skidding across the rusted damp to stop just short of hitting the hull. He charged, catching Mercuri around the waist in a tackle that sent him both sliding across the murky floor.

Harris laid into Mercuri's side with a barrage of punches, but hit the floor face first when Mercuri punished his spine with an elbow to the center of his back. While Harris recovered from the blow, Mercuri relieved himself of the belts, straps and holsters that secured his weapons.

The items were hitting the crate with a clatter just as Harris rushed Mercuri from behind and repaid his elbow to the back with one of his own. The impact had Mercuri grimacing, yet he followed the attack by bringing his elbow up and back squarely into Harris' cheek. The satisfying crunch of shattering bone followed. Harris kicked out and the heel of his boot caught Mercuri's ankle, sending him to his knees.

Mercuri rounded rapidly for a man his size and caught Harris' already abused cheek with a ferocious slam from his fist. The contact sent Harris landing on his ass. He connected with the crate and sent it crashing to its side. Mercuri caught Harris' ankle and dragged him back for more punishment. He brutalized the man's face, intent on inflicting the same savagery Patroclus Kostas suffered as he died.

Harris' nose fountained blood, but he had yet to play his final card. From a small sheath along his belt, he retrieved a gleaming switch blade. Mercuri's fist was staged for another blow, but Harris swiped the blade, slicing it across Mercuri's wrist. He then put another gash along the inside of Mercuri's bicep. Blood poured from the rip in the sleeve of the army green crew shirt he wore.

Mercuri managed to catch Harris' wrist, squeezing until he'd forced open the hand that wielded the knife. The blade clattered to the rusted metal hull. Mercuri tightened his grip on Harris' wrist, his intention to crush the bone.

Harris struggled in earnest, working to free his other wrist that Mercuri had trapped beneath his knee. Harris achieved success and, catching the handle of the flashlight, used it to punish Mercuri's jaw.

The pain radiating along the side of his face, had Mercuri grunting. Harris staggered to take a knee and next drove a fist into Mercuri's jaw. Harris got to his feet and took additional advantage of the opportunity to drive a vicious kick into his adversary's ribs.

"Thanks for suggesting I use my hands," Harris panted, "and feet," he followed up the kick to Mercuri's ribs with another. He bent, and from an ankle holster, produced a small caliber gun. "If it's all the same to you now, I'm ready to see you die."

"I agree," Mercuri breathed. Rearing up, his fist connected with the nickel plated pistol. The force of the blow had the gun flying into the darkened distance. Seamlessly, he slipped Harris' neck into a vice hold that took the man off his feet. A moment passed and then Mercuri was dropping Harris on his ass. He followed, kneeling behind his enemy on the ship's grimy bottom.

Harris fought for his breath. Mercuri cupped his chin in one hand while the other lay flat across the crown of his head. "The power," Harris shuddered out the words. "Did you ever want it? Even a little?"

"I never wanted it," Mercuri's voice carried the same shuddering intensity. "Not even a little." He gave a ruthless jerk that turned Harris chin and forehead in opposing directions.

The air carried the echo of the telling snap that signaled Harris Van Deer's neck breaking.

~~~

Mercuri's weary expression gave way to one of renewed outrage when he stumbled out of the ship's hatch to find his men and his friends waiting along with Tee. She looked both out of place and right at home seated on the tailgate with her short, shapely legs swinging rhythmically.

She spotted him first and, even as she raced into his arms, Mercuri was eyeing Slayte, Rutger and Pope with lingering glares of lethal promise.

Pope was first to step forward and test his bravery. "She refused to leave," he explained.

Mercuri's expression was then one of surprised amusement. "Refused? And you let her?" Faint laughter colored his words.

"She threatened us," Slayte supplied while shutting the SUVs tailgate. "Made us promise to only give you ten more minutes before we went in after you."

"Threatened you?" Despite the pain still radiating and a general sense of being pissed off, Mercuri's laughter flowed a bit more noticeably. "With what?"

"Jeez Merc, isn't our admission of being threatened, enough?" Rutger gave his argument on a hushed breath. "Don't make us relive the humiliation by repeating it."

Mercuri looked down at Tee who seemed more interested in the bruise beginning to darken his jaw.

"I'll give you details, later," she told him in an absent tone, still focused on his jaw.

"Suffice it to say we believed her," Pope added.

Tee gasped suddenly, having noticed the blood streaming Mercuri's arm. In seconds, she'd waved over men armed with treatment kits. They surrounded Mercuri, escorting him to the back of a waiting van. Tee followed, standing nearby as he sat.

"What'll we find in there?" Rutger asked.

Mercuri shook his head. "It was just Harris- I'm pretty sure he was alone."

Nodding in sync, Pope, Slayte and Rutger led a band of men into the waiting ship.

Tee watched as the MTs cutaway Mercuri's shirt sleeve and began treating and dressing the wound. Repeatedly, she slid her fingers through the sweat slicked hair matted at his forehead and temples.

"You're an idiot," she told him dryly.

"But you still love me, right?" He studied her coolly, the mesmerizing pools of his exotic gaze stirred with helpless adoration.

"Definitely," There was no stopping her smile when she confirmed his query as fact. "But you're still an idiot. He could've killed you."

He shrugged, then grunted as something stingingly cold was pressed to a bloody scrape along his cheek. He bowed his head reverently. "I knew I had the advantage going in. Thanks for softening him up for me."

She gave a playful wave. "Anytime."

"This was the only time. Count on that," there was no playfulness in his tone. He looked to one of the MTs investigating his ribs. "Could you give us a minute, Reg?"

Reginald Soloway gave a brief nod and then made himself scarce.

Mercuri caught the edge of Tee's shirt and drew her closer. "This was the last time. Harris was unfinished business- that's finished now."

"Thank you for coming to find me."

Mercuri slipped his injured arm about her waist, but made no indication that the move caused him pain. "Did you think I wouldn't?"

"I knew you would. I just didn't see how you could. What were the odds of you finding me in there?" She jerked her head toward the ship in the distance.

"Odds were pretty good," he winced, "I put a tracker on your phone."

"When?"

"The night your friends came to the house," he slanted a wink when she gaped. "Forgive me?" he asked.

Tee spared a few more seconds to gape and then shook her head on a sigh. "Since it resulted in saving my life, I'd have to say 'yes'." Her expression turned somber. "I'm sorry about Kevin and Vince."

"I'll never be able to repay them for what they did," Mercuri was somber as well. "Harris may not have been the only one in there with you if it weren't for them."

Tee shook her head again, the gesture held the lightness of relief. "What do you think the odds are of us living a drama free life?"

Mercuri winced a second time. "Not sure about that, but what do you say we give it a try anyway? You game?"

"Game." She gave a single, stern nod. "But first things first."

"Oh yeah?" his brilliant eyes lowered suggestively to her chest heaving provocatively beneath her T-shirt. His fingers were skimming the hem when he saw her wave to the MTs.

She cupped his face when he breathed a curse. "Still love me?"

Mercuri pretended to consider his response and then leaned on the one she'd given earlier to his same question.

"Definitely."

~CHAPTER 33~

Four Days Later...

"How did you do this?" Tee's voice carried the distinct flavor of bewildered amazement. The bottomless dark of her expressive eyes mirrored the same wonderment as her words. She'd spent the last 25 minutes riveted by the play of image and voice across the flat screen in Mercuri's bedroom.

Mercuri wasn't nearly as riveted by the television broadcast. While Tee sat up on the enormous bed, her legs folded beneath her, Mercuri rested content while grazing his bruised knuckles across the small of her back.

He wasn't missing anything. Randall Cafrey had already instructed his team at the FNN to provide an advanced copy which Mercuri had viewed the night before. Regardless of whether he'd been privy to the sneak peek, Mercuri knew he favored the way he was spending his time.

Once the MTs had ceased their relentless prodding at the shipyard, Mercuri was transported home-flat on his back in the treatment van. His doctor subjected him to a more relentless prodding and diagnosed him with three bruised ribs and a mild concussion. The slice he'd suffered along his bicep had been deep, but there would be no lasting tendon damage.

Still, the doctor had restricted his patient's movements, ordering bedrest and limited movement. Mercuri despised the last order as it limited his enjoyment of his houseguest. Sadly for Mercuri, Tee was all too devoted to following the doctor's orders. She agreed to stay with Mercuri so long as they kept to separate sleeping quarters.

Following the shootout between Grant Zubin and a recovering Vince Folksom, Mercuri's men had arrived on scene at Tee's apartment. Mercuri had given them instructions to have her belongings removed. He'd even made space in his closet for her stuff, but Tee had spent every night alone in a bed three rooms away.

"This is amazing," she shook her head while the closing credits flashed for *In Scope* FNNs award-winning news documentary program.

"You didn't have the discs long enough for them to come up with something this thorough," she said.

Mercuri closed his eyes, sheer relaxation coursing his body as he stroked her back. "Helps to have someone on the inside. 'Specially when that someone is a former member of the GAN."

Tee shifted, folded her legs beneath her when she faced Mercuri in bed. "This was your plan?"

"This was my plan. Some of it." He rolled a beefy shoulder and appeared nonplussed. "I didn't expect Rand to have it done so fast- guess he was motivated."

"The reporter said the footage and the questions it raises could put the GAN in a scandalous spotlight-one that could foreshadow its ruin."

"Yeah," Mercuri sighed over her words, but still portrayed an image of serenity. "It could at that."

"Doesn't feel right for me to thank you."

"Then don't."

"What I mean is," she shifted a bit more on the bed. "Grodins Alberts they…my involvement with them was abstract, on the fringe, I wasn't…involved the way you were."

He opened his eyes then, covered her clasped hands beneath one of his. "What happened to you, happened to too many others. It had to end one way or another. You were that way."

"Incidentally."

"And effectively. Don't second guess what's done, Tee and for Christ's sake, don't pity them. They were filth. A stain that deepened every year they existed. My mother, my friends' mothers, they were no more than breeding stock to them- a way to keep their ranks replenished. That practice would always be a relevant one to them which means there would always be a woman lured by the promise of a new and better life only to discover too late what was required of her, when she was forced to give up the thing she loves." His rare eyes turned hard and haunted then.

"For that Tee, I wish I could send them all to hell."

She turned her palm up, linked her fingers through his. "Maybe you have," she squeezed his hand.

Mercuri took advantage of the innocent contact to tug her close. Tee resisted with a hand to the center of his chest but found herself on her back beneath him in a few second's time.

"Mercuri no-"

"But I'm all better," he settled some of his crushing form against her and allowed her to feel the weight of his erection on her thigh.

"See?" He taunted when he saw her lashes flutter.

Tee rolled her eyes. "That part of you was never injured."

"It's starting to feel that way."

"The doctor said no," her voice was a shudder when he began a lusty assault on her earlobe.

"I won't tell him."

The rumble of his voice was an inducement all its own.

"I will." She still managed to resist, but gave a throaty gasp when his fingers were thrusting and rotating inside her.

"I'll make it fast. I promise," he suckled harder on her lobe.

"'Kay..." she slipped silkily into submission. "And after that I'll be forced to go stay with my girls..."

His fingers slowed and then withdrew. He raised his head and fixed her with a look of playful disappointment. "You're a traitor, you know?" He slid back to his preferred side of the bed.

Pitying him a little, Tee leaned in to put a sweet kiss to his temple.

Mercuri merely grunted. "That's not helping. Don't go," he said when she began to scoot from the bed.

"I'll be right back," she smiled at the doubt in his expression as her own mounted.

~~~

She made good on her promise and was returning to Mercuri's bedroom suite in less than five minutes. His eyes sparkled with the hope that she'd changed her mind, but soon he was appearing crestfallen having noticed what she brought along with her.

"Tee-"

"I know. I know you didn't ask to see it, but I-*I* need you to." She held the disc case in both hands as though it were some kind of sacred offering.

"I've been told on many occasions that I'm all types of fools for wanting to show you this, but I need you to know I-I know we both have things in our pasts, but this is one I just don't want between us. I think about it all the time-not so much since I met you but...I know you've wondered where I go when I zone out. Sometimes I'm afraid I'm not done with it- that the need to do...what I did might creep up again and I...I just," she gave a weary shake of her head, "I just want you to have answers."

"I don't need any, babe."

"I know." She tried for a smile but only managed a miserable tremble of her lips. She descended the short stairway to the bed and sat the disc on the corner.

"I'll be in my room if you want to talk," she said and then all but ran from the room.

~~~

Rain ushered in the next day. Unlike previous mornings, Tee didn't visit Mercuri's room to check on him. He hadn't come by to talk the night before. She didn't think it wise to take that as her answer but she had a hard time doing anything but.

To take her mind off her nerves and to prepare for the worst, she decided to pack a bag. She was finishing up when the disc dropped down next to the bag on the bed.

Mercuri. God would she ever get over how silently he moved for someone so big? She remained still for only a moment, before worry had her skirting the bed in order to face him from the other side.

"I was just packing my stuff." Nerves had her stating the obvious.

He nodded. "That's a good idea."

Tee felt her heart sink and figured she'd be next. She forced herself to meet his gaze, but saw that his eyes were on the floor when she looked at his face.

Nice goin', Tee. She would've kicked herself, but she'd already done so much of that since she'd left the disc with him, that she feared she was numb.

"It won't be a good idea for you to stay here, Tee."

"It's okay Mercuri. I get it." She lifted a hand to urge his quiet. She didn't trust herself to last much longer without breaking down into a humiliating display of emotion and grabbed the strap of the brown leather bag before she was making her way out of the room.

"What the hell are you doing?"

She stopped on the fourth stair down the wide case and half turned to stare at him. "I'm leaving."

"What the hell for?"

Her eyes went almost as wide as the O formed by her mouth. "You said it wouldn't work for me to stay here."

He sighed as though she had completely overlooked the obvious. "'Course it won't, Sprite." He leaned against a wall and folded his arms across his superb chest. "People who love each other usually stay in the same room when they live together."

Like before, his words had her heart falling and threatening to take the rest of her along with it.

Mercuri's expression had grown hard. "This setup won't work for me any longer. To hell with what Doc Stanley said. Course, I do realize you're gonna need your space," Unmindful of her; still stunned on the stairway, Mercuri left his position against the wall.

As bewildered then as she was curious, Tee left her bag on the stairs and followed him. He was heading back to his bedroom where he disappeared through his wardrobe. Tee saw a recessed panel in the rear that she hadn't noticed before. She watched him slide it open and wave for her to precede him.

"Mercuri!"

His name was a gasp, wrapped up in a squeal, airbrushed with cautious delight. Tee found her entire living room re-created there. Furnishings, rugs, even her prized collection of framed opera posters adorned the walls.

"It was a tricky move, but easy enough to slip by you since the house is so large." He stood just outside the spacious adjoining room he'd yet to find a use for. He found the enchanted look on her pixie face to be priceless as he watched her stroll the area. Timidly, she stroked the furnishings as though she couldn't quite believe they were really there.

"So I'll just leave you to enjoy," he called, and then snapped his fingers. "Oh yeah, hurry up and pick another opera, will you? Our box is waiting." He was grinning wildly as he retraced his steps through the wardrobe and bedroom.

"Mercuri?"

He was on his way down the front staircase when she called out. "The disc?"

He faked confusion for only a second. "I watched it the night you were here with your friends."

Her gasp seemed to echo throughout the lower level.

"I was thinking about putting the tracker on your phone, looked through your bag to find it- saw the disc on the table. I realized it wasn't the one I expected, a little too late."

"God," she leaned into the banister.

Mercuri walked back up the stairway to meet her. "I thought for sure you'd ask me about it when you found it in your bag instead of on the table where you left it."

"You-you saw it?"

"I saw it." His eyes narrowed in mock agitation. "I don't believe you intentionally wanted me to put that shit inside my head. Now I'll only be able to imagine all the ways I could've enjoyed killing them instead of really getting to do it."

Tee was still suspended by her disbelief. "You saw it and you- you still…" she sent a weak wave up the stairs.

Mercuri took her hand. "And I still," he kissed her palm.

"Mercuri who I was that night…it'll always be part of who I am. There's no getting rid of it."

"And I don't want you to. All those parts are part of the woman I love."

312

"And you're sure." It wasn't a question then. She could see that he was.

He nodded. "I'm sure. I'm sure I'll spend every minute in this house hounding you until you say you'll marry me."

She used her free hand to squeeze the banister in hopes of keeping herself upright. Mercuri scooped her close before her legs failed her.

"I'm sure," his stirring eyes were soft, yet as heated as molten gold. "I'm sure I love you. Sure I'm taking you downstairs," he began to do just that.

"Later, we'll spend the night in front of the fire," he continued, "we'll eat in front of the fire, watch that damned disc burn in the fire," he joined in when she laughed and then kissed her mouth when she quieted.

"I love you," she said.

"Even though we just met?"

"Looks like," her mouth curved into an alluring smile. "We aren't being cautious at all here, are we?"

"Hell Tee, where's the fun in that?"

There was more laughter as Mercuri's steps carried them to the den Tee had marveled over during her very first visit. Now, she marveled over something just as breathtaking- a life she never thought could be hers.

"So what happens after all this fire stuff?" She teased, as he dropped to an armchair and kept her snug on his lap.

"Well then, Ms. Shaw, that's the best part." Mystery colored his voice. "We get to make up the rest of this stuff as we go along."

Her deep gaze widened with playful expectancy. "What kind of stuff?"

"All kinds," his voice was a whisper as his mouth skimmed the line of her neck.

"Sounds very good," Tee inclined her head to give him more room to explore.

Mercuri ceased his slow glide along her neck. He stood then with plans to retrace his path back upstairs.

"Trust me," he said. "It'll feel even better."

Dear Reader,

     When I say this story hit me out of nowhere, I mean it! I was actually in the process of crafting another project when I went off on a tangent-what I thought was just a brief, distracting thought. Next thing I knew, I was in the grips of this sexy, dangerous, depraved and seductive story.

     I won't hold you with a lengthy letter. I'd just like to say thank you for taking a chance on this new world of drama that I've conjured. I hope Mercuri's and Tee's adventure kept you in as much suspense, intrigue and delight as it did me. There's more to come and I do hope you'll be on board for the ride.

     Email me with your thoughts.

Very Sincerely,
Ally Fleming aka AlTonya Washington
altonya@lovealtonya.com
www.allyfleming.weebly.com

"INTOXICATED" CAST OF CHARACTERS
(In Alphabetical Order)

A

Brody Alberts- Son of Nathan Alberts
Nathan Alberts- Co Founder of the GAN
Pope Apostolou- Best Friend Mercuri Nikolaides

B

Zeke Baylis- Diner Owner & Tee's Landlord
Nolan Booker- Las Vegas Police Officer
Denise Brassels-Pope's Aspen Neighbor
Steve Brassels- Pope's Aspen Neighbor

C

Randall Cafrey- VP Programming Feature News Network
Floyd Chapin- Actor
Berrill Clayton- Best Friend Etienne 'Tee' Shaw

D

Gerard Deese- Wilmington Vermont Sheriff

E

Vera Earl- eShaw Assistant to Tee
Rutger Eliades- Best Friend Mercuri Nikolaides

F

Vince Folksom- Tee's Security Detail
Leonard Fowler- Ops Commander
Rita Friedrich- LuCarolyn's Assistant
Robert Fritz- Co Leader of The Ten

G

The GAN- Grodins Alberts Network
Jake Grodins- Lorne Grodin's Son
Lorne Grodins- Co Founder of The GAN

H

Sumter Hamisch- Co Leader of The Ten
Prin Holland- Best Friend Etienne 'Tee' Shaw
Mike Hough- Bear Arms Assistant to Berrill Clayton

J

Kevin Jonas- Tee's Security Detail

K

Moira Kent- eShaw Receptionist
Patroclus Kostas- Best Friend Mercuri Nikolaides

L

Jerome Lehman- Congressman Morrow's Campaign Manager

M

Slayte Miltiades- Best Friend Mercuri Nikolaides
Christopher Morrow- Congressman

N

Mercuri Nikolaides- Hero of "Intoxicated"

O

Shaun Oates- Bear Arms Assistant to Berrill Clayton
James O'Hara- Mercuri's Head of Security

P

Dorinda Patterson- Brothel Owner

R

Luke Robb- Member of the GAN
Les Rollins- GAN Soldier
Eduardo Roya- Son of Enrique Roya
Enrique Roya- Personal Pimp to the GAN
Jack Rylance- Member of Grant Zubin's Team

S

Etienne 'Tee' Shaw- Heroine of "Intoxicated"
Caleb Stein- Member of the GAN

T

Lamar Tilson- Officer for Rutger's Security Team

V

Harris Van Deer- Member of the GAN

W

Ben Weiss- Rutger's Security Chief

Y

Basil Yost~ GAN Soldier
LuCarolyn Young- Best Friend Etienne 'Tee' Shaw

Z

Grant Zubin- Member of the GAN

An AlTonya Exclusive